MY BIG FAT FABULOUS CHRISTMAS

The coldest holiday of the year is about to get blisteringly hot...

LYNDSEY GALLAGHER

Copyright © Lyndsey Gallagher 2022

All Rights Reserved

No part of this book may be reproduced in any form or by any electronic means, including information storage and retrieval systems, without written permission from the author, except for the brief use of quotations in a book review.

This is a work of fiction and any characters that bear a resemblance to anyone living or dead is a coincidence. The events are imagined by the author and bear no similarities to actual events.

ASIN B09X6B9KT3

*For Martha,
the queen of Christmas
and glossy hair.*

PROLOGUE

SASHA

The six-foot Christmas tree glints from the corner of the double-height living room. Twinkling multicoloured lights glow, then darken on a calming, repetitive cycle. Admiring the dazzling scarlet and gleaming gold baubles, a grin twitches at my lips as I recall precious memories from only a few hours earlier.

Ryan and I started something I'm determined to finish tonight – and I'm not referring to the decorations.

Nothing prepared me for falling in love. Everything I've ever read or heard failed to convey the dizzying, all-consuming, exhilarating sensations. Every lust-fuelled glance sends electricity pulsing through my veins, surging through every cell. Every fleeting touch. Every shared kiss.

Ryan Cooper is resplendent. We might only be eighteen, but I know I've found the man I'm going to marry.

We both agree we're meant to be.

Tall, dark and handsome, he's the epitome of the fairy tale

prince, except he emits a delicious bad-boy vibe with his leather jacket and shadowy stubble.

Our relationship is obsessive. Addictive. When I'm not with him, thoughts of him devour me.

As I wait for him to return to the luxury cabin his family rents from mine, my skin pricks with an incessant longing for his touch.

Six cabins flank my family's estate, Huxley Castle. Each similarly decorated by my slightly bohemian mother. Opulent, yet understated.

The entrance boasts full-length windows, making it spacious and bright. The living area's open plan, impressively minimalistic and tastefully decorated in varying shades of cream, with a large open fire. The only touch of colour and sign of the season is the tree.

I glance at the clock impatiently. Ryan had to meet his band, Imagination. They haven't secured many gigs yet, but last week, their social media blew up after a video of them covering a Paul Weller song went viral. It's only a matter of time before the offers start rolling in. As the lead singer, he has a bright future ahead.

I should be in my four-poster bed half a kilometre away. If my parents catch me, I'll be confined to the four walls of my stately bedroom for years. They're aware of our relationship. They actually like Ryan, approving of his musical creativity and ambition. But if they catch me here, in this low-cut black dress, at this hour of the night, that will quickly change.

The bang of the front door startles me. The familiar thud of boots approaching makes my heart rate triple.

'I missed you.' Ryan enters the living room, striding purposefully towards me. Confidence radiates from his every movement. Strong hands yank me towards his lithe torso as if I'm weightless. He's bigger than most guys I know. Inky black hair cascades over thick, neat eyebrows framing a face that wrenches my insides.

He's my catnip. My perfect match. As if he's been created specifically for my appreciation. Not only was he gifted a voice fit for the radio, he's blessed with a face for television too. Even without the viral video, he's going to go far in this life.

He's adamant he's bringing me with him.

He flicks stray strands of hair from his face, his huge lash-framed eyes boring into mine, so dark it's difficult to distinguish his pupils from his irises, two swirling pools of molten beauty.

He practically steals the breath from my chest simply by looking at me, yet I manage to utter, 'How was practice?'

'It was torturous, knowing you were here waiting for me. Billy's a good guitarist, but I'm not sure he has what it takes to make it to the big time.' His fingers sweep my unruly hair from my face, tucking it tenderly behind my ear.

For a big guy, he's so gentle.

'And you *are* heading for the big time. There's no doubt about it.'

His head tilts to the side, a flicker crossing his chiselled face. '*We* are heading for the big time, Sasha. I'm not going anywhere without you.'

I trace a finger across the curve of his jaw, revelling in the roughness of his five o'clock shadow. Masculinity radiates from him, igniting a blazing fire in the pit of my stomach and lower.

'Hmm. I'll remind you of that when you have a hundred thousand groupies in a stadium, screaming your name and throwing their underwear at you.'

'If only you'd get over your stage fright, you could be up there alongside me. Think about it.'

'I have thought about it. It's all I ever think about. I will come to the States with you, but as your secret songwriter, and your girlfriend – not your guitarist.'

My parents expect me to at least get a college degree, if not some sort of doctorate. Bohemian or not, they'll hit the roof when they realise I'm leaving with him next year, but we've spent the last year of our lives planning this. Scheming how we'll break free straight after our final exams, before we get bogged down and caught up with mortgages and adult stuff. Before the dream is forever confined to just that.

The plan is to escape the castle under the ruse of taking a year out. Hopefully when the year passes, we'll be so successful my parents won't even question my failure to return for college.

It sounds like a giddy childhood dream.

It's not.

Ryan will be a huge star. He's too talented for it to go any other way.

'Why can't you be my girlfriend, guitarist and secret songwriter?' He nuzzles my neck, teasing me with his tender touch. Tonight, I'm finally ready for so much more.

'I told you, I'm shy. I prefer hiding behind a pretty notepad and a pink fluffy biro. The thought of playing something I've written in front of a crowd is too much. Too personal. It scares the shit out of me.'

'But you play in front of me all the time.' He cups my face in his hands, pretending to pout.

'That's different. I love you.'

'And I love you. That's why we make such an awesome partnership. Imagine what we'd be like together on stage.' Darting far enough back to meet my eye, he gazes at me, intoxicating me with his familiar scent; raw masculinity, tinged with hints of citrus.

Snaking my arms around his waist, my body crushes against his. Shivers rip across my forearms, nothing to do with the crisp white snow falling outside the cabin window. The first snow of the year.

'Hmm. We'll see.' Deep down, part of me longs to be on that stage with him. Logistically though, even if I could get my head around it, I don't know if my legs would support the weight of my nerves for it ever to be a realistic option.

'We're in this together, Sasha. You'll see. You and me are meant to be. On and off the stage.'

I'm silenced before I can protest. His lips find mine again, parting them with his tongue.

Over his shoulder I glimpse the huge cream clock mounted over the open fire. Dragging my mouth away, I reluctantly warn him, 'I don't have long. My parents will be back within the hour.'

They've gone to watch my youngest sister, Victoria, perform in her school Christmas concert. The only reason I'm not watching a load of giddy seven-year-olds stammer their way through a nativity play, is under the pretence of studying.

A devilish grin exposes huge white teeth. 'I can do a lot with you in an hour.'

Supple hands grip my backside, lifting me to grind against him. His mouth returns to the sensitive skin of my neck, teeth gently nipping and teasing.

'Where's your dad?'

Being caught like this would be beyond embarrassing, and if my parents got wind of it, I wouldn't get as far as the castle walls, let alone the States.

'He's out. Another dodgy business deal, no doubt.' Ryan pauses, a flicker of annoyance flashing over his face.

His father's business is the one thing we don't talk about. Ever. I know it's less than legitimate, but I don't judge and I never pry.

'And your brother?'

Jayden's a year older than Ryan and equally as exquisite to look at. Though his arrogance leaves a lot to be desired.

'He's probably doing exactly what we're about to do, with one of your housekeeping staff. Jacinta? Janine? I can't remember her name, but they've had something casual going on for a few weeks now. Don't tell your parents.'

I scoff. 'As if.'

Mam and Dad are madly in love even after all these years, but they barely have enough time to listen to each other between the day-to-day running of the estate, let alone listen to me.

They love me unconditionally, I know they do, but dealing with hotel guests and managing staff makes spending time doing normal mundane family things, like having a meal together, a rarity.

Which actually suits right now, because stealing time with Ryan Cooper is my favourite pastime.

His mouth captures mine and I'm transported directly to my own personal heaven. A space so familiar, yet still so breathtakingly rousing. Mind-blowing, yet so damn natural.

Pulling me back towards the couch, he breaks our kiss. 'Are you sure about this?'

We've fooled around, come close so many times before. We've done everything but *it*. Before he left, I said I was ready to take things to the next level. I wasn't lying.

'Never been more certain about anything in my life.'

I sink onto the ebony leather couch, while Ryan throws another log on the smouldering fire. He goes to draw the blinds, shutting out the snow, the sky and the entire world as we know it.

'Don't.' I point to the light switch instead and he crosses the room, killing the intrusive beams.

The moon looms full in the starry sky giving a romantic

iridescent glow. Crisp snowflakes flutter against the glass of the window pane.

Pulling his sweatshirt over his head in one swift manoeuvre, Ryan crosses the room to rest his knees on the oak flooring in front of the couch. Scorching eyes search mine with a lingering question. A tenderness floods my heart fast enough to make it explode.

I nod and he pounces, parting my legs, wriggling his hips inside my thighs, pressing his excitement against mine. Hungry lips ravage my skin as warm hands slip beneath my dress, fingers tracing the underside of my breast until I feel like I can't breathe.

I yank the little black number over my head as a low whistle slips from his lips.

'Sasha Sexton, you're the most beautiful girl in the universe.' He tuts and stares appreciatively.

Unhooking my bra, I lay myself bare for him. Eager eyes roam my chest and his head dips, mouth darting to capture my flesh. His hands wander beneath the hem of my underwear, removing every scrap of material separating us.

As our bodies unite, skin on skin, Ryan caresses every inch of me, kissing away the initial sharp burst of discomfort as we embark on the most delicious, intimate, loving act.

My raspy moan echoes around the otherwise silent room. He takes my body to places I've only ever dreamed of. Blistering heat invisibly sears us, marking us for each other, and each other alone.

I thought I knew pleasure before, but it was nothing compared to this.

Afterwards, we lie entangled, embracing each other in a vice-like grip, the leather sticking to our clammy backs. The hammering thud of my heart rings through my ears as my breathing struggles to regulate.

'I never thought it would be so...' It's hard to summon the

right word. A word big enough to represent what we just did. What passed between us.

Ryan's lips press against my forehead, tugging me even tighter against his bare chest. 'You're amazing.'

An ear-splitting pounding on the front door sends the two of us leaping from the couch. Panic rises in my chest as I scramble around for my hastily discarded clothes.

'Is that your dad?'

'No, he'd hardly be knocking.' Ryan's eyebrows knit in a frown as he glances at the clock. It's almost ten p.m. If I haven't already been busted, I need to get back before I'm missed.

Worry worms at my stomach. 'Shall I sneak out the back door?'

Ryan shakes his head vigorously. 'No way. Give me two minutes to see who it is, then I'll walk you back to the castle. It's too dark for you to be out there alone.'

Even as my gaze rolls skywards, I'm flattered at the value he puts on my welfare. The pounding resumes again, replaced shortly by the sound of a flustered female voice drifting through the letterbox.

A voice I'd know anywhere.

Ryan yanks open the heavy front door and my middle sister, Chloe, bursts through, white-faced, wide-eyed and panic stricken.

With less than a year between us, we're practically twins. I can read her every micro-expression like an open book. Though, nobody would need that ability to see the face she's wearing now depicts serious cause for alarm.

My first thought is, I've been busted. My parents have discovered my whereabouts, and while they might be comfortable with us dating, they most certainly won't be comfortable with me offering him my V-card on a crisp December night.

'Shit! Is it Mam and Dad?' My hands fly to my cheeks in a poor attempt to hide the burn.

She nods, a rare unnerving look of bewilderment in her eyes.

'You need to come now,' Chloe says, tugging me out of the cabin.

Within minutes life as I know it is blown into a devastating oblivion.

CHAPTER ONE

SASHA

Ten years later
16th November

'Quick, that's the photographer arriving!' In the distance, car headlights swing into the winding gravel driveway.

A small crowd congregates on the paving in front of Huxley Castle Estate, awaiting the official switching on of the impressive Christmas lights. Our resident pianist plays traditional carols on a white grand piano from his station beside the ornately sculpted water feature of three entwined dolphins.

Thankfully, the weather's behaving, for now at least. A fresh crispness lingers in the chilly evening air, but there's no sign of rain.

My fingers trace the long-sleeved crimson silk dress I'm wearing, smoothing it into position. Patting my hair into place, I take a deep breath.

'Relax.' My best friend and the castle's manager, Megan, pats my arm in a reassuring gesture. She begins to hum a familiar tune under her breath, the same one she always hums when I'm anxious.

'Huh! You have no idea how hard it was to get *Tatler* to agree to come here at all! I practically had to beg. I offered the damn woman two nights free accommodation in one of our most luxurious suites, in exchange for twenty minutes work and a half-page slot in next month's magazine, and that's if I'm lucky! And do you know what her response was? She asked if the room had a sea view. Unbelievable.'

When my parents were alive, the glossy magazines used to fight over who got the exclusive at Huxley Castle. The switching on of the lights is a tradition they started long ago, and one of many that I've tried desperately hard to keep alive in honour of their memory.

When they died, I inherited the business, the entire estate and custody of my seventeen-and seven-year-old sisters.

Running the castle estate alone hasn't been easy.

Raising a teenager alone hasn't been easy.

But every time I worry if I'm doing a good enough job with either, a staff member reports an issue demanding an immediate solution, leaving me zero time to dwell on it. Not sure if that's a blessing or a curse.

A few years ago it emerged some parts of the castle had a rare form of dry rot. It cost a mint to rebuild those areas and now I'm in debt up to my eyeballs trying to keep the place afloat– a fact I'm desperately trying to hide from not only my own sisters, but my father's two as well.

Aunty Mags is a dream; she'd do anything to help, even sacrifice her own trust fund if she had any idea of the financial difficulties this family is in. I'll never allow that to happen.

Aunty Evelyn, on the other hand, makes Cinderella's evil step-sisters seem positively amiable. As my father's eldest sibling, Evelyn was adamant the estate should have fallen to her when he passed. Thankfully, I was eighteen and legally old enough to claim everything, including sole care of my sisters.

Chloe emigrated to Dubai the day after she turned twenty-one, carving her way in the world as a super successful events manager. Having founded her own company, she employs fifteen full-time staff and deals with the Emirates' most elite.

Victoria is seventeen and the sole cause for the single strand of grey I found in my otherwise glossy chestnut locks this morning. Her happiness concerns me more than anything else. She was with our parents when the accident happened and, though she's never spoken of it, it must haunt her subconscious. It has to. She still has night terrors. Especially this time of year.

So, beneath the intentionally well-presented exterior of both myself and the castle, I'm secretly struggling. The long and short of the situation is – I'm praying for Prince Charming to rock up on his white horse and save us, or a Hallmark-worthy Christmas fucking miracle, because without some sort of divine intervention, according to our accountant, this could well be our last Christmas at Huxley Castle, our family home for the previous three generations.

Swallowing hard, I whisper to Megan, 'You know Christmas isn't my favourite time of year. All those memories.' It's as close as I can bring myself to mentioning it.

'I know, Sasha. I know. You're doing a great job though.' Megan's sympathetic smile brims with reassurance and love. She's one of the few friends I kept from my school days. When everyone else left for college, I became a parent, business owner and a hot fucking mess. It didn't leave much common ground with my peers.

So, when Megan graduated from UCD with a degree in hospitality, she was the obvious choice when the previous manager retired. Not only is she the most loyal friend a girl could wish for, she's efficient, savvy and unafraid of hard work.

Crunching tyres grind to an abrupt halt at the castle pillars, ending our conversation before it really begins.

My favourite porter, James, descends the concrete steps to assist. He's been like a father figure to me these past ten years. Ever ready with a hot coffee and the ability to lend a thoughtful ear, he's seen me at my best and worst and always keeps my confidence.

As he opens the driver door, a sharply dressed woman with jet-black hair secured in a severe-looking chignon steps out. She drops the car key into his hand without so much as offering him a glance, preoccupied with scrutinising the castle and its subtly eroding but charming features.

Its grandeur is unquestionable, but under close inspection, so is the fact it needs a small fortune spent on it. One I don't currently have.

Megan imparts a swift dig to my ribs and sniggers. 'Cruella has arrived.'

I shoot her a warning glare, then present an air of confidence I don't truly feel. 'Miriam, delighted you could make it. Welcome to Huxley Castle.'

Miriam, the Tatler journalist, glances round at the locals, my regular supporters, mostly comprised of family friends, neighbours, and the families that currently rent the cabins. 'I thought there'd be more of a crowd.'

It's hard to get huge numbers these days without the presence of a fashion-setting blogger or trendy celebrity. Exotic canapés and mulled wine help, though.

'Didn't you see the news? There's a rain warning in place,' Megan interjects. I might not have many friends, but the few I do always have my back.

James attempts to squash his burly six-foot-five frame into Miriam's Mini Cooper, wincing at the cramped space.

'Wait!' Miriam barks and I flinch. 'I need my cameras from the boot.'

James steps out, sighs with relief and opens the tiny compact boot. As he retrieves Miriam's equipment, one of the younger porters slips into the driver's seat and offers James a thumbs-up.

The estate might not be the most financially viable, but the staff are the best. Many have been with my family for years. Most have become more like friends than employees.

It's a blessing and a curse, because if I don't pull something spectacular out of the bag, people I care deeply for might not have jobs this time next year. And it'll be all my fault.

Waitresses in crisp black-and-white uniforms circulate offering delicious canapés, champagne and mulled wine from gleaming silver trays. The poor girls have been polishing them like mad all week, warned of the importance of maintaining a convincing display of luxury.

Miriam takes a champagne flute, knocks back its contents in three mouthfuls, then scans the premises, hopefully for where she might capture the best photos.

'It's probably better to leave her to it.' Megan grips my elbow, steering me in the other direction. 'We don't want to look desperate.'

She halts a passing waitress, takes two champagne flutes from her tray and presses one firmly into my hand.

'You know how much is riding on the Christmas turnover. I need bookings to go through the roof. I need to be hosting Christmas parties every single night of the week if we have a hope in hell of staying open next year.'

Megan smooths her auburn spiral curls from her face and takes a sip from her own crystal flute. 'Don't panic until the meeting with the accountant on Monday. It might not be as bad as you think.'

It already is. I've just been burying my head in the sand.

The bookings simply haven't materialised this year, or last for that matter. Yet due to the poor insulation and utterly unpredictable Irish weather, the entire estate still needs to be heated year round, ever ready, just in case.

Ever the optimist, I've a habit of over-ordering produce for the kitchen. Most of which ends up being donated to Dublin's homeless shelters. It's far from ideal but it warms my heart to know it doesn't go to waste.

But the extent of my problems isn't something I wish to share with anyone, not even my best friend and most valued member of staff. Megan has her own responsibilities, caring for her sick mother, and overseeing the running of her family's farm until her brother is discharged from the army next year, as well as working full-time for me.

'Sasha, Sasha!' Victoria, my youngest sister bursts from between the castle's humongous wrought-iron doors. She leaps down the steps two at a time.

'Careful, child! You'll break your neck on those stairs!' I warn as she bounds over like an excited Labrador, her long hazel hair trailing in her wake. Placing my arm round her shoulder, I attempt to shelter her bare skin from the chill.

'Child? I'll be eighteen next year!' Horror taints her tone.

'Where's your jacket? It's freezing out here.' It's official – at the age of twenty-eight – I've turned into my mother.

Many women my age are hanging round elegant wine bars, sipping post-work drinks after a long and gruelling day at the office.

Me? I'm nagging my sister to do her homework, floss her teeth and stay away from irrefutably attractive, but utterly unreliable boys. She's a late developer, but one can't be too careful. I wish my mother had instilled that wise gem of advice into me.

Ten years after Ryan's instant and shocking departure, my

heart still aches when he springs to mind. I try not to think about him, but despite my best efforts it's pretty fucking difficult when his voice regularly booms out over the radio and his exquisite face hijacks my television.

In these instances, I remind myself the asshole upped and left without a backwards glance when I needed him the most, and kill the noise source as quickly as my size-five feet will carry me. Unfortunately, it isn't fast enough to avoid the searing pain which still stupidly penetrates my heart.

The very same night I tragically lost my parents in a car accident, I lost my boyfriend too. He didn't get taken from me though. He chose to leave. It hurt every bit as much, possibly even more.

I returned from the hospital with my sister to find Ryan's cabin empty. He'd vanished along with his father and brother.

Never to be seen or heard from again, until seven years ago when an American record label signed him and he became an international superstar practically overnight.

Every time he pops up somewhere it rips my heart into a million shreds. I've banned radios in the castle kitchens, but only Megan and Conor, our gorgeous and talented head chef, know why.

'Sasha, you're not listening to me!' Victoria tugs at the front of my dress. She's almost as tall as me now, almost the same age I was when I inherited her and this estate.

'Sorry, honey. I'm a bit distracted with these lights. What is it?'

'Never mind the lights! James has everything under control.' She points to my favourite porter, who does indeed seem to be doing a grand job rounding up the crowd, regaling them with some sort of Christmas story involving the castle's history. He's an absolute gem. I'd love to double his Christmas bonus, but at this rate he'll be lucky to even get one.

'Chloe's on the phone.' Victoria thrusts her iPhone under my nose and the familiar tanned features of our middle sister light the screen before me.

'Chloe, how are you? You look fantastic.' It's the truth. The Middle Eastern climate suits her. I'm so pale I'd fry under a full moon, but Chloe takes a beautiful bronze tan. Stunning freckles adorn sharp, high cheekbones and her eyes glint as blue as a tropical ocean. Her wavy chocolate-coloured hair's pulled into a loose ponytail on top of her head; her shoulders barely covered by the summer dress she wears.

'I didn't want to miss the switching on of the lights.' Chloe's voice travels through the hands-free and Megan takes a step back, leaving Victoria and me to chat to our sister in private.

'I'll turn the phone round so you can see. It won't be long now.'

Glancing round, I check Miriam's in position. Thankfully, she's smiling as her camera clicks and flashes in the distance. I can only pray it's a good sign – pray she enjoys her stay here with us.

As the castle walls and immaculately kept grounds burst into a magnificent, festive display of elegant twinkling stars, sophisticated angel silhouettes and tastefully positioned reindeer, the crowd burst into a collective rounds of 'ohhhs' and 'ahhhhs'.

A twenty-five-foot tree stands proudly on the perfectly manicured lawn as the castle's centrepiece, its white lights gleaming.

'You went for all white lights *again* this year?' Chloe says, her fingers drumming against her lips on the screen before us.

'I'm a stickler for routine.'

I don't tell her that every time I see multicoloured lights on a tree it transports me directly back to *that* night. The night I thought I'd gained the world, but in actual fact, lost everything.

Almost everything anyway.

Taking Victoria's hand, I squeeze it gratefully. She's my everything now. My sole focus. Her and the castle. I only hope I can find a way to turn things around and do both of them justice.

'I wish you were here,' Victoria croons to Chloe.

Chloe's the trendy, successful sister. She never nags, and always sends Victoria the coolest gifts. Chloe got out of here the second she was able. She never voiced why but deep down I know she couldn't bear being reminded of our loss. It's probably the same reason she rarely comes home.

'Actually, funnily enough, that's why I'm ringing.' She clears her throat and I usher Victoria further from the crowd to hear Chloe better.

'I'm between projects at the minute. I've decided to come home for Christmas.'

Victoria's resounding shriek pierces my ear drum and I flinch, certain Chloe could hear her in Dubai without the help of an iPhone. 'Are you serious?'

'Yes. It's time. It'll be lovely to see you both. To be home for Christmas.'

It certainly will. In this split second, I vow to put all worries aside and concentrate on making this year the most fabulous Christmas ever, because apart from the fact Chloe hasn't made it home for one in six years, there's a good chance it could be our last here.

Unless something drastic occurs.

CHAPTER TWO

RYAN

17th November

November in LA is one of my favourite months. With the madness of summer over, the weather's finally at a temperature I'm comfortable with.

I'm Irish. We aren't made for extreme heat.

The twenty-five metre turquoise shimmering pool is as inviting as the two unopened beer bottles on the neighbouring marble-topped table, but business always comes before pleasure. From the look on Jayden's face, today, he means business.

He might be my brother, but he's also one of the most ruthless agents in Hollywood and I'm grateful for him every day, even if he is a pain in the arse ninety-nine per cent of the time.

I have a reputation for being a bit of a bad boy. Truth is, Jayden's worse than I've ever been, or ever will be. The man can be merciless at times, both professionally and personally. And his arrogance is notorious across several continents.

He pushes his Ray-Bans onto his head, shooting me a piercing stare from his steely grey eyes. 'You need to sort your shit out and pull something out of the bag, or Diamond Records *will* pull the plug on you, permanently.'

Older than me by a year, he's never had any problem bossing me around. Even if I am supposed to be a fucking rockstar.

He has a point, a valid one, but voicing the worst-case scenario is a dick move.

'Look, I know. Believe me, I'm working on it.'

His eyebrows raise as his hand sweeps the expansive landscape in front of him. 'Yeah, I can see precisely how hard you're working on things.'

'Oh come on! You of all people know my job isn't your typical nine-to-five. I can't just sit at a desk and force out unfelt lyrics. They need to resonate with people, and in order for that to happen, I need to feel inspired. I can't simply magic them out of thin air.' I scrape a hand through my jet-black hair. It's well overdue a trim, but I can't even face the thought of leaving the comfort of my own mansion, because every time I do, someone asks me when the next album is coming out and the truth is, I don't fucking know.

I've never struggled this way before. It's like the creative part of my brain has run drier than the Sahara Desert. The words just refuse to come. I can't even muster a single artistic idea.

I've been shutting down my emotions for the last ten years. Running from the overwhelm of my own obfuscated feelings.

Now I'm feeling brave enough to attempt to open Pandora's box again – the code's changed or something. I'm utterly incapable of any kind of meaningful emotion, let alone able to write about it. I'm emotionally frigid or something. I can't, or maybe I just don't want to feel.

'You're contractually obliged to provide two more albums, one before the end of January. You have roughly a month until the three concerts at The Colosseum in Vegas to pull something out the bag. Even a few new songs might convince the world, and Diamond Records, that a new album is imminent.'

We've had this conversation multiple times this year. I might have five multi-platinum albums to my name, but it's been years since I've even attempted to write anything. Cruising shamelessly along on the gravelly voice I was born with, and old material from many moons ago, which had the most exquisite muse.

One I've tried not to dwell on – unsuccessfully I might add- since the day I left her.

'Believe me, I'm well aware of my contractual obligations.' Aware that, more than likely, I'm not going to be able to fulfil them.

'The press are swooping in like vultures, printing crap about your writer's block, claiming you're a "has-been". If we don't do something, Diamond will drop you and no one else is going to snap up an artist who can't uphold basic contractual obligations. We need to give them something.'

My considerate housekeeper, Mrs Garcia, chooses this moment to stick her head out of the patio doors. 'You boys about ready for some lunch?'

Sara Garcia has been with me for the past five years. She makes the best steak sandwich known to man, and turns a blind eye to the countless women who traipse hopefully through here, before being rapidly replaced by the next.

I make no secret of the fact I'm a commitment-phobe. It's their fault if they think they can change me.

Eyeing the cool condensation dripping across the length of the beer bottle, I call back, 'Lunch would be amazing! Thanks.'

At the same time Jayden shouts, 'Not yet, we haven't quite finished talking shop.'

'There's nothing more to say.' I pop the top from one of the bottles and hand it to him. He pauses for a split second before reluctantly accepting it.

'You better find something to fucking say. The world is waiting.' Jayden adjusts his glasses back on his nose, then gulps down a couple of noisy mouthfuls.

'I will. Don't panic. I just need a little inspiration.' My gaze falls back to the water, as if the answer might be lurking at the bottom of the pool.

'Well, for the love of god, find some! I don't care if you have to go to Timbuktu to get it.'

He might have a point, because sitting here, holed up in this luxurious self-imposed prison, certainly isn't helping. But where would?

So desperate to change the topic of conversation, I bring up the only thing I know will distract him.

'Have you heard from Dad?'

'Nope. Probably drinking himself into a stupor somewhere. For a man who rushed us back to this country in such a fucking hurry, he sure doesn't seem happy to be here.'

And what a rush it was. A shudder rips through me as memory of that night flashes to the forefront of my brain.

Dad's a liability. Truthfully, he always has been. If it wasn't a dodgy investment, it was a get-rich-quick scheme. Both of which landed this family in a ton of shit. Enough that we had to flee the country I loved.

And the woman I loved.

I squeeze my eyes shut, refusing to go there. Even after all these years it's still a raw gaping wound, deep enough that no amount of one-night stands can plug it. It's the song I can't write. Ten years later, it's still too fucking painful to confront, let alone analyse.

I shrug off the memories. 'He'll get in touch when he needs something.'

'Don't I know it,' Jayden says, his fingers brushing his designer stubble.

Attempting to lighten the mood, I change the subject once again. 'Any plans for the weekend?'

'Nah. I was supposed to be going to the *Bond* premiere with Cindy, but then she asked if I wanted to spend next weekend at her parents' beach house and alarm bells blasted. I'm not signing up for that *Brady Bunch* shit. No fucking way.'

'And there was me thinking she might be "the one".' A smirk twitches at my lips at my outright lie. My brother's never been interested in anything remotely serious. Though he usually spends a few weeks before moving on, which is more than I can manage.

A hearty belly laugh explodes from his chest and he flashes a rare grin. 'Bollocks! Anyway, you can hardly point the finger. Not exactly "Mr Committed" yourself, are you?'

I shrug off his remark. The difference is, I was once and I would have remained that way, given half the chance. Sadly, life had other plans.

My brother stays long enough to finish three more beers and a pile of tacos, and give me another pep talk about finding inspiration.

As the evening draws in, I remain on the marble-tiled terrace, the sun pleasantly seeping through the designer polo shirt on my back, straight into my bones. Yet, a chill lingers somewhere in the depth of my core.

Hours after Jayden leaves, I'm still dwelling on his warning.

I need to produce something, and fast, unless I want to be axed faster than a row of ripe Christmas trees in December. Gathering the empty bottles, I head inside the spacious four walls of my pad.

I have more than I ever dreamed of. Another huge villa in San Francisco, a penthouse apartment in New York, a Ferrari, a Porsche and more money than I could spend in several lifetimes. What I don't have, is any fresh ideas.

Pacing the wide corridors, I can't settle, never more aware of the ominous ticking of the grandfather clock in the bright, airy hall. It's like it's ticking specifically on my career, tormenting me. I need to find that inspiration. And I need to find it now.

Vegas gigs are notoriously prestigious. The Colosseum only hosts the biggest and best artists. The pressure to deliver something original weighs profoundly on my chest. Leave the crowd desperate for more. Show them Ryan Cooper is not a has-been.

Because without my career, what am I?

Flopping onto the massive suede couch, I grab the remote and turn on the TV, searching for something mindless enough to wind down. Christmas movies are airing already. *Home Alone* is showing on CBS. I watch for a few minutes before resuming my restless, futile channel hopping.

Fox News display the official switching on of the New York Christmas lights at Time Square and, not for the first time today, I'm instantly transported back to another time. Another life.

A memory of just days before we promptly skipped the country hits me like a freight train, wreaking havoc with my long-buried emotions.

Sasha and I, hand in hand, gazing at the lavish display of lights radiating from her family's castle. Back then, I was as much in awe of that place as I was her.

We were classes apart, and though her parents welcomed me as warmly as one of their own, deep down, despite my outward show of confidence, I never truly felt good enough to justify the title of her boyfriend.

Mr and Mrs Sexton are two of the kindest, most admirable people. I loved her parents almost as much as I loved her. Thanks to my dad's illegal investments catching up with him, I had no chance to even utter a goodbye to any of them.

Long pent-up emotion swells in my chest, forcing its way up my throat until I'm certain I might actually explode. It hits me like a brick – the most emotion I've felt in years. And it hurts like fuck.

Though I don't want to face it, to feel the loss of my previous life, maybe that's exactly what I need to get over this blip in my career.

Perhaps it's finally time to go back to Ireland? To face the life I left behind.

I'm not stupid enough to think Sasha will be there. She had every chance to find me if that's what she wanted. Clearly, she didn't.

But the thought of returning to the lush lands of my roots is suddenly growing legs with every passing second.

It's been ten years since I stepped foot on Irish soil. Ten years since I witnessed the flourishing green of my homeland. It might be exactly the type of inspiration I need. If that flashback is anything to go by, it might just be the only way to unlock the elusive compartment in my brain that controls my emotions- or lack of them.

If I confront the place I mentally locked away all those years ago, deal with the pain I've shied away from, perhaps I'll return lighter and with some sort of clarity?

At least less emotionally frigid, with any luck.

A sense of acceptance settles in my core. It's time.

CHAPTER THREE

SASHA

19th November

Wringing my hands beneath the privacy of my father's old maple desk, I glance around the office that's now mine, trying to view it as Harry, our accountant, might.

A huge landscape oil painting of Velvet Strand hangs as centrepiece on the back wall. It's an original. For a fleeting second I wonder how much it's worth. Things are getting bad when I'm considering selling my father's treasured collection.

Mind you, he wasn't the only one with a soft spot for that particular beach.

Huge sash windows overlook the expansive grounds of the estate, intense greens meet the vivid cobalt afternoon sky. Yet, no matter how much winter sun streams outside the glass, I can't bring myself to feel bright.

Harry clears his throat and pulls some papers from his briefcase, rustling them noisily on his lap. 'Did you think any more about what we discussed last month, Miss Sexton?'

He's alluding to his suggestion of selling the estate, or even parts of it initially.

I've done nothing but think about it – anytime I have a free second to myself, that is.

'Call me Sasha, please.' Harry's been the estate's accountant for twenty years. He knew my parents well. That's why it's even harder to hear him say I should consider selling.

Even though his tone has never so much as hinted at being judgemental, I can't help feel he's disappointed at the terrible job I'm doing running the place. Or maybe it's just me who's disappointed and I'm projecting. Whatever.

He sighs before continuing. 'How would you feel about selling the cabins? That would potentially raise enough revenue to pay off most of the castle's outstanding debts.'

The word 'most' lingers in the air between us. We both know if even another millimetre of dry rot is found, this place is finished. And it's a real possibility.

If I sold the cabins, I'd still likely be a few hundred thousand short. And I need cash to keep the business afloat, pay the staff, keep the fridges stocked and the lights on.

The cabins were my mother's pride and joy. They were her forte. She designed every inch of them. Selling them would be like selling a part of her memory. But if it meant I could hang on to the castle, find some way to increase the revenue... resuscitate a bit of life into the place.

'You don't have to decide now, Sasha. But as things are, the way this estate is being run is not sustainable. It hasn't been for a long time. Something has to give.' His eyes fall to the paperwork in front of him. 'What about starting with the cabin that's not in use?'

My palm instinctively covers my stomach as hot bile blazes through my oesophagus, burning a path to the back of my throat. I haven't been in that cabin since that night. Nor has anyone else. And I'm not ready to deal with that yet, even if it has been ten years.

'Is there anywhere else I can cut back?'

Harry offers me a sympathetic smile. 'The staff wages alone equate to over half a million, annually. You know how much the electricity costs, and that's without the extravagant display of Christmas lights.' He arches an eyebrow at me. 'The general maintenance is substantial. The bookings have only dwindled since...' he winces before correcting himself, 'over the last ten years. If you want to emerge with enough to secure a modest future for yourself and your sisters, it might be wise to considering selling everything. If another single block of dry rot is discovered, it will ruin you. It might be better to quit while you're ahead. Marginally, that is. Unless you have another plan? Something I don't know about?'

Harry places the paperwork on the desk between us, gently nudging it towards me before helping himself to a cup of tea from a tray, Tilly, one of my favourite young waitresses, dropped in ten minutes earlier.

The truth is, I don't have a plan. I can't make any staff cutbacks. Each and every one of them, myself included, does the work of two people. The few times I tried to skimp on ordering food, we were unseasonably busy and ran out. It's so hard to make money in the hospitality industry, especially when bookings are as unpredictable as the Irish weather.

The lavish sheets, guest treats and sublime menu can't be forsaken if I'm to keep charging hundreds of euro for a standard double room per night.

Silence descends on us as I silently wrack my brain for a miraculous solution.

Truth is, there isn't one.

Harry's been warning me for years that the estate isn't making a profit. I blamed Brexit, Covid and everything in between, but maybe it was simply poor management?

I just don't have a head for business. I've been spreading myself so thinly trying to keep everything going the way Mam and Dad had, and trying to raise Victoria to the best of my ability. I don't think I've been particularly good at either.

'If you see Santa on your travels, tell him I'm looking for him. I have a Christmas wish.' It's a joke of course. A feeble one. I need more than a wish; I need a fucking Christmas miracle. I pick up the remaining china cup and pour steaming hot liquid into it from the pot, just to do something with my clammy hands.

'Get December over and then make a decision.' Harry clears his throat. 'You've done brilliantly, Sasha. It wasn't easy being left such a responsibility at such a young age. You've managed to keep your staff in employment for ten years. Your sister is growing into a marvellous young lady. Don't be so hard on yourself. Selling up might offer you a sense of freedom you never realised you missed.'

I don't want freedom.

Whereas Chloe left the second she could, despite my teenage fantasies of swanning off to the States, you couldn't pay me to move now. Well, I might have to, but it certainly won't be my choice. I'm a home bird, and this is my home. If I have to sell it, I will, but it will break every single cell in my heart.

A knock on the office door saves me from having to respond to Harry's kind, but misplaced, concern.

'Come in,' I call, pleasantly. I like the staff to know they can approach me with anything, at any time. My door is always open, even when it's not.

Tilly steps into the room, beaming from ear to ear. Her long blonde hair's piled on top of her head into a stylish, messy knot that the teenagers favour these days.

God, when did I get so fucking old? Raising a child does

that you. The flat of my palm instinctively goes to my stomach the same way it always does.

'Louise asked me to give you this.' Louise is the head receptionist. She's been with me for three years now – efficient, organised and a pleasure to have around.

Tilly passes me a sheet of neatly folded A4 paper, her hand trembling as it extends in my direction. She looks fit to burst with excitement.

Harry and I exchange a curious stare before I unfold it.

It's a booking reference for a reservation. My eyes must be deceiving me because it looks like someone has hired the penthouse for the next six weeks. The penthouse costs almost four thousand euro a night. It's three thousand square feet of top-floor luxury with its own private terrace, complete with hot tub overlooking the grounds. Bar the odd wedding, it's rarely used.

My eyebrows shoot skywards. Who on earth would book the penthouse for six weeks? It'd have to be some sort of royalty to justify that. And if it is royalty, imagine the publicity it could bring?

Do I dare to dream my luck could be improving?

The name on the booking is Mickey Mouse. Celebrities always do that. Whoever it is, must be a really big fish.

'Wow. Any idea who it is?'

'You will never believe it!' Tilly's shrill tone is ten octaves higher than usual, she's practically squealing.

'Who?' The suspense is killing me.

'Ryan Cooper. Oh my *fucking* god! The man is an absolute legend.' Her fingers fly to her lips, like she can't quite believe she said 'fuck' in front of her boss.

She needn't worry. The second *his* name fell from her lips, nothing else mattered.

'It'll be good for business at least,' Megan says, nursing a glass of wine, perched on the purple plush velvet sofa of my private quarters, which just so happens to be adjacent to the penthouse suite.

'It won't be good for me.'

I've opted for the hard stuff, swirling amber liquid round a crystal tumbler before pressing it to my lips. It burns, but not nearly as much as the knowledge that Ryan Cooper thinks he can waltz back into my home, after ten years of nothingness.

Like he didn't abandon me when I needed him the most.

Like he didn't obliterate my heart into a trillion tiny shards, when it was already in bits with the sudden shocking loss of my parents. He didn't even stick around long enough to offer his sympathies.

How dare he? The sheer audacity of him. Now he's a superstar, does he think he's above the common laws of human decency? Or is he clueless enough to think it's all in the past now?

I deliberately don't have my face on the castle website or social media, preferring to use the youthful faces of my star-quality employees. Perhaps he thinks I've left? Moved on with my life. Huh. Part of me will probably never move on.

'Call the front desk.' I point at the old-fashioned landline. Each room in the castle has one, but they're only ever used to ring reception. 'Tell Louise to ring back our VIP guest.'

'You can't cancel him, Sasha. You said it yourself, the estate needs an injection of cash.' Megan shoots me a pleading look. She needs this job as much as I need this castle.

'I know. That's why Louise's going to tell him she made a mistake. She's going to apologise for using last year's pricing. Inform him the suite is actually eight thousand a night. Let's see that flashy git put his money where his mouth is.' A small smile forms on my lips for the first time since the news broke. It might be petty but it makes me feel better – marginally. Like I have some sort of control of the situation, when clearly I don't.

Megan's green eyes widen. 'You can't do that!'

'You better believe I can. If I am going to even contemplate suffering that man under my roof, he's damn well going to pay the price for it.'

A snort of laughter bursts from my best friend. 'He'll know you did it deliberately.'

'I don't care.' More like, I wish I didn't care. The thought of seeing him again in the flesh after all these years, literally turns me into a brandy-drinking quivering mess.

He was everything to me, once upon a time. When he left, he took a part of me with him. He scarred my soul with a wound so deep, I've never been able to let anyone else get near me for fear they'll do the same.

Even Conor Riley, my gorgeous head chef. He's the only other man I've ever secretly contemplated getting close to after Ryan. And even at that – it's been years and I'm still contemplating, no further forward than when he first started at the castle. Three years older than me, he joined us straight after he graduated, ten months after my parents passed.

'What if it puts him off and we lose his business?'

It's no coincidence he booked into my castle.

'It won't, trust me. It's pittance to him. If he's booked this place, it's because he wants to come back.'

Why though?

From the look of it – and believe me when I say I try not to – it appears he's living the high life in the States. Each glossy photo plastered front page of the tabloids boasts a different singer or actress on his arm.

My stomach churns.

'Why would he come back now? After all these years?' Megan's thoughts mirror my own.

'No idea.'

She bites her lip thoughtfully. 'You know, the gossip rags are claiming he has writer's block.' She takes a sip from her glass to avoid looking at me. She's the only one who knows what Ryan and I had. That we used to spend hours composing songs together. So many times she's hinted half the songs on his album were basically written by me. I wouldn't know, I could never bring myself to listen to them.

She stands and stalks towards the phone. 'You know what, I'd call it compensation for smashing your heart into a trillion pieces. Eight grand a night's a bargain!' She winks as she relays the message to Louise.

I sip my drink and wait for my shaking hands to steady.

Ten minutes later, the phone rings. It can only be reception calling back. Perhaps Mr Flash-Ass isn't prepared to put his money where his mouth is after all.

'Everything ok?' I ask.

'Yes, I just wanted to confirm that the new price was fine for our, erm... special guest. Also he booked an extra room – a deluxe suite with sea views for his, erm, companion. I took the liberty of adding a fifty per cent increase on to our usual price, I hope that's ok?'

I should be delighted. It's a huge boost for the castle. Yet, the thought of Ryan and his 'companion' makes me violently nauseous. Bad enough he's coming back, but to bring a woman with him too. It maims like a rusty dagger.

'Great initiative, Louise. You've just earned yourself a bonus. Thank you.'

Megan rolls her eyes, having overheard the entire exchange. 'Companion! Pah! What a tosser! It'll be weird, you know, seeing him after all these years.'

'You're telling me.' It's the understatement of the century.

'Does Victoria know you used to date him?' Megan glances at Victoria's closed bedroom door.

'Yeah, Ryan used to chase her round and play tag with her. She used to adore him. Funny, she never brings it up now.'

As young as she is, she seems to know it hurts. It's safely in the firmly taped box of 'we don't discuss' – along with *that* night, and everything else that might rip open any other barely closed wounds.

'Is she still seeing the counsellor?' Megan's voice drops to a hushed whisper even though it's only the two of us here.

'Yeah. It seems to help.'

I could probably do with a few sessions myself, though I don't need a professional to tell me why I can't let anyone get close to me.

'I know it's less than ideal, but maybe this is exactly what Huxley Castle needs, you know, some excitement. Ryan's arrival will certainly put us back on the map.'

It's exactly what the castle needs. But the return of Ryan Cooper is precisely everything *I* don't need.

CHAPTER FOUR

RYAN

20th November

'I think you're making a mistake.' Jayden runs his fingers over his ever present designer stubble.

'You were the one who told me to find some inspiration.'

I throw an assortment of random clothes haphazardly into a suitcase. Anything I forget, I'll buy.

'Is it even safe?' Jayden alludes to our father's previous misdemeanours.

'Well, I'm pretty sure there's no arrest warrant out for me. If there was, I'd have heard about it by now. I've not exactly been in hiding – unless you count from the paparazzi.'

Jayden tuts. 'I wasn't just referring to Dad's illegal endeavours.'

I pile in three of my thickest sweaters, the temperature's likely to a be shock after the warmth of LA. 'Well then, what exactly are you referring to?'

He looms by my open patio doors, gazing out at the

bright lights of Hollywood. 'Is this about that girl you used to bang?'

'Don't be ridiculous.' Even as I swat off his remark, I don't dare question the truth of it.

Admittedly, I'm looking for inspiration. Something that came in abundance when we were together. I've been emotionally incapacitated for the last ten years. Leaving her like that, disappearing into the black night, especially *that* night, was the hardest thing I've ever had to do.

Dad left me with no choice. As we fled, he stressed repeatedly that any contact with anyone from our previous life would directly result in him being banged up. We were forbidden from using phones and social media. Hell, he wouldn't even let me send an email.

Then when we got to the States he pretty much abandoned us.

I didn't finish my schooling. I have zero formal qualifications. Thankfully, I didn't end up needing them, but it was less than ideal on so many levels.

Against all his warnings, I did leave Sasha a brief note in the cabin before we fled. Fat lot of good it did. I never got so much as a Christmas card from her.

It was that point that I became emotionally stunted. When I left her, it was like I'd left half of myself behind. When months passed and I heard nothing, I assumed she'd heard about my father's illegal activity.

Seeing the switching on of the Times Square Christmas lights, and the memories it evoked, sparked the first real emotion I've felt in years. Turns out I'm not just a great singer, I'm a fucking brilliant actor too, because that's exactly what I've been doing these past ten years. Plastering the all-American smile on my face and performing like a circus animal, while my internal well was running dry enough to bleed out every ounce of anything real.

If I see Sasha, I'll deal with it, but I'm not looking for her.

I'm looking for the me I was back then. The man who was capable of banging out song lyrics by the hour. Respectable ones too.

Jayden sighs, entirely unconvinced. I'm not sure if his concerns stem from his role as my agent, or my brother. 'When are you leaving?'

'Now.' I glance at the chunky piece of Swiss metal on my wrist. 'My flight leaves in four hours. Pierce's coming with me.'

Jayden's face pinches into a frown and he rubs the bridge of his nose. 'That's something, I suppose.'

Pierce is my private protection. He goes everywhere with me. Another eternal bachelor, and trained Marine, he's every bit as deadly with his bare hands as a rifle. No one in their right mind would cross him.

He lives in a smaller section of my house, never usually seen or heard unless there's a problem. Which recently, there hasn't been, thank goodness.

'When will you be home?' Jayden begins pacing the carpet fast enough to wear a hole in it.

'I booked the castle for six weeks, give or take. I'm not sure how long I need.'

'You're staying in the fucking castle?' He stares at me like I've lost my mind. Maybe I have, but there's no point doing half a job. If I'm going back, I'm going right back to the beginning.

'Yes. It's been ten years. I'll barely know anyone there.'

I'm under no illusion Sasha will be there. She's probably married with kids by now. She always wanted to be a mother. Did she study music at college? Or did she veer in a more academic direction, like her father hoped?

I need to stop thinking about her. Obsessing about Sasha. It's not healthy. Going back is one thing. Going down a long overgrown rabbit hole is an entirely different matter. We've both moved on.

Except maybe I haven't.

'You're due to perform in Vegas in the middle of December.' Jayden enunciates every word as if I'm eight, not twenty-eight.

'No fucking shit, Sherlock.' I roll my eyes at him. 'That is exactly why it's imperative I get the fuck out of here and get some work done in preparation.'

He shoves a hand through his hair for what seems like the hundredth time. 'Do you want me to come with you?' His tone is weighted with a reluctance, suggesting he'd rather walk the fucking plank.

Thankfully, I feel the same.

'No, I don't. The whole point is to get away. To find myself. The last thing I want is company. Bad enough Pierce has to come.' I shoot a look towards the doorway in time to see my burly bodyguard, hovering pensively. 'Sorry, Pierce, no offence. It's just hard to think straight in permanent company.'

'You won't even know I'm there.' Pierce crosses his enormous, muscular arms over his chest and nods once before continuing down the corridor.

Jayden's face is scrunched up as though he's in pain. 'Are you sure you don't want me to come with you? My schedule is pretty flexible – most of my other signings are behaving themselves.' He shoots me another glare.

Mocking him, I click my fingers like I've just remembered her name, biting back the smirk threatening my lips. 'Does this have anything to do with that girl you used to bang? Jacinta? Or Janine?'

'Don't be fucking ridiculous,' he huffs.

'Well, now you know how I feel. Stop fussing and let me

get on with what I have to do.' I slam the suitcase closed and lock it, fiddling to set the code.

'The difference is, little brother, I was never in love with Jacinta. You, on the other hand, spent years mooning over Sasha Sexton.'

'Oh, now you remember her name? Besides, there's an embarrassingly large number of women in LA who would beg to differ.'

'Really? Remind me again how many of those women you used those three life-changing little words on again? Or how many of those women you composed song after song about?' He stops pacing, long enough to tower in front of me.

'Whatever, Jayden. You'll be smiling all the way to the bank when I come back with enough songs to fill ten new albums.'

'You really think that's gonna be the case?' He takes a step backwards to scrutinise my face. I've never been able to lie to him. We've always been close. Mam left when we were toddlers and, before he left us, Dad worked every hour god sent to provide for us, though definitely not as honourably as we'd have liked.

'Why else would I go back to Ireland at the start of the coldest season of the year?'

I amble out into the hallway and down the marble circular staircase, with Jayden tight at my heels.

'Just be careful, ok?' Not exactly the affectionate type, Jayden slaps my back in a manly gesture.

'Gee, maybe there's a heart in that chest of yours, after all.' Though none of the women in this city would concur. I might be a love-them-and-leave-them type, but I least I do it with honesty and a kind smile. Jayden's always been the treat-them-mean type.

'Whatever. Call me if you need me.' He strides purposefully towards the front door.

'Will do. Try not to break any more hearts this week.' I loiter in the doorway as he marches over my paving.

'We all have our talents.' He opens the door to his shiny new Mercedes SLK, shouting over his shoulder as an afterthought, 'Can I borrow your Ferrari while you're gone?'

'Not a fucking chance. Buy your own.'

He sniggers and offers me his middle finger as a parting gesture. 'Write that fucking album and I might just do that.'

That's the whole idea.

I only hope it's a good one, because if it turns out not to be, I don't have a whole heap of others.

CHAPTER FIVE

SASHA

21st November

I spend the entire morning getting ready for the arrival of Ryan- Runaway-Cooper and his 'companion'.

Excuse me if I sound bitter. I'm not. It's not in my nature. But I want to be here when they arrive, to face any potential awkwardness head-on – with a professional smile and a formal aloof welcome – before making my excuses and avoiding him, and her, for the next six weeks, or however long he actually hangs around for this time.

Curiosity burns at the prospect of seeing him in the flesh after all these years. My insecure inner eighteen-year-old lurks, desperate to prove his rapid departure didn't affect me, even though Chloe would testify it almost killed me.

He might be living the high life in the States, but it's imperative he knows my life here is perfectly fulfilling too. I don't need him, and I never did. I want for nothing. I have my sisters; I have Megan; I have my staff and I have my castle. For now, at least.

My stomach flips as I sneak a discreet glance through the gleaming sash window of the large private quarters I share with Victoria.

He's here. After all, who else would be crushing up the driveway in a brand-new lustrous black limo? The windows are noticeably tinted, obviously, but it's him.

Even from this distance, his sheer proximity pricks something deep inside my core, sending a hit of heat crusading through my bloodstream.

With a deep breath, I take a final peek at my reflection in the vanity station. First thing this morning I visited the castle's spa. It's pretty mediocre compared to most and something I'd love to invest in if I ever manage to turn this place around. A prospect that's looking less likely with each passing day. The facilities are basic, but Tara, one of the beauty therapists, worked her magic on me nevertheless. It's a perk I never usually avail of, too busy working to worry about my appearance.

Ryan's ageing well. The odd time I've glimpsed a flash of his tanned chiselled face was enough to ascertain the man is as beautiful as ever, on the outside at least. No doubt the woman he's bringing will be equally stunning.

Precisely why I need all the help I can get today. Tara managed to create an effortlessly chic look. The scrub she used on my face has my skin gleaming with a radiance I usually only dream of. The foundation she applied provides a natural luminosity. Some sort of magic mascara renders my eyelashes a foot longer.

I should avail of Tara's talents more often.

Ha! Where would I get the time? I almost choke on my own snort.

My hair hangs loosely in bouncing curls that fall down my back. Where Megan hates her spiralling locks, I pay good money to have mine set this way. It's the only regular vanity I indulge in. Nothing says confidence like bouncing curls.

I turn to the side, hating that I'm wondering what he'll think of me after all these years. If he'll like my appearance, like he seemed to before.

It shouldn't matter. Yet, it somehow does.

Smoothing down the black fitted pencil dress that clings to my frame, I examine my silhouette. I'm slimmer than I was back then, which can only be attributed to stress, or the fact I never stand still long enough to gain a single ounce. Every cloud, I suppose.

As the car halts outside the window below, I count to five, exhaling slowly through my nose, before descending the wide walnut staircase. White knuckles grip the intricately carved banister, my shaky legs faltering is a real possibility.

Forcing a smile, I fix my gaze on the reception desk below instead of the front door. I'd hate for him to think I'm eagerly awaiting his entrance, when, curiosity aside, it's actually the polar opposite.

Vibrant crimson and emerald garlands adorn the reception area. A lush, bushy, shimmering sixteen-foot Christmas tree towers proudly, welcoming guests as they come through the door – no colours, simply white lights again.

I mentally repeat the same mantra I've been privately practicing since I learned of his impending arrival.

Be cool.
Calm.
Collected.
Indifferent.
Unaffected.
He's just another guy.
A childhood ex.
Just another paying customer, albeit a very wealthy one.

The rich scent of cinnamon and pine wafts through the

air as the heavy front door swings open, dramatically banging against the inside stone wall.

The manly form that enters is a far cry from the boy that left all those years ago. He's inexplicably more exquisite. A magnetising aura radiates far and wide in every direction. His star quality is undeniable. With that jet-black hair and powerful physique, even from across the room, he's impossibly striking.

For fuck's sake. Someone upstairs is testing me. Haven't I endured enough?

A discreet, fleeting glance allows a quick closer inspection. The worst is confirmed. Ryan Cooper, aged twenty-eight is utterly fucking arresting. If I didn't already know the man was a rockstar, it wouldn't be hard to imagine.

He exudes a unique confidence. Still rocking the bad boy vibe, a fitted black leather jacket sculpts his powerful shoulders before nipping in his lean waistline. Low hanging jeans drape below his hips, sculpting a ridiculously pert backside.

My stiletto comes to an abrupt stop, hovering an inch above the bottom step as I drink him in. His hair is longer than it used to be, shaggier. The way it frames the familiar contours of his face begs me to rake my fingers through it. Stubble dusts his jaw.

And that mouth.

Oh my god.

His full Cupid's bow – plush, plump lips. The memory of exactly what they're capable of springs to the forefront of my mind.

Close your mouth, Sasha fucking Sexton.

Despite my best efforts, a tiny, barely audible gasp escapes my throat.

His head whips round. The rucksack he clutches drops to the floor as his chin lifts, and inquisitive eyes seek out mine.

They're a warm dark chocolate, only accentuated by his Californian tan.

In one eternally damning split second, he manages to transport me back to my swooning teenage self. The naive, hopeful girl brimming with absolute awe and adoration for the boy before her. Heat floods my veins as spiralling chemicals surge to parts of me that have been in an unrousable slumber since he left.

The natural light accentuates tiny amber flecks in his smouldering eyes. Torrid golden flames ignite in his irises, dancing dangerously as his tongue flicks over his lower lip before disappearing again.

Our eyes lock and something powerful passes between us – an undeniable connection so raw that it penetrates every inch of my body, searing my soul.

Fuck. Fuck. Fuckity fuck.

So much for remaining cool. Three seconds after his untimely return, the man has my insides blistering and my blood boiling.

He takes a step forward as my foot eventually connects with the bottom step.

'Sasha,' Ryan's gravelly voice pronounces my name like it's the most precious word to fall from his tongue. 'It's been a while.'

He strides across the grey mosaic tiled flooring to stand directly before me.

I offer my hand to shake his, at the same time as he bends to press a kiss against my face, leaving our hands joined while his hot lips press against my cheek. I'm on the verge of spontaneous combustion. The contact further fuels the growing, dizzying lust inside; the lure of his touch as promising as ever.

Mustering the strength of an army, I manage to utter three tiny words. 'It certainly has.'

Tearing my eyes from his, I sidestep his hold, channelling

my inner Beyonce as I sashay towards reception to Louise, who's standing wide-eyed and open-mouthed watching our unusual exchange from behind the polished walnut desk.

If there are whispers around the castle regarding my history with Ryan, none of the staff have said it to my face, but this little encounter will likely spread like wildfire. Even the best staff gossip.

'Louise, this is Mr Cooper. Please ensure he has everything he needs for the duration of his visit.' My tone can only be described as pleasant. And distant. Which is exactly what I'm aiming for. Attractive he might be. He's also the bastard who disappeared after taking my V-card, and smashing my heart to smithereens the same night my parents died.

I'd do well to remember it.

There's no sign of his companion yet. Perhaps she's arriving separately. It's none of my business. I'm not supposed to care. Turning abruptly on my heels, I get halfway back to the staircase in my attempt to escape *him* and the gut-wrenching, world-spinning effect he creates, before he catches my wrist.

Yanking free from his grip, I glare up at him. Beyonce and her cool demeanour have officially left the building, ten years' worth of rage and hurt rise dangerously close to the surface.

He towers over me. 'That's it? After all these years?'

My eyebrows lift so high into the air I wonder if they need an oxygen mask up there. 'What exactly did you expect?'

The man has the neck of a giraffe. He's used to being pandered to in LA with his screaming groupies, an army of adoring fans. Does he expect me to bow down and join them? Hell will freeze over first.

'Not this, obviously. Not you.' A hint of hurt lingers in his tone. 'I must say, it's a surprise. A pleasant one, of course.' His velvet voice is deeper, even more masculine than I remember. An American twang weaves through his Dublin accent.

'You book in to my castle, yet you don't expect to see me?' Tossing my hair off my shoulder, I wonder if he's winding me up, or what.

'Well, I knew there was a chance, but truthfully I thought you might have left...' His eyes fall to my left hand. 'Got married maybe...'

'Oh you thought so, did you?' Hot rage boils beneath my skin. My voice drops to barely more than a hiss. 'Funny how you thought that, yet you didn't think to say goodbye before you vanished from the face of the earth all those years ago.'

Fuck. Fuck. Fuck. I promised myself I wouldn't bring it up. I swore not to let him see how he affected me.

How he still apparently affects me.

He's been here less than a minute and I've failed epically on all of the above.

Thick tanned fingers sweep through his hair as a huge weighted sigh rushes from his chest. His face falls and his eyes drop to the floor. 'You're right, Sasha. I'm sorry. It's none of my business.'

For a split second, I almost feel sorry for him. Almost.

'The past is the past, Ryan. Let's leave it there. Truly, I hope you enjoy your stay at Huxley Castle. My staff will be sure to cater for your every need. If anything arises surplus to the usual requirements, the General Manager will assist you.'

Oh God, ground swallow me whole, please! If anything arises! That sounded shockingly sexual!

I need to get away from him this second because I'm liable to blurt out anything with his intoxicating masculinity wreaking havoc with my newly awakened pheromones.

'*Your* staff?' His turn to raise eyebrows.

'Yes.' Has the man gone deaf since he was here the last time? Who the hell else would be running the show?

'Where are your parents?'

As he glances round the dome-ceilinged room with a quizzical expression carved onto his chiselled face, my gut twists painfully.

This has to be some sort of sick joke, right? Why would he even say that? Pretend not to know? He was even there when Chloe arrived at the door.

My lips part, then close again as the blood drains from my cheeks, rushing to my rapidly hammering heart.

Dark pupils search mine, piercing my soul, scratching the thinly formed surface barely sheathing the scars beneath.

I take deep breaths, concentrating on measured inhalations and exhalations, as my hand fumbles around clumsily for the handrail of the staircase once again. It's paramount that I drag myself away from here right now. Away from him.

'Sasha?' Concern colours his molten eyes.

'My parents are dead, Ryan.'

Horror rips across his features. He visibly recoils in shock. A hand lunges towards me again, but I'm quicker this time. His condolences are ten years too late.

'Oh my god. I had no idea, Sasha. I'm so unbelievably sorry for your loss.'

Still confused, I shrug off his sympathy, even as my heart tears opens in my chest once again. 'It's life.'

'When did they pass?'

I glance up to see a six-foot-five, burly soldier type entering the castle, staring intently at Ryan. Covered in tattoos and protruding muscles, he looks like he stepped straight out of the army. James is at his heels, laden with two plastic Samsonite suitcases.

Ryan barely glances in their direction, but he raises a hand at the man as if to tell him to wait. His eyes are trained solely on me. 'That's Pierce. My travel companion.'

His companion?

Of course the man travels with security. He's a fucking superstar. In fact I'm surprised he didn't bring the full entourage.

A shiver of simultaneous relief and stupidity rips through me. Relief I don't have to watch him parade around my family home with another woman hanging off his arm. Stupidity for thinking he'd book a separate suite for another woman in the first place. And extreme stupidity for caring either way.

His deep sultry voice lowers to barely more than a whisper. 'When, Sasha?'

'Does it matter?' Crossing my arms across my chest, my chin tilts in a defiant stance.

'It matters to me.' His tone is almost pleading.

Huffing like Victoria might, I manage to utter, 'It'll be ten years next month,' before turning on my heels and fleeing to the Ryan-free safety of my own private quarters before he can completely unravel me.

The continued attraction between us is inconvenient to say the least, but the man abandoned me. He took my heart, my soul and my ability to trust anyone.

He broke me for anyone that might come after him. No way will I ever fall under the spell of Ryan Cooper ever again. I barely survived the first time.

CHAPTER SIX

RYAN

In the enormous, elaborately decorated atrium, I'm left reeling from both Sasha's shocking revelation and the intoxicating sensation of being in her proximity after all this time.

The castle has barely changed, but she certainly has. She's matured into one sophisticated beauty. Exquisite jade eyes are still piercing, but where they were once bright and inviting, they're now pensively wary.

The urge to grab her waist was barely controllable. My fingers ached to stroke the porcelain complexion of her face, naturally dewy and fresh, a stark contrast to the women I've met in LA.

Sasha might be slimmer, but her self-assured, stoic presence makes her bigger than ever, smashing down the carefully constructed shield within my chest, once again stealing my heart from within. So much for being emotionally frigid. Apparently, I was merely on the wrong side of the Atlantic.

Fuck.

I'm under no mad illusion that she'll ever feel the same. I

left her with no explanation, abandoning all our plans. I barely had time to pen a hastily scrawled note, no wonder it didn't cut it.

And now I discover her parents died, the same month I disappeared. It must have been the worst time of her life and she had to face it alone. There's no rebuttal. How could there be?

The night my father piled us into a black taxi and ushered us through the airport to his sister's remote ranch in Texas, every single cell of my body shrivelled and died.

The iniquitous investment he'd championed had gone spectacularly up in smoke, along with the cash he'd acquired from several corrupt sources. He had to flee the country or risk going down for the rest of his life.

Nausea rips through me as I glimpse a hint of the horror that Sasha must have gone through. Losing them and me in the same month. Especially after what we'd done. What she'd given me.

A million questions spark and burn inside of me. Questions I have no right to ask, and less right to be given answers to.

Pierce's steel-toe capped boots clunk against the mosaic floor, snapping me back to the present and I finally turn away from the recently vacated staircase to check in.

Louise, the girl on reception, stutters and stammers her way through her welcome speech.

At the risk of sounding like a total douche, I tend to have that effect on women. I'm not vain enough to believe I'm irresistible or anything, it's just the shock of seeing someone you're used to watching on a big screen in the flesh. It was the same for me and Jayden when we first moved to LA.

A handful of babbling women pass through the grand hallway, slowing to almost a standstill, inquisitive eyes darting between Pierce and me.

Noting the increasing interest, Pierce assumes command. 'Upstairs. To wherever the penthouse is. I'll deal with the formalities in a minute.'

Louise slips from her position behind the desk and gesticulates in the direction of the stairs. Good. The penthouse must be near Sasha. The draw to slip away and seek her out is growing with every passing second.

I've been back less than three minutes and she has me utterly enamoured with her again already. Though god knows what I'm hoping for. From the way she briskly bolted, she made it quite clear she doesn't want to be anywhere near me. I can't blame her. The fairest thing I can do is leave her the fuck alone.

In a matter of minutes I have more inspiration for an album than I've had in years. The loss of her burns acutely, as if it was yesterday. The loss of our relationship, of everything that could have been. My soul's been ripped open and is finally fit to bleed straight out onto a notepad.

We climb the vast staircase to the spacious landing above. Window seats, lined with plump navy velvet cushions, offer extensive views of the gardens and woodlands. The only view I'm interested in seeing again is Sasha Sexton.

I'm addicted to her once again.

Was I ever not?

Every intimate encounter I ever had in LA was fucking laughable in comparison to what I feel for her. What I've always felt for her.

But she deserves better than me. She did then and she does now.

A variety of oil paintings adorn the walls, lush landscapes and authentic beach scenes. They're evenly spaced and beautifully framed with gilded wood. The carpet's thick underfoot, in the same shade of dove grey as the flooring below. Dense grey and navy curtains frame the window, clasped back with threaded silver tassels. It's like taking a step back ten years. The decor appears almost exactly the same as when Sasha's mother and father ran the place.

Navy, discreet double doors are nestled to my right. If I didn't already know they were there, I might have missed them. I can only assume that was Sasha's parents' intention when they claimed this area of the castle as their family home.

I know the inside of that area well – intimate memories of a misspent youth, (or well-spent some might argue) have haunted my dreams for a decade.

'If you'd like to follow me, sir.' Louise beckons us across the corridor to the entrance of the penthouse. There's no missing it, with its majestic maple door and burnished wall plaque.

Using a touch key card, she opens the door before standing back and allowing us to enter.

The suite is enormous and bright, despite the dark regal decor within. A colossal lounge area boasts sliding doors opening onto a huge terrace overlooking the extensive landscape, gloriously stretching all the way to the Irish Sea. The balustrade is comprised entirely of glass and chrome offering the perception of infinity. A hot tub sits next to a slate-grey Elementi fire pit.

I thought someone was having one over on me, but I can see the justification of the price. This is worth every cent.

LA has some stunning spots, but there's no place like home, and that's even without The Sasha Effect.

A porter enters with my luggage, and Pierce leaves with Louise to find his own suite next door.

'I won't bother you, boss. But I'll be listening. Shout if you need anything.'

'Thanks, Pierce.' I appreciate his discretion, but the only thing I really need right now, is to get my head straight.

Because every single bone in my body is screaming at me to bang on the door of Sasha's private quarters and beg for her forgiveness. Something which is not only utterly futile, but completely undeserved.

We had our time. Our chance. It wasn't to be. Her life's here. Mine's in LA. It's pointless starting something I won't be able to finish. Again.

Opening my suitcase, I begin to unpack. The crisp white designer shirts and tailored leather jackets seemed so appropriate in LA, here they just highlight how colourless my life is.

For the first time in months, my guitar calls to me from where the porter left it in the lounge area. My fingers itch to strum. To find a way to vent this emotion I'm finally feeling, to channel it outside of my body, because I've just been given a crash course in why I suppressed it for so long – it has the potential to consume me.

I need to expel it one way or another before it tears me apart. And though it might hurt like hell, this is exactly why I came here.

Grabbing the Huxley Castle stationery, I take my guitar onto the terrace and finally put pen to paper.

CHAPTER SEVEN

SASHA

22nd November

Despite the dark ungodly hour, my mobile vibrates from the pillow next to me. Assuming it's my alarm, I hit the red button. Within seconds, it's buzzing again. I cancel it for the second time.

Rolling face first into my pillow, I bury myself further under the duck-down duvet, hiding from the day ahead. Another day of trying to avoid Ryan. Though he made it easy yesterday, not emerging from his suite once.

Not that I was watching, I simply happened to notice the door didn't open across the hall. But he won't stay holed up in there forever.

When the phone vibrates for a third time, I know it can only be Chloe. She's four hours ahead in Dubai and has a horrible habit of ringing me at appalling hours.

'Hello?'

'Hey, Sasha, put the light on. I can't see a thing!' Her chirpy voice singsongs through the receiver.

'That's because it's the middle of the night.' I groan, flicking the bedside lamp on nonetheless.

Squinting at the image of my sister sitting on her beachside balcony, I can't help but admire her peach short-sleeved blouse. The sun beams on the horizon behind her and tendrils of her hair sway in the soft breeze.

How can anyone be this chipper in the mornings?

'It's time you were getting up anyway, you have a multimillion euro castle to run!' She jokes, oblivious to the true financial difficulty this multimillion castle is actually in.

'Hmm. You could at least wait until I've had my coffee to call.'

'Get one of the breakfast staff to bring you one up.' She shrugs. 'You are the boss.'

'Yes, I'm the boss, not the fucking queen. Jesus, Chloe, I swear you've been watching too much *Downton Abbey* or something. Either that or you've been away too long. This might be a castle, but I'm no princess! There's never a dull moment. Every single person works their ass off here.'

'Oh stop complaining, you love it really!' she scoffs.

She's right. I do love it. Which is why I need to think of a plan, and fast, if I'm going to make this place profitable before I lose it forever.

'Anyway, enough of the small talk! Did Ryan-Runaway-Cooper arrive yet or what?' She raises her sunglasses from her face up onto her head, peering intently across the screen like she's trying to see inside my soul.

My eyes roll skywards. 'Who told you about that?'

'Victoria, of course. Do you even have to ask?' She smirks. We both know when it comes to our baby sister, Chloe's the good cop and I'm the bad cop, and that's just the way it has to be.

'But even if she didn't, it's all over the Irish news channels.'

I'm still half asleep. 'You get Irish news channels in Dubai?'

She rolls her eyes at me. 'On the internet. Get with the times, sister.'

Unlike Chloe, I don't have time to search the internet, surf social media, watch *Downton Abbey* or anything else of the sort. I'm too busy. But like she said, I love it. It gives me a sense of purpose.

'Have the press started hounding the place yet? Are the paps circling like crazy? How have the bookings been? I bet the place is swamped with calls!'

If it is, it's news to me. Mind you, I've been locked in our family quarters since yesterday lunchtime sorting through a mountain of paperwork I've been putting off all year. Funny how yesterday suddenly seemed like the perfect afternoon to tackle it.

When I don't reply, Chloe continues the interrogation. 'So, what was it like seeing him again? Tell me, is he as hot as he looks on TV these days?'

'Eurgh, Chloe! Do we have to do this? You know I hate talking about him! He might look good on the outside, but remember what Mam used to say? *"There's many a good-looking bastard."* Ryan is a prime example. It's just a shame that at eighteen I wasn't equipped to see it.'

'Oh, please. He was never a bastard. He was utterly enamoured with you.'

'So enamoured he left,' I remind her. 'Why are you taking his side? You know what he did to me.'

'I'm not taking his side! You've spent the last ten years avoiding the issue of Ryan Cooper. Now he's sleeping under the same roof as you, it might finally be time to confront it. Find out what the fuck actually happened.'

'I know what happened. He left. I stayed. End of story.'

'But why? Did he say why? Honestly, Sash, I know we

were all kids, but I could have sworn you two were the real deal.'

So could I, that's why it hurt so much when he disappeared. It was so unexpected.

It should be comforting that I wasn't the only one he fooled, but Chloe isn't exactly the best judge of character either. The last serious boyfriend she had was her office manager. He took half her clients, big names she acquired through her own sheer hard work and determination. She too was left high and dry, well almost. She managed to claw them back, eventually, and so many more.

Fast-forward three years and her events company has overseen some of the biggest occasions in the Middle East, going from strength to strength with each passing year. She's one of the most successful women I know, but she learned her lessons the hard way. These days, she's ruthless.

Chloe is permanently dating, dining in fancy restaurants and living the high life on private yachts, schmoozing men over business deals. And I hear way too much detail than any sibling should have to endure about her sex life, but she never lets anyone into her heart or into her life, refusing to be taken for a fool twice. These days she point-blank refuses to date the same guy more than once.

I've tried to tell her that not all men are the same, but I'm not exactly blazing a trail. Apart from an awkward couple of dates with the son of a friend of Aunty Mags, I haven't really been on many dates.

There's always been an underlying attraction with Conor, my gorgeous and exceptionally talented head chef, but neither of us have acted on it. Megan perpetually teases me about it. She swears he's in love with me, and has been for years. I'm not completely unaware there might be some grain of truth to it.

When Conor first started here he asked me out a couple

of times, but it was always under the guise of a joke so I never knew if he was serious or not. Either way, it wasn't a chance I was willing to take. I needed a chef, and friend, more than anything else.

Now time has passed and the attraction still lingers, but we have such a great friendship, I'd hate to mess it up.

Besides, it has no comparison to the connection I had with Ryan-Runaway-Cooper back in the day. That was intoxicating stuff. Wild horses wouldn't have stopped me acting on that. It was feral. Though the manageable attraction to Conor is probably far healthier.

Maybe what Ryan and I experienced was just teenage lusty hormones? Maybe adult attraction is supposed to be calmer, slow building?

'Sasha, are you still there? The screen looks like it's frozen.'

The screen is fine. It's me that's frozen.

'I'm here. I just don't know what to say to be honest. I don't know where to start.'

'Start at the beginning. Did you see him? Or did you let the minions do your dirty work?' She sticks her tongue out, knowing her words will get a rise out of me.

'They're not my minions, Chloe! You know how much I value each and every one of them.' I take a deep breath. She might be ruthless in business, but I prefer the staff here to feel like part of the family.

'Sasha, spill the FECKIN' beans! Did you see Ryan?'

'Yes, I saw him.' Colour floods my cheeks even picturing our brief but heated exchange.

'And?' She rubs her hands together expectantly.

'And what?' What am I supposed to say? The man is an even bigger ride than ever, speaking of which, that's all I've thought about doing since I laid eyes on him again. Even though part of me actually hates him, I can't deny the attraction still burns like a forest fire.

I guess I can rule out it being synonymous with being a teenager, because clearly I'm still battling it.

'Did you talk? Did he apologise? Did he say why he left?'

'We talked briefly. He didn't apologise and he didn't explain why.' I close my mouth before I can blurt the rest. The part that really shocked me. The part that might potentially allow the rage in my heart to still long enough to even contemplate forgiving him.

Canny as ever, Chloe picks up on my hesitation. 'What? What else? You were about to say something then before you clammed up again.'

Swallowing hard, I stare at my sister who looks so much like me, but is so wildly different. So much stronger, assertive, less damaged.

'He didn't know.'

She leans so far into the screen I'd swear she's about to crash though it.

'About Mam and Dad – about the accident. He asked where they were.'

Her sharp intake of breath reminds me that perhaps she's not as strong as the front she puts on. 'How could he not know? The night I came to get you… And then it was front-page news in every single paper.'

I shrug. Before I can say any more on the matter, my bedroom door bangs open and Victoria bounds in. I swear, I don't know where she gets the energy. She was up half the night watching strangers doing random dances on TikTok. Still, I suppose it's better than what I was up to at her age.

'Sasha, have you looked out the window?' Hazel eyes spark with excitement.

Leaping from the bed, I hand Victoria the phone to talk to Chloe, racing to the window. 'Don't tell me it's snowing already? It's not even December yet. I'll have to get the paths gritted.'

The fact I can't afford a lawsuit on top of everything else, is something I deliberately don't voice. My fingers grip the heavy velvet curtains, yanking them back. Below, the castle is absolutely crawling with people, most of whom are laden down with enormous cameras, circling like vultures hunting for easy prey.

'What the...?'

Victoria holds the phone up to the window so Chloe can witness the commotion.

Her laugh echoes round the high ceiling of the bedroom that used to belong to our parents. 'I told you Ryan's return to Ireland is all over the news! He's bigger than Bono ever was. And a million times hotter. You need to up your security. Or at least see what he has planned in that department.'

'He only came with one other man.'

'You're joking? You better hope the women of Ireland don't get wind of that! There will be a full-on siege! They'll be bashing the castle door in before the day is done. There will be zero regard that it's an original wrought-iron door from the early eighteenth century and one of Daddy's favourite features!' Though she jokes, a fondness taints her tone at the memory of our father. He really did love that front door.

I'm not fond of it at all, but I can't bring myself to change a thing they loved, so keen to keep their memory alive.

'Chloe, I better go and sort this mess out before they scare all the other paying patrons away.' I grab my favourite fleece dressing gown from the back of my bedroom door and cross the varnished cherrywood flooring to my ensuite.

'You've got to be joking? No one's going to be scared away. This is the best thing to happen to the castle in years. Up the prices for the month of December. Ryan Cooper is the biggest tourist attraction you'll ever have. You may as well cash in on it.'

Though I hate to admit it, she might be right. The prospect of overcharging people makes my skin crawl, but Megan's been telling me we've been under-pricing for years. Some of our competitors are charging twice our standard bed and breakfast rate. I suppose it's no wonder the castle hasn't been turning a profit.

'I'll call you tomorrow.' I blow a kiss across the room to where Victoria sits on my bed, holding up the phone.

'You'll call me later you mean! With a full update! And we still need to talk about the Christmas ball!'

Damn. Annually hosted on the 23rd, I'd hoped it was the one tradition our parents started that she might forget. Even if I wanted to, there's no way the castle can afford to host a lavish ball this year. We couldn't last year and I did it anyway, racking up further debt.

I seriously need to reconsider the pricing.

'I'm so excited, I've tried on like three hundred dresses in the mall! Which band did you book this year? Are we going jazz? Or something more modern? Did Conor come up with a menu yet?'

I haven't so much as thought about it.

Shit.

Less than a week ago, I promised I'd make this the most fabulous Christmas ever.

It's a promise I need to make good on, no matter how much it costs. Hung for a sheep as a lamb, right? If it's going to be our last one here, we might as well go out with a bang, I suppose.

'I'm on it. Chat later.' Disappearing into the privacy of my bathroom, I switch on the shower, pondering how I'm going to pull it all off.

The extra income from the rental of the presidential suite

should cover the initial cost of a ball. I hate doing it, but the ticket prices are going to have to soar this year. After all, if Huxley Castle is good enough for one of America's biggest rockstars, it's got to be worth every penny.

Maybe Ryan's arrival will prove beneficial after all.

Huh. Tell that to my bleeding heart. It hasn't got the memo yet.

CHAPTER EIGHT

RYAN

'Looks like you've been busted.' Pierce pulls back the curtain, nodding to the infuriating source of noise below.

Huxley Castle has always been a place of sanctuary. It's one of the reasons my father was so desperate to rent a cabin here. After our mother left, he wanted his sons to be raised in peace and privacy, safely away from whatever illegitimate business he dabbled in.

I've barely been here a day and the place has transformed into a paparazzi-fuelled circus. I can only imagine Sasha's displeasure.

'It's inconvenient to say the least.' I suppose it was inevitable, but I'd hoped to get at least a few days grace.

Celebrity status has its perks, but you can't just switch it off. People I've never laid eyes on feel like they know everything about me. Like they own me. Like I'm public property.

I don't want to relocate, and not simply because I managed to bang out three new songs last night. Songs which flew effortlessly from my soul, straight to the strings of my guitar.

Jayden will finally be able to tell Diamond Records I have some new material, but even if I'm able to keep up this rate of production, which is unlikely, I'll need more than a couple of nights here to fill an album, let alone two.

'Either we move on, or we're going to have to do something drastic about the security around here.' Pierce gazes out the window, assessing the situation below.

'I'd prefer not to leave.'

Pierce nods, glancing at my guitar, which I discarded on the sofa before falling into a deep fitful sleep, haunted by dreams of my past.

'You managed to come up with something?' His normally subdued tone rings with hope.

'Yep.'

'What is it about this place?' Pierce's huge hands lift in question.

I join him at the window, careful to stay far enough back from any prying long-lensed cameras. Pointing to the row of cabins, I say, 'This is where we lived before we moved to the States.'

'And the girl?' Pierce raises his eyebrows knowingly.

He never pries, so I can only assume he's assessing how she might react to his security requests because if we have a hope in hell of staying here, there will be many.

'We were...' I search my soul for the right words. Words that have enough weight to justify what we had, what we were to each other.

Pierce nods and I know he gets it. 'Will I make the security arrangements?'

'Yes. Whatever it takes. Whatever it costs to make staying here a viable option.' I've only just got back. I'm nowhere near ready to leave and truthfully, it has less to do with finishing the album, and more to do with seeing Sasha Sexton again. Even if she does hate the ground I walk on.

Besides, I've got something I have to give to her. My dick twitches in my pants. *You wish, buddy.*

'I'll speak to the manager.' Pierce strides across the room.

'And I'll speak to the owner.' It's a valid excuse to get close to her, even for a couple of minutes.

'Do not leave this floor.' His features pinch into a frown and his voice resonates with unquestionable authority. And there was me thinking *he* worked for *me*.

At least he cares. Though his loyalty has never been in question. He's saved me multiple times from sketchy situations. Female fans can be equally as dangerous as men, especially alcohol fuelled and in large numbers. They travel in hyena-like packs, occasionally managing to tear strips from my clothes at least.

The door clicks closed, leaving me in silence, bar the squawking racket below.

In the spacious bathroom, I shower, shave and try not to think about Sasha. If she's showering fifty metres away from me. If she thinks of me when her soapy hands glide over her body. It's not helpful. Not only are my emotional senses awakened, but the way my dick's poking up at me, it would appear my physical ones are on high alert too.

I've spent the last ten years in LA seeking physical release without any emotion. Here, I'm reminded exactly how powerful it can be when the two are combined.

I push that pointless observation away before I can dwell on it any further. Just because I'm still overwhelmingly attracted to her, it doesn't mean anything.

Her life is here. Mine is in the States. But my body refuses to get the memo, every cell alight at the prospect of seeing her again.

Though the castle's heating is on full whack, there's a chill in the air stemming from the crisp white frost coating the frames of the thin sash windows. I pull on a thick grey jumper and a pair of Levi's, and brush my teeth.

My stomach growls, reminding me I haven't eaten in over twelve hours. The thought of room service, eating alone again, does nothing to satiate my hunger. I'm hankering for food, but I can't deny I'm also hankering for some company. Preferably a five-foot-six brunette who hates my guts.

Opening the door of the suite, I peer out, left and right, checking for any potential screaming fangirls after this morning's shitshow outside the window.

Having a singing career offers a multitude of advantages: wealth, luxury, status, access to places most people can only dream of. On the flipside, it can be claustrophobic, imprisoning and suffocating, stripping me of even the simple ability to walk around like a normal person.

The coast is clear. Banging the door shut behind me, I saunter leisurely across the humongous corridor. The pale morning sun slants through the window panes, illuminating the art lining the walls. A depiction of one of my favourite childhood haunts, Velvet Strand, catches my eye and I pause to admire it, memories of a summer with Sasha hit me like a train.

How have I managed to suppress this for years? These feelings. These emotions. And why?

Survival.

'There he is! Ahhhhh!' Shrieks and screams pierce the air as a stampede of crazed women sprint up the walnut staircase with an alarming sense of urgency and purpose.

I'm metres away from the penthouse door. Pierce will kill me, if one of these women don't.

Last time I performed in Times Square, two unassuming-looking women held me at knifepoint, while their boyfriends attempted to bring round a car to kidnap me for ransom.

Pierce and his team intervened and the crisis was averted, but it was a lesson learned. Or perhaps not, given the current situation.

My eyes dart between the suite door and the rapidly approaching women. I could just smile and pose for a picture and get it over with? Lightning doesn't strike twice, right?

Before I can decide, the navy doors open beside me, and I'm yanked backwards, practically ten years backwards to be precise, against the full, heaving chest of Sasha, into the familiar confines of the Sexton family's private quarters.

The door bangs unceremoniously behind us. A low gasp slips from her lips as the furious pumping of her heart rattles in ribs which are pressed against mine.

Does she feel my every inch as acutely as I feel hers? Is she remembering how much better we feel against each other without any material between us, simply skin on skin? Or does she hate me too much to even contemplate it?

For fuck's sake, Ryan! Get a grip.

She takes a step back and my body silently screams, aching for her closeness.

Her cheeks flame and her sweet, ragged breath permeates the air between us.

Oh, she feels it.

This hot, flustered Sasha's way more attractive than the ice queen who greeted me yesterday. Probably because I remember clearly the last time I saw her cheeks flush like that. Oh that connection is definitely still there, and it's more alive than ever. That chemistry. It smoulders between us.

'What the hell are you thinking? You can't just wander around the castle corridors on your own.' Her arms fold tightly across the chiffon shirt clinging to her breasts in an indecently decent manner.

'I was thinking I was hungry.' I bite back my smirk. She's

so adorable when she's trying to hide her arousal. 'Good morning, by the way.'

'Huh! Good morning? It might be if my estate wasn't swamped with unwanted guests.' She takes another three steps back and glares at me.

A throaty chuckle bursts from my chest. 'Ouch. My wounded heart bleeds.'

'Hmm. I don't care about your wounded heart and I wasn't simply referring to you.' Her eyes dart towards the window of her own suite.

This place is like a relic. Every single ornate detail has been preserved. It's like stepping back in time.

'Yeah.' I shove a hand through my hair. 'Sorry about that.'

She stalks towards the open-plan kitchen/living area, heading straight for what looks like the only new addition to the place in a decade, a coffee machine.

Following her through, I drop onto the velvet couch, watching as she loads a capsule and fetches two mugs. A black pencil skirt hugs her pert backside in a way I can only dream of.

'I suppose you can wait here until the fuss dies down. I'd hate you to get ambushed in my castle. It wouldn't exactly inspire other celebrities to book in.' She doesn't turn round. 'Tea or coffee?'

I'm under no illusion this woman is impressed by my fame or celebrity status. All she sees is the boy who ran away. I can't even blame her.

'Coffee, please.'

'Black, no sugar,' we say simultaneously, and I can't help the grin inching onto my lips. She remembers.

She makes two mugs, hands me one, then perches on the other end of the couch, as though she's afraid she might catch something.

'So, about this security issue...' I blow on the steaming hot liquid before taking a sip. 'I'm sorry. I didn't mean to bring trouble to your door.'

She shrugs. 'It's not ideal, I mean we're not geared up for this kind of attention, but it's certainly getting Huxley Castle in the press again, so I guess it's not all bad.'

'Was Huxley Castle *ever* out of the press? This place was always the leading hotel for luxury.'

'Things change.' Her perfectly shaped eyebrows furrow together for a split second before she seems to remember to rearrange them into their natural, defensive stance. 'It's nothing I don't have under control.'

She smooths the material of her skirt, running her hand over her thighs, and my pulse rushes at the sight. It's an effort not to stare.

Bright jade eyes meet mine. They're the same shade I inadvertently painted my Californian bedroom. Now I know why. 'So, what do you need?'

What do I need? I need you to slip off your underwear, straddle my lap, wrap your arms and legs around me, put your full lips on mine and make the past ten years disappear.

Wow. If Jayden could see me now he'd give me a short sharp shove. He'd knock some sort of sense into me. Someone should, anyway.

I hurt her beyond forgiveness. I could accidentally do it again in a heartbeat, because if she invited me into her bed, I'd hop into it willingly. My body craves her. It's not even a want, it's a need. But my life is not here. Despite the crackling chemistry between us, we are worlds apart these days. It would be like déjà vu, both wounded all over again.

She stares at me from under those elongated lashes, her expression a mix of wariness and want. I know her too well to miss it.

She can practice her ice queen routine all she likes, but her body wants mine the same way mine wants hers.

Her tongue darts over her lips, and she subtly presses her thighs together. The air's thick with anticipation.

For a man who's made millions from his voice, it isn't doing much for me now. But what can I say? There's no way to make up for the past, and there's no hope of a future.

'To up the security around here?' she prompts, breaking the sexually charged silence between us.

The security, of course. She doesn't care about my other needs. I lost that right the night I left.

'Does the front gate still close? That would be a start. If we could cordon off the premises for hotel residents only, stop the paps lurking outside the gate. Ask the cabin residents to restrict their visitors for a few weeks. I'll compensate them heavily for their trouble, and you, of course.'

Sasha bites her lower lip, as if she's in deep thought. 'What about extra security staff?'

'Pierce is on it. He has contacts everywhere. He'll hire a few heavies to patrol the place.'

'Would it be too much to ask if they might wear a castle uniform? I don't want the other guests to feel intimidated.'

'Of course. Consider it done. And truly, I'm sorry for the inconvenience...'

Our eyes meet again and I chance shimmying a few inches closer along the couch. My body instinctively gravitates towards her, like there's an invisible thread tugging, weaving us closer together.

Only a foot remains between us, but she's rigid, like a deer in the headlights.

'Sasha, I—'

'Oh my fucking god! Ryan Cooper is in my living room!' A taller, ganglier-looking version of Sasha bounds into the lounge, and I dart back a few inches, the moment spectacularly broken.

Gazing over the teenager before me, a smile rips across

my face. 'Victoria Sexton? Oh my goodness! Have you been standing in a tonne of manure since I left, or what? Look at the height of you!'

Jumping to my feet, I stride across the room to greet her, but she leaps into my arms, the same way she did at seven years old. Her slim frame offers a squeeze tighter than she looks capable of and her hazel eyes dance with excitement.

'I can't believe you're back!' she squeals.

'I can't believe you're all grown up! Who will I play tag with now?' I gently place her at arm's length to inspect her.

Thick-rimmed glasses frame her eyes, and a red headband sweeps her thick fringe from her face, but other than the size of her, she hasn't changed a bit from the sweet, adorable kid who used to beg to be chased round the castle grounds.

'You could barely catch me then, I'm pretty sure you won't be able to now!' She smirks and turns to Sasha, who's staring with her jaw almost on the floor. 'Sash, did you tell him I'm cross-country running champion at my school?'

A maternal flicker of pride flashes across Sasha's face and only as she grins at her little sister, do I realise the full weight of Sasha's responsibilities.

Not only did she inherit the castle, but by the look of it, she inherited a sister/daughter to raise too.

The enormity of what this woman has been through strikes like a tsunami. I'm utterly in awe of her.

'Vic, Ryan and I were just talking about how we can up the security round here, perhaps you could give us a few minutes.'

Victoria rolls her eyes and winks at me. 'Is it like when you guys used to tell me you'd play hide and seek with me? I used to hide for hours and when I actually gave up, I'd find you sucking each other's faces off on that precise couch.'

A snort erupts from my chest at the same time as Sasha shoots her sister a warning look.

'Fine.' Victoria rolls her eyes once more. She turns as if to stomp out of the room, but doubles back on herself, taps my shoulder roughly and shouts, 'tag!' before running out of the room giggling.

I turn to Sasha, who's shaking with laughter. It's probably killing her that the ice-queen routine's just been blown to smithereens. She wipes a stray tear from the corner of her eye.

'Sorry about that.' Her lips twitch as she continues to battle control them.

I sit once again. 'You've got your work cut out there.'

She rolls her eyes and I see where Victoria gets it from. 'Oh, you have no idea.'

She's right, I had no idea she was here alone, raising her sister, running an estate. None of it can be easy. The woman's a fucking warrior.

She shakes her head and stands, running her palms over that skirt again, stoking a smouldering fire in my boxers.

Her eyes meet mine again, all trace of laughter replaced with a heat that sears my skin. 'Right, I'll get on top of it.'

Oh, I wish, Sasha. I fucking wish.

Still, the ice has thawed, marginally at least.

CHAPTER NINE

SASHA

24th November

'Unsurprisingly, the bookings have gone through the roof.' Megan reports in my office, handing over a double espresso. 'And that's with a fifty per cent price increase on all room rates. I know you hate overcharging but inflation is crazy right now. You're running a business, not a charity.'

'What about the restaurant bookings? We might have to hire more staff.'

'We will, but they're going to have to be security vetted if our rockstar guest is staying for the foreseeable future.' She winks at me and licks her lips saucily.

'Is that make-up you're wearing – again? Come on, Sasha, spill the fucking beans. You don't think I came down here to talk about work, did you?'

'Well, it is your job! You *are* the hotel manager!'

'And I'm also your oldest and wisest friend, which also makes it my job to make sure you're ok.' She perches on the edge of my desk, peering down at me.

'I'm fine. Everything's fine.'

'Course it is.' Megan shrugs, sarcasm heavy in her tone. 'The rockstar you've spent the last ten years hating and pining over in equal measure has just returned to your family home. He's walking round like a smoking-hot pile of sex on a stick, and you're absolutely fine.'

'I have a job to do, an estate to run, and a child to raise, in case you've forgotten. I don't have oodles of time to squander thinking about him.'

'Ah ha! But, if the whispers are true, the estate may be going on the market in the new year, and the child you've been hiding behind raising is only months away from turning eighteen. Edinburgh, isn't it? The college Victoria's looking at?' She shoots me a knowing look.

It was foolish to think she had no idea about the extent of our financial difficulties. She's as much a part of this place as I am. She wouldn't be much of a manager if she wasn't.

'What are you going to do then? Sasha Sexton, twenty-eight years old, with no responsibilities, footloose and fancy free. God forbid, you might have to put yourself first, because, girl, you wouldn't know where to start! It seems like a bit too much of a coincidence that Ryan-Runaway-Cooper returns when you might just be free enough to run after him this time.'

A less than ladylike snort bursts from my mouth. 'I'm not running anywhere, and I'll NEVER run after him!'

'Pah! Word it however you like, run *with* him. Whatever.'

'Even if I wanted to, which I don't – I can't actually stand the man – who's to say he'd want me to?' I flick my hair from my face, looking anywhere but directly at my best friend.

Megan shakes her head and grins. 'You don't hate him. You love him. You never stopped.'

'Bullshit,' I snort again.

'You have no idea, do you? And the feeling is obviously

mutual. Apart from the fact that Louise has told every single person in the building that Ryan Cooper was all over you like a bad rash, and, by all accounts, the smouldering looks you were giving each other almost set the estate on fire, if you actually listen to any of his albums, it doesn't take a genius to work out who his muse is!'

Thankfully, the door swings open and Louise pops her head around, ticking off a checklist on her right hand. 'The extra security have arrived. The front gate's been replaced with one wired to open electronically. Two of Mr Cooper's men will police it themselves, checking residents' bookings as they approach. Oh, and we might want to consider hiring someone to maintain this role after they leave, but I guess we don't need to worry about that quite yet.'

'Thanks, Louise. Anything else?'

'The castle's been inundated with bookings. There's a cancellation list as long as my arm extending right up until the end of next year.'

I shoot Megan a smug, I-might-not-be-finished-yet look to which she rolls her eyes.

'Conor's asking for you in the kitchen. And we've had over two hundred email enquiries demanding to know if we're hosting a Christmas ball this year.'

'Well, that's encouraging.'

Chloe will be pleased. There might just be hope for the castle after all. As much as I hate to credit Ryan with anything, his arrival has definitely helped my home, if not my heart.

Louise leaves. I down my coffee and push back my chair before Megan can continue her interrogation. She raises her eyebrows at me once again and nods to the humongous artwork of Velvet Strand.

'Remind me again, exactly how many pictures of that beach hang around the castle?'

Heat creeps into my cheeks. 'It was my parents' favourite place.'

'Hmm. The "parents" card! Can't argue with that, can I?' she teases. 'Though, isn't that the spot where you and lover-boy had your first kiss?'

That's the trouble with having the same friend since forever. They know too much about everything.

'Coincidence.' I shrug, forcing down the memory of the first day Ryan's hot lips touched mine. The day I was pretty much ruined for anyone else, and that was before the man became a world-famous sex symbol.

'Now, if you'll excuse me, I have work to do. Can you work up some projected figures for next year and email them to the accountant? For once, he might be marginally optimistic about our situation.'

Sashaying through the wide corridors, I make my way to the enormous kitchen. It's filled with shiny chrome and steel worktops and appliances. The smell of rosemary, caramelised onions and simmering garlic assaults my senses. Soft jazz infiltrates the room through discreet speakers positioned around the room, barely audible over the low rustling sound of people at work, chopping and peeling, preparing tonight's dinner.

Conor glances up from his station in the centre of the room, where he keeps a watchful eye on the chefs under his command. Cobalt eyes light when they land on me. His lips part and spread into a warm wide grin.

'Hey, boss lady. Slumming it in the mere shallows?' His joviality immediately brings a smile to my own face.

Placing down his knife, he uses his forearm to sweep his blond hair from his face before striding towards me.

Conor, like Megan, is one of my biggest champions. He's so dear to me. Not only is he absolutely gorgeous, but simply being in his company is the equivalent of being enveloped in a deliciously safe and warm hug.

I drop an affectionate pat on his arm, noticing the swell of the bicep beneath the crisp white chef uniform. 'I heard you wanted me.'

'Oh, Sash, I've wanted you for years, please tell me you've finally copped on?' He winks and drops an arm round my shoulder, squeezing me in an affectionate gesture.

'Funny, Conor. You know, if you weren't such a fantastic chef, I'd recommend you take up a career in comedy.'

His eyes sparkle and he shrugs again. 'A man can only try.'

He says that, yet he never did try. Not really. Though neither did I, because if I did and then lost him, like I lost everyone else, it would have been the final straw in my fragile existence.

'Is it about the influx of bookings? I'm going to email the agency this afternoon. I'll have more staff by the weekend, even if it kills me.'

'That's good to know, but it's not just that. I heard you're going ahead with the ball. Is it a sit down meal? Do you want the full five courses? Or will we go with canapés and champagne this year?'

Last year, the sit down meal had been pretty much a disaster. So much waste. At least the homeless shelter had a mouth-watering Christmas dinner.

'Let's go with canapés, it's safer, but make them really extravagant. I'm talking lobster, oysters, caviar. Go wild! Work your magic.'

'Oh, I plan to.' Conor presses a kiss on the top of my forehead. 'Will you spare me an evening soon?'

Saliva floods my mouth. Conor's perpetual teasing and flirting is commonplace, but is he finally asking me out properly? I never know when to take him seriously. And why now? Is it because of Ryan's return? He's one of few people who knows the whole story. I confessed the whole sorry debacle one night after too much red wine.

When I don't answer, he says, 'For the tasting. You have to sample the goods. When you finally do, I know you'll never want to put another thing anywhere near those lips.' His finger brushes over my mouth and a low chuckle escapes his throat.

Ok. He's definitely cranking up the heat. Last week, it probably would have had me swooning. The man is undeniably attractive. Effortless to be around. He radiates warmth like a summer's day. This week, with Ryan here, I don't know how to feel.

'It's not like my social calendar is hopping. You know where to find me.' Patting his arm again, I shoot him a smile as I leave.

Ryan's return is doing funny things to me. Awakening parts of my body I've squashed for years. Since our close encounter, apart from the rage that simmers beneath my surface, I'm in a permanent state of hot-and-bothered.

I decide to email the agency from the privacy of my own suite, away from Conor, and Ryan, who thankfully, I haven't laid eyes on since I saved his ass from the shameless stalkers.

That's not to say I haven't thought about him though. Lusty thoughts invade my brain mercilessly, even when I'm asleep.

I'm a woman, with wants and needs, but it's only now they've begun to stir in me again. With Victoria turning eighteen soon, maybe Megan's right. Maybe it's time to address those wants and needs.

Am I finally ready to look for a relationship? If I am, Conor would make the perfect partner.

If only I could feel the way about him that I did for Ryan all those years ago. I've got a horrible feeling he's permanently ruined me for anyone else.

When I reach the top of the walnut staircase, the gentle thrumming of an acoustic guitar rings through the air, its soft, lulling melody calling to the fragmented parts of my soul. Its draw is so powerful, I unwittingly follow, seeking the origin.

Subconsciously, I know the source. I just don't expect it to be in my private quarters.

Opening the navy double doors, I slip into my living area. Ryan perches on my couch, oozing sex appeal by the bucket load.

He's bigger now, more powerful looking. His perfect features are carved into an expression of lustful longing. A sharp burst of heat stokes my lady parts.

A muscled forearm supports the guitar. Slow, deliberate strokes across the strings send shivers rattling over my spine, simultaneously chilling and heating my skin in a silent war between the devil and angel inside. The devil urges me to throw myself at him. Straddle him like I've done so many times before on this very couch. There was some serious make-out sessions in the build-up to the actual V-card event.

With his eyes closed tight in concentration, his husky, rich voice croons so softly, I almost don't catch the words.

Almost.

Something about a lost love. A hurt so deep it drowns a person from within.

The angel inside wants me to hold him, hug away his hurt, because it's clear from his expression, he's harbouring something similar to me.

Tears well, threatening to spill over my hastily applied foundation. I haven't cried in years. I fear if I do, it'll be the equivalent of a dam bursting.

I watch, paralysed, hypnotised, until he strums the final chord. His eyes open, and he stares at me, through me. Instead of being surprised at my presence, it's almost like he expected it.

'You heard me?' His voice is thick, sensual, weighted with emotion.

I get the impression he's asking if I heard what he was trying to tell me, not the tune he was playing.

'Is it new?' The urge to know that is bigger than the urge to know why exactly he's playing it in my lounge.

'It is.' He sighs and pats the couch next to him, inviting me to sit.

I do because I'm terrified if I don't my legs might buckle beneath me.

'I've been struggling,' he begins.

His dark eyes exude heat and vulnerability as they search mine for something. Understanding? Acceptance? Reassurance? I don't know.

'That's the first song I've written in years. The words wouldn't come, the feelings, they wouldn't come.' He glances round wistfully. 'Here, they flood me to the point I feel like I might drown.'

I know what he means. Little by little, my anger at him thaws, melting with each passing second, each smouldering glance.

'Sorry for the intrusion, by the way. I thought you'd be in your father's office. I mean your office... Victoria said...' He shrugs. 'It's not like I can wander round freely, there are limited places I can hang out and the penthouse was getting claustrophobic.'

'It's fine.' It's worryingly more than fine. Forgetting I'm supposed to be mad at him, I like that he finds his creativity here, in our home. The place where we made so many memories.

He hands me his guitar. It looks suspiciously like the same guitar he had ten years ago. 'Here, you try.'

'No.' I push it back forcefully. I couldn't, even if my limbs weren't trembling like a fawn trying to stand for the first time. 'I don't play anymore. I haven't since...'

His eyebrows stretch skyward. 'Not at all?'

'No.' I shake my head. 'The girl who played the guitar and wrote silly love songs died with her parents.'

'If I could have one wish, it would be that you'd play with me.'

'I'm sure you could think of a better wish than that.' My lip catches between my teeth but it's too late to bite back the flirtation that slipped out. 'Besides, I've played with you enough to last a lifetime.'

'Nowhere near.' An earnest vulnerability exudes from his expression and the anger that simmers below the surface of my skin thaws further. 'I've been meaning to talk to you about something... I have something for you. I thought you'd come looking... but you never did.' His voice cracks and he inches towards me, setting the instrument down on the coffee table in front of us.

His Adam's apple bobs as he swallows. My eyes return to his mouth. Those full perfect lips that have the power to set every nerve in my body alight with the lightest of brushes. The tongue that's stroked the most sensitive parts of me. Being with him, near him, it's hard to remain resentful when I can clearly see the boy he once was still lingering inside.

Maybe I'm not the only one with wounds. It's on the tip of my tongue to ask him why he left. What happened. But my pride refuses to permit it.

He slides closer, closing the distance between us, until his lips are mere millimetres from mine. The rockstar melts before me. All I see when I gaze into those swirling chocolate pools, is the boy I loved.

The boy I would have done anything for.

The boy who left me.

Abruptly, the scalding blood pulsing through me runs cold.

Darting back, I leap from the couch as if I've been stung, because I have – ten years ago, and I can't let it happen again. I can understand Ryan coming back to find some of his original creativity again, but I'm not stupid enough to be used as a part of that. When he's written his album, he'll swan off into the sunset again and I'll be left just as heartbroken as I was the first time.

'Work away.' I gesture to his guitar. 'I'll be in my office.'

I bolt out the door, needing to put some distance between us. Between me and the sound of his perfect voice, the unique scent of his musky skin, and the very come-to-bed eyes that ruined me.

CHAPTER TEN

RYAN

27th November

I've been here less than a week and managed to produce more material than I have in the last four years. Once I work out the time difference, I pick up the phone to call my brother. Tired Jayden is even more grumpy than hungry Jayden.

He answers on the first ring. 'Yo. I was literally just thinking about you.'

LA traffic rushes in the background. Sirens, horns and white noise from a world away. It sounds like he's outside, but the noise passes too fast for him to be walking. An engine roars. He must have got a new convertible.

Unless the cheeky bollocks has 'borrowed my Ferrari'.

What a douche.

'Driving a person's car does tend to remind you of them, especially when you do it without their permission.'

The snigger that follows confirms my suspicions. 'It was

sitting in your garage, all lonely. I thought I'd blow the cobwebs off it for you.'

I shake my head, but can't help but grin. 'Just don't ding it.'

'Huh, so much for drive safely, brother.' He pretends to be offended.

'Don't push it, Jayden.'

'Don't worry. I'll mind it for you. I'll even wipe down these gorgeous leather seats if Cindy agrees to have sex in it later.' Clearly, he's nowhere near done winding me up yet.

Sex is at the forefront of my mind since I've been reunited with Sasha Sexton. During the day, I manage to focus on the emotion, on the songs. At night, all I can focus on is the fact she's metres away from me, possibly naked.

Jayden mistakes my groan of frustration for irritation.

'Hey, bro, you know I'm only joking. Besides, Cindy and I aren't having sex at the moment. She's still punishing me for not going to her parents' beach house. I think it's over, but I haven't got round to having the conversation yet. Hey, maybe she'll give me one for old times' sake. You know the "I really hate you and I'm totally glad we're separating, but let's have one final dirty goodbye shag to make sure".'

'For fuck's sake, Jay.' I shake my head again, open the sliding doors and step out into the crisp November night. The castle's Christmas lights are as spectacular as ever; Sasha's really outdone herself with this display. It's far more extravagant than I remember her parents ever executing; the purely white and silver lights add a rich touch of class. It's a far cry from the tacky flashing Christmas trees of my childhood. And of LA.

'So, how's it going in the Emerald Isle?' he says before swearing and beeping his horn – my horn. I wince and try not to think about it.

'It's going well.' Apart from the swift, harsh emotional

awakening and my Sasha-induced blue balls, but he doesn't need to know that.

'Manage to write anything yet?' He sounds about as optimistic as a pig en route to the abattoir.

'Actually, yes.' I send up a silent thank you to the clear midnight sky above.

'Seriously?'

'Yep. Check your email. I've sent you a couple of videos, for your eyes only, of course.'

I imagine him rolling his eyes heavenwards. He might be an arrogant, Ferrari-stealing douche, but he's my brother and I trust him with my life. Besides, his career's riding on this as much as mine. A leak would deem my work financially worthless.

'How many are we talking?' He's yet to shake the scepticism from his tone.

'Eight, so far. I'm working on another right now, but I needed a break.'

A couple below stroll hand in hand through the manicured lawn, admiring the lights and sights. A ripple of envy whips through me. I haven't had a girlfriend since Sasha, not a proper one anyway. There were a few staged efforts in the early years to up my profile but never anything meaningful. It never occurred to me to care, until now.

'Eight? Holy fucking shit, man!' He beeps the horn again but this time it sounds three times in a triumphant symphony. 'At this rate, you'll be home by next week.'

Home. The word is so subjective.

Though I love the climate in LA this time of year, I've never felt truly at home there. And especially not at Christmas. Christmases are meant to be cold. Spent snuggling with loved ones round a roaring fire, not tucked between two models I don't know or care about.

Which is probably why I'm the songwriter and Jay is the

agent. Underneath the hard exterior, I'm a soft shite, whereas Jay's arrogant assertiveness is likely his true personality. If he has a softer side, he's yet to show it to the world.

'You know, this still kind of feels like home.' I run my fingers across the top of the glass balustrade, swiping the silvery frost and pinching it between my index finger and thumb. Its damp chill is sharp on my skin but it makes me feel alive. Being here makes me feel alive.

'You know I'm Irish, through and through, but would I swap my life in the sun for the damp dreary mist and rain of our motherland? Not in a million fucking years.'

'I quite like it.'

'Oh oh. Does this have something to do with that girl you used to fuck?'

'Oh come on, Jay, have a bit of respect!'

'Ha! I knew it! Tell me, are you fucking her again? You are! Course you are! What woman in their right mind would turn down Hollywood's hottest bachelor? You did see you're on the front cover of *GQ* this month ahead of the Vegas concerts?'

'No, I'm not fucking her. Do you have to be so obscene, man?' My own mind is perfectly capable of being obscene enough without Jayden adding fuel to the fire. 'And no, I didn't see it. You know I hate the media.'

'So, what's the deal then?'

'There is no deal. I've barely got near her.' A sigh of frustration disappears into the night with the steam from my breath. Yesterday I thought she might... I thought we might... I almost kissed her but then she bolted.

'You know what you need, brother?' Jayden voice drops, like he's about to let me in on some worldly secret.

I do know what I need – she's about five-foot-six, with an ass to die for and about as much love for me as a soggy shit stuck to her shoe, but I don't tell him that. 'Go on, enlighten me.'

'You know that, "I really hate you and I'm totally glad we're separating, but let's have one final dirty goodbye shag to make sure" thing I mentioned... you might want to do that with Sasha and then you might finally be able to draw a line under her.'

'You have no idea.'

'I do. She was your first love. It got ripped apart before it could naturally run its inevitable course, that's all. Trust me, what you need is closure.'

'I doubt it.'

I don't think I'll ever get closure on what Sasha and I had. Even at eighteen, it felt like a once-in-a-lifetime love. And if her continued icy demeanour is anything to go by, that's the way it's going to stay. Rockstar or no rockstar. Despite the obvious attraction, she'd never let her guard down enough to act on it. And she's right. Apart from mind-blowing sex, what can I offer her? Her life is here, mine is a million miles away.

'Look, I gotta go.' I can't listen to anymore shite. My brother is a lost cause. 'Listen to the tracks I sent you and let me know what you think.'

'I will do.' Jayden hesitates for a second. 'Despite the piss taking, I'm proud of you, man.'

'Thanks.' Maybe he's not a lost cause after all.

'Still think you should give her one, bro. For old times' sake.'

Scratch that. 'Bye, Jayden.' I hang up, wondering what to do with myself for the rest of the night. It's late, but my body clock's all over the show with the time difference.

My stomach growls; I've missed dinner again, so lost in my lyrics. I could ring room service, but I've been holed up in this suite most of the day again and cabin fever's beginning to set in.

Is it too late to call to the only other suite I know I won't be hounded by women?

Huh, if only.

Sasha has too much class to hound anyone, even if she wanted to. The other day, she leapt from the couch like she'd been burned.

Stepping out of my suite I amble across the corridor to hover outside the Sexton family quarters. Only silence lurks behind the door. Victoria's probably in bed. Teenager or not, she's still a kid at the end of the day, with a full day of school tomorrow.

A door opens further up the corridor. Pierce sticks his head out. 'You ok, boss?'

'Fine, just stretching my legs.'

'There's security downstairs if you want to go for a walk. Or I can come with you, if you like?' He glances down at his vest and tracksuit bottoms and I shake my head.

'It's fine. I'll just take a walk to the kitchen. See if I can grab a bite. I'll be back up in half an hour, tops.' Any chance I have of slipping around unnoticed evaporates with a man like Pierce flanking me.

He throws me a baseball cap to put on. 'Buzz if you need me.' He taps the pager attached to his waist.

'Sure.' I don't mention I left mine in my room.

Sauntering through the castle, I take my time, soaking it all in. Not much has changed. I'm surprised Sasha hasn't put her own stamp on the place.

Ha! It's laughable that I consider myself qualified to make assumptions about a woman I knew ten years ago. That Sasha was carefree and brimming with love. The woman who greeted me seems as cold and closed up as I have been myself for the last decade.

Did I do that to her? Or is that just wild vanity on my part? She lost a lot more than me that weekend.

I want to tell her about my dad. To explain I was dragged away, that I didn't flee willingly, that I'd never have chosen to leave her.

But what's the point? It doesn't change anything. If she'd wanted to know she would have asked. I left her a note. She could have found me. I've been sprawled over every goddamn newspaper and television station. It's not like I was in hiding.

No. The best thing I can do is keep my mouth shut and my head down. As soon as I have enough material for two albums, I'll be back on the first flight to LA, back to the sunny afternoons jamming by the pool. I'll even be able to strum something that's not ten years old.

It should be heaven.

So, why does the prospect suddenly seem so empty?

The plan was to come, deal, and go.

I've a horrible inkling it might not be as straightforward as that.

Passing through the warm, inviting atrium, I pause to admire the neoclassical features. Gold and auburn flames flicker and dance on the traditional open fireplace, the scent of burning wood and cinnamon lingers enchantingly in the air. A million images hit me consecutively like a slideshow of my eighteenth year, each and every one of them stars Sasha.

Her smile.

Her infectious laugh.

Her hand in mine.

Her mouth all over me.

Shaking off the memories, I pass through unnoticed, bar the receptionist who offers a discreet nod and smile before returning to her computer. With the paparazzi taken care of and the place locked down to residents only, it feels pretty secure.

Having snuck around this castle for the best part of my youth, I know exactly where the kitchen is.

The main restaurant's empty at this late hour. Lurking at the kitchen's double doors, I glimpse the lights still blazing brightly behind the circular panes of glass. This kitchen used to be the heart of the castle, perhaps it still is.

Nudging the door open a crack, I hear a sound I haven't heard in years. One that no passage of time would ever allow me to forget; Sasha's unreserved vivacious laughter.

Perched on top of a stainless steel countertop, her long legs cross under one of her trademark pencil skirts. This one's leather, just to rightly set my pulse racing. The top button of her charcoal coloured blouse is open, displaying a hint of creamy porcelain cleavage. In her right hand, she clutches a glass of red wine.

Her hair is as unrestrained as the smile that lights her face and her jade eyes sparkle and glint with an abandonment that renders me grinning foolishly at the sight. Blood pounds and rushes below. She's fucking beautiful. One hundred per cent natural and utterly out of this world.

I follow her eye line, seeking the source of her amusement and my grin freezes on my face. A six-foot version of what looks like a lifelike Ken doll stands adjacent to her, his blond floppy hair falling over one bright blue eye. He looks utterly enamoured with the woman before him. Hell, there isn't a man in this world that would blame him, but it still makes me want to go all GI Joe on him and hand him his ass.

It didn't occur to me she might have a fucking boyfriend.

Envy rips through me. Yet another emotion I haven't felt in years. I have no right, but the urge to swoop in and mark my territory is overwhelming. She's not mine. She hasn't been for years, but the urge to claim her is feral.

My feet move before I can stop them, directing me straight towards them. Yanking off Pierce's stupid baseball cap, I toss it on one of the gleaming chrome counters as I march across the room, all previous rationale evaporating.

Ken steps in front of Sasha, his hand rising to her lips. The way she parts her mouth for him sends a shiver of longing shooting through every single cell in me. Fuck.

My breath's trapped in my throat while I wait for him to kiss her, but instead he simply pops a tiny morsel of food in. Instead of staring into his eyes, she closes them.

There might be hope yet.

I know now with complete certainty that I won't be able to leave until she parts them like that for me. For my tongue. Even if there's no hope of a future between us. I need to taste her again. And not just her lips.

It defeats logic. She lives here. My life's in the States, but I've never been more certain of anything. Maybe Jayden's right. Maybe we need closure.

Though it has nothing to do with a, 'I really hate you and I'm totally glad we're separating but let's have one final dirty goodbye shag to make sure,' and everything to do with 'I know what your body needs because it's haunted my dreams every single fucking day since the last time I touched it.'

Random images of what might have been if Sasha had come to the States with me all those years ago bombard me.

If I could have only hung on for six more months. Ifs don't change a thing though, but after all these years, she is still the full package for me. She's a goddamn work of art. I'm sure we'd have been happy. We'd have made a life together.

She was mine first. And I need her to be again. Even if only for a while.

CHAPTER ELEVEN

SASHA

'Ryan.' I hop down from my less than professional position on the kitchen counter and wipe my mouth, hoping Conor's buttery pastry isn't stuck to my lips.

Ryan marches deliberately towards me – his eyes glinting like a hungry predator. It's accurate. He's the only man with the ability to eat me alive, chew me up and spit me out. He's the polar opposite to Conor's safe, easy-going demeanour. I'd be a fool to forget it.

Yet, despite the obvious danger, the heat exuding from his blackening pupils beckons me, drawing me in, urging me to connect with him somewhere deep inside his chest. And his pants.

Guess who's on their third glass of wine? My thoughts are in the gutter.

He looms in front of me, forcing Conor to sidestep out of his way.

I watch in slow motion as a fluid hand rises. His thumb flicks sensually over my lower lip. Pulling it back, he examines it for a split second before seductively placing it onto his own tongue in a way that has my panties melting.

'Pastry. Not bad, maybe slightly heavy on the butter.' He turns to Conor, eyeing him with a steely composure.

Conor's blue eyes shift to a positively icy shade. 'Sasha seemed to be enjoying it.'

'We're menu tasting for the Christmas ball.' Why the hell am I explaining myself to Ryan-Runaway-Cooper of all people?

'I look forward to trying more of them then.' His eyes bore into mine with an intensity that's only quadrupled over the last decade.

Mr Hollywood has clearly perfected the art of the drop-your-panties stare because it's all I can think about, regardless of the fact Conor is standing right next to us.

Who am I kidding? Even at eighteen, he'd mastered that stare.

What's he playing at tonight, barging in here like this? Interrupting my one evening off. It's the first time I've relaxed in months, an effortless task in Conor's lovely sunny company.

If Conor's gentle aura projects picnics, sunshine, strawberries and champagne, Ryan's projects dark nights, tangled limbs and a lust that burns hotter than neat whiskey.

I guess it's safe to say, Ryan's arrival has eclipsed everything.

'You're staying for the ball?' I take a sip of wine to stop myself staring at the god-like creature before me.

'I think I will.' He gently prises the glass from my hand, swirls the liquid it contains and takes a thoughtful sip. His espresso coloured eyes linger on mine, heavy with want and clear in their intention as they press against the crystal.

If Ryan were a dog, he would have literally just peed on me. I'm torn between being flattered and outraged. He's a fucking international superstar. The man was on the front page of *GQ* today as one the most eligible bachelors in the world. I know because Chloe forwarded the link and I opened it before I realised what it was.

He left me. He had his chance. I should be running for the hills, but there's a part of me that wants to run straight into the fire, straight into his arms and his bed. And that's even with the certainty he'll leave me again the second his album's finished.

'2012 Cab Sav?'

'Someone got an education while they were away.' Conor rolls his eyes. He might just be the only person in the entire estate who is utterly unimpressed by Ryan Cooper. Ahem, other than me, I mean...Who am I kidding?

'You could call it that, I suppose.' Ryan shrugs, barely glancing in Conor's direction. His gaze remains intently fixed on me. It's an effort not to squirm under the intensity.

Swallowing back the saliva pooling in my throat, I manage to utter, 'Is there something you were looking for?'

A smirk rips across Ryan's full lips. 'Yeah, I was kind of hungry. I still am, actually.' His stare drops to my cleavage for a millisecond, enough for me to know he's not simply hungry for food. He was confident at eighteen. At twenty-eight, the man has no shame.

Ryan hovers closely in front of me, while Conor flanks my back. 'Tell me what you want and I'll get someone to bring it up to your room. We're kind of busy, if you hadn't noticed.'

'You know I always loved the balls here. One year there was New Year's Eve ball...' Ryan's eyes scan the kitchen with a mischievous glint in them, before focusing on the pantry.

Heat suffuses my skin at a memory I know for certain I'm not the only one reliving. Aged seventeen, it was the first time I let him touch me down there, minutes before the bells rang. Ryan had no problem sullying the black lace dress I wore. I'd never known pleasure like it. Addictive, explosive, life-altering carnality. And he was the instigator of it.

Ryan winks and colour floods my cheeks.

Again, so much for cold and distant. The man has me burning so hot I'm liable to combust.

'Tell me, was that the year you abruptly left for stardom? Or was that the year prior to that?' Conor folds his arms over his chest, his voice thick with sarcasm.

'Believe me, I didn't leave willingly.' Ryan's eyes don't leave mine, though all trace of his smirk has evaporated.

Sandwiched between the only two men I've ever truly been attracted to, I'm too flustered to ask for more details.

Ryan sips from my glass again, before reaching for the open bottle placed to his right, generously topping it up. 'Don't mind if I do. It's not often I get to have a drink with an old friend.'

'I'm not sure which of us you think is your friend, but either way, I'm pretty sure you're mistaken.' Conor's hand brushes my right arm at the same time as Ryan reaches out to stroke my left. Goosebumps rip across my skin and it takes a second to realise what that hot pain searing my lower tummy is – hot, savage longing.

'Oh, we're much more than old friends, aren't we, Sasha?' Ryan leans close enough for me to inhale his intoxicating masculine scent before turning his attention to the man behind me. 'What exactly are you two to each other again?'

Despite his close proximity, I can't see Conor's face, but from Ryan's widespread grin I assume enough flashed across it to portray we haven't been intimate. Not yet, anyway.

'I thought as much.'

In some wild fantasy, being wedged between the only two men I've ever been attracted to might be next-level sexy, but in reality, I can't bear the heat any longer. Slipping out from between them – one light, dependable and amusing, the other dark, dangerous, and exhilaratingly sexy – I cross the room and open a window. The crisp cold breeze cools my flushed face.

'Seeing as you're drinking my wine, the least you can do is get me another.' I point to the glasses hanging from the ceiling rack above his head. By moving Ryan from Conor's immediate vicinity, I'm hoping to shatter the tension that's rippling between them in turbulent ominous waves.

Conor tuts. 'If you're playing waiter, you can pour me one, too.'

Seeing the opportunity for some sort of truce I leap on it. 'Perhaps Ryan can help with the menu tasting, that'll save you cooking anything else at this time of night, and it'll save my waistline.'

Ryan mutters, 'Your waistline looks perfect to me.'

Conor nods in reluctant agreement.

This is quickly shaping up to be one of the most surreal nights of my life. First Conor finally starts showing some initiative with his seductive feeding, then Ryan struts in all alpha wiping up the crumbs. Wait until Megan hears about this.

Ryan shares the burgundy liquid between three glasses, placing one on Conor's work station. He hands me a fresh glass, brushing his lips over my original one, precisely where my lipstick mark stains it.

'How's the writing going?' That at least should be a safe topic.

'Surprisingly well. Something about this place inspires me. Or someone.' The glint is back. So is the grin.

Conor snorts, busying himself with the next appetiser, giant tiger prawns on some sort of wafer-thin red cracker. I watch, impressed, as the minute details in the presentation blend decoratively together.

'Did you book a band yet?' Conor turns to me, his bright-blue eyes vivid with enthusiasm. Even with Ryan here trying to overshadow him, he's still in great humour.

'No, but I need to. To be honest, I hadn't even planned on having a Christmas ball this year. Not after last year. It's all for Chloe. She rarely ever comes home, so I want to make sure it's the best Christmas ever.'

'Where is Chloe?' Ryan asks, like her absence only occurred to him.

'Dubai,' Conor and I say in unison.

'She runs a successful event management company these days, breaking balls by day, and hearts by night.' I shrug and take a sip of my wine.

'Ha. She reminds me of Jayden. Well, he's brokering record deals all day, but they definitely have the heart thing in common.'

'Chloe has this one-date rule.' I'm probably oversharing but it's a relief to be talking about someone other than us.

'And that is?' Ryan arches an eyebrow.

'They only get one date. Ever. No repeats. No matter how well it goes.' I shrug.

'And what about you?' Ryan takes a step towards me, gauging my expression. 'Do you ever do repeats?'

Despite my best intentions, my gaze falls to his lips. The memories steal the breath straight from my lungs and it's an effort to remember why I'm supposed to fight this feeling.

'Try this one.' Conor saves me from having to answer. He hands me a succulent looking prawn. Dressed with a beetroot trim, it's almost too pretty to eat.

'What about Matt's band? I'm pretty sure they'd love to perform at the ball if you're stuck.'

'Thanks, Conor, I might just take you up on that.' Matt is Conor's cousin and another gorgeous budding musician. He's five years younger than Conor and an only child. Conor's always looked out for him like a younger brother. It would be nice to give him the business. 'Text me the number and I'll ring him in the morning.'

It'll be one more job I can tick from my ever-growing list.

Ryan puts his drink down and accepts the canapé Conor hands him. 'Thanks.'

Wow. He almost sounded civil.

'You know, I could do it...' he says, before taking a bite.

My head whips up to check if there's a stupid grin on his face, because surely he has to be joking. The man is a fucking rockstar. People pay hundreds for a single ticket to see him in concert. I'm pretty sure I can't afford his prices, no matter how much revenue his visit is bringing to the castle.

As if he can read my mind, he says, 'No charge, of course. It's the least I can do for intruding on your Christmas.'

'Too right.' Conor huffs.

'Are you serious?' The tickets will fly off the printer. It would certainly ensure we didn't have a repeat of last year's disaster. And it would justify a substantial increase in ticket prices.

He steps closer to me again, his hand brushing over my arm in a reassuring gesture. 'I've never been more serious in my life.'

'Well, in that case, you've got yourself your first Irish gig in what, ten years?'

'Looks like it.' He smirks.

Conor steps between us again. 'What about Matt? Will you need a band?'

My shoulders tense. Performing with a world-famous artist on stage would give Matt and the other young lads the biggest boost of their life. I don't know Ryan well enough anymore to know if he's the kind of man to do that for them.

Ryan glances thoughtfully at me, before turning his attention to Conor. 'I will. Apart from anything, I'll need breaks to steal a few dances myself.'

Is it possible Ryan's arrival might be the one thing to save us all?

In the rush of excitement, I throw my arms around him in a spontaneous gesture. 'Thank you so much. This will mean the world to the lads. And to Victoria and Chloe. Honestly, I don't know how I'll ever repay you.'

Strong, muscular arms envelop me in a crushing hug that feels like home. Warm wine-scented breath brushes my ear as he whispers, 'Meet me in the pantry before midnight and I'll show you.'

A nervous, excited burst of laughter escapes from my chest and I slap his arm in gentle chastisement.

'Been there, done that. I'd be a fool to do it again.' Though with three glasses of red wine working their magic, I'm beginning to wonder if I'd be a fool not to. Even if it results in getting my heart broken for a second time.

The coldest months of the year are shaping up to be exceptionally hot.

CHAPTER TWELVE

RYAN

1st December

Pierce's shaven head pops through the doorway of the penthouse suite. 'You need anything, boss?'

Placing the guitar on the couch beside me, I flip my notebook closed. My unruly scrawling's finished for today. Being back here's allowed me to dig deep. Every lyric emerged from some profound unfathomable source within. I've got a feeling these words will resonate with millions.

Jayden was ecstatic when he listened to what I sent him. So much so, he begged me to fly back right away, but I can't. And it has nothing to do with the second album, and everything to do with Sasha Sexton. Slowly but surely, I'm breaking down her barriers and I'm nowhere near ready to stop.

'No thanks. Are you going out?' I glance out the window where the winter sun rapidly plummets from the sky, sinking into the Irish Sea.

'I was thinking about hitting the city for a couple of

hours, if that's ok with you? Frank and Archie are here and there's six more security lads downstairs.'

'You don't have to justify it to me. I don't expect you to hang around twenty-four seven. Go see the sights of Dublin.'

I wouldn't mind seeing them myself, but nothing in this world would tear me away from this castle tonight. With it being Friday night, I'm planning on making a visit to my two favourite Sexton sisters.

The urge to call in has plagued me all week, but it's not fair to distract Victoria too much when she has school the next morning and Sasha mentioned she was up to her eyeballs running the estate.

'Cabin fever, you know.' Pierce gestures out the window to the vast expanse of countryside.

Other than in this penthouse suite, it's not something I suffer with here.

Cabin fever feels way worse in LA. Cooped up, hiding from paparazzi in a hot crowded city. I know it's quiet here, but it's tranquil. I've taken to early morning running through the woodlands again. The crisp crunching of twigs underfoot and the sight of my own breath clouding the space in front of my face is fucking liberating.

'Don't rush back on my account.' With the gates closed and extra security, there hasn't been an issue. Well, apart from the obvious stares at breakfast. I've posed for a few photos but haven't been mobbed again, thankfully. Mind you, I've been so busy working, nobody's had a chance to mob me.

Pierce nods and closes the door behind him.

I shower, change into a pair of jeans and a navy fitted pullover. My hair could do with a cut but I don't care enough to go out for one. I squirt my favourite aftershave onto my neck, the same one I've worn since forever, and slip out the door into the corridor.

Frank and Archie spring to attention, but I motion for them to relax, nodding at Sasha's door, across the hallway.

'Is she in there?'

Archie nods and Frank wiggles his eyebrows suggestively. These two are Jayden's guys. They probably think I'm the same as him. Hell, until I got back here, I wasn't much better. But Sasha's different. I might be desperate to get into her knickers, but I'm also desperate to get in her good favour again. I can't bear the idea of unresolved conflict between us. We were everything to each other before, the least I'd like is for us to be friends again. And after I offered to perform at the Christmas ball, I think she's beginning to feel the same.

Knocking on the navy doors, my ears prick at the sound of a scuffle from behind it. It sounds like something heavy's being dragged across the floor.

'Not like that. I like it the other way.' Sasha's voice is as clear as day.

She wouldn't have to tell me which way she likes it.

Who the fuck is she talking to? If it's Conor, I might actually die.

Turning back towards Frank and Archie, I raise my eyebrows and thumb the door questioningly.

Archie shakes his head and Frank sniggers. 'Go on. I think they might need your help in there.'

I don't need telling twice. Pushing the door open, I let myself into the Sexton's private quarters. The scent of cinnamon, cloves and the tang of fresh oranges lingers enticingly in the air. The source isn't hard to locate. A pot of mulled wine's simmering on the cooker, two goblet glasses adjacent at the ready.

In the corner of the room, Victoria and Sasha are just about done struggling to erect a seven-foot Christmas tree, a trail of pine needles lining the floor in its wake.

'There, it's much better that way.' Sasha nods, eyeing its

final resting place. She dusts her hands together, brushing off a couple of stray needles.

'Hi.' Once again, I feel like the eighteen-year-old boy who doesn't really deserve to be here. Maybe this was a bad idea.

Sasha's head whips round and I catch her grin a second before she manages to straighten it into her polished, distant ice-queen routine.

Victoria bounds across the open-plan living space to greet me with a bear hug. As a child she was overflowing with affection. As a teenager, she hasn't changed. She carries an air of innocence about her. One that Sasha certainly didn't have at her age.

'Ryan!' Genuine enthusiasm resonates in her excited squeal. 'Do you know that every single girl in my class wants to be me right now?' She flicks her hair from her face and beams.

'Because you're amazing and talented and you're going to ace your final exams next year?'

'Duh. No. because I have this mega-famous superstar staying in my family home and they all want to run off and marry you.' She wiggles her eyebrows at me and Sasha rolls her eyes. 'I told them you were just as goofy as you were ten years ago, but they don't seem to believe it.'

'Goofy? Me?' I don't know whether to laugh or be outraged. I've been called many things in Hollywood – arrogant, eligible but aloof, talented. Even a has-been lately. Goofy was definitely never mentioned.

'Yeah. Do you remember you guys used to play dress-up with me, and you'd always pretend you wanted to be the princess? You used to parade around with my favourite tiara until I laughed so much my stomach hurt.'

I'm surprised Victoria remembers because until this very second, I'd forgotten.

'It's a hard mental image to get rid of, especially when it

was imprinted at such a formative age in my development. You could sell a billion records and be half-naked on the front of every magazine cover in the world, but to me, you'll always be my big sister's goofy boyfriend – sorry.' She shrugs as a giggle slips from her lips.

My eyes dart to Sasha at the boyfriend remark, but she's suddenly become engrossed in something outside the window, even though it's pitch-black out there now.

'Now, if you happen to know Adam Draker's phone number and you wanted to hook me up with him, then I might be impressed.'

It's my turn to eye roll. 'Adam Draker? Is that who you're into? The guy spends longer doing his hair for a gig than he does actually performing one.'

I've met him numerous times; he's a raging diva. He makes Mariah look like a pussy cat.

'Seriously? You know him?' Victoria squeals as her hands fly to her flaming cheeks.

'If you're ever in LA, I promise I'll introduce you.'

Sasha clears her throat and spins to glare at me from ten feet away. 'Don't make promises you can't keep.' Her tone could cut through glass.

'I mean every word of it.' Crossing the room, I stand next to the Christmas tree on the pretence of admiring it, when it's really Sasha I'm desperate to admire up close.

She's dressed casually this evening. Her long dark waves are pulled back into a simple ponytail that shows off her long slender neck. An emerald V-neck top drapes across her top half, revealing sharp, sexy collarbones. Tight navy jeans hug her peachy backside. Lucky them.

'We were about to decorate the tree. Want to help?' Victoria asks.

It sounds like the perfect way to spend the evening, but before I accept, I glance sideways at Sasha to make sure I'm not intruding. Bright jade eyes flick towards mine and she shrugs.

'At least you might be able to reach the top.' She nods towards the silver star sitting on the huge opulent dining room table, overflowing with Christmas decorations. They're all silver and white frosted, not a scrap of colour to be seen, just like the other trees in the castle.

'Is everything white?'

She used to love the clashing, cascading colours when we were young. Our last night together, the night before my father turned my life upside down, we decorated the tree in my family's cabin together and it was she who insisted on coloured lights and thick bushy multi-coloured tinsel.

I assumed the theme of white and silver outside the castle was aiming to be tasteful and classy, not a personal preference.

Victoria rolls her eyes and points at Sasha. 'Yep. Queen of the castle over there insists. For some reason she can't stand twinkling, flashing multi-coloured lights.'

Sasha stalks towards the kitchen. Towards the mulled wine to be precise. 'They're not entirely white. You got your crimson garland, didn't you? And what about the beautiful wreaths and candle displays? Now, who's for a drink?'

'Can we go to the Christmas markets tomorrow, or are they too bright for you as well?' Victoria calls to Sasha across the room.

'We can go to the Christmas markets, I suppose.' Sasha stirs the mulled wine, dips a finger and places it in her mouth thoughtfully. 'You know what would be spectacular? London. The Winter Wonderland. I've always wanted to go. Maybe next year?'

'I'll hold you to that,' Victoria promises.

A sadness sparks inside of me. I long to ask Sasha why she stopped liking bright and beautiful things, but I hold my tongue. It doesn't take a genius to guess it has something to do with me. With the last time we decorated a tree together.

'You know what day it is?' Sasha's voice is slightly subdued. Using a chrome ladle, she fills the two goblet glasses, then hands one to Victoria and me.

'Are you old enough to drink that?' I nudge Victoria.

'Almost.' Her eyes flicker towards me but she doesn't smile, instead she returns her gaze to her older sister, who reaches into a cupboard, removes another glass and fills it to the brim.

Sasha takes a huge mouthful before continuing.

'It's the first of December.' Her words are weighted with significance and it takes me only a millisecond to realise what she's reminding me of. It's the date I left, ten years ago. The blood drains from my cheeks. I lick my lips, wracking my brain for an adequate response, even though I know there isn't one.

Victoria swallows hard, a lump forming in her throat. She raises her glass against Sasha's, clinking it in a sombre gesture. 'To Mam and Dad. Ten years without them.'

Sasha takes a shaky breath. 'May they be sipping their own glasses of mulled wine and watching us make a mess of this tree, after we've had ours.'

Time freezes for what seems like an age as the full enormity of what I'm learning hits me square on the jaw.

However horrific I felt before, knowing that Sasha's parents died the same month I left, I'm absolutely fucking appalled to know it happened the same night. There's no forgiving that.

'I.. I..' I'm utterly speechless.

Victoria clinks her goblet against mine and eyes me with firm encouragement. 'To Mam and Dad,' she repeats again, until I get the memo.

It's about them. Not me. I need to get over myself. Fucking Hollywood's gone to my head after all.

Losing me was probably insignificant to losing them.

'To Mr and Mrs Sexton. The finest parents I ever met.'

Sasha nods, seemingly satisfied for now. Looks like I've just walked in on a ten-year tradition between the remaining Sextons. For the first time since I arrived in Ireland, I get the distinct feeling I probably shouldn't be here. They should have thrown me out.

'Come on. Let's get this party started.' Victoria pulls me by the arm towards the decorations. 'Mam and Dad would hate to see us wallowing. Let's make them proud.' She fiddles with her phone and two seconds later, Shakin' Stephens blasts through the suite and the moment's instantly transformed from subdued to celebratory.

CHAPTER THIRTEEN

SASHA

The mulled wine went straight to Victoria's head. She's currently face down on the violet velvet couch, decorating it with her drool. Soft gentle snores wheeze through her nose.

Brushing the hair from her face, I gaze at my youngest sister, wondering for the millionth time if I'm doing a good enough job raising her.

She's less mature than I was at her age. Some might have expected her to go the other way after the crash, but Vic went into herself, cocooning in her own bubble. She barely spoke in the year that followed, surrounding herself with stuffed animals, playing with them long after the other girls her age moved onto make-up and fashion.

Ryan materialises next to me from his position by the tree, the only one of us tall enough to reach the top few branches.

His arm's so close it brushes mine. As if he can read my mind, he says, 'You've done an absolutely amazing job with her.'

Staring down at the peaceful expression resting on Victoria's face, I can only hope he's right.

Hovering close enough that our elbows are touching, his voice drops to a breathy whisper, 'You know, you'll make a great mam one day.'

A low sigh whistles from my lips and the palm of my hand instinctively spreads across my stomach.

I came close to finding out once, but it wasn't to be. Ryan doesn't need to know that our child would have been nine years old, had I managed to keep him inside of me.

Maybe it was the grief of losing my parents, or the stress of inheriting my sisters and the castle. Or perhaps it just wasn't meant to be. I'll never know. And neither will Ryan. I don't need or want his sympathy, not when he didn't want me. Didn't want us. Megan and Conor are my only two confidantes on the matter and that's the way it's going to stay.

There's no denying the explosive attraction's still there. And I'm not naive enough to miss its reciprocation. The chemistry crackling between us is so powerful it's painful, especially after that night in the kitchen.

As much as my body begs me to, I'd be a fool to act on it. Apart from the fact he'll run back to the States as soon as he gets his album done, leaving me pining after him for a second time, there's a part of me that's still furious with him, even after all these years.

We were so good together. At least, I thought we were. When he left, I didn't see it coming. It's the sole reason I'm terrified to let anyone else get close to me. Even Conor. I can't be certain it won't happen again.

Soft snores continue from the couch. There's no way I can carry her to her room, and I hate waking her when she looks so peaceful, especially today of all days.

'Will you help me put her to bed?' I nod towards her bedroom door and watch as a frown flickers across his face.

It takes me a second, but I realise he assumed that was still my room. It was mine, once upon a time. Then again, so was he. Things change.

He nods, places his half-full goblet on the coffee table and sweeps my baby sister up into his arms as if she's weightless. Slumping against his chest, she barely opens her eyes as he carries her through to her four-poster bed. Smoothing her hair from her face, I place a heavy grey throw over her, switch off the light and close her door.

Ryan's already back in the kitchen area refilling his glass, and mine. Talk about presumptuous. The way he's carrying on anyone would think he was the most eligible bachelor in the country. Oh wait... he is.

He swings between being this confident, gorgeous, god-like stranger, to being the sensitive boyfriend I once knew and loved.

'Thank you.' I don't just mean for filling my glass.

The music's still playing from Victoria's phone. Christmas songs about love infiltrate the air surrounding us.

We gaze at each other for several seconds without uttering a word. A charged intensity penetrates my pupils from his blackening ones, causing butterflies in my stomach to flutter, swirl and soar. Dark irises beckon. Like the smoothest, silkiest chocolate, I know he'd taste amazing, but he's so not good for my health.

Muscular arms extend. Fingers tentatively search for mine. Heat pulses through me. I can't decide if I'm blazing with anger, or lust. Both probably. But I can't even berate myself for it because the man is not only my first and only love, but he's a fucking rockstar.

It doesn't mean I'm going to act on it though.

His fingers reach their destination, entwining with mine. I don't pull away, but neither do I return the sensual strokes.

'Sasha, I—'

'Don't, Ryan. Just don't.' There's no need. There are no words.

'Sasha, please. I need to explain. I can't bear you thinking I just waltzed off and left you. I had no idea about your parents—'

'It's not even about my parents. Regardless of that...'

It hangs unspoken in the air between us, the weight of what we had, what he left, because there really are no words. Not for me anyway. Nothing could adequately describe the connection we had. The connection he broke. It was sacrosanct.

'I would never have chosen to leave you.' Pain weaves into every syllable of every word so convincingly, I almost believe him. 'I had no choice.' Grabbing my hands, he lowers his face until his forehead presses against mine. 'I can't fully elaborate, but it was my dad.' He pulls back, shaking his head, an angry expression scrunching his features.

Swallowing down the million questions sparking inside, I wait, even though it kills me. For years I've wondered, contemplating every possible reason under the sun.

I wait with bated breath, silently pleading for him to open up to me. To give me a sliver of proof he didn't leave me willingly. That I wasn't wrong about what we had. That one day I might trust myself to move on, because it wasn't something I did or didn't do. That our relationship wasn't something I misinterpreted.

Ryan sighs, running a hand through his floppy hair. 'I don't know the specific details, but my father said if we didn't leave for the States that night he would be imprisoned or killed. The haunted look in his eyes was different to any I'd ever seen before. He was even more shaken than the months following my mother's departure. I didn't doubt the truth of his words, they were etched into every deepening line on his face. He hinted Jayden and I could be in danger if we stayed. He was so ashen.'

Ryan's father was a crook, white-collar crime his speciality. Even my own father was aware of Mr Cooper's business dealings, but his rent was always on time and they were excellent tenants, so he kept his nose out of it.

'I might have been eighteen, but I was still a kid. Just a boy. I was terrified for my father, and of him. He had one hell of a temper.'

He shifts from one foot to the other, an enigmatic expression carved on his face. Any remaining resentment I harboured thaws, melting to a wetness that heads straight for my underwear.

'I assumed a financial scandal large enough to have us fleeing the country must have hit the headlines – that you and your family had been as disgusted as the rest of the country. I never felt good enough for you, Sasha. And I didn't get the chance to prove myself worthy of you while you were mine.'

He didn't feel good enough for me?

'I spent the first two months in Texas praying to hear something, anything from you. Even if it was your disgust at my father's illegal activities. I had no idea you were dealing with a bigger trauma of your own.'

Ryan didn't choose to leave me.

It was out of his control.

A numbness settles inside of me.

He tugs me towards him, enveloping me in his strong, familiar embrace. The scent of his skin, soap and masculinity, has my insides on fire with longing.

'I am so so sorry, sweetheart. For everything. I had no idea that you lost everything that night, but believe me when I say I lost everything when I left you.'

'Couldn't you have been honest with me? You could have trusted me with anything. You could have told me just enough to know it wasn't me. I spent years wondering what I'd done to drive you away. Driving myself crazy.'

'And I spent years thinking you were disgusted with me. I had no idea what you'd been through.' His grip on me intensifies. 'I'm so sorry, sweetheart.'

Melting into his chest, the tears stream uncontrollably across my cheeks. Tears for what we lost. Tears for what could have been. Tears for my parents. Tears for him. Tears for our baby.

When his hot full lips seek me out, I can't fight it. His mouth presses against mine with an urgency fuelled by both passion and pain. Our tongues entwine, stroking, dancing, devouring. My chest crushes deliciously against his. Every nerve ending inside sparks to life with a scorching, fervent passion I didn't realise I still possessed.

His palms cup my face before dropping to my waist. To the underside of my breast. He lifts me onto the counter without breaking our kiss. Urgent hands grip my backside before tracing my thighs, parting them enough for him to insert his hips between them.

My breath's laboured and my heart thrashes erratically in my chest – it's so loud every single person in the castle must be able to hear it. Gripping his shoulders, I wiggle closer to the edge of the worktop, pressing every inch of me against him. He murmurs something incoherent but appreciative into my mouth, grinding against me.

Ryan's here.

Ryan's kissing me.

Ryan didn't choose to leave me.

His fingers slip underneath the front of my top, caressing the skin below. Goosebumps ripple across my flesh, and he chases them with light sensual strokes.

I shouldn't be doing this. I shouldn't make it so easy for him, though I'm not doing it for his benefit. It's for mine. My body's need is so primal, I can't bring myself to stop.

Ryan's the one who's returned, yet it's me who's finally come home.

A thud sounds from the bedroom. He pauses, but doesn't pull away.

'Sasha?' Victoria calls from her bedroom, her voice cracked with emotion. She might not talk about the night our parents died, but I know it still haunts her dreams.

I push Ryan away from me, even though it physically pains me.

'Coming, Vic. Give me two seconds.' I try not to stare at the bulge in Ryan's trousers and fail. Epically.

'Sorry. It's the hardest night of the year for her.' Wiping my lips with the back of my hand, I jump down from the kitchen counter.

'No, it's ok. Go.' He ushers me towards her bedroom door.

It's probably for the best. Things were spiralling out of control. My hormones assumed control of all rational thought.

We cross the room together and he catches me by the hand. 'Can I see you tomorrow?'

It's an effort not to beam in his face. 'I'm sure we'll bump into each other at some point.'

'That's not what I mean and you know it.' He tugs me close to him again, pressing his torso unfairly against mine. It's a battle to think straight with the heady effect he has on me, and that's before his lips seek out mine again. My tongue slips hungrily inside his mouth before I can stop it.

'Sash?' Victoria calls again.

'I'm going to take that as a yes. Call me if I can help.' He nods sombrely towards Victoria and slips from the room, leaving a Ryan-scented trail in his wake.

What have I done?

CHAPTER FOURTEEN

RYAN

2nd December

Waking up alone in the penthouse bedroom isn't the worst feeling in the world, especially with the memory of last night's kiss pressed firmly on my lips. Though it would be immeasurably more satisfying waking up across the hall with my favourite brunette. Blood's pulsating to my dick so quickly I'm about to burst out of the boxers I slept in.

Considering it's winter, it's seriously fucking hot in here.

I hit the shower and give myself a release under the streaming hot water. I can't think straight with blue balls, and I need my wits about me if I want to get anywhere with Sasha at all.

Kissing her is one thing, but what now? Will we pick up where we left off last night? How will this end well when we live in two separate countries?

Wow.

I need to slow the fuck down before my brain explodes. For all I know, it could have been the wine. She could be full of regret today. If she is, I need to show her she needn't be.

I glance at my watch. It's barely seven, but sleep alluded me hours ago and the need to see her is making me physically itch.

I want to do something special for her. Show her how much I care. Prove how sorry I am. Nothing could ever make up for leaving her, but she's had such a hard life I want to spoil her for a while at least. But how? Sending her breakfast in bed in her own hotel just isn't going to cut it.

How do you impress the woman who has everything? Because *GQ's* most eligible fucking bachelor or not, I have a feeling if I'm going to get into Sasha's favour, I'm going to have my work cut out for me. Even now she has some idea why I left.

Wracking my brains, I search for some sort of inspiration to show her how much I care.

I have it! I fucking have it! An idea bursts through my brain so spontaneously that my own shocking laughter reverberates round the suite like a mad man's.

I'm going to need help.

I dial reception. The receptionist answers on the first ring.

'Huxley Reception, how may I assist you?' A chirpy voice sings down the phone.

'Hi. It's Ryan Cooper.' I always feel like such a douche pulling the celebrity card but I need help. 'Is it possible to speak to the manager?'

The receptionist clears her throat. 'Certainly, Mr Cooper. I'm not exactly sure where she is at the moment, but I'll page her and get her to call you back the second I locate her.'

'Would it be possible to send her up to my suite? It's a discreet matter I need to discuss.'

'Certainly, sir.'

'Thanks.' I replace the receiver and throw back the curtains.

The winter sun's barely beginning to rise, the sky a deep burnt rusty orange. Grabbing a sweater and my guitar, I head out to the terrace. The air is cold and crisp, yet somehow welcoming. I love it. I love it here. The prospect of leaving at the end of the month is already one that saddens me. I push it to the back of my brain for now.

My fingers instinctively strum the chords of one of my newest songs. It's about Sasha. It's always been about Sasha. I'm still amazed how it flew out of me. How after years of feeling nothing, I now feel everything.

Grief.

Loss.

Sorrow.

Longing.

Gratitude.

Hope.

I don't know what I'm hoping for exactly. I don't know how this will go. But when I'm near her, a spark of life ignites inside of me again and I'm going to cling onto it for dear life.

It's why I've struggled to summon any real emotion. Why no other woman has managed to get close to me in the last ten years. My damn heart has been here in this estate the whole time. She had it.

Even when I thought I'd clawed it back, it was only an illusion. It was given so unreservedly the first time, there wasn't a chance in hell of ever reclaiming it. Everybody has something in life they'll never get over. Sasha Sexton is mine.

The door slides open behind me and for split second, I dare to hope it's her. The woman I'm driving myself demented pining over.

Sadly, it isn't.

Though it is her best friend.

'So, Ryan-Runaway-Cooper finally returns...' Megan Harper stands in the open doorway, leaning against the frame with her arms folded and a grin on her face. Her auburn spirals flap in the breeze, as unruly as they ever were.

'Ryan-Runaway-Cooper?' I snort, standing to greet her with a kiss on the cheek, but she punches my arm instead. She hasn't changed a bit.

'Believe me, you've been called much worse than that.' She winks knowingly.

Only now do I register she's wearing a version of the castle uniform: a black fitted suit, a crisp white shirt, and a name tag that says, "General Manager."

'I can't believe she lets you run this place!' Actually I can. It's Sasha through and through. She keeps her friends close. Loyalty is one of her finest qualities.

'Huh.' It's Megan's turn to snort. 'At least she knows I won't disappear into the night.'

'Ouch.' My palm jokingly rests across my heart, but my tone is serious. 'I had my reasons. Believe me, if I could have stayed I would.'

'I always liked you, Ryan. I knew you'd come back at some stage. Just do me one favour? Whatever you do, don't break her fucking heart again. I know she's projecting this whole ice-queen persona right now, but believe me, it's all an act. The girl is still as soft and warm as she ever was – only now she can't afford to be, because she has a lot more responsibility to deal with.'

Megan turns back to the suite, grabs a tray she must have brought up with her and carries it outside to the patio furniture. She fills two china cups with steaming coffee from a gleaming silver pot. Handing one to me, she motions for me to sit.

'Is it too cold out here?' She's only got that blazer on and it doesn't look particularly thick.

'Don't be daft. I'm not the one who's used to the Californian climate.'

I raise my hands in resignation. It's fucking freezing, but there's no way I'll let her see me squirm.

'Welcome home.' She clinks her coffee cup against mine.

'Thanks. It's great to be back.' I mean every word. 'So, how've you been? What's been happening the last ten years?' I wrack my brains trying to remember her brother's name to ask how he is. When I asked to see the manager, I certainly didn't expect her.

'Same old, same old.' Megan rolls her eyes. 'Not much changes here. You're the one with all the excitement going on. How does it feel to be world famous? Is LA crazy cool or what? It looks like you're living the dream over there.'

My mind returns to my plush villa, the lavish cars, the vibrant city and the rat race that's my life there as I try and summon the words to describe it. 'It's big, bright, flashy. Some people love the constant parties and the lifestyle. I've done my fair share of it along the way, don't get me wrong. But it's kind of soulless or something. Lacking in reality and meaning. I prefer to chill by my pool a lot of the time. I can't go out without getting hounded, so it's just easier that way.'

'First world problems.' Megan nudges me with her elbow and smirks. 'Speaking of problems, is there something wrong? I believe you requested to see the manager?'

'Nothing's wrong exactly. I just need a bit of help.'

She nudges my ribs again jovially. 'If you've blocked the toilet with a huge murky shite or something you're supposed to call housekeeping not the manager.'

'I'm *GQ's* most eligible bachelor – I shit rainbows, I'll have you know.'

Her lips part and hot breathy laughter clouds the winter air between us.

'On a serious note, does this place have a landing pad still?'

'Oh god, who are you flying in? Not that arrogant brother of yours, I hope?' She arches an eyebrow in question.

'It's not so much who I'm flying in, as who I'd like to fly out for a while.'

'Ah ha. That, I can help you with.'

Megan winks, approval stamped all over her face. At least she seems to be onside because god knows I'm going to need all the help I can get.

CHAPTER FIFTEEN

SASHA

I wake in Victoria's bed. She's spreadeagled across the centre, leaving me clinging on the edge. Through the dim morning light filtering through the edge of the curtains, I see her eyelids are closed, a peaceful expression on her face. She might be turning eighteen next year, but she'll always be my kid sister.

Slipping out of bed, I pull on a kimono-type robe and pad across to the coffee machine. The opening of the suite door causes my head to jolt round in alarm. None of the staff ever let themselves in here, not even to clean the place. My office door is always open, my bedroom door is distinctly more private.

Familiar auburn curls appear a split second before the rest of my best friend's head and body.

'Megan? What the hell are you doing in here at this hour? Is everything ok?'

I race through a variety of scenarios that might require

attention this early, none of them pleasant, but her self-assured grin reassures me nothing's too wrong.

She turns to the doorway and beckons for someone else to enter, only piquing my curiosity further.

Tilly arrives, carrying a huge tray. On it sits the most beautiful display of two dozen crimson roses elaborately tied with a gorgeous lace bow, a pot of fresh coffee and a plate full of Danish pastries, which smell like they're straight out of the oven.

'Is it my birthday or something?' Suspicion taints my tone.

'No.' Megan's smirk is decidedly smug.

'What have you done then?' I cross the room to where Tilly places the tray on the coffee table and help myself to a Danish, never more aware of the mulled wine I drank last night.

Oh god.

Last night.

The memories of practically dry humping Ryan flood back to me, along with a rush of blood straight to my cheeks.

I should have pushed him away. I shouldn't have let him kiss me. I'm no better than the groupies congregated outside my castle walls, waiting for any opportunity to throw themselves at Mr Eligible himself.

Oh god.

Shame washes over me. I've let myself down. How on earth can I expect him to respect me if I carry on like that?

Mind you, if I remember rightly, I wasn't looking for his respect. I was looking for his...

Megan interrupts before my thoughts can fully disappear into the gutter.

'I haven't done anything. Don't shoot the messenger...' She nods towards a tiny envelope nestled amongst the flowers.

My fingers snatch the envelope quicker than if it was the last cream cake on the baker's shelf. My name's scrawled across the front. I'd recognise the writing anywhere, even ten years later.

Megan watches on, smugly triumphant, as I slip the note out.

Have your passports at the ready... R xx

Blood pounds through every vein and artery so powerfully I'm sure it'll wake Victoria. Where does Ryan think he's taking me? Surely not back to the States with him? And I thought I'd been forward? Jesus, one kiss and the man thinks I'm his again.

'He can't be serious.' I stare at it in disbelief.

'Oh, he's deadly serious.' Megan nods, her eyes gleaming with excitement. 'The helicopter's on the pad waiting to take you and Victoria. Estimated time of departure is ten o'clock. You better get that skinny butt of yours in the shower and wake your sister.'

My mouth opens and closes like a goldfish; saliva pools in my throat.

Surely he doesn't expect me to up and leave and drag my sister with me? No wonder Megan's sporting her 'I told you so' face. She called this the second we heard he was coming.

I swallow thickly. 'I don't know what type of mushrooms you've been eating for breakfast, but I can't just swan off to the States with a rockstar I used to know, and I certainly won't leave my home or drag my sister out of her final year of school to do so.'

Megan's laughter erupts around the room like a hyena and

she slaps her thighs repeatedly as the guffawing continues. Every time she tries to open her mouth to speak, she dissolves into fits again.

'You think it's funny? The man's made it as a celebrity, so now he thinks he can just click his fingers and I'll go running back to him. How entitled and presumptuous of him.' I might have promised to go to the States with him once upon a time, but that was a very long time ago.

The deliberate clearing of a deep masculine throat echoes from the doorway. Tilly must have left it ajar on her way out.

Ryan leans against it. He looks ready to hit the road, or sky, in a pair of dark jeans and a grey jumper that hugs his torso in all the right places.

His shoulders shake with pent-up laughter as he rakes his shaggy hair from those enormous smouldering eyes. He looks like a grown-up version of the boy I used to love, but the two beefy security guards flanking him remind me he's so much more. More powerful. More successful. More proficient. And seemingly, even more used to getting what he wants, when he wants.

'Oh, Sasha honey, if I thought it was as easy as that, I'd have clicked my fingers first thing this morning and had you running straight to my bed.' His gravelly voice, loaded with promise, sends shivers through my stomach and lower.

'I can't just up and leave, Ryan! I have a life here!'

Ryan crosses the room, closing the distance between us. Warm, strong hands hold my waist as he drops a kiss on my head. 'Relax. It's only a day trip. One you'll enjoy, I promise.'

As his words sink in, colour floods my cheeks again. Since the man arrived I seem to be in a permanent state of hot and bothered, anger, embarrassment, or all-consuming arousal.

'Now who's the presumptuous one, sweetheart?' His chest brushes against mine as he heads towards the coffee. I cross my arms over my chest to cover the effect he creates on my treacherous body.

'Well? What are you waiting for?' Megan shoots me a wink. 'Go get ready.'

'But what about the castle?'

I'm off today. I'm simply looking for any excuse not to go on a day trip with Ryan-Runaway-Cooper.

It was hard enough to get over him the first time round. He's barely been back two weeks and I already know when he leaves again it will crush me. Spending time with him certainly won't help the situation. Yet, the way my body screams at me, I know I'll do it anyway.

'I have everything under control. Go get ready. Put something warm on.' She ushers me towards my bedroom while Ryan watches on from the couch.

'Conor's cousin's band's coming tomorrow night to talk about the ball.'

'You'll be back later tonight, don't sweat it,' Ryan promises through a mouthful of pastry.

I never realised it was possible to be jealous of a Danish until this very second, but the way his tongue licks it from his lips has me infuriatingly envious.

'Fine.' I stalk off to get ready under the pretence of reluctance.

I'm not kidding anyone.

Least of all myself.

***

'Holy fucking shit, I can't believe we're in a helicopter,' Victoria shrieks over the noise of the blades and the engine.

'Language,' I remind her and she sticks out her tongue.

Ryan squeezes my leg through my leather trousers as he glances sideways from his seat adjacent to mine.

He's bringing us to London. To the Winter Wonderland. He's made Victoria's year, and mine. Who knew the power and influence being a superstar held? I feel a million miles away from Huxley Castle and all the responsibilities that go with it.

The view over London is incredible. The Thames. The London Eye. The Christmas trees. The lights. The hustle and bustle. Even the manic traffic swarming below appears beautiful from this height.

Mind you, the view inside isn't too bad either. Despite my best efforts, Ryan's caught me staring at him multiple times. I'm only human. The guy is a rockstar. Panty-melting hot. And my first and so far, only love. And for some reason, he's acting as though he's enamoured with me.

I've never been great with heights, but the butterflies swirling in my stomach have nothing to do with the flight and everything to do with the hand that rests on my thigh.

Victoria sits behind us with Pierce, Frankie and Archie, more of Ryan's security. They're three huge, intimidating-looking men, yet they are fawning over Vic as though she's their own daughter and she's lapping up the attention.

With every passing day the child I raised is becoming more of a woman.

Twenty minutes later the pilot eases us into a gentle landing on a helipad atop a building I don't recognise. We take a mirrored elevator forty floors down, the six of us squashed together with Victoria giggling in the centre. Ryan's back is to the wall. His front's pressed to my back. I'm left under no illusion how he feels about this unexpected cosy confinement.

A tight bulge presses against my backside in a way that makes my body burn in all the right places. With the subtlest flick of my hips, I push back against him before pulling away again. The resounding sigh that follows sends heat searing through me, and a grin settles on my lips.

Ha. Mr Eligible Bachelor is as human as the rest of us.

A couple of minutes brisk walk sees us at a side entrance to Hyde Park, to the Winter Wonderland. This must be specifically reserved for VIPs because it's heavily staffed with security guards.

Pierce pulls out a grey beanie hat and passes it to Ryan, his eyes darting round our immediate vicinity, and I gather it's not to keep him warm.

'Me and Frankie will flank you. Archie will stroll with Victoria,' Pierce says, the voice of authority. 'No one knows you're here – everyone thinks you're holed up in an Irish castle – if we could keep it that way, it'd make my job a lot easier.'

Ryan nods and offers me his arm. Archie follows suit, taking Victoria's next to us.

'If anyone gets lost, or if there's a situation, meet back here at this gate and the security team will put you in an SUV until the situation's resolved. Is everybody clear?'

'Yes, boss.' Ryan nods, solemn for once, and I get the impression his safety's been jeopardised more than once. It's not something I'd ever considered when I imagined him living the good life in LA, not that I spent a lot of time thinking about it. Much.

We take off, strolling through the bustle of the Christmas markets. Twinkling multi-coloured lights glint and flicker but today, hanging off Ryan's reassuring arm, they don't bother me.

Throngs of people bustle by, but nobody offers us a second glance, each engrossed in absorbing the festive magic.

It's an effort to take it all in, my senses on overload. Row upon row of charming chalets. Gingerbread, mulled wine, ornaments, sparkling baubles. Scented candles and intricately carved wooden figures. Chocolate fountains and marshmallow sticks.

Victoria's eyes shine with excitement as she points out each and every attraction. The Cirque Berserk. The carousels. The Ice Bar.

Frankie and Pierce linger a couple of feet behind us as promised. Nobody would even guess they're with us. It's so surreal.

Victoria stops at a mini fudge factory, reaching into her purse to purchase some but Archie pushes her hand away, instead buying her an overflowing assortment that he carries as if he really were her dutiful date.

We spend hours exploring the stalls and sights. Gazing around, I realise we're no different from anyone else here, well apart from the superstar amongst us of course. The one whose body huddles against mine. The one who's taking my hand and slipping it inside his coat pocket so his fingers entwine with mine.

He looks down to meet my stare. 'What next?'

I gather he means at the Winter Wonderland because if he's talking about us, I have no idea.

'The Ferris wheel!' Victoria squeals and Ryan grins.

'Still hate heights, Sasha?' he whispers into my ear, warm breath skimming over my cold earlobe.

'I see you haven't lost your memory in your old age.'

'Old age? Sweetheart, I haven't even hit my prime yet.' His breath tickles my ear again and I'd almost swear his tongue flicked over it too.

'Is that right?' It's a battle to form a coherent sentence when he's this close.

'Play your cards right later, and I might even show you...'

He winks and I use the hand that's not in his pocket to slap his shoulder.

'Been there, done that... Thankfully, I don't have the t-shirt because I never quite made it to one of your concerts.'

'We'll have to rectify that,' he says, dragging me towards the queue for the Ferris wheel.

Pierce intervenes, ushering us to a side entrance again, skipping the queue of probably hundreds of people. He nods to another security guard who leads us directly to a carriage.

My heart plummets. Ryan had it in one. I'm petrified of heights. The helicopter was one thing, but this hazardous transportable machine is another thing altogether. What if the damn thing gets stuck up there? What if the hinges snap and we plummet to the ground? My shaky breath presses tightly against my chest.

'You don't have to do this,' Ryan whispers into my ear as Victoria and Archie hop in first. Her face is a picture of excitement. She's glowing like I've never seen her glow before.

I can't let her down.

I won't let her down.

'I'm fine,' I lie, hopping in across from them.

Ryan slides in beside me and asks the security guard for something. I can't hear what.

He squashes against me, wrapping his huge arm around my shoulder, forcing me into his chest. I'm not complaining. It was once my favourite spot in the whole world.

Who am I kidding? It still is.

The guards returns with a woman who looks about twenty. She carries a tray containing a bottle of Dom Perignon and four champagne flutes, which she places on the small metal table in the centre of the carriage.

'So this is what it feels like to be a VIP...' I manage to mutter in Ryan's ear as Archie takes the bottle. The delightful cork pop is usually one of my favourite sounds in the world but today it sends me hopping further into Ryan's arms.

'Sasha, Queen of the Castle, you already know what if feels like to be a VIP,' he teases straight back. 'But you haven't yet found out what it's like to be *my* VIP...'

My stomach flips and this time it has nothing to do with the Ferris wheel that's slowly beginning to rise in the air.

Christmas songs blast from speakers everywhere.

Archie hands us each a glass of champagne. I eye Victoria's with an arched eyebrow, but she arches one straight back, deliberately glancing between Ryan and me. I'm only grateful she hasn't taken a picture and sent it to Chloe because no doubt she'll have a lot to say about this development.

Ryan eyes Archie's glass, and Archie places it down on the table between us.

He is at work, I suppose. I never noticed before but he's really young looking. Way younger than Pierce and Frankie. Maybe even younger than me.

'This is incredible.' Victoria raises her voice to be heard over the noise as she scans the crowd below, an awe-filled look on her face.

She isn't wrong.

Raucous children queue outside a cute looking wooden grotto to see Santa, hopping from one foot to the other in excitement. Others squeal as they venture up a daunting slide made of ice nearby. A Santa train chugs by, transporting tiny waving toddlers clutching candy-floss and gingerbread men. Chubby grinning faces press against the steamy glass of the windows.

What's truly incredible though is the god-like creature next to me. His face. His lips. That mouth.

Despite the freezing cold afternoon, a promising heat

emanates from Ryan's eager pupils as they roam my face before meeting mine.

Oh I'm in trouble. It might be safer if this damn thing does plummet from the sky, because I'm well on my way to falling again anyway. And I'm not sure which prospect is more dangerous.

CHAPTER SIXTEEN

RYAN

'Ok, who's for the ice slide?' Victoria squeals as we step out of the Ferris wheel carriage.

'You've got to be joking.' Sasha shakes her head firmly. 'I've had enough excitement for one day.'

That's what she thinks.

If I get my way, she'll see a lot more excitement before the day is over. Spending time with her, being with her, it's addictive. Years have passed, yet I still feel that pull, that innate connection like we're tethered together with some sort of invisible string.

This whole emotional awakening is turning me into a fucking pussy because as much as I am desperate to get my hands all over her ridiculously enticing body, I'm also desperate to spoon her all night, to wake up next to her – something we never got to do as kids.

'I'll bring you on the ice slide,' Archie offers before turning to me. 'If that's ok with you, boss?'

It's perfect with me. It means I get Sasha alone. Something I've craved from the second I laid eyes on her again.

'Sure. Do you want to go for a drink?' I point out the Fire Pit, the perfect place to soak up the atmosphere.

Sasha's shoulders sag in visible relief and she nods.

'We'll get a table and wait for you there.' I turn to Archie. 'Guard her with your life.'

Archie nods solemnly and links Victoria's arm again. 'We'll come straight back to you when we're done.'

Pierce and Frankie lead the way through the throng of Christmas revellers to the Fire Pit. Pierce locates a high table with two bar stools tucked in the corner of the bar area.

'Sit here. Back to the wall. Eyes peeled. Me and Frankie will be at the bar keeping an eye out. Keep the hat on. It's one thing walking around and people getting a fleeting glance, but with you sitting still, someone might recognise you.'

I nod in reluctant acceptance and hand over my credit card to pay for the drinks he'll have to order. If anyone had any suspicion who I am, my accent would only confirm it.

Sasha glides onto one of the high stools and slips the little satchel bag off her shoulders, placing it on the table between us.

Scanning the surroundings, a comfortable quiet settles between us. When her gaze finally returns to me, I meet her keen stare evenly, memorising every inch of her perfect face.

Jayden's wrong. It's not because we were forced to separate prematurely. It's because she's so fucking beautiful. She has a heart the size of Africa, a quick mind, and even quicker tongue. Plus, she oozes a type of sublime class I've never come across since. It's safe to say Sasha Sexton is one of a kind.

Though she's given me access to her lips and her hands in

the last twenty-four hours, I get the distinct impression her heart, big as it is, is still off limits. To me, at least.

An image of her sitting on the kitchen worktop beaming at Conor bursts to the forefront of my mind, generating a queasiness in my stomach. She trusts him, there's no doubt about it. And as much as I hate to admit it, the two of them definitely have some sort of chemistry.

Not like what we have though.

Not judging by the way her body responded so explosively to mine last night.

Still, Conor's a safer bet for her. I'd be reckless to underestimate the threat he poses. He doesn't have a track record of abandoning her. And he lives in the same country.

We could be so fucking good together. I just need her to trust me enough to let me in. Even if we live in different countries, even if we have very different lives, I know for certain I need her in mine in some capacity. She's always been her own woman. The question is, how do I get her to be mine?

If I can only gain her trust again, I know we could have something phenomenal. I deliberately ignore the geographic logistics of the situation. I can buy a plane if needs be. I could buy a hundred fucking planes. What I can't buy is her.

She finally breaks the silence between us. 'What's going on in that mysterious mind of yours?'

I bite my lip, trying to think of something witty for a couple of seconds before deciding to go with the simple truth.

'I'm wondering how I can make you mine again.' Stretching my hand across the table, I find hers and rub my thumb over the back of her hand.

She sighs, and a sad smile forms on lips that are painted a festive, seductive shade of crimson. 'Ryan.'

Her words are weighted with a heavy acceptance. She's written us off before we've even tried.

'You live in the States. You're a goddamn rockstar for heaven's sake. It wouldn't work.'

'What I feel for you is real. I spent years closed up, emotionally stunted, unable to move on. When I'm with you I feel fucking alive again. I know you feel it too. It might have been ten years, but even after all this time there's something blazing between us. Don't even try to deny it.'

'I'm not denying anything. But we are worlds apart.' Her hand squeezes mine back, but it's with sympathy or empathy or some other negativity. She's right, I know she is, but I'm still compelled to try.

Pierce interrupts briefly with our drinks: another bottle of champagne. The old romantic clearly has experience wooing a woman. Either that or he's been employed directly by Cupid himself.

When he returns to his stake-out position at the bar, I lean as far across the table as my torso will allow. 'You're wrong. I know I broke your heart. Give me another chance and I swear to god, I'll prove to you how right we are together.'

I have no idea how to embark on a real relationship, let alone a long-distance one, but I'm practically begging and I don't care. The need for her to be mine is all-consuming.

An influx of rowdy women arrive and congregate next to us, queuing for the bar. The laughter and cackling suggest this isn't the first pub they've hit today.

Centrally positioned within the gaggle stands a blonde woman wearing a flashing white tiara, a knee-length white coat and high white boots. The red flashing sash draped over her shoulder says *Bride-To-Be*. Two others sport *Bridesmaid* ones. The others wear red and white outfits in support.

These women are the exact demographic of my typical fan base.

Pierce arches an eyebrow and takes an inconspicuous sip from his drink. Frankie stands taller and takes a step in our direction. I slink down into my seat, wishing for Harry Potter's invisibility cloak because I've got an awful feeling my peaceful afternoon with Sasha's about to be horribly interrupted.

The women examine their surroundings like sharks searching for seals. Searching for prey. It's a look I know well. Jayden wears it regularly. Specifically when he's on the hunt for a shag.

As if in slow motion, one of the bridesmaids turns in our direction. Her eyes flick towards us and just as her head twists away, she yanks it back in a double take.

I know in that split second I've been busted.

Frankie and Pierce join us at the table. 'Think we should probably go, boss. I've paged the park security. They'll have a car at the back entrance in three minutes. We just need to get you out of here without starting a goddamn riot.'

Sasha squeezes my hand, biting her lip as she watches the scene unfold in front of her.

Sure enough, the bridesmaid elbows the girl next to her, who elbows the girl next to her. The hushed whispers become full-blown squeals.

As I stand from the stool I hear, 'Oh my god, is that Ryan Cooper over there?'

The news reaches the bride before I'm out of my seat. She marches over to our table with the expression of a soldier charging into war. Her mission is clear.

'I wish I had a newspaper to hide your face,' Pierce mutters. 'Even a fucking bin bag would be helpful at this point.'

Before the blonde gets within three feet of the table, Sasha stands, blocking her path to me.

'Is that mistletoe up there?' She points upwards and my gaze turns to festive foliage, which is indeed bursting with fresh mistletoe. When I look down again, her mouth's an inch from mine. With her bust against my chest, the scent of her skin surrounds me, the warmth of her breath on my lips. Snaking my arms around her waist, I wrench her into my arms, ready to flip her behind me if things get out of control.

From the corner of my eye I see the blonde pause, hovering beside us, questioning herself and my identity. Frankie and Pierce insert themselves behind Sasha so there are three people blocking the bride-to-be's path to me.

Seconds pass. Sasha's eyes remain focused intently on mine – huge, burning pools of longing. An intensity she can't deny. We're caught in limbo waiting for the car.

'Excuse me...' the blonde calls hopefully.

Sasha's lips crash against mine, her head blocking the view of my face. Everything else melts away. She can fake that she's doing it to hide me, but she can't fake the way her tongue hungrily seeks out mine. Tiny teasing strokes scorching my insides, igniting an inferno in my chest and stomach.

I need to get out of here, and it has nothing to do with the mob of women desperate to make my acquaintance and everything to do with the woman I'm desperate to get reacquainted with.

Her palms reach for my neck. Fingers rake exploratively beneath my beanie grabbing a fistful of hair. There's no way this is a simple distraction technique.

Sasha Sexton is as hot for me as she ever was. And I'm going to make sure she stays that way.

Pierce's elbow rudely interrupts the hottest kiss of my life. 'They're here.'

Reluctantly, I tear my mouth from Sasha but not my eyes.

Cameras flash from phones in every direction. The bride stands with her mouth open as Pierce and Frankie rapidly usher us out. The back door of a black SUV opens and I push Sasha in before hopping in behind her.

'Victoria...' Sasha's eyes widen as the door closes.

'Don't worry.' Pierce glances round from the front passenger seat. 'Frankie's gone to find her and Archie. They'll meet us back at the helipad.'

She slumps back in the car with apparent relief and I chance taking her hand again.

'Welcome to my world.' I wink at her. 'Turns out, you fit in fucking perfectly. Just like I knew you would.'

When we're safely back inside the castle reception area, Sasha turns to me thoughtfully. She nods towards her sister who's laughing at something Archie says as he escorts her up the grand staircase, the fudge tucked under his right arm. 'Thank you so much for today, Ryan. It meant the world to Victoria.'

Now we're back, the ice queen's trying to make a reappearance. Given half the chance, I'm going to crank the heat so high she'll melt for good.

'To Victoria, huh?' She's not making this easy on me. Even if she did save me from getting mobbed by a crowd of starstruck groupies.

A blush creeps into her cheeks as her eyes meet mine. 'And me.'

'Have dinner with me.' It's out of my mouth before I've even thought about it.

She bites her lower lip while she thinks about it. 'But what will people say?'

My laughter echoes all the way around the huge atrium. 'That's your only concern? Sweetheart, there were more phones flashing in the Fire Pit today than camera flashes at a wedding. I'm pretty sure your face, or the back of your head at least, will be all over the nine o'clock news.'

'Well, I never said it was my *only* concern, but it's up there with – What will my staff think of me? What will Victoria think? What will Conor think?'

She ticks them off each finger, but I interrupt her before she finishes.

'You're worried about Conor?'

'I don't want to hurt his feelings.'

'But what about my feelings? Saying no might hurt them...' I pout and she snorts.

'You'd get over it, Mr Eligible.'

'I wouldn't, trust me. Conor might though.' I scratch my head. 'Over time. A very long time...'

I'm lying. He'll never get over Sasha Sexton. Trust me, I know from experience. I've had ten fucking years and I'm no closer to getting over her than I am to getting under her.

'Besides, I hadn't finished...' She holds her hand up again and checks off a final question. 'Last but not least. Will Ryan-Runaway-Cooper make a fool out of me for a second time?'

'Sasha, I swear to you, I will not make a fool of you. Give us a chance. I can't make it up to you if you won't even let me try.'

She deliberates for a few seconds, chewing that lip hard enough to draw a dot of scarlet liquid. It's so tempting to lick it better, but we're already attracting enough attention from the receptionists huddled behind the huge maple desk.

'If, and I mean if, I were to agree to dinner, or anything else. I need something from you, Ryan.'

'Anything.' I mean it.

'I need honesty. If there's a problem; if you need to leave abruptly; if something happens I need to know. Don't keep anything from me for any reason, I don't care whose secret it is. It won't go any further than between us, but offer me that respect at least.'

It's a done deal. A no-brainer. In fact, it goes without saying, though I fully understand her need to say it after last time.

I give her my scout's honour sign.

'I need to hear you say it.'

'I swear. One hundred per cent honesty, transparency, and no secrets.'

She offers a curt nod, seemingly satisfied, for now. 'Fine. Dinner. But not in the restaurant.'

Even better. No prying eyes or social etiquette.

'My place or yours?' I ask, even though technically, they're all hers.

'Yours. Unless you want Victoria badgering you about Adam Draker and every other teenage fantasy she might have.'

'As much as I adore your kid sister, I'd really like some time alone with you.' My mind wanders to the outdoor hot tub. It's the perfect night for it, if I can only persuade her to get into it with me.

She swallows hard as her eyes meet mine. I'm not imagining it. There's a fire burning in her soul for me. What we have is real. It's no ordinary love.

Love? I catch myself. Is it possible to have fallen in love with her again already?

Fuck that. If the lyrics that burst out of me are anything to go by, I never fell out of love with her in the first place. Love was never a question. It was everything else.

'Give me an hour to get changed and organise food to be sent up.'

'Don't go to any trouble.' I meant with the clothes, because I have every intention of stripping them straight off her the second she permits it.

'I take it you still like your steak medium rare?'

Hmm. She's not quite on the same page yet.

'I'll take it any way I can get it.' I shoot her a wink and she slaps my arm.

'I said dinner.' A smirk twitches at her lip, which she tries desperately to hide.

'I'm already thinking about dessert.'

From the way her breath catches in her chest, she remembers exactly what I prefer to eat for dessert.

'See you soon.' I plant a kiss on her mouth before she can pull away, then head up to my suite to get myself ready.

I need a shower, and not just to wash. There's no way I'm peaking early tonight. I've spent ten years thinking about this. I need to ensure it's memorable for the next ten.

CHAPTER SEVENTEEN

SASHA

Rummaging through the contents of my wardrobe, I discard five different outfits before settling on a classic black dress. Its cut is simple, skimming all the right places but without actually revealing much flesh.

I need to order dinner, but the thought of asking Conor to cook for Ryan and me feels like sticking a knife in, even though Conor and I have never been together.

To avoid any awkward questions, I ring Megan to arrange the food instead. She's due to finish her shift in ten minutes, but she never leaves on time.

'Well? Tell me everything!' Her shriek practically pierces my eardrum.

'Hi, to you too.' I turn the taps on to run a bath and pour in a generous amount of scented salts.

'Oh, don't be all coy now, Sasha! The ice-queen routine doesn't work with me. I need details!'

'You'll have them, but not right now.'

'Oh my god, is he there? Do I hear a bath running?' I

didn't think it was possible for her voice to get any louder. Clearly, I was wrong.

'Shh, will you, please! He's not here, but he asked me to have dinner with him. In his suite.'

'Oh my god. You are totally going to have sex with Ryan-Runaway-Cooper! Again!'

I pray to god she's in some quiet corner of the castle – alone. 'I am not!'

'Are too!'

'Am not.'

I'm not planning to, if at all possible. Though I wouldn't bet my life on it. Especially after the way my body lost control last night.

'Please, Meg, seriously, I need a favour.'

'Condoms, right? I think there are some stashed somewhere, I'll just ask Louise—'

At that prospect, I almost drop the phone into the bath.

'Don't you dare, Megan Jane Harper, or I swear to god you won't be my best friend anymore!' It's an 'in joke' we've used since we were kids.

'Ok, ok! I was only joking! Keep your knickers on! Or don't! But either way, I NEED details.'

'Tomorrow. I promise. But tonight can you get room service sent to Ryan's suite? I don't want to have to ask Conor.'

'Ah.' Understanding rings in her tone.

'I know we've never been together or anything, but you know better than anyone there's this underlying energy between us.'

'He's gonna be kicking himself he didn't make a move sooner,' Megan says with a sigh.

I turn off the bath taps. 'Honestly, it wouldn't have mattered either way.'

'Why? Are you and Ryan getting back together?'

'No, but the way I feel about him blows everyone else out the water. There's no comparison. And whether I end up with him or not – which is super unlikely by the way, given the logistics of the situation – I won't settle for anything less than that feeling. Even if I never find it again.'

With Ryan's return, so have the enormity of my feelings. I won't be able to settle for a love that's less than phenomenal – not when I know it's out there.

'You guys did have something sensational. Maybe you could again?'

'Ah, Meg. It's complicated. I can't think straight when I'm around him. I know I should have said no to dinner tonight, I've been with him all day, but he's like my own personal brand of chilled champagne or something. He makes me feel so good. I'm utterly addicted.'

It's a relief to admit it out loud.

'You know he feels the same way about you. Give him a chance.'

'I'm just terrified he'll disappear again.'

'Lightning doesn't strike twice. He told me he had no choice. This time, nothing and no one in this world can tell him what to do.'

She's right. The man has the world at his fingertips. Literally. Look at what he managed to do for me today.

Maybe I should trust him and just go with this?

'Shave your legs, just in case.' Megan snorts, lightening the mood again. 'Now, what do you want to eat?'

***

An hour and a half later, when I've checked on Victoria and answered three million questions on FaceTime from Chloe, I knock the door of the penthouse suite, ignoring the smirking security guards positioned either side of it.

Pierce must be taking a rest, because I don't recognise either of them.

Ryan opens the door wearing a pair of black jeans that hang from his hips like he's a male model. The rolled-up sleeves of his shirt cling to his pronounced biceps in a way that makes me want to grab them, pin him to the nearest available surface and jump his bones.

Well, one bone.

Several times.

As if he can read my mind, a sassy smirk on his lips sends butterflies crusading through my stomach. And lower.

'Come in. Welcome to my humble abode.' He gesticulates around the spacious room and winks.

'I think you mean *my* humble abode.' I arch an eyebrow at him.

'No. For eight grand a night, it's definitely mine. For the time being at least.' He winks again, and a ripple of guilt flashes through me at my anger-induced price increase.

I follow him through to the living area. The curtains aren't drawn. Thousands of tiny lights twinkle in the distant horizon, glittering in the distance.

Ryan's taken the liberty of ordering a bottle of the castle's most expensive champagne and it's sitting in a gleaming chrome bucket filled with ice.

'Can I get you a drink? Seeing as we had to abandon the last one?' Without waiting for my answer, he pours fizzing, bubbling liquid into two flutes before handing one to me.

Taking a sip from the glass, I stride towards the patio doors to look out, and to put some space between us. Every cell in my body silently screams and writhes in protest.

To distract myself, I babble, 'How does it feel to be back after all this time?'

'Honestly? I love it. For years, I wondered about this place. About you.'

He crosses the room to linger behind me. Resting his chin on my shoulder, he slips an arm round my waist, pulling my back against his chest. My pulse quickens as we gaze out at the horizon.

I turn to face him, drinking in his intoxicating scent. The delectable mouth that's begging to be kissed. Those lust-filled chocolate eyes. His incredible bone structure. The man is a work of art. The boy I once knew is gone. The man before me is a fucking god.

Our eyes lock. Chemistry cracks the air between us, and his lips land on mine with the same maddening urgency as the night before. His tongue seeks mine and once again I'm incapable of rational thought. Every nerve ending pricks to attention, desperate for more. More of him. More of this feeling.

A knock from the door sends me leaping away from him like a naughty school girl. I suppose last time we were together, that's pretty much what I was.

Megan herself strides in wheeling a trolley full of steaming goodies. An array of appetising scents permeate the air, but they're still not nearly as mouth-watering as the man next to me.

'Hope I'm not interrupting anything?' Her smirk says otherwise.

'You were supposed to finish hours ago.' My eyes roll heavenwards.

'Yes, but you two need discretion, so I thought I'd hang on a little longer to deliver this myself.'

Huh. More like she wanted to witness the action firsthand.

'Well, thank you. But you can go now.'

She wheels the trolley across the room and leaves it next to the dining room table, which is big enough to comfortably lie across. Heat burns in my cheeks and I push the image away immediately.

Ryan grins at me, as if the same thought occurred to him.

'Call me in the morning. I'm not due in until the afternoon.' The nudge she delivers with her elbow is firm enough to make me yelp. For someone supposedly concerned with discretion, she certainly isn't subtle. She gives me the thumbs up before finally closing the door.

'Are you hungry?' Lifting the polished silver lids, I inhale the succulent aromas.

'Yes.' Ryan's gaze drops over my body in a deliberate motion and the butterflies swarm and soar once again.

I pull out a chair and motion for him to sit. Reluctantly, he drops into the cushioned chair and tuts, as if eating is a waste of his time. I don't remind him dinner was his idea.

He soon changes his mind, devouring mouthful after mouthful of juicy fillet, dripping in a red wine jus. 'It's unbelievably good.'

'Conor is very talented.' I pop another melt-in-the-mouth bite on my tongue and close my eyes. When I open them, Ryan's staring at me.

'Oh, he is, is he?' Jealousy flares in his pupils.

Now he knows how I felt any time I caught a glimpse of him on the front page of a glossy with some beautiful high-flying actress on his arm.

I shrug and nod, stoking the fire, unable to help myself.

He places his knife and fork on his plate in a slow deliberate motion. I do the same, and put my plate back on the trolley, no longer hungry all of a sudden.

Using his index finger, he beckons me to where he sits at the head of the table. I shake my head, unconvincingly. My body begs me to leap across to him, but my hammering heart still urges caution.

He rolls his eyes in borderline arrogance. 'Playing hard to

get, Sash? We both know where this is going to end.' The legs of his chair screech against the floor as he stands, stalking deliberately towards me.

I rise to my feet and raise my hands in surrender. 'I'm not playing anything. I'm just trying to act with caution.'

He turns my body to meet his, pushing his powerful frame against my front, pinning my bum to the table behind me.

Saliva pools in my mouth and heat rages through my core, and lower. I want him. I can't deny it. I've always wanted him.

My thinly veiled self-control is pushed to the limits when his hips press against mine, leaving nothing to my imagination.

'I'm done with caution. I want to make you mine again, right here, right now.' His deep velvety voice commands my attention, as do the fingers that tilt my chin to meet his smouldering stare.

My tongue darts over my lips as my hips buck defiantly back at him, refusing to meet the lips that linger tormentingly, millimetres from mine, because once I do all sense of self-preservation evaporates. 'Who says I want you to?'

Laughter dances in his eyes. 'Oh, Sasha, I can read every minute signal from your beautiful body. And like every other instrument I put my hands on, I can and will play it perfectly.'

As if to prove his point, he drops a hand to my bare knee, sliding his finger up the inside of my thigh. When he slips it inside my silk underwear, the gasp that slips from my lips has him grinning.

'You know, you're quite persuasive when you want to be, but you can't just walk back in here after ten years and expect me to roll over for you.' I'm soaked. I can barely stand and my tone's weighted with wanting and he knows it.

His index finger glides up and down my centre. Raw lust rips through me. Burning desire swells in every single cell, yet I manage to hang back, to not bury my tongue in his mouth.

'I never said anything about you rolling over,' his husky voice growls into my ear.

My legs tremble as his index finger continues its maddening, addictive stroke. I haven't even come yet, but I already know once won't be enough. It's been ten long years and I have craved this body for each and every day of them.

The hand that's not inside my underwear strays to the back of my dress searching for a way to undo it. The sweet metallic swish of the zip lowering is the sexiest sound in the world. When he removes his fingers from my sex to whip the dress over my head, I whimper out loud. The ice queen has officially melted.

The satisfaction sparkling in his pupils shows he knows it.

'Oh, Sasha, what am I going to do with you?' Hungry eyes roam my body as I stand before him in nothing but an ebony silk thong and matching Agent Provocateur bra.

It's on the tip of my tongue to beg him to continue exactly what he was doing but somehow I manage to keep my mouth shut. I want him to decide. I want him to do whatever he wants to me. Because I know, whatever it is, I'm going to enjoy every single second of it. I never stood a chance fighting this.

His burning pupils bore into mine as he sits in the seat I just vacated, pushing me backwards on to the table, until I'm flat on my back. Greedy eyes drink me in as his fingers nudge my thighs apart, inching higher until they're at my underwear again.

In one swift animalistic wrench, he rips them from me and I'm laid bare for him.

Hot lust radiates from his gaze as his face drops to the most sensitive parts of me. When his tongue finally reaches its destination, I cry out in sheer relief. It's short lived as he begins to tease me with swift maddening strokes. As I wriggle and writhe beneath his mouth, he grabs my hands and pins them to the table either side of me.

The man is trying to kill me in the most infuriatingly seductive way.

Just when I think I can't take it anymore, he changes tack, his tongue swirling, sucking, worshipping in a perfect rhythm.

Pressure builds inside and I'm so close to exploding. Maddeningly, he pauses, his face hovering millimetres from where I need him to be.

'Now tell me who's talented, Sasha?' A deliciously alluring wickedness resounds in his tone and the slow deliberate exhale over my body is enough to send goosebumps rippling across my flesh. He's got me exactly where he wants me and he knows it.

'Whose girl are you, Sasha?' He prompts me again, confident, poised and sexy as hell. I love his possessiveness. The way he seeks to claim me.

It was always going to end this way. No one else can, or will, ever compare to him, and that was before he took the world by storm.

I'm so busy panting and squirming, I can barely form a coherent sentence. 'You. You. It's always been you.'

'Good girl.' His grinning lips resume their position – his tongue returns to my centre with slow and sensual strokes. I'm so close. Within seconds, he brings me to the point of powerful, delicious explosion. A myriad of blinding stars burst behind my tightly shut eyelids.

He releases my hands from the table as I cry out his name. My fingers rake through his hair as he laps at me like I'm the sweetest thing he's ever tasted. He offers my sex one final kiss before sitting back in the chair, a victorious expression carved on his magnificent face.

Hauling myself to a sitting position, I inch off the table to straddle his lap. The bulge from his trousers just begs to be touched.

'You've still got it.' I press a kiss to his lips and his hands tug at my bra until my breasts spill over the top. He teases my nipples as I hastily yank at his jeans, needing him to fill me up.

'And you are going to get everything I've got, sweetheart.' His mouth drops to my breast, as my fingers unfasten the buttons of his shirt before discarding it on the floor.

Strong hands grip my waist, lifting me onto the table again as if I'm weightless. His ripped chest glistens as he slides on top of me, minus his trousers. Spreading myself for him, I wait while he opens a condom. When he finally thrusts inside me, the cry that comes from my lips is unrecognisable as my own.

He moves inside me like he's specifically made to be there. The tear that slips from the corner of my eye is one of sheer relief and unparalleled pleasure. And love. I love him. I always have.

Quickening the pace, his hands slip under my backside to angle himself better inside me.

'Sasha.' His mouth traces on my neck, my collarbone, my breasts.

I wrap my arms round his muscular shoulders as we shudder in a mind-blowing climax together.

CHAPTER EIGHTEEN

RYAN

3rd December

Waking up with Sasha Sexton in my arms is the single most transcendent moment of my life. The electric atmosphere of an arena rammed with a hundred thousand screaming fans has absolutely nothing on the sensations rippling through my body and my, until recently, cold fucking heart.

A contented sigh resounds through the blackness of the early morning and she snuggles deeper against my chest. Memories of last night flood me. The table. The sofa. This bed.

There have been plenty of other women in my life, but not one of them ever came close to creating what we had last night. From her lusty cries, I can only assume it's the same for her.

Were there many men after I left? I can't imagine it, but equally, it's hard to imagine her short of offers. Thank god Conor was slow off the mark. Imagine if she'd married him...

The thought of her with another man perforates my heart like a shiny switchblade. One thing's for sure, it'll never happen again.

Because she is mine. And I'm hers. And that's the way it's always been.

My mind plays devil's advocate with worrying consequences.

What if the condom split? What if I got her pregnant?

Instead of alarming me, the prospect incites a yearning I didn't realise I was capable of. The image of Sasha carrying my baby in her swollen belly is enough to set my dick hard again.

One day, I'm going to make it our reality. I'm not sure how, but I won't give her up now I've found her again.

I push away the niggle that reminds me we live in different countries. This time I'll do whatever it takes to keep her in my life. No matter what. Nothing in this world will make me leave her.

New lyrics bombard my brain, begging me to put pen to paper, but I can't drag myself out of this bed, unable to tear myself away from my woman.

The intrusive vibration of a phone ringing breaks through the silence. It's Sasha's, not mine. She groans as she stirs, planting a kiss on my chest before reaching for it where it's relentlessly flashing on the bedside locker.

'For fuck's sake.' She groans, cancelling the call.

'Good morning, gorgeous.' I haul her back into my arms, desperate for skin-on-skin contact. My dick's solid with a burning longing only she can soothe.

Seeking her mouth with mine, I nudge her backwards, sliding on top of her. Her grin is audible, though I can't see it.

'Good morning to you, too.' She parts her legs, allowing me access, but before I can slip inside her, her phone rings again.

'For fuck's sake.' Patting the bed next to her, she finds it and cancels it again. 'She won't stop, you know.' She warns me as she scratches round the bedside locker, hopefully in search of another condom.

'Who won't?'

'Chloe. She's like a hound with the trace of a scent. She's called every single day since you got here, desperate to know what's going on.'

As if on cue, Sasha's phone rings again.

'Give it to me. I'll get rid of her, once and for all.'

She grinds beneath me and giggles. I'm not joking.

Snatching the phone, I hit the green button and an image of Chloe Sexton on a beachside balcony fills the screen. Bar a few more freckles decorating her high cheekbones, she hasn't changed a bit.

'Sasha? I can't see you. Turn the light on!' she demands from a thousand miles away.

'That won't be possible right now, I'm afraid.' My voice is as weighted as my dick.

'Oh my frickin god, is that you, Ryan-Runaway-Cooper?' It's practically a squeal.

My eyes roll skywards. That's one name I need to lose with immediate effect.

'Are you in my sister's bed?' Her hand flies to her mouth but not before she flashes a humongous grin.

'Technically, she's in mine. Though I suppose they're all hers really. Unless I can convince her to marry me at least.' I kiss Sasha's lips, which are parted in a delicious O. She thinks she's in shock now, she has no idea.

'Oh my frickin god,' Chloe repeats, squealing again. 'Well, I was ringing for an update. Clearly I got one.'

'Can you look for updates past nine a.m. going forward? Because Sasha's going to be otherwise engaged every night and every morning from now on.'

'Confident, isn't he?' Sasha's amused voice cuts through the darkness.

'He always was. It was one of the things you used to love about him.' Chloe pulls a face. 'I don't know if I'm delighted or disgusted to know my big sister's been having filthy mind-blowing sex all night.'

'Oh, come on. I've had to listen to enough tales from you over the years. Besides, who said it was filthy? Or mind-blowing?' Sasha sticks her tongue out, her face just about visible through the glare of screen light.

My hips buck against her. I'll show her mind-blowing.

'Oh, please!' Chloe swats her hand in front of her face. 'You've been pining over each other since he left. I don't doubt it was explosive.'

'And as much as I'm sure she'd like to share all the gory details with you, I haven't quite finished with her just yet.' I drop the phone onto Sasha's chest, slide downwards ready to worship her in my favourite way.

'FYI, I'm not the only one who wants the gory details. You guys made front-page news this morning. That London mistletoe kiss caused a media frenzy. The only difference is, I would recognise my sister's head from behind, wherever she is in the continent. The world wants to know who Ryan Cooper's new woman is.'

'I'd shout it from the fucking rooftops, but we're kind of busy right now.' My tone rings with impatience.

'Call you later, sis.' Sasha hangs up and flings the phone across the room in a rebellious motion.

'Now, I'll show you mind-blowing.'

Her pelvis squirms as my tongue gets to work.

***

. . .

Sasha leaves before ten to check on Victoria and sort some castle business. Even though her absence from my immediate proximity kills me, I suppose she does have an entire estate to run.

I manage to bang out another song. It's far from perfect, but the bones are solid. Maybe, if I play my cards right, Sasha might help me improve on them later. She always did have an ear for a compelling lyric. Perhaps I'll even convince her to pick up her guitar again.

Just as I set my own down, my phone rings. It's Jayden. He's up early this morning.

'Jayden, what's up, man?'

'Well, if it isn't fucking Romeo himself. Tell me, the brunette you're pictured sucking the face off in London, is it Sasha Sexton, by any chance?'

A tut clicks from my tongue. There's nothing sacred in my life.

'And what if it is?'

'Please tell me you gave her a filthy final goodbye shag and that you're on the next flight home.'

There it is again. That word. Home.

The only place I truly feel at home is between Sasha's legs.

'You may be my brother and my agent, but my love life is none of your business.'

'Oh fucking hell, dude! Did you just drop the L bomb? Things are worse than I thought.' He fakes disgust but I know him well enough to detect his underlying surprise.

I sigh, desperate to talk about what happened. He's probably not the right person to listen, given his feelings on long-term relationships but there's no one else.

'There's just something about her, Jay. It's always been her.'

'It's probably just an infatuation that you need to get out

your system. Stay until Vegas, see how you feel after that. When you're back under the bright lights you'll see things clearly again.'

It's more than infatuation, I know it is. Wrapped in my Sasha-infused Irish bubble, I'd miraculously forgotten about Vegas. The thought of leaving her, even for a few days, causes my stomach to churn.

'I don't think so, Jay. I think I want to marry her.'

Actually, I don't think. I know.

'Holy fuck, dude. Have you been drinking moonshine? Because you are coming out with some seriously crazy shit right now. You barely know the woman. You haven't seen her in ten years.'

'I know enough.' I'm adamant. 'But don't worry, I'm not going to tell her that. She'd probably run a fucking a mile.'

'Yeah, right. You're the world's most eligible bachelor, for fuck's sake. Apart from me, of course, only I prefer to keep a lower profile.' He snorts.

'Hmmm. Is that what you were doing cruising round LA in my Ferrari? Keeping a low profile? How is it by the way? Still in one piece, I hope?'

'It's doing better than you, apparently...'

'Whatever. You'll be pleased to know I've got more material since we last spoke. A lot more.'

'Well thank fuck for that. At least this lovey dovey phase is proving beneficial in some way.'

'Oh, trust me, brother, it's not a phase. And it's super beneficial to those involved.' My dick twitches at the flashbacks dancing through my mind.

'Don't make me come over there and beat some sense into you.' He sighs. I can practically see him rolling his eyes.

'I think you should. Then you'll see it's the real deal.'

'The only place you're going to see me is Vegas. Send me

the material so I can see exactly how beneficial your new beau is.'

'Ok. Talk later. Don't bang my fucking car.'

'Of course I won't. Does banging *in* it count? Coz me and Cindy...'

I hang up before I have to listen to any more of his shit.

It's early afternoon before I emerge from my suite. Padding across the corridor, Archie informs me Sasha's not there before I knock.

Ambling down the wide staircase, I seek her out. My fingers literally itch to touch her. I knock the door to her office. It used to be her father's, once upon a time. We used to creep past it en route to the kitchen to raid the leftover desserts. A smile inches onto my face at the memory.

Pushing open the door, disappointment surges. She's not here, but I take a minute to examine its huge wood-panelled walls. My attention's drawn to the magnificent art work – the glorious landscape of Velvet Strand. An impulsive urge to visit presses at my chest. It's not only beautiful, but it holds some fabulous sun-soaked memories.

Memories I'd love to recreate.

I don't know how I'm going to make things work with Sasha, from a practical point of view. LA is where all the big dicks hang out. It's where I need to be to further my career. I'm not ready to retire just yet. Would she consider coming with me? She would have done, at one point. Megan could run the castle in our absence.

What about Victoria? Where does she plan on going to college? Maybe she'd like the States?

Jesus, I'm getting ahead of myself again.

Slipping out of the office, I make my way towards the restaurant. At four p.m., the lunch rush is over and the dinner reservations have yet to begin. Immaculate white napkins line the tables, expertly folded into crisp, starched triangles. The silverware gleams under the chandelier as I pass through to the kitchen.

Peeping through the circular window, I'm slapped by a sense of déjà vu. Sasha's perched on the kitchen counter again. Conor hovers in front of her with his back to me. Several other chefs work at various stations, paying no attention to their boss's presence, so I can only assume her visits and the comfortable way she sits with Conor is a fairly regular occurrence.

Her hand lingers on his shoulder. I can't hear what she's saying but her cheeks colour at something he says, her smile wide enough to display perfect ivory teeth. Red-hot jealousy rips through me like an out-of-control bush fire.

I march halfway across the kitchen just in time to hear Conor say, 'I care about you, that's all.'

So do I, dickhead.

Sasha's head whips up to look in my direction, like she instinctively knows I'm there.

'Ryan.' She shoots Conor a glance as if to warn him to hold his tongue.

I'd like to give him a warning of my own. Like stay the fuck away from my woman.

Instead, I force my lips to smile graciously at him. I won, after all. It was my bed she woke up in. And it's my bed she'll fall into tonight. I won't have it any other way.

'More menu tasting?' Conor steps back as I reach Sasha and plant a kiss on her mouth.

'No, actually Conor's cousin is on his way in. Remember, the band for the ball?'

'Of course.' It had totally slipped my mind, but I'm glad I'm here to meet them, music being my only other interest bar the woman sitting in front of me.

A flashback of her legs spread on the dining table springs

to mind and from the way she bites her lower lip, I gather I'm not the only one.

'So what are your plans?' Conor eyes me with obvious trepidation.

'For the ball?' I cross my hands over my chest defensively, positive that's not what he's referring to.

'For the future.' He glares.

Sasha hops down from the counter and inserts herself between us, raising her hands to calm us down. 'Conor, please.'

'That's the beauty of life, isn't it?' I meet his stare with one of my own. 'None of us know what the future will bring. The only thing I'm certain of right now, is that this woman' – my hands slip round her waist, tugging her back to lean on my chest – 'is going to be the epicentre of mine.'

Conor scoffs. 'Just try not to break her heart. Again.'

He turns his back just as Megan waltzes in. Her eyes flick from Sasha, to Conor, to me, and back to Sasha. If she senses the tension, she doesn't comment.

'Your cousin and his band have set up in the ballroom. They're doing a soundcheck whenever you're ready.'

'Great.' Sasha claps her hands together.

'And the tickets sold out in two minutes once word got out that lover-boy here is the entertainment.'

'That's absolutely fantastic.' Sasha's tone is infused with genuine joy. I didn't realise the ball meant so much to her.

'I emailed Harry everything. Obviously it won't clear the loan, but combined with the new prices and the fact we're booked solid for the next two years, even he's finally optimistic about the future of the castle.'

Sasha shoots Megan a look as if to tell her to shut her mouth. Megan glances in my direction, then back to Sasha, visibly wincing.

I'm missing something here.

Before I can ask any questions, Conor wipes his hands on his chef whites and whips his top over his head revealing his torso.

For fuck's sake. Could he be any more obvious?

Megan hands him a shirt I didn't notice she was holding and takes his whites from him. 'The ballroom. Let's go. Your cousin awaits.'

I shoot a meaningful look at the pantry, which causes the blush to creep into Sasha's cheeks once again. Her lower lip catches between her teeth and heat suffuses her bright eyes.

'We'll be right behind you,' I tell them, nudging Sasha in the opposite direction as my dick turns to stone in my trousers.

CHAPTER NINETEEN

SASHA

Not for the first time in my life, I find myself in the pantry with Ryan's hand underneath my skirt.

With the hand that's not currently inching up my inner thigh, he flicks the switch inside the door and harsh spotlights illuminate every corner of the room.

'What are you doing?' My breath rasps in my throat.

'I want to watch while I make you come.' His fingers inch higher. 'Stockings? Are you trying to fucking kill me, woman?' Skimming over the lace tops, he groans, drops to his knees and hitches my skirt up around my waist.

He won't have to wait long. The way his eyes focus intently on mine is enough to get me off alone.

Conor and Megan might be gone but there are plenty of kitchen staff on the other side of this door ready to deal with room service requests, the bar menu and afternoon teas, yet I can't bring myself to care. Carnal lust is blinding.

Ryan's wandering hands search inside the lace of my thong.

'You're wet.' He nudges my legs apart, then his hot breath brushes the most sensitive parts of me while his fingers simultaneously deliver maddeningly delicious strokes.

'You're surprised?'

'I'm in awe of you, woman. You literally have me on my knees.' His tongue skirts over the lace hold-up, darting higher.

'Ryan, if you do that, I won't be able to help myself.' Just seeing him there, on his knees for me – watching him relishing the effect he has on me – is the hottest thing I've ever witnessed.

His smirking lips crush against my sex and my legs tremble. It's an effort to support myself. Strong hands grip my backside, taking the weight from me, squeezing my cheeks as he buries his tongue inside me. Lust rips through me and within seconds, a trillion stars shoot and cascade behind my eyelids.

How have I gone without this for ten years?

Because he's the only man who has the power to do this to you and he hasn't been here.

'That's my girl.' Ryan plants a final kiss below before repositioning the lace.

'Oh no you don't.' My gaze turns to the bulge pressing in his pants as he springs to his feet.

'I can wait,' he says, but the story in his trousers tells me otherwise.

I yank open his jeans and free him. It's my turn to drop to my knees.

'Sasha, you don't have to,' he says, even as hot hunger scorches his pupils.

'I want to.' Licking his tip, I can taste his slickness already. 'Mmm.'

Half the world would kill to be in my position right now.

The thought sparks a possessive streak I didn't know I owned.

Taking him into my mouth, I work him teasingly at first, before switching to low and slow. As his quads tense and jerk, I cup his balls, taking as much of him as my mouth will physically permit. His grip on my shoulder tightens as he shudders to an inevitable climax.

Pulling me to my feet, his index finger lifts my chin, turning my face to meet his. 'Fucking mind-blowing, Sash.' He presses a kiss to my nose as I button up his trousers. No one else is getting a look inside these. Not if I have anything to do with it.

'Do we have to go to the ballroom?' His low husky voice is fuelled with the promise of so much more.

'We do. For a few minutes at least.' Smoothing down my skirt, I try to reassume the respectable role of castle owner and adoptive mother, while the earth beneath my feet still shakes from my own superlative orgasm.

'Then what?' His lips lunge for the sensitive spot on my neck.

'Whatever you like…'

'Seriously? Anything at all?'

I shrug. Hung for a sheep as a lamb. The last twenty-four hours prove I can't say no to this man if my life depended on it. I'm hooked on his touch, his proximity and his every breath, and with no idea how long he's going to hang around for, greedily, I want as much as I can get.

A wolfish grin rips across his face. 'Well, what are we waiting for? Let's get this meeting done so we can crack on with the rest of our evening.'

His hand finds mine and yanks me out of the pantry.

Three of the sous chefs raise eyebrows as we tumble out, and Tilly almost drops the plates she's carrying.

Some of the guests stare as we walk hand in hand through

my family's estate. The photo from the Winter Wonderland is all over the news. The cat is well and truly out of the bag. There's no point being coy now.

Conor even took it better than I thought, though there was no mistaking the flicker of hurt in his eyes. He's probably grateful we never got involved, because no one in this world could miss the way Ryan makes me glow.

His sheer presence eclipses everything and everyone else.

Breathing in the fresh pine of the Christmas trees lining the corridor, an intense surge of gratitude envelops me. Not only is the love of my life back in my life, and promising to stay that way, but his arrival has dissipated my worries for the castle. Chloe's coming for Christmas. Victoria is healthy, happy and almost ready to spread her wings.

I send a silent thanks up to the sky. A tiny sliver of me dares to believe my parents are looking out for us from somewhere up there. It's the one idea that's offered me a modicum of comfort on my darkest days. But now Ryan's here, I'm getting my comfort from other sources.

Life is good.

Really good.

As long as I don't focus on the logistics of him living an entirely different life to me, in a far-flung country. He practically begged for another chance. He won't leave me again. He won't.

***

Ryan is ridiculously good with the band; he's kind and interested, and offers Matt some sound advice and encouraging praise. Even Conor looks grateful.

The guys shake hands and arrange to meet to practise

with Ryan the week before the ball. This gig for them, as small as it is compared to the likes of Vegas and New York gigs, will give Matt's band the biggest kickstart they could ever have hoped for. It will inevitably end up all over the news and social media. They'll get more exposure this way than if they played in the O2, Dublin's most popular venue.

Ryan perches against one of the ballroom tables, its white starched cloth hidden beneath his insanely toned backside. He gazes on, waiting for me as Megan goes through the logistics of the ball. I'm only half concentrating, acutely aware of his eyes on my body. He's not even attempting to be subtle about it.

From my periphery, I notice Conor approaching the table. He extends a hand to Ryan, who pauses for a split second before taking it. Conor, thankfully, isn't one to hold a grudge and even he can't deny how much Ryan's presence has helped everyone, even his own family.

'Thanks, man. I appreciate what you're doing for Matt.'

Ryan nods, his eyes still lingering on me, searing straight through my shirt.

'We all had to start somewhere. He seems like a good kid.' From the way he talks, you'd swear he was forty-eight, not twenty-eight, but I guess he has more life experience than most.

'He is. And she's a good girl, too.' Conor nods at me. Megan even pauses from running through the stage production suggestions in order to eavesdrop.

'She's all woman,' Ryan says. 'And not just a good one, she's the best.'

'I meant what I said earlier. Don't break her heart. She barely survived the first time. What with her parents, and then the baby.'

Ryan's head snaps up as mine instinctively twists in his direction.

'It was fucking cruel she had to endure that alone,' Conor continues his warning, oblivious that he's spilled the only secret I deliberately kept from Ryan.

A thunderous look consumes his face as he yanks his hand back from Conor's grip, folding his arms across his chest.

Conor, used to Ryan's stand-offish behaviour towards him, is none the wiser.

Megan's nostrils flare as she glances from Ryan to me. In a flash he's by my side, the palm of his hand pressing against the small of my back.

'Upstairs, please.'

It's the words I've been longing for him to say since we left the pantry, just not under these circumstances.

CHAPTER TWENTY

RYAN

My head's reeling from Conor's revelation. Was it my baby?

Or was it someone after me?

That night, on the couch... the night I left.

It's a possibility.

One I never even considered.

We'd fooled around so many times before but it was the first time she let me take her properly. It was the single most beautiful experience of my life. The thought that it might have caused her so much subsequent sadness sickens me.

Guiding Sasha upstairs, I steer her towards the penthouse rather than her own family quarters. I need answers and I won't get them if Victoria happens to be vegging out watching *I'm A Celebrity, Get Me Out of Here* on full blast like only a teenager can.

Nodding at the security guards, I close the door firmly behind us.

The colour's drained entirely from Sasha's already porcelain complexion. She looks positively ghostly.

Pinning her against the wall, my hands resting either side of her head, I search her eyes with mine. 'Is it true?'

She swallows hard. 'Yes.'

'Was it mine?' A growl hisses from my lips.

'Of course it was yours.' She tears her watery gaze away, staring at the floor.

Shock knocks the breath from my chest.

She was carrying my baby. Our baby. And she had to deal with that loss on her own, on top of everything else.

Shame surges through my veins, rapidly chased by a hot ugly anger. My fists bang the wall above her head. 'Why didn't you tell me?'

'You weren't here.' Her words are a definitively damning kick in the balls. I can't even argue with her. She's right. Nausea surges within.

'Why didn't you tell me when we...' I'm at a loss to describe our current situation.

'What difference does it make? What's done is done. Nothing will bring him back. I didn't want to put that hurt on you. I never wanted you to feel a fraction of the loss I felt. Time passes, but it doesn't lessen. Not really. I've just learned how to live with it.'

Her confession kills me, almost as much as her compassion for my feelings. It literally doubles me over. My head buries into her bust. To think she went through this alone. I'm so fucking angry.

'You could tell Conor, but you couldn't tell me?' I hate the hurt in my tone. Hate the bitterness.

'It was a long time ago. Conor and I... he was here. And interested. I needed him to understand why I couldn't just jump into something. Then, in the meantime, we became friends...'

Rage courses furiously through my hammering heart.

It's not Sasha I'm angry with.

It's not even Conor.

It's me.

I should have been there. For as long as I live, I'll never forgive myself. How Sasha grew into the amazing woman before me, I'll never know. She has the strength of lioness with the heart of Mother fucking Theresa.

Eventually, I manage to raise my face enough to meet her eye. 'Him?'

She nods, her eyes welling with tears. Wrenching her into my arms, I hold her head as she sobs into my chest. Tears flow freely from my own eyes, saturating her hair. Together, we mourn the baby I didn't know we'd made. Every milestone that might have been.

'How far on did you get?'

'Five months. I had no idea what was happening. One day I was in the restaurant and I just got this urge to push. Megan called the ambulance and he delivered an hour later.'

'Did he live at all?'

She shakes her head, her face awash with fresh horror at the memory.

Slumping to the floor, I pull her on to my knees, rocking her back and forth as the salty liquid streaks her otherwise flawless face.

'Shhh. Shhh. I'm here now. I'm so sorry, baby. I'll never leave you again. Everything will be ok. We can't bring him back, but I'd like to go and see where he's...'

She nods, rubbing her eyes, nestling closer to my chest.

'It might not be the right time to say this, Sasha, but I need to say it anyway. I'm going to marry you. We are going to have a houseful of babies. And you will never go through anything alone again in your life. I swear to you.'

She wraps her arms around my neck, pressing her lips zealously against mine. Sitting up, she straddles me on the floor, my back to the wall. I pull a condom out of my pocket as trembling fingers undo my zipper with a sense of urgency, but when she slides onto my dick, it's anything but urgent.

It's slow.

It's sensual.

It's expressive.

It's momentous.

It's actual love making.

My hands slide under her shirt, seizing her breasts as she works me at a deliciously languorous pace.

Her tongue traces my jawline. She rolls it from my mouth to my neck and back again before licking my lips in a seductive technique that should be illegal.

When she finally presses her hot mouth against mine again, I pull my head away. The need to look into her eyes is overwhelming.

'I love you.' The weight of my words hangs in the air between us as she hovers at the top of my dick.

'I love you too,' she says, sliding deliciously downwards again.

Her climactic moan sends my own release pulsing through me, straight to the depths of her.

Plunging my hands into her hair, I rest my head against her breasts once more.

'I never stopped, you know...' She must know. It doesn't take a genius to work out my first three albums were entirely based on her. On us.

'Neither did I.'

We remain wrapped in each other's arms for a long time.

Hours later, in the hot tub on the penthouse balcony, we share a bottle of red wine as the stars sparkle above us. Below, a million glinting Christmas lights twinkle from the castle grounds.

It's cold enough that my breath plumes like smoke before my face, but between the scorching hot-tub bubbles and the fact Sasha is utterly naked beside me, I'm hotter than hell.

Soft fingers entwine with mine beneath the wet blanket of water as she slips closer to rest her head against my shoulder.

'You know it feels cold enough to snow.' Sasha gazes up before talking a sip from her glass.

'I don't know. It feels pretty hot to me.'

She smirks. 'I hope you use better lines than that in your songs.'

'Of course I do. Do you remember the line in "The Mark You Made"?'

'What's "The Mark You Made"?' She's still stargazing. If it were anyone else, I'd bet a million dollars they were teasing me right now, but her face is perfectly straight and given our history, I'm pretty skilled at reading her.

'You have to be joking?'

'About what?' She finally tears her eyes from the sky to look at me.

'"The Mark You Made". The song I wrote. The title of my first album.

'Oh. I can't say I know it.' She shrugs, and offers a half-apologetic smile.

I can practically feel my jaw hit the floor of the tub. 'You what?'

'I don't know it.' She looks down. 'I couldn't... I never listened.'

'Holy fuck. At the risk of sounding like a totally entitled twat of a rockstar, how the fuck did you miss it? The album went platinum. The song was used on a multi-billion dollar Hollywood movie soundtrack.'

'Yeah, actually I think I heard that somewhere. You must be super proud of yourself. You've done so well, Ryan.' Her fingers squeeze mine.

The woman has managed to do literally the impossible – escape my music for ten years solid. The enormity of what she's telling me hits me like a truck.

She didn't simply happen to escape it. She must have deliberately avoided it. Which reminds me, I still have something for her, and whether she needs it or not, it's only right. I'm sidetracked once again by the bigger bombshell she just dropped.

'Is that why we have to listen to that dull jazz on repeat all through the castle? For fear of hearing anything that might remind you of me? Did you seriously hate me that much?'

She gently shakes her head, her emerald eyes slant towards mine. 'It wasn't because I hated you.' She bites her lower lip. 'It was because I loved you. And the hurt was unbearable.'

Crushing her into my chest, I repeatedly kiss her head, her face, anywhere I can reach. 'Sweetheart, I am so fucking sorry. But if you'd have listened, you would have known. "The Mark You Made" is entirely about you. You should listen to it, then you'll never doubt me again.'

She takes a drink from her glass before placing it on the adjacent side table. Floating towards the middle of the hot tub to face me, she grabs both my hands, pulling me into the middle with her. 'Sing it to me.'

'What, now?' For some reason I'm oddly shy. I've sung this song a million times before, yet this is different. It's about her. And it bears my soul.

'No time like the present.' She winks.

'Hmm.' I'm stalling for time. 'The one person in this world who has actively avoided my music, now wants a front row seat. You know people normally pay a lot of money for tickets to my concerts. What do you think it's worth for private show of your own?'

Her palm pushes my chest. 'Cat got your tongue? Don't go getting all shy on me now, Ryan-Rockstar-Cooper.'

At least we've finally lost the runaway bit.

'I'm not shy, I just think you need to work for it.' My lips curl into a grin as my hands find her bum under the water, pulling her towards me.

'Is that right? If anyone has to work for anything round here, I think it's you.'

'I'll do you a deal. Come to Vegas with me in a couple of weeks and I'll sing that song just for you.' Gripping a thigh in each hand, my fingers blaze a trail upwards and her head rolls back as she sighs.

'No deal.'

I slide my hands back towards her knees and a disappointed sigh clouds the air between us.

'Please. I'd love you to come.' My eyes silently plead with her.

She rolls them straight back at me and shimmies herself onto my quads and wriggles suggestively. 'I'd love to come.'

From the lust-filled look in her dilating pupils, I gather she's no longer talking about Vegas, but I'm not ready to give up yet.

'Then make a deal with me. Come to Vegas, I'll sing for you, and the rest...' I purposefully glide my hands upwards again, this time allowing my fingers to find her sensitive spots.

'I want to come.' Her eyes glaze over as a gasp slips from those deliciously full lips. I pause what I'm doing, anticipating there's a "but" coming.

'But what about the castle? And the upcoming ball? What about Victoria?' She sighs again.

'She's almost eighteen.' I continue teasing her, driving her closer to the edge.

'Almost.'

My fingers slide into her, desperate to feel her release on me. 'Think about it.' My mouth silences hers, before she remembers her initial request.

I want her in Vegas with me. Not just because three nights without her feels like the worst kind of torture, but because I want to show the world my woman. And show my woman, she is my world.

CHAPTER TWENTY-ONE

SASHA

9th December

The press are still wild with speculation surrounding Ryan's mysterious brunette, though they haven't caught sight of either of us since. Primarily because we've been hiding out in places where our limbs can be permanently entangled.

I've slept in his bed every night since he brought me to London. I love being with him. But I'm happy being anonymous. I'd hate to live in the spotlight, scrutinised every time one of us is pictured without the other, or god forbid we dare to have a bad day and get caught without a smile.

I've seen enough tabloids to realise being rich and famous isn't all it's cracked up to be. I'm silently praying that Ryan feels the same. That he'll want to settle this side of the Atlantic eventually. He says he won't leave me, yet we both know he'll have to at some point. His life is there. Mine is here.

It's hard to see how it's going to work out between us. The penthouse is his until the week before Christmas. He committed to the ball on the 23rd. But what then? Will he leave? Have Christmas with his brother?

He hasn't mentioned it, and I can't bring myself to ask. The prospect of Christmas without Ryan is like the thought of a birthday party without cake. But at least he's back in my life again.

If we have to do long distance for a while, I'm ok with that. I've unintentionally waited ten years for the man. A couple more won't hurt, if that's the way it has to be, but long term, I don't see myself settling anywhere other than this castle. Any childish notions I'd had about moving to the States were exactly that.

Conor's revelation wasn't exactly ideal, but it's brought us closer. While the loss isn't any easier, the weight of it feels shared.

I think I might finally have learned how to trust him again.

All in all, things are better than I ever dreamed of. As long as I don't overthink the logistics.

Sitting in my office, I take a sip of the double espresso Megan brought in, along with the accounts to look over. Many of the bookings for next year have paid in advance due to the discount we offered online. The castle's bank account is out of the red for the first time in years.

Before I have too much time to congratulate myself, my mobile vibrates on the desk in front of me. It's Chloe. She's actually been abiding by Ryan's post nine a.m. request. If only he could have enforced that particular rule years ago.

I swipe to accept and an image of my sun-kissed sister fills the screen. She sits poolside, sipping from a coffee cup. Against her tan, her eyes appear so blue they're blinding.

'Well?' She sniggers, raising her eyebrows.

'Good morning, to you, too.' I stick out my tongue.

'Oh, put it away, I can practically see Ryan's pubes stuck to it.' She rolls her eyes and pretends to vomit.

'I thought you'd be delighted I finally have something to overshare. God knows, I've listened to enough from you.'

'That's different! You don't know any of the guys I've had sex with. Ryan, on the other hand...' Her hand flies over her eyes as if he actually stands before her.

'Don't pretend you're horrified. The man is a goddamn sex symbol.'

'That he may be, but an image of him drilling into my sister is something I'd rather not have imprinted on my brain. There is such a thing as too much visual. It's a bit like reading *Fifty Shades* versus watching the movie. Nobody in the world needed the visual of Anastasia's unwaxed, virgin v—'

I hold my hand up in protest. 'Okay, okay, I get it! Just for the record, I might have been a born-again virgin for the last ten years but my personal hygiene, waxing down there, has always been a priority.'

'That's enough.' Chloe squeezes her eyes shut. 'I know originally I wanted details, but frankly, I've heard enough. All I need to know is that you're happy.'

In case the smile that extends to each earlobe isn't enough, I nod to confirm it.

'And he's treating you well?' she asks. And there was me thinking I was the oldest sister.

'Like a queen.' My mind wanders to the way he worships my body. The way if I even move a millimetre in the night, he moves with me. If spooning were a sport the man would be a world champion, hands down.

He watches over me with a protective tenderness. His hands are permanently on me. On my thigh. Round my waist. Entwined with mine. He's constantly touching me. Glancing down, my body feels bare without him.

'So, how's it going to work?' Chloe flicks her chestnut hair from her shoulders.

My gaze returns to the screen. 'How's what going to work?'

'Well, I assume he's staying for Christmas, but what happens after that?'

My stomach lurches. She assumes more than me.

'Well, I guess he'll come back when he can… He'll be on tour for weeks, maybe months at a time.'

A mad thought enters my head… surely he doesn't assume I'll go with him?

No. That's ridiculous. I have a business to run. A child to raise. A home. A life.

Yes, but it was empty without him.

'I guess at some point, we'll have to iron things out, but for now, we're just taking things one day at a time.'

Chloe huffs. 'I see.'

'What's that supposed to mean?'

'Just don't let him walk all over you this time…' The implied suggestion that she's not around to help pick up the pieces lingers in the air.

Just to say something positive I tell her he asked me to go to Vegas with him.

'Oh my god! You have to go, Sash! Vegas is like the coolest place on the planet. And you've wanted to go to the States for years!'

'Hello… you're forgetting I have a castle to run. And Victoria to mind. I know she's nearly eighteen, but she's way more innocent than you and I were at her age. I worry about her, you know…'

'Pah! Speak for yourself. I was a virgin until nineteen years of age when James Doherty brought me out to Westport for the weekend to climb Croke Patrick. Needless to say, the mountain was not the only thing I climbed.'

'Chloe! Seriously! Don't make me tell you Ryan licked my...'

'Ahhh! Enough! Okay.' She visibly shudders and I snigger, delighted to get my own back for once.

'Payback's a bitch.' I wink at her.

'I can't disagree. Especially when I'm not getting any at the moment. Things have run unseasonably dry in the desert lately.' She shrugs.

'Maybe you'll pull a Christmas cracker when you come home, and it'll be so explosive, you'll end up staying here forever, and we'll all live happily ever after...' I sigh, blissfully.

A look of mock horror etches on to her neat, even features. 'Have you been reading those crappy romance novels again?'

'Sis, I'm a walking fucking romance novel at the minute. I should get a pen and start writing this shit down. It'll be worth millions.' My smile freezes on my face.

Fuck. Is that what Ryan's doing? Using us to alleviate his writer's block.

And if so, should I be horrified or flattered? I can't decide, but I guess it depends on the outcome of our relationship.

Old habits die hard. He promised he'd never leave me again. For frig's sake, the man swore blind he was going to marry me. Ok, so it wasn't an actual proposal, but he did lay his cards out in front of me. Perhaps I haven't fully learnt to trust him again yet after all.

Chloe mistakes my sudden silence for something else.

'I'm so sorry I'm not there to help. If I was, you might have some hope of going to Vegas. Signing off on the final contract of the year is taking longer than I hoped. Worst-case scenario I'll be back the twenty-second. There's no way I'm going to miss the ball.'

I offer her a distracted smile.

'And don't worry about Vic, she's fine. She might be a little naive for her age but that's what happens when you live in a castle and attend a private all-girls school. She's probably waiting for a handsome prince to ask for her hand in marriage before she goes on a date. Just be grateful she's not veering the other way. Then you'd really have something to worry about.'

She's right. I know she is. And even though I'd love to go to Vegas, it's simply not practical. If Ryan and I are serious, I'm sure there will be other opportunities.

Life is good. Scratch that. Life is fucking fantastic.

'Can't wait to see you,' I tell my sister, honestly.

'You too. I'm sorry I left it so long.' Her sombre expression turns to one of immediate excitement and she leans closer to the phone. 'I would say I don't want you to go to any trouble for my arrival, but you know it's not true! I'm expecting the full Irish welcome; the food, the drink, the Christmas lights! All the traditions that get utterly overlooked in this strange, empty city! Let's go all out. Maybe lover-boy will bring us all back to the Christmas markets? It's been years since we ice skated!' Her blue eyes positively shine at the prospect.

I stifle the laughter as it erupts from my mouth. 'Sure. I'll see what I can do. Either way, it's going to be the best Christmas ever.' Even if Ryan isn't here to share it with me. As an afterthought I find myself asking, 'Chloe, did you ever listen to Ryan's songs?'

'Duh. Who didn't? Other than you, I mean?' She rolls her eyes at me.

'What were they about?'

'Listen to them and you'll find out.' She dares, knowing exactly how hard and for how long, I've worked to avoid them.

'I told you before. The man's been pining for you since he left.'

'I asked him to sing one to me and that's when he said about Vegas. He wouldn't do it in the hot tub. Sorry, he wouldn't *sing* in the hot tub. He had no problem doing the other stuff.'

'Eww. And ahh. I see why you want to go to Vegas.' She squints at the phone.

'I'm intrigued, but what if I hate them? Or read them wrong? We're only just getting back on track. It seems like the past is the past, so maybe I should leave it there?

'You could always have a sneaky listen on YouTube. Or just google the lyrics? Then you'll be alone and if you hate them – which you won't – it won't matter.'

'It feels like cheating at this stage. I'd love to hear them from his mouth. Anything else seems like second rate. But equally, I'm terrified. "The Mark You Made" – with a title like that, it can't be good, right? But if it isn't, why would he want me to go to Vegas to watch him perform?'

'You'll love it, trust me. Damn. I'm getting an incoming call. It's the client I'm waiting for. I'm sorry, sis. I have to go. Chat later.'

I blow her a kiss as she ends the call, my belly buzzing with the warm fuzzies that the excitement of a giddy festive season with family, and a boyfriend, brings.

That fuzzy feeling rapidly evaporates as Megan enters the office again. Her expression dark with despair.

'What? What is it?' I rise from behind the desk quicker than a speeding bullet.

'It's the ballroom.'

Relief floods through me. My first thoughts were for Victoria. Then Ryan.

'What's up with the ballroom?' It's probably not big enough to hold all the people currently engaged in a bidding war for tickets to the Christmas ball.

'I found a new crack. Several actually.' Megan shuffles

from foot to foot, every bit of her aware of the devastating blow she's just landed on me.

'Not more dry rot?' It's barely a whisper.

This will finish us. Just when the future was looking bright, it's ripped away, yet again.

She nods. 'Looks like it. I'm so sorry, Sash. There's no way we can hold a ball there. We couldn't even hold a tea party for two. The insurance simply won't cover us. The whole thing is going to have to be knocked down and rebuilt. It's a health and safety nightmare.'

My legs give way beneath me and my bottom hits the cushioned chair.

I nod and she leaves, knowing I need a few minutes to process. Hell, it's going to take more than a few minutes.

So much for the warm and fuzzies. Merry fucking Christmas.

I'm still slumped over my desk when Ryan's head pops unexpectedly round the door. The smile freezes on his face the second he catches sight of me.

'Sash? What is it? What's wrong?' He's by my side in a one swift leap, kneeling on the floor next to me. His eyes gleam so darkly, they're practically black.

I can't find the words to tell him. To explain. The dry rot has been the bane of my life for the past three years, but even before that the castle was haemorrhaging cash. The truth of the matter is I just don't think I'm fit to run the place, and this is the final straw.

'We need to cancel the ball.' It's the truth, but it's the least of my concerns. My family home will more than likely have to be sold because no matter what I do, I can't seem to turn things around.

'Oh thank god! You scared the shit out of me. From the

expression on your face, I thought it was going to be way worse.'

'It is way worse. That's just it.' Silent tears streak my cheeks. I swipe them away with the back of my hand. I'm not a crier, not normally, but the situation is so desperate.

'What happened? You know you can talk to me about anything.' Ryan perches on the desk in front of me and takes both my hands in his. His stare penetrates my soul, pleading with me to open up. 'I wasn't here for you before, but I am now, Sash. Let me help you.'

I'm so ashamed. So embarrassed. I feel like such a failure. My parents ran this place like a well-oiled machine and I can't even manage to turn a profit. I've ruined everything.

'I take it you know what dry rot is?'

'Of course.' A puzzled expression furrows his features.

'The ballroom is apparently riddled with it. We've had this problem in other areas of the estate and barely survived the demolition and rebuild of them. And now, the cracks are beginning to appear again – literally.'

He swallows, confusion mists in his swirling eyes. 'Sasha, it's only bricks and mortar. We can fix it.'

I shake my head and the tears fall again. 'The estate's been struggling for years. I can't turn a profit. I don't know how my parents did it, they made it look effortless, but since I've been in charge I've fucked up everything. The accountant warned me I'd probably have to sell up, and that was before we found the latest cracks.'

Ryan pulls me upwards into his strong embrace. 'Sweetheart, we will fix this. Whatever it costs. Money is not an issue. Nor will it ever be again. There's no way I'm going to stand by and watch you sell this place. I've only just found my way back, and I'm kind of fond of it.' A small smile curls at his lips.

Ok, so the man probably has millions in the bank. It

didn't exactly come up in conversation. But even if he does, I won't take his charity.

I shake my head against his chest. 'This is my mess. I got this family into it and it's my responsibility to get us out.'

'Oh, so I'm not family, no?' His fingers tickle my waist, teasingly. 'Don't make me put a ring on that finger already.'

It's not the first time he's joked about it, but there's still no way I can let him sort out the financial wreck of my family estate.

'It might not be the best time. There's not much of a dowry.' I can't even bring myself to smile.

'Sasha, do not worry about the money. I've been meaning to give you something since I got here. It's actually why I was looking for you. Well, that and a burning, relentless urge to take you on your father's desk.' He glances up as if my dad's actually watching. 'Sorry, Mr Sexton, but I'm sure you've been here yourself with Mrs S.'

'Oh my god, you're gross.' It's one thing joking with Chloe and entirely another to think of my parents like that.

Ryan reaches into his back pocket and pulls out a white folded envelope. Pressing it into my palms, he urges me to open it.

Instinctively, I shake my head. I won't take his charity.

Though if it's charity, how did he know I needed it?

I pause, my fingers hesitating over the seal.

'Go on.' He nods in encouragement.

I open the envelope gently, sliding out the contents with reluctant caution.

My eyes nearly burst out of my head at the insane figure written on a cheque addressed to me. Six million dollars. What the fuck?

I immediately press it back against his chest and jerk away from him. I might be surrounded by a crumbling mess of an estate, but I do have some pride.

'I can't, Ryan. I just can't. But thank you for the offer. I'll work something out.'

'What are you thanking me for? It's your money. You earnt it fair and square.' He pushes it back at me. 'Look at the signature on the bottom of the cheque. It's not my name.'

The guy probably put it under a different name, sure he could have a hundred businesses for all I know. We haven't spoken too much about his life over in the States because he's slipped so effortlessly back into this one.

Squinting cautiously through my puffy slits, I glance down at the cheque.

'Diamond Records?'

'It's the record label that signed me. I know you haven't listened to the albums, but there are some tracks that I can't take credit for.' He glances at the floor, as if he's ashamed.

'Seriously? You used the songs we wrote together?'

'Some of the lyrics. The music producers changed up the melodies and tempo, but yes, I used some of them. I had your name put on the copyright alongside my own. I was so sure you'd come and find me when you realised, that you'd want your share. Somehow, far away, amongst all the LA drama queens, I forgot you've got way too much class for that. Then out of stubbornness, and hurt from your rejection, the fact you ignored my note and never once tried to contact me, I held back from delivering it earlier. I was actually mad with you. I thought you'd heard about my dad and tarred me with the same brush. You were always so far out of my league, a princess living in an actual castle. I never felt good enough for you.'

Wrapping my arms around his neck, I rest my forehead against his. Our noses tip to tip.

'I needed you.'

'I know. I didn't realise what you were going through.

That you might need the cash either. I'm so fucking sorry, Sash.'

It's too much to process.

He used the lyrics we wrote together.

Some of my most private and intimate words are out in the world – and have been for years. I need to listen to the albums. Jesus, if I hadn't been so pig-headed, no, heartbroken, I might have realised earlier.

Wait.

'You left me a note?' I never found one. The first place I went in the aftermath of Chloe's devastating arrival that night, was straight back to Ryan's cabin in search of his strong arms. Where I needed him to be. There was definitely no note.

'I did try and tell you that when I got here, but you were having none of it.'

His eyebrows deepen in a pensive expression.

He's telling the truth. I feel it with every bit of my body.

Where did it go?

It might finally be time to go back to the cabin.

CHAPTER TWENTY-TWO

RYAN

'Come on.' Sasha stuffs the cheque in her top drawer, grabs a bunch of keys and pulls me towards the door with a sense of urgency.

I'm still not fully sure if she's mad at me for using her lyrics, or relieved she has the means to take care of her family estate and pretty much anything else her heart desires.

Her family were always super affluent. I had no idea she was struggling financially. A fresh wave of shame washes over me.

I should have reached out.

I could have helped her.

I could have loved her.

What a waste of ten years.

She tugs my hand, guiding us through the castle, past the huge Christmas tree in the dome-shaped atrium and out into the bitter December day. A flurry of tiny fresh snowflakes drift across our faces and frost the ferns and bushes lining the walkway towards the far end of the estate.

'Where are we going?' Even in heels and on icy ground, she moves past the life-sized reindeer statues at a serious pace.

'To the cabin.'

'Why?'

I have no idea who lives in it now. The lights were off the few times I've passed by it.

The snow falls thick and fast as an easterly wind howls around us. Neither of us have a jacket. It's a relief when we reach the front door.

A weird sense of déjà vu envelops me. Though it shouldn't be weird, because I've been here before. Many times. It just feels like it was in another life.

The boy who lived here was young and foolish with big dreams. Dreams that thankfully became a reality. Most of them anyway. Some of them still need work, namely, keeping hold of the woman next to me.

Sasha's fingers fumble with the key, trembling with the cold. Prising them from her, I insert the key into the lock and twist it. As the door swings open, a pungent stench of dust and staleness assaults my nostrils.

Curiosity burns my tongue, but I hold it, waiting until Sash is ready to explain what we're doing here and why the place is like a fucking mausoleum.

As we step through the dust and grime, I note nothing's changed. I lived here for two years of my life and I could almost swear it is exactly how it was then. As if it's been completely untouched.

Oh fuck.

That's exactly it. It literally hasn't been touched.

The filthy-looking Christmas tree glaring from the corner of the lounge confirms it.

'Sasha, what the actual fuck?' So much for holding my tongue.

'Where did you leave the note?' She scans the room apprehensively, stepping gingerly towards the kitchen area. Her tone isn't accusatory; I'm pretty sure she believes me. Nevertheless, a grimace remains pressed upon her lips. As if she's in physical pain, or it's taking everything she's got to hold it together.

I cross the large open-plan space, glancing at the couch as I pass. Memories flood back with the force of a rising riptide, so I can only imagine how Sasha feels. That night was always going to be memorable for both of us. It should have been the best night of our lives, yet it turned into the worst, for both of us.

So much pain.

So much sadness.

I point at the dust-covered kettle. 'I left it propped here.'

'Well it wasn't here when I came back.' Her voice shakes with emotion, but not anger.

I drop to the floor, checking the surrounding areas, then behind the kettle, even pulling the unit from the wall to check it didn't slip behind it.

'You're certain no one was in here?' I don't mention that that fact alone has shocked me to the core.

'No one. It was bad enough sorting through Mam and Dad's stuff. I couldn't sort through yours as well. You think I'm a total weirdo...' Her eyes fill with unshed tears.

'No, I'm just a little shocked. You could have rented this place to another family all this time...'

'I couldn't deal with it. And no, before you think I'm crazy, it's not because you turned into a super massive sex symbol and I wanted to preserve the fact you'd ever been here. It was more like I wanted to freeze the memory of before, when everything was perfect. When the whole world was ahead of us and my parents were the responsible adults. That, and truthfully, I just couldn't deal with coming in here again. This is the first time I've stepped foot in here in years. Harry, my accountant, wanted me to sell it, along with the other cabins, but they were my mother's idea and, in case you haven't noticed, I've tried to keep things pretty much the same as she did...'

'Until the dry rot...'

She nods glumly. 'It forced a slight modicum of modernisation.'

'You know you could probably sue someone for that. The bricks they used mustn't have been certified.'

Sasha rolls her eyes. 'Come on, Ryan, this isn't the States. Those bricks are as old as the hills. Even if I could find someone alive to hold responsible, it would cost me more to sue than I'd ever get back. Not to mention I could die of old age before it even got to court in this country.'

She has a point.

'So what now?' I lean on the dusty kitchen counter top, drinking in the woman before me like I did so many times as a boy.

'I guess I'll have to wonder...unless you want to tell me what it said?' She's talking about the note, but I meant with the castle.

'When you come to Vegas and hear me sing, everything will become crystal clear, I promise. Don't cheat beforehand. You've come this far without listening, just wait another few days. I'll make it worth your while, I promise you.'

'Ryan, I told you, I can't. Especially not now. Even if I didn't have to look out for Victoria, I'm going to have to call the architect out and source a construction company asap.'

'I'll help you with everything. You're not on your own anymore. You don't have to personally oversee everything. We'll arrange everything before we go and Megan can oversee it. I'll leave Pierce here too, he's great at managing this type of stuff.' Pulling her knuckles to my lips, I kiss each of her fingers persuasively.

She groans. 'I can't. One day I'll make it to the States. But not this time.'

'Wait... one day? You never made it to the States? Not even for a holiday?' I kind of assumed she would have gone at some point. Hell, it was her idea, initially. We've spent so much time together this past week, but I've barely scratched the surface of the last ten years. I want to know everything.

'I never got round to it with everything else that happened... Been kind of busy...' Her voice trails off, loaded with longing.

She *is* going to Vegas with me next week, come hell or high water. She's missed out on so much already, given up her twenties for so much responsibility she didn't ask for.

And in the meantime, I'm going to help sort out everything to do with this estate, starting with this cabin.

'You know, you don't have to keep everything the way it was. Especially not now. You're stuck with me whether you like it or not. You've done an amazing job with the castle and your sister, despite all the shit that's been thrown your way. Your parents would be so proud, but you know, I think it's time we changed the place from a shrine to those who have passed, to a home for those who are yet to arrive in our future.'

Her head snaps up as my hand trails across her belly.

I need her to have my babies. The sooner the better. Maybe that's utterly selfish. She's spent the last ten years raising her sister. Now Victoria's almost an adult, she might prefer some time to herself.

But if that's the case, why is she gazing up at me with a lust-filled look. Does she want what we once almost had, as much as I do?

CHAPTER TWENTY-THREE

SASHA

13th December

As good as his word, Ryan waved a magic wand – his figurative one – although he's been using the one in his pants a good bit too.

He hired the country's hottest architect, the same woman all the Irish home building TV shows employ, and miraculously, I even have the money to pay her.

The ball will go ahead. We've hired a luxury marquee. It's almost the same size as the castle, complete with all the fairy tale trimmings. The number of tickets available has now quadrupled, though the second they went on the castle website they sold out in under two minutes – again.

Taking money for Ryan's work doesn't exactly sit easily with me, but seeing my name in black and white on the paperwork makes it easier to swallow. Even though I've yet to hear how they've been polished and delivered, they are technically and legally co-written.

The amount is enough to clear the castle debts and

provide a giant cushion. For the first time in years, I'm confident my family's home will be mine to pass on to the next generation. Which from the way Ryan's taking, might not be in the too distant future...

The landline rings on my desk in front of me. It can only be reception.

'Hi.' I balance the receiver between my shoulder and ear, resting it in the crook of my neck, sifting through the pile of paperwork in front of me.

'Hi, Sasha, sorry to bother you.' It's Jess, one of the receptionists.

'You're fine, Jess, go on. What's up?' My fingers trace the lines of my eyebrows as I listen. I had one of the girls in the spa tint and shape them yesterday.

'There's a phone call for you. A woman called Miriam wants to talk to you. She said she's from *Tatler*. I tried to palm her off on Megan, but she's having none of it.'

My lips lift in a wry smile.

When Miriam departed after her two-night stay she was less than impressed, according to Megan, Louise and the barely half a page mediocre mention in that week's edition of *Tatler*.

'She said she was so impressed with her recent stay she wanted to purchase tickets for the Christmas ball, and of course she'd cover it in this year's final edition of *Tatler*.

'Hmmm.' I bet. It wouldn't take a genius to work out which male rockstar she's hoping to bump into.

'Also, representatives from *Hello*, *The Irish Independent* and *Women's Weekly Magazine* have all expressed an interest in coverage of the ball too. I have emails from a dozen others looking for tickets in return for publicity. Just something to bear in mind if you do speak to Miriam.'

'I see. Thank you, Jess.'

'Will I put her through?'

'No. Tell her I'll call her back.' The woman made me wait months before returning my call with her demands. The least I can do is make her wait a few hours while I come up with a few of my own.

Front-page mention perhaps? With a double-page spread. I snigger at the thought. For the first time in years, publicity isn't going to be a problem.

Everything is finally coming together. The relief is momentous. And it's all thanks to Ryan.

'Is there anything else?' I take the phone in my hand, stretching my neck to the side.

'Well, there are the relentless phone calls from journalists brazen enough to ask if Ryan has a woman here. If anyone knows who the brunette he was pictured in London with is...' Though her voice trails off, a smile is evident in her tone.

I know I can't hide from the media forever. If Ryan and I have any chance of making it as a couple, I'll have to embrace being in the spotlight at some point, but my plan is to stay anonymous for as long as possible.

The authorities never caught the driver who recklessly ran my parents from the road. It used to torment me day and night that he or she was still out there walking around, living life when my parents no longer have the chance to.

Even though the end result is the same, it kills me that they didn't get justice. I know it's not going to bring them back. I'd like answers, and I'd like the culprit behind bars, even though the harshest punishment a person could endure is the knowledge of the destruction he or she caused.

But the prospect of the whole tragic event being dragged through the media is not one I relish. Victoria wasn't old enough to read the papers then, but she is now. I don't want the kind of attention it might bring her, especially in her final year of school. She has her exams to focus on.

Her dream is to study medicine. I don't doubt her drive to

save people stems from her own loss. She'd make an excellent doctor. Her academic ability is out of this world; I only hope she wants to pursue it for the right reasons.

'Say nothing. We don't disclose private information about our guests.'

Especially not when they're sleeping with me.

'Absolutely. I'd never dream of repeating anything that goes on inside this castle.' Jess's reassurance is unwavering, both in her words and her delivery. 'I just want you to be aware the sharks are circling.'

'Thanks. I appreciate it.' For the hundredth time I thank my lucky stars for my loyal staff.

The receiver clicks as it slots back into the handset. Stretching my hands over my head, I yawn. Even though the late nights are sublimely satisfying, I'm officially wrecked. The clock overhead shows it's five-forty-five; an acceptable time to call it a day.

Especially because Ryan is leaving for Vegas tonight on a midnight flight and I'm determined to make sure he leaves with an explosively sexy bang, literally.

Vegas. I've mulled it over in my head so many times but I just can't leave Victoria, or the castle. Not for four nights anyway. It's too much. She's a minor after all. And this time of year her night terrors are always worse.

And though my heart aches at the thought of even a few days without Ryan, if we have any hope of sustaining a lasting relationship, I need to get used to the long distance. And the fact that there are literally millions of women lusting after my boyfriend at any given time of the day. I have to trust him.

When he's here, it's easy to forget the outside world. But that's the real world. In here, we're cocooned in an unrealistic love-filled bubble.

The niggling anxiety that once he leaves, he may never

return (again), haunts me, despite my best efforts to force it away.

A shivery anxious sensation ripples across my spine, pricking the tiny fine hairs on my neck.

No, Sasha. Stop it.

He came back.

Ten years later.

If he did it again, I'd be thirty-eight next time.

Stop it, Sasha. He's coming back. He promised he'd always come back.

I hate the irrational neediness that creeps in. The fear of losing him again. It's as raw as it was the first time.

Stop it!

Pushing my chair back from behind my desk, I slip out of the office and along the corridor, towards the sanctuary of Ryan and the penthouse, practically sprinting up the stairs to be with him after the afternoon apart.

He wanted to practise before he left. Ten years ago he could have comfortably performed a concert with his eyes closed. I'm pretty sure he could do it in his sleep now.

The past few evenings he's been strumming snippets of his recent compositions while I hum along, dreaming up words and phrases that suit the melody as he scribbles and nods encouragingly.

So when I open the door to the penthouse, I'm not surprised to see he's resting on the edge of the couch in front of a blazing fire with the guitar resting on his bare, toned chest. Every inch of him oozes a blistering masculinity.

Whatever *GQ* have on the front cover, nothing compares to the image before me. It's next-level sexy, not only stealing my heart, but my ability to focus on anything else.

I could stand and silently stare at him forever, drinking him in for the rest of my life without ever feeling full, but I don't get the chance.

Hooded eyes lift, lasciviously roaming over me. Devastatingly sexy pupils pin me in an impenetrable stare. Without uttering a word, he nods to the spot on the couch next to him, his thick, strong fingers continuing to strum a familiar hypnotising tune.

When his mouth parts, his low velvety voice penetrates the room, sucking the air from my lungs. Words paralyse me to a position that I'd happily adopt for the rest of my life if it meant I got to enjoy this show.

Once again, I'm hit with the devastation that I can't leave with him tonight. The thought of the electric atmosphere, the deep unwavering bass that blasts from a live concert. And the man before me, centre stage, commanding the arena before him.

One day, I'll get to see him in action.

A frown inches onto his brows. I'm still standing gawping, worse than any desperate groupie. He gestures to the couch again, finishing the final few bars before lowering his guitar, leaning over it to press his hot, luscious lips against mine.

'Am I completely mistaken, or is that the same guitar you've had like forever?'

He nods. 'I should probably invest in a new one, but it has sentimental value.'

I know what he's alluding to. All the times we spent strumming it together, composing with the innocence of youth, big plans and even bigger dreams.

A resounding sigh permeates the air. It could have come from either of us. All I know is it simultaneously screams relief and a longing for more.

When eventually he pulls back from another dizzying kiss, I'm left breathless.

'Hello to you too.'

'I need you, before you leave me again.' The words jump bluntly from my subconscious.

'I told you, Sasha, I'll never leave you.' Earnest eyes bore into mine, radiating a deep unquestionable love. How is it possible we've fallen so far, and fast, in love again?

I prise the guitar from where it rests between his thick fingers. He passes it over willingly, but when I try and place it on the table he stops me, gently pushing it back towards me.

'Play for me.' He pouts with lips that are hard to say no to.

Hard, but not impossible.

I shake my head, the guitar oddly hot in my hands. 'I told you. I don't play anymore.'

'You didn't do a lot of things while I was gone, apparently.' He arches an eyebrow, meaningfully.

'I'll have you know I went on five dates without you.' I huff, cradling the guitar in my lap because he's blocking me from putting it down on the table and I don't know what else to do with it.

'Is that right?' Ryan stands, then slips in behind me on the couch, placing a large thigh either side of mine, his bare chest pressing against my back, his chin resting on my shoulder.

'So who were these five lucky guys? And should I be worried?' From his playful tone, it's obvious he's not overly concerned.

'It was five dates with the one guy. A son of Aunty Mags' friend.'

The growl that vibrates in his throat sends a ripple of pleasure through me. I never had myself down as one of those women who go for the whole alpha thing, but when he growls like one, it makes my panties melt.

Heated breath grazes my neck as he presses tiny sweeping kisses across the sensitive skin.

'Did he kiss you like this?' It's barely more than a whisper.

One hand slips under my shirt, sliding upwards across my stomach towards the silk of my bra, which he yanks low enough for my breast to spill out over the top.

'Did he touch you like this?' Fingers circle my nipple, gently teasing. His growing arousal presses into my lower spine as he nudges himself against me.

Giddy with lust, I can't even bring myself to form a coherent answer.

'Did he do it for you like I do?'

'No.' Sizzling desire emanates from my every pore.

He removes his hand and his mouth in the same second. The whimper that passes through my lips incites a smirk. I can't see it, but I know it's there.

'Play for me,' he insists again.

'Play with me.' I'm not referring to the guitar.

'I will if you will.' His suppressed laughter shakes through both of us.

'Urgh. You are so annoying.'

'You weren't saying that ten seconds ago.'

'Ten seconds ago you were making me feel all dizzy and delicious. Don't tease me, it's not fair. Especially when you're leaving tonight.'

'I told you, I'm not leaving you.' He accentuates every word for effect.

Resting his palms over the back of my hands, he uses them to lift the instrument again, positioning it higher in my lap, balancing it against my middle. His right hand places my fingers over the strings, while his left slips back under my shirt, inching upwards again.

'This is so unfair. It's like sexual blackmail or something.' I huff.

I can't bring myself to play. I just can't. It reminds me of all my broken hopes and dreams.

He circles my nipple again, long enough for my eyes to flutter close in sheer bliss, until he mischievously removes his fingers again.

'Ryan!' It's practically a shriek.

'Sasha.'

'If you don't stop teasing me now I'm going to spontaneously combust and it won't be pretty.'

'Baby, if you play a few little chords for me, I'll make you "cum-bust" so deliciously hard, they'll hear you all the way in Vegas.'

Lusty flutters ripple through my stomach.

I sigh, repositioning my fingers over the metal strings.

'Good girl.' His hand moves back to my breast, his lips on my neck and eventually I play out of fear of him ripping them away again. My physical need for this man overrides the fear of any emotion playing might unleash.

I begin to play the last melody we ever wrote together. Its every chord engrained into the rawest part of my memory. Ryan's lips gently work over my neck as the music fills the room.

Closing my eyes, under the protection of Ryan's embrace, I allow myself to feel everything for the first time in years.

The shock.

The loss.

The grief.

It's nowhere near as raw as I anticipated.

And I know precisely the reason why.

He sits behind me, loving me, teasing me, torturing me in the most delicious fashion.

As I strum the final chords, a smile eclipses all other emotion. I did it! And ultimately, I enjoyed it! But not nearly as much as I'm going to enjoy what comes next.

Placing the guitar down on the coffee table, I spin round to straddle Ryan, who's wearing a wistful grin.

'Happy now?' I wiggle on top of him, placing his other hand underneath my shirt in search of my reward.

'You have no idea how happy I am.' He smirks, eyes darkening in a distinctly predatory manner.

I grind myself against the bulge beneath me. 'Ah, I think I have some idea.'

Our lips crash together, teeth scraping like the first time as we urgently claw each other's clothing. Through the grinding and panting, I pause long enough to ask a question I can't get out of my mind.

'Did you use that song? Is it one from your album?'

His tongue dips to my collarbone, fingers wrestling with the top button of my blouse.

'Yes.'

Fervent hungry kissing resumes until another question pops into my head.

'What did you call it?'

A thunderous rap strikes the door of the penthouse, causing both of us to jump as though we're still sneaking around like naughty teenagers.

'Who's that?' I straighten my shirt.

Ryan shrugs, but I can tell from the glint in his eye he's suppressing a smile. 'Open it and find out.'

'Is there something wrong with your legs, all of a sudden?' I nudge him in the ribs.

'Only that I have a third one.' He thrusts upwards and I snort, reluctantly sliding from his lap.

This better be good. Nothing less will justify the interruption.

Striding across the carpet, I fling open the door, ready to give Pierce, Frankie, or whoever else, hell for the interruption.

Instead an actual whoop escapes my mouth and I throw myself at the only other person I'm desperate to hug.

Chloe.

Tanned, gorgeous and laden with bags, she returns my embrace, before stepping back to eye me from head to toe.

'You've got that "getting-loads-of-sex-multiple-times-daily" glow about you.'

'What are you doing here?' I drag her into Ryan's living quarters before she can disappear from my sight.

Her mouth parts in a wide grin, flashing brilliant white teeth. 'I'm your fairy fucking godmother, sweetheart. You're going to Vegas, baby.'

CHAPTER TWENTY-FOUR

RYAN

14th December

A private jet propels us through the night sky.

'Thank you for organising this with Chloe,' Sasha says, glancing at me from under thick long eyelashes as though she's suddenly shy.

The flight attendant hands us each a glass of amber whiskey before nodding and exiting the cabin, leaving us entirely alone.

'I told you I wouldn't leave you. Perhaps next time, you'll believe me.'

Intelligent green eyes gaze over the rim of the crystal tumbler she grips between her fingers. Staring thoughtfully around the camel-coloured plush leather interior, she asks, 'What's it like?'

'What's what like?'

She gestures round the plane. 'Being super rich and famous and having all of this at your fingertips.'

I wink to show I'm joking. 'Don't forget super-talented

too. And I'm not just talking about my voice.' My hand instinctively falls to her thigh. The need to touch her all the time is overwhelming.

'And vain too.' She laughs, then takes a sip of the liquid.

'If my memory serves me correctly, it was you who always used to say confidence is the most attractive trait in a man.'

'True.' She shrugs, her lips curling into a coy smile.

There's no doubt about it, Sasha is about to see another side to me. It's actually funny she's never seen it before because it's the only side I show the rest of the world.

Talking her hand, I press my lips to the back of it. 'You tell me, sweetheart. What does it feel like? Because you too are super rich, and the second the media works out who you are, you're about to become super famous too.' She flinches at that comment, but I continue anyway.

'And all of this' – I motion around us – 'is at your fingertips now too.'

'I'm terrified and excited in equal measures.' She takes another sip of whiskey. Impressively, she doesn't so much as flinch at the burn.

'You're going to love it.' A man can only hope. Because if she doesn't, there's no way I can break the news to Jayden I'm moving back to Ireland to live a simple life. I scoff internally. There's nothing simple about living in a fucking castle. Especially if it means giving up the success I worked so hard for. When Victoria goes to college maybe Sasha will consider moving Stateside for a while. Especially now the estate is financially secure.

'So, your house is in LA... will we have time to go there?' She tucks a glossy strand of hair between her ear.

'Not this time. It's about two hundred and fifty miles away from where we need to be. Unless you want to stay an extra night and I can change the flight schedule?' I'd love to show her my place. Though I gave Mrs Garcia the month off, she'd probably come in for a few hours to get the place ready for us.

'I'd love to, but I feel bad enough already. I don't want to take the piss. It's such a busy time of year at the castle.'

'Early in the new year then.'

She nods but her expression isn't exactly convincing. 'What about Christmas? Where are you spending it?'

Jerking the glass from my mouth, my lips curl downwards. 'Is that a joke?'

'No. I, ah.' She swallows thickly. 'It's just you never said what happens after the ball, I didn't want to assume...'

Cupping her chin, I tilt until her gaze meets mine. 'Christmas is the time of year to be with loved ones, isn't it?'

'Yes.'

'Well, I love you. So that's it sorted.'

'You'll stay at the castle for Christmas?' Her voice is a triumphant shriek.

'Of course. I mean, I'll have to give you a present, right?'

A dirty snigger slips from her tongue. 'I don't mind if it's something I've already seen before.'

My mouth instinctively lunges for hers. 'That's a given.' But I'm going to buy her something phenomenal too. Something I should have bought her years ago.

Within seconds, she pulls back like she's just thought of something. 'So where is home for the next few days?'

'We're staying in the Nobu Penthouse at Caesars Palace. It's amazing, I've stayed there a couple of times. You're going to love it.'

She looks down at the jeans she's wearing, and a tiny frown pinches her eyebrows. 'I don't think I'm appropriately dressed for that kind of place, Ryan. I know I'm only twenty-eight but some days I feel positively ancient. Like, I can barely remember the last time I got dolled up to actually go out anywhere. I've been rocking the same little black dress for years. I've never really had the need to buy much else...'

Her forlorn expression is fucking adorable. 'I love that black dress. Though I love it more when it's up round your waist, or better yet, on the floor.'

Pulling out my phone, I type a quick email to Angela, my PA, asking her to schedule an appointment for us at the Bellagio. I'm going to take my girl shopping. It's the least I can do. I want to ruin her. She deserves to be spoiled.

Angela's staying at The Colosseum to deal with the press and publicity aspects of my concerts.

Jayden will land at some point, he always does, but with whom and in what... I have no idea.

'So, the nights are going to be kind of busy with the show, but is there anything you want to see during the day?'

She sucks on her lower lip, deliberating. 'I'd love to see the Grand Canyon.'

'Consider it done. What else?' It's weird thinking like a tourist for a change. Normally I avoid attractions at all costs for fear of getting mobbed.

'A couple of nice dinners, something we don't usually have in the castle would be nice...' she muses.

'You're easily pleased.' I shoot her a wink.

'Easy when you know how.' She licks her lips.

I take her glass from her hands before reclining her chair.

Fourteen hours later, we're eventually through airport security and my own security has arrived to accompany us to the hotel. And they aren't the only ones to welcome us.

Jayden lounges against the limo outside the airport sucking a lollipop as if he's nine, not twenty-nine. The winter sunshine pleasantly warms my face as I step forward to greet him.

His coal-black hair is shorter than the last time I saw him, which reminds me mine is in serious need of attention.

'Just couldn't wait to see me, hey?' I go in for a man hug, but he sidesteps me and lunges straight for Sasha, sweeping her into an over-familiar embrace. The way his hand lingers on her waist a few seconds longer than appropriate sets my blood boiling. From the glint in his eyes, it's deliberate. He's testing me.

'Sasha, welcome to Vegas, baby.' His megawatt grin serves purely to annoy me, I'm certain of it. He might be a massive shit-stirrer but he's built a thriving career around his reputation for being the most aggressive agent in LA.

If he signs an act, it's their golden ticket to stardom. He's fucking brilliant at what he does. His tongue cuts through bullshit like a brand-new machete and he drives a brutal bargain. If he's in your corner, no one will fuck with you, be it a record label or the press.

'Jayden.' Sasha's wary eyes light with surprise at the welcome.

She's right to be wary. He's my brother and I love him to bits, but I don't trust him. Especially not around her. Not that I expect he'll leap on her, but he has an annoying tendency to wreak havoc for his own amusement. And no doubt he's intrigued by our reunion, probably because he can't actually fathom being in love with anyone but himself.

'Okay, okay, that's enough.' I swipe his hand from her body and shoot him a look conveying, *I will actually kill you if you fuck this up for me.*

'What's wrong, baby brother? You worried your woman's going to want a real man, now she sees one?'

Sasha snorts. 'Firstly, I'm my own woman. Secondly, I've been enjoying your brother's unmistakable masculinity daily – multiple times. The kind of masculinity *you* radiate reminds me of a neutered chihuahua dry humping a table leg.'

Deep throaty laughter bellows from Jayden's chest. He hangs onto the stick of his lolly so as not to spit it out. Finally reaching out to me, he shakes my hand firmly. 'Congratulations, brother, you've got yourself a feisty one.'

'She can take care of herself, for sure.' I don't add she's had no other choice but to do exactly that.

'How's Cindy?' Ushering Sasha into the back of the limo, I slip in behind, to stop Jayden cosying up next to her. The air con feels deliciously fresh inside.

'We broke up. For good this time.' Jayden smirks as he removes a bottle of champagne from its cooler and pops it without bothering to ask if we want any. He must be satisfied with the new material I sent over, because normally it's always business first.

'She kept going on about the trip to the beach house to meet her family and I continued to be brutally honest about my intentions, or lack of intentions towards her. And that was that.'

'At least that put a stop to you shagging in my car.' I roll my eyes.

Jayden bites his lip. 'Yeah, about your car...'

My chest tightens in annoyance as I wait for the punchline. 'My car that I specifically told you not to borrow, yet you took it anyway and had sex in.'

'Yeah, that's not the worst part. Cindy went mental after our little chat and keyed the side of it.'

'What the fuck? Could you not have broken up with her in your own fucking car.'

'Relax, bro, it's in getting fixed as we speak, okay.' He holds his hands up like it's no big deal. I suppose it isn't when you live the lifestyle we do. It's the principle of the situation that irritates me.

Shaking it off, I turn to the woman next to me. Sasha

stares quietly out the tinted windows, drinking it all in as the familiar sights of the city whizz by.

The heaving, crawling traffic; the ostentatious buildings; the flamboyant lights of the city. The showiness seems almost vulgar in comparison to the country we just left.

For a split second, I wonder if living in Ireland full time would be impossible after all?

CHAPTER TWENTY-FIVE

SASHA

The three-bedroomed, ten-thousand-square-foot Nobu Villa at Caesars Palace makes Huxley Castle look like a three-star resort in comparison.

The luxury is next level. It's out of this world. The Japanese-inspired rooftop villa boasts an exquisite patio overlooking the Strip below. Gazing out across the city, I'm awestruck, desperate to soak in every single detail.

Brightly decorated flashing Christmas lights glint and glimmer from every building and window. A life-sized snow globe sits on the street below, tourists posing adjacent for photo after photo.

An enormous inflatable Santa floats airborne from the next building, for a split second it feels like he's waving specifically to me. Like his jolly, knowing smile is responsible for all the good in my life right now.

Spinning round, I admire the extravagant decorative foliage of the terrace, tinsel trimmed and preened to perfection. There's a barbecue pit, a full bar, a fire and water feature and even a secluded Zen garden with an Italian-made whirlpool.

Yep, it definitely makes Huxley look mediocre.

Mind you, it is thirty-five thousand dollars a night. I know for a fact, because it was the first thing Megan texted when I sent her a picture. I guess as a hotel manager, it's her job to know these things. Eight grand a night for the Huxley penthouse seems laughable.

As I wait for Ryan to emerge from the shower, I steal a few moments to myself, trying to get my head around the whole thing. Not just the shock of his lifestyle, because clearly, this is his normal lifestyle. He didn't bat an eyelid at this off-the-chart luxury, so I gather he's well accustomed to it at this point in his career.

No, it's the shocking way life can take a tornado-like spiralling turn that I'm struggling to get my head around.

This life is something else, so morally decadent. So startlingly foreign to me. But it's his life. Being here makes me wonder if Ryan would seriously give it up – partially anyway, if we're going to make a go of it – for me.

Strolling back inside, I commit every single detail to memory. The interior is just as impressive as the exterior. A sprawling, formal dining room features elegant ultra-modern lighting and a table large enough to seat twenty. The opulent Japanese-inspired flourishes continue throughout. A curved staircase overlooks the terrace and a stone hearth wall. Everything about the place screams upscale extravagance.

It's sophisticated and quirky. The wall art is eclectic. Trendy furnishings are every travel blogger's dream.

Ryan emerges from the gigantic bathroom, striding across the room like he owns the place. Yeah, he's definitely used to the high life. In a pair of low hanging navy jeans and a navy t-shirt that frames his huge powerful shoulders, he looks positively delectable. Ray-Bans balance across his forehead, his shaggy hair damp from the shower. Ink-coloured stubble lines his powerful jawline.

Right here, right now, in the middle of Vegas, I've never been more aware that the man is a fucking rockstar.

My legs wobble beneath me as the internal swoon surges through me. Then the anxiety kicks in.

How will I ever be enough for him?

A man who is habitually acquainted with utter luxury, utter perfection.

Shit, he is utter perfection.

Imposter syndrome is real. Glancing down at my Spanx jeans and off-the-shoulder white t-shirt only reinforces the feeling.

'You okay?' Ryan's warm hand strokes the back of my arm before he tilts my chin upwards to meet his eye.

Swallowing hard, I nod, unable to trust myself to speak. How do I ask if I'm enough without coming across like an insecure loon? The man already thinks I'm half-crazy after preserving his family's cabin since the day he left. Any more craziness might just push him over the edge.

Away from Huxley Castle, I'm a fish out of water. I don't know what I am. Other than seriously overwhelmed.

As if he innately knows I need reassurance, he grabs my waist and hoists me onto the table. Hot, full lips graze my ear as he murmurs, 'I missed you in the shower.'

The yearning in his liquid espresso eyes set a fresh shiver of longing rippling across my spine.

'You think you can show me something more impressive than Vegas?' My tongue streaks across his neck as I speak. Masculinity rolls off him in unmistakable undulating waves.

'Oh I know I can.' He smirks, slipping a hand under my t-shirt, skimming the curve of my breast. 'But sadly, we have somewhere else to be.' My body silently shrieks in protest as he removes his hand.

I thought we'd have hours before the concert. It's not supposed to start until ten. It's only early afternoon yet.

'Where are we going?' It's an effort not to pout as he drags me towards the front door.

A firm seductive slap lands on my bum in full view of the entourage of private security congregating in the corridor

'You'll see.' Devilish eyes glint with mischief.

Oh god, what am I even doing here?

Who even knew the Bellagio had its own mini shopping centre? I feel like I've stepped right into that scene from *Pretty Woman* where Julia Roberts goes shopping. The only difference being Ryan Cooper is way hotter than Richard Gere ever was (and that's saying something), oh, and I'm not a prostitute.

Also, I mustn't forget I actually have millions in my bank account, thanks to a few childhood lyrics and Ryan's multi-platinum albums.

We do a quick tour of the touristy stuff; walk the Strip, as much as possible anyway, when we have a security entourage as big as Ryan's flanking us. Women scream at him from miles away. At one point I worry we'll have to abandon the sight-seeing altogether, but the suits have it all under control in a matter of seconds.

Ryan indulges my own excited squeals, even letting me photograph him under the Welcome To Vegas sign. We devour the most delicious steak lunch at the Top of the World restaurant on the 106th floor of Stratosphere Tower, ogling the panoramic vistas while sipping champagne.

But the highlight of the day so far, has to be the Bellagio.

Stepping out of the bright white, spacious changing rooms, I twirl in front of the biggest mirror I've ever seen in my life and cautiously glance at Ryan, who lounges on a chaise longue sipping an iced water like he's part of the furniture.

As if this is a totally normal, regular occurrence for him. It might be, who knows. But it's certainly not for me.

I'm in fucking Vegas!

In the Bellagio.

In an exclusive celebrity boutique trying on a Evangeline Araceli dress that costs four figures. I have another heap of clothes on the white leather couch adjacent, clothes that I've tried, loved, and am about to purchase.

'Fucking hell.' A low whistle surges through Ryan's teeth. He leaps to his feet, prowling in circles around me like a lion ready to pounce on his prey.

The way his pupils dilate and his nostrils flare indicate he likes the dress. I like it too. Slim-fitting rose gold silk draping in all the right places, jees, what's not to like? The front only delivers a hint of cleavage, but the back drops low enough to practically see my tailbone, which Ryan's fingers skim over appreciatively as his tongue darts out to wet his lower lip.

'She'll take it,' he says to the smartly dressed assistant in her thirties, whose shell-shocked eyes are darting between us faster than a shuttlecock in a professional badminton match.

I imagine, working in a place like this, she must be used to dealing with celebrities. Though I suppose Ryan's devastatingly good-looking in addition to being off-the-chart famous, so I'll have to cut her some slack. Hell, I know exactly how she feels in his proximity.

Though she recovers quicker than I'm ever able to do around him. Mind you, I get the benefits – touching him, and having him touch me – which is something no woman in the world would ever recover from quickly.

Oh god, the mere thought of Ryan touching another woman sends a stabbing pain through my chest.

'Of course. Is there anything else I can get for you to try?'

Her voice is polished and professional, though her eyes continue to flit.

I shake my head. We already spent a bomb in Chanel and Louis Vuitton before even stepping foot in here.

'Thank god.' Ryan's shoulders sag with relief. It's nothing to do with the money. Or the act of shopping itself. It's because he's not used to being limited to looking, not touching.

We've been gone from the villa for hours. It's probably the longest we've gone without being intimate since we've been reacquainted. He's not the only one getting restless for some earth-shattering physicality. I shoot him an agreeable wink, which triggers both a grin and a subtle sigh of relief.

He tosses the sales assistant a credit card.

'No, Ryan. I'm getting these.' Colour floods my cheeks. The last thing I want is him thinking I'm taking advantage of him. He already bought me every other item I tried on today.

'What's mine is yours. Get used to it, sweetheart.'

My eyes instinctively drop to his crotch.

'That too.' It's his turn to wink.

CHAPTER TWENTY-SIX

RYAN

Even the knowledge that there are six of my security detail outside the front door at any given time doesn't prevent me from making Sasha scream behind it. The bedroom is too far away in this ridiculous palatial mansion.

Making her come, anyway and every way is incurably addictive. I need to hear her desperate, delirious moans this second.

'I would get you to put on that dress again, but apart from the fact I don't have the patience, it would be a shame to ruin it before you got to actually wear it.' Peeling her t-shirt from her poster-perfect body, my face dips to her collarbone, then her breasts. Ripping the white lace down, her pert, full breasts stiffen in response. Creamy coloured and smooth as silk, I could worship them all fucking day.

She reaches for my buckle.

'Not yet, baby. Not yet.' We've barely got the front door closed and already my hard-on is unbearable, but the carnal craving to hear her cry my name, to feel the sharp tug of fingers in my hair as I taste her, trumps my own throbbing need every time.

'Ryan, I need you.' Desperation sounds in her every word. So much that I almost abandon my original plan. Almost.

'I need to taste you. I need you on my mouth. Are you ready?' I tug her jeans down to find the skimpiest scrap of white lace.

'Going for the good-girl look, were you?' Yanking it to the side, my fingers part her, gliding over the most sensitive parts of her. 'There's nothing innocent about what you've got there, no matter how you dress it up, sexy girl. I'm going to remind you just how good a bad boy can make you feel.'

Muffled cries resound against my throat as I lift one of her legs and position it round my waist giving me unlimited access to my favourite place. Backed against the wall, she couldn't get away from me if she wanted to. Judging by the slickness on my fingers, I'd say she wouldn't be anywhere else in the world.

'You're driving me crazy.' Hot, lust-filled eyes bore up at mine.

'That's the plan, sweetheart. But don't worry. I'm going to make it worth your while, I promise.'

She clenches and shudders at my touch. 'You always do.'

'I love playing with you. Touching you. Tasting you. You're mine, you know that don't you?' Something about being here, back in the States, back in the limelight, sends an uneasiness through me. It's like a reminder of what life was like before Sasha became a part of it again. Bright and glitzy from the outside looking in, but seriously lacking in any real depth. The need to possess her, every inch of her, claws at me. And as much as it's a physical reaction, it's an emotional one too.

She nods, her tongue fervently pushing against mine. A glistening sheen dusts her luminous skin and I fall to my knees, taking her in my mouth. Her cry of relief is the sweetest sound I ever heard. Draping her leg over my shoulder, I support her weight while my tongue relentlessly seeks her pleasure.

Gripping my hair, she thrusts herself against my tongue as her quads tighten and tremble. 'Ryan, I... fuck, you're so fucking good at that. I think... I'm...'

'Give it up for me, baby.' My hands grip her backside, tilting her pelvis further into my face and she cries out my name as her body peaks and spectacularly shatters in my mouth.

Before she can recover, I stand, pulling her legs round my waist and fumbling with the buckle of my belt. It's too much effort to take my trousers off. The need to be inside her is all-consuming.

Fire pricks and burns in every single cell of my body as I shimmy my jeans low enough to get free. To reach my final destination. Amongst the greatest luxury in the world, being able to luxuriate in the lust of the only woman I've ever loved, is the ultimate indulgence.

Following two more rounds of mind-blowing sex, the ringing of my phone rouses me from a coma-like sleep.

Nestled beneath the silk sheets, with the glistening lights of the city hidden behind the finest blackout blinds money can buy, Sasha stirs next to me. Between the sex, the shopping and the jetlag, I'd swear she'd happily stay there all night. But we have somewhere else we need to be – again.

Four thousand people are waiting to see Ryan Cooper, multi-platinum-selling singer/songwriter. It's like having a split personality, or an alter ego.

Disassociated to the man everyone else seems to love, I don't even know who he is. It's not imposter syndrome – I've lived too long with the mask to feel that way. It's just an odd sort of distance between my true self, and the one the media and the public think they know so well.

I can flick it on and off like a switch, but it can be so draining projecting that part of me for too long.

What the world sees is merely a tiny sliver of me. One dimensional. The most polished one. The side that oozes confidence and presence.

Maybe it's self-preservation? Keeping the real side private?

The only time I feel utterly myself is with Sasha, and Jayden to some extent, but that's very different. Though both of them knew me before I hit the big time, so I guess that's no surprise.

As much as Jayden's Jayden, I know he'd kill for me. When he gives me a hard time it's usually because I need a kick up the arse. Though there's only a year between us, he's sort of become paternal towards me since Dad lost the plot and started drinking as soon as we got to the States.

And as for Sasha, being with her just feels so fucking natural. Like she knows me better than myself. I can't believe I wasted ten years without her. A shudder rips through me at all the heartache she went through on her own. But tonight, she's about to find out she wasn't ever truly alone in it. She's about to hear first-hand how much heartbreak I went through without her.

I saw her discomfort earlier. Jitters at this life. The luxury. The extravagance. As if any of it could ever compare to her, or what we have.

After tonight, she'll never doubt my feelings for her again. Excitement fizzles inside, whizzing through my blood on adrenaline fuelled shots.

I've always loved performing live. The electric, hair-raising atmosphere. The incommunicable buzz. No words could describe that rapturous feeling. The only thing in the world that beats it is being inside Sasha Sexton.

Having both in the one day, and getting to perform to the one woman who helped shaped the original dream, is the biggest dream I've ever had.

'Are you going to answer that?' Sasha squints through the dark at me.

'Yeah, sorry.' I hit the accept button, still adjusting to being accountable after the few restful weeks hiding in the idyllic Irish countryside.

'Ange?'

'I'll be there to collect you in twenty minutes. Get those vocal chords warmed up, Rhino. Every woman in the city wants to feel like you're singing specifically to them. Except me of course. I want you to sing directly into my bank account.' Her low American drawl ends with a snigger.

Angela says it as it is. She possesses military-level organisational skills. No amount of smouldering glances will get me out of a gig she's organised. Her girlfriend says she's exactly the same way at home.

'Good evening to you too.'

'Make sure it is, Romeo. Sing like your career depends on it – because rumour is, it does.'

Ha. She has no idea. The material I wrote in the past few weeks is the best I've written in my life. Glancing at the gorgeous, naked woman beside me, it doesn't take a genius to work out why.

'Now, now Angela, don't be so dramatic. You're in for a real treat tonight, trust me.' I stick my tongue out at the phone, winding her up is too easy to pass up. Maybe I'm more like Jayden than I realised?

'The last man who said that to me ended up with his balls

being stuffed up his hairy arsehole. Eyes on the prize tonight, Ryan.'

Oh my eyes are firmly fixed on the prize. Fixated even. I can't wait to see her face when she sees me up there. When she hears the songs we wrote as kids. I just hope they mean as much to her now, as they did back then.

CHAPTER TWENTY-SEVEN

SASHA

The Colosseum at Caesars Palace is like nothing I've ever seen before; huge but intimate; grand yet homely; unique, yet somehow familiar – like I've been here before in another life. Or that I was meant to be here.

A weird but reassuring feeling of déjà vu seeps into my skin as I take my seat in the plush, padded, central box. It's the best seat in the house.

Wearing the Evangeline Araceli from earlier, I feel a million fucking dollars, even if I did only have four minutes to apply my make-up, thanks to Ryan's incessant but highly gratifying urges.

The theatre below is packed tighter than the London Underground during rush hour. A sea of crimson Santa hats bob and jerk below. Several women have dressed as sexy Mrs Clause, others clutch signs declaring their undying love for my boyfriend. It's utterly surreal.

A monstrously large Christmas tree fills half the stage. Thankfully I've got over my aversion to twinkling, glittering multicoloured lights because it's one of the biggest, tackiest things I've ever seen.

Despite the reasons that initiated the switch, I honestly do prefer white shimmering tasteful Christmas decorations to the eyesores I've witnessed today. Oh, don't get me wrong, I enjoyed seeing them, and photographing them, but they're definitely a case of what goes on in Vegas, stays in Vegas. Apart from what Ryan did behind the door earlier, he can bring that trick home every day of the week.

Home. My mind wanders to Chloe and Victoria and my heart fills at the thought of them bonding, spending time together. I know Chloe had her reasons for leaving, we all have our own way of dealing with the difficulties life threw our way, but honestly, I would have loved her to stay. Not just to help out, but to keep our family united.

When Victoria goes to college next year, we'll be spread across three countries and it's not a thought I relish.

A rustling sound next to me catches my attention. I turn, assuming it's a waiter but it's not.

It's Jayden.

If Ryan is to be believed, his brother is the biggest player around. He looks every bit the part as he slides into the seat beside me, a wolfish grin adorning his lips. Lips that are full and plump, so similar to his brother's.

'Sasha.' He greets me the French way, with a kiss on each cheek, though where we were raised is far from the Riviera.

'Jayden.' I can't work him out and the wariness in my tone is clear.

'Have you ever watched him perform?' Steel grey eyes flit from mine to the stage, then back again.

'Not since we were kids.' My shaking head reinforces my words.

'You're in for a treat then.' He clicks his fingers and a waiter arrives instantaneously. 'Champagne please. Not the usual shit. Give me the best you've got. I don't care how much it costs.'

I offer the waiter a reassuring smile because frankly, he looks terrified of Jayden, whatever that's about. He turns on his heels almost tripping out of the box in his quest for the drink.

When my head angles back to the stage, Jayden's face is almost touching mine. 'I hope you're going to be good for him. That you understand he's not going to have much time for a relationship.'

Stupidly, his remark sends a surge of heat pulsating through me, finishing with a spectacular rose-coloured finale scorching my cheeks.

Before I can utter a response, his features furrow into a ferocious frown as he whispers, 'Just don't break his fucking heart – again.'

My head does a double take, my neck creaking at the whiplash effect. Hello? The man abandoned me hours after popping my much protected cherry. The same fucking day I lost my parents.

A surge of adverse energy rises inside. 'What the...'

Before I can continue a thunderous beat erupts from the stage. The main man is on his way.

The waiter returns with the champagne in a chrome cooler. He sets two flutes on the tables either side of us but neither of us so much as give him a second glance.

With bated breath I wait to see the man of my fucking dreams, literally, performing in front of thousands.

Ryan steps out from behind a thick crimson curtain, takes a half bow and smiles with a confidence that oozes both gratitude and sheer sexuality.

Ovaries combust from every direction, my own included.

In the short time he's been backstage, someone's cut his

hair. The way it sweeps higher, revealing sensual dark swirling eyes, sets my insides alight.

He taps the microphone in front of him with the same fingers that were inside me only an hour earlier and a wicked thrill sweeps through me at the memory.

'Welcome to The Colosseum. Thank you so much for coming tonight. It's my absolute pleasure to perform for you.' Every word that rolls from his tongue sounds sexual. That Irish lilt, so familiar at home, stands out a mile here.

No wonder he was voted *GQ*'s most eligible bachelor. Even if I didn't know what he was capable of, I'd still be drowning in my own juices right now.

The crowd erupts with applause and for a split second I see a flash of exultation from the eighteen-year-old Ryan I once knew. Confident though he was, he was never arrogant. Self-assured but eternally grateful and graceful. It only adds to his appeal.

The second the noise dies down he continues, 'I can't tell you how good it feels being back.' As the crowd roars, my heart plummets to my feet. Of course he must feel amazing up there.

How can I compete with that level of adoration?

The excitement.

The fulfilment.

The sheer electric buzz.

I can't.

No matter what we have. Even I can appreciate how exhilarating it must feel centre stage, worshipped by a myriad of adoring fans.

Ryan's gaze travels upwards, homing in on the box I sit mesmerised in. I raise the glass Jayden poured for me in a toast to him.

He struts towards the edge of the stage leaning towards the crowd with his microphone in hand. He winks conspicuously, like he's about to divulge his deepest darkest secret and the audience fall stonily silent with anticipation.

'Tonight is super special for me, guys.'

A chorus of 'ooohhhs' and 'ahhhs' resound around the soundproofed walls before bouncing inwards and reverberating again.

'Tonight, there's someone really special here.' His eyes bore into me across the room with a heat that makes me squirm in my seat.

'The brunette from London?' Someone shouts from the front row, and I sink lower into my seat, grateful for the low lighting.

'All will be revealed.' Ryan offers a dazzling wink as he breaks every heart in the room, bar mine, which has trebled in size.

'I've got some insane, brand-new material for you tonight, but how about I start with a classic?'

Foot stomping and deafening applause ensues.

The opening bars of a song I didn't realise I was familiar with echoes around the room, created with a few elegant strokes from the guitar Ryan clutches to his front.

How do I know that tune?

Even as I allow its hypnotic, enchanting melody to envelop me, I can't fully relax into it because it's bugging me relentlessly as to how I know it. I've never listened to Ryan's music – deliberately.

I associate the soothing lull with reassurance, protection and a feeble sense of hope.

Suddenly, it hits me like a truck.

Megan. She hums this tune over and over again. Usually at a time when I'm so low, I think I'll never be able to see the light again. But when I hear it, I know with unwavering uncertainty I will.

I never realised it was *his* song.

Thick fingers pluck the strings with expertise. Dark entrancing eyes search out mine again, then he stares at me with a heat that melts away every other person in the room.

He leans into the microphone, his lips brushing the metal in a way that flips my stomach. 'For any of you who haven't heard this song before, or have never truly listened to the lyrics, this song is for you.'

While a murmur of disbelieving laughter ripples through the crowd, his eyes remain locked on mine. It's so intense I feel the world might actually have ceased moving.

'It's called "The Mark You Made."'

He closes his eyes as if entering the song on a deeper level.

'Once upon a time,
A long time ago,
I gave my heart to a girl,
A girl I used to know.

She said she loved me,
She offered her heart too,
I didn't mean to break it.
To break it clean in two.

Hearts and limbs united
In the most intrinsic way.
Enmeshed together
Entangled more than words can say.

The mark you made,

Seared harrowingly on my heart,
I never imagined we'd ever be apart.
That we'd be forced to part.

The night I had to leave,
   I couldn't say goodbye,
   Bound by unforeseen circumstance
   That left nothing left to chance.

Agonising hurt,
   Replaced the love we shared,
   Forbidden to say goodbye,
   Though my soul you had ensnared.

The mark you made,
   Seared harrowingly on my heart,
   I never imagined we'd ever be apart.
   That we'd be forced to part.

And though you never came,
   My heart still holds high hopes.
   Hopes you'll come knocking
   When we're free of these binding ropes.

But if I see you on the street
   With another man.
   I'll wish you all the best,
   Though he'll never give you what I can.

                              . . .

The mark you made,
  Seared harrowingly on my heart.
  I never imagined we'd ever be apart.
  Perhaps one day.... We'll no longer be apart...

No longer be apart....'

Time stops. Emotions swell as the weight of Ryan's words force the breath clean out of my chest.

With just his voice, those words and that guitar, he's succeeding in ruining me for anyone else. As if he hadn't already done so in every other way. Hot salty tears spill from my eyes, streaking my cheeks, but they're happy tears.

He gets it.

He hurt as much as I did.

He wasn't simply placating me.

I'm not in this alone.

Though the circumstances aren't ideal, we'll work out the logistics. He needs me as much as I need him.

Jayden leans towards me to murmur into my ear, 'He always had it bad for you.'

The urge to know more, to understand what their father did consumes me. Feigning ignorance, I ask, 'Why exactly did you have to leave?'

'Two words: our father. And I'm not talking about the mysterious dude in heaven. I'm taking about the living, breathing, drinking arsehole who drops in and out of our lives when he needs an injection of cash.'

Though I'd always been aware Ryan's dad's activities were less than legal, it's hard to imagine what could be serious enough that they had to flee the country. Maybe I'm better not knowing. Perhaps that's why Ryan didn't fully elaborate.

'He survived sleeping on the streets of LA better than he survived the loss of you. Don't dream of rejecting him again.'

Jayden's words shock, as they intended to. The streets? I had no idea of the hardships they endured before getting where they are today. So lost in my own misery, in my mind it was plain sailing all the way to the bright lights. No wonder he didn't elaborate. There's still so much we haven't caught up on.

My voice is barely more than a whisper. 'I never rejected him.'

'He said he left you a note.' Steely eyes penetrate mine with an unspoken question.

'If he did, I never found it.'

'Either way, he's not exactly been in hiding. You could have reached out, if you wanted to. He spent years pining after you.'

'I had no idea.' It dawns on me that if Ryan didn't know about my parents, there's a good chance Jayden doesn't too. 'I lost more than just Ryan the night you left.'

His head whips round in a curious motion.

Oh I lost that alright, Jayden, but that's not what I was referring to.

'My parents were killed in a traffic accident the same night you left. If there was a note, perhaps it got lost in the commotion? While you've been monopolising the bright lights of this city, I've been trying to keep my own on, back at the castle. No mean feat with two younger sisters, a mountain of staff to pay and a pile of dry rot.' My eyebrow arches in defiance as the enormity of what I've been doing hits us both in unison.

Ryan's right. Megan's right. Though their memory is sacred, I can finally appreciate I've done my parents proud. It's time I started living for me now.

Granite grey eyes darken and a burn with a brand-new

empathy. 'Sasha, I had no idea.'

I shrug. 'Just like I had no idea why you all disappeared into the night. Or that you'd been sleeping rough until you got a break. None of us wear our scars on the outside. Such is life I guess...'

'Speaking of which...' Jayden nods in the direction of the stage where the familiar chords of a song I know from a decade ago float through the theatre.

It's been years, but I'll never forget that melody. I practically composed it myself. The lyrics were written fireside in the very cabin I've avoided for years.

Over the haunting rhythmic melody, Ryan says, 'This one's for you, Sasha Sexton. Scratch that, baby, they're all for you. That's my girl up there everyone. She's the most amazing woman I know. It's always been her.'

A chorus of 'ohhs' and 'ahhhs' erupt again and it feels like every single person in the theatre is craning their neck to catch a glimpse of the woman who's stolen the heart of the most eligible bachelor around. Thank god for the security positioned directly outside my box. Initially, I thought they were overkill. I hadn't realised Ryan was planning on outing us to the world.

Instead of shying away from the attention, I flash the goofiest grin – I can't help it – before blowing Ryan a kiss.

He's still strumming that haunting melody. This is the song he put my name to, both on the paperwork and to the world.

'I called this song "Such is Life." You might remember it?'

The crowd gasp and coo as though they're being let in on Ryan's deepest secrets, which truthfully they are. Though they're not just his secrets. They're mine too. Right now, I can't bring myself to care about the repercussions his announcement might bring.

Such is life, indeed.

CHAPTER TWENTY-EIGHT

RYAN

17th December

As amazing as Vegas was, it was fucking exhausting. Or perhaps I've just lost the horn for it now I have more meaningful things in my life again. Namely, my relationship with Sasha and the prospect of our first Christmas together.

It's only five p.m. but I could cheerfully drag her straight to my bed. I might even let her sleep, once I've satisfied both of us, that is.

The temperature has dropped since we left. Crisp frost embellishes the ferns lining the driveway, hundreds of tiny stars sequin the clear sky above. White fairy lights adorning the castle twinkle, dipping and brightening in a soothing cycle.

It's the perfect night for a hot tub on the terrace, if I can prise my girlfriend away from her sisters.

Chloe and Victoria practically fly out the castle door to greet us. From the welcome they extend, you'd think we'd been gone months not days.

'How was it?' Chloe asks at the same time as Victoria shrieks, 'Did you bring me back a present?'

Both Sasha's sisters envelop her in a ginormous hug, creating a Sasha sandwich.

One of the porters takes Sasha's bags. 'Thank you so much, James,' she calls over Victoria's shoulder.

'Is that a Louis Vuitton bag I see?' Victoria's animated shriek has me visibly wincing.

Pierce arrives with Frankie and Archie, relieving the security staff that travelled with us. The castle gates are absolutely crawling with paparazzi. It's my own fault. I gave them Sasha's name. Though it's an inconvenience being swamped again, I can't bring myself to regret it. I wanted the world to know she's mine – now they do.

Pictures of us strolling the Strip in Vegas headline every single newspaper both sides of the Atlantic.

Sasha got her own double-page spread in most of them, but because she's been keeping a low profile for the last ten years, there were hardly any pictures of her online. Smart girl. Everyone wants to know more about my mysterious brunette, the unofficial queen of Huxley Castle. It's probably one of the reasons we've been offered millions in exclusive interview deals, none of which we've accepted yet, though to me, it's a no-brainer.

It's not like we need the cash, but Sasha could invest it straight back into the castle. Honestly, I'd just love to get our story out to the world and then maybe they'll let us crack on with actually living it.

Megan greets us in the reception area, also throwing her arms around my girlfriend. 'Oh. My. God. It looks like you had an amazing time! Do you know that Evangeline Araceli dress you wore to the concert has sold out everywhere? It's all over social media, pictures of you sipping champagne in your private booth, draped in that stunning rose gold silk. You looked like you were made for that life.'

Sasha glances at me, squirming uncomfortably for some reason as Megan ushers us into one of the castle's private drawing rooms behind the reception desk. The double-height, rectangular room is tastefully decorated with the usual navy and white theme, and thick expensive wallpaper lines the fireplace where flaming orange logs offer a welcoming warmth.

'Actually, I did hear it sold out. Evangeline called me yesterday to ask if she could send over a few more items that I might wear to any events we have.'

'Evangeline called me yesterday," Megan imitates Sasha in an extremely poor fashion. 'Holy fucking shit that's unbelievable. The woman is one of the hottest fashion designers to grace this earth.' Her hand clamps over her mouth but it does nothing to silence her shrieks.

Sasha nods, but her smile doesn't quite reach her eyes. She perches on a navy velour couch, motioning for the rest of us to sit. 'How's everything been here?'

Between the last few days, the concerts and the jetlag, I'm beat, but I sit anyway. She sat through three concerts in a row, the least I can do is sit through a cup of tea and an update on the castle.

Chloe and Victoria take the couch opposite us and one of the young waiting staff wheels in a trolly loaded with tea and fancy triangular-cut sandwiches, placing them on the table between us.

'Also unbelievable. That new quantity surveyor has whipped everyone into shape. When she shouts jump, every construction worker in the country asks how high. She's fantastic. There's no denying the place is going to be a bit of a building site for a while but the way she's going, the rebuild will be finished in a matter of weeks rather than months.'

Sasha lets out a sigh of relief, her tense shoulders visibly relaxing a full inch lower.

'I know you've only just arrived in the door, but we need to talk about a rebrand. I get you always wanted to preserve things, do things the way your parents did.' Megan shoots a sympathetic look at the three sisters before continuing. 'But seriously, the interest you and lover-boy have caused in this place is sensational. With a bit of modernisation, and a few clever tweaks, this place could be turning over millions each year.'

Sasha swallows hard, glances at each of her sisters and nods. 'I've been thinking about it a lot and I think it's time. I've been honouring Mam and Dad's legacy, and it nearly cost us our own. It's time we moved with the times, as long as you both agree?'

I'm not surprised. She said as much over the past few days. Perhaps the break provided a little more clarity. Or dare I dream to believe she might hand over the reins to someone else and come and live stateside with me?

Fuck, do I even want to live stateside anymore? There's no doubt I love my LA villa, but it's a completely different world over there.

I palm the stubble dotting my jawline, not certain if I know anymore.

Did I enjoy Vegas? Yes, of course.

Do I want to go on tour again? Forty-eight cities in as many days – no fucking way. It sounds like torture.

Contractually, I'm obliged to provide another two albums and world tours, but dates have yet to be confirmed.

Perhaps I can negotiate extra album material, for fewer dates? Jayden should be able to do it. That's what I pay him for. If he can't swing it, no one can. But there is no way I'll be able to escape the tours completely, and though my priorities have changed and I'd like to take it a bit easier, I'm not ready to give up the music industry entirely yet. I've enjoyed the creativity of composing again.

I have no idea how to juggle everything. How it will work between us. But it's becoming increasingly clear that Sasha and I need to have a frank and serious conversation in the imminent future. While the women discuss the latest on the Christmas ball, I'm wondering how to juggle all the balls.

***

I manage to persuade Sasha to hop into the hot tub with me. Her head rests on my shoulder as I balance her between my thighs, supporting her weightless frame with an arm across her chest. My hands refuse to stay away from her body. They have a mind of their own.

'What was your favourite part of the trip?' I ask before taking a sip of a smoky twenty-year-old whiskey, distilled here in Dublin.

She inhales a long breath as she quietly contemplates.

'I loved the private helicopter trip to the Grand Canyon. I loved the shopping. The bright lights. The winter sunshine. The suite that made my own fabulous castle appear simple.' Her head twists round to make eye contact. 'Most of all, I loved seeing you perform. You were born to be on that stage. I knew it when we were kids, but watching you up there in all your magnificent glory simply reinforced it. Watching you was...' She bites her lower lip while she struggles to find the right word.

'Mesmerising.' Bright jade eyes glitter under the night sky.

'Thanks, but you're wrong. What I was made to do, was you.' My fingers trace the underside of her breast. It's only been a couple of hours but my need for her rises again.

A tiny sigh escapes her but it doesn't sound like the usual sigh of contentment. The one I've come to love, along with everything else about her.

'You don't agree?' I swallow down the concern rising in my chest.

'I do agree, but I'm not the only factor at play here.' She wiggles free from my arm, turning to face me. 'Jayden told me about the world tours.'

I bet he did.

'Nothing's confirmed yet.' Swirling the amber liquid in the glass, I can't quite meet her gaze.

'But you are contractually obliged, right?' Loose tendrils of hair drift across her face in the winter wind and she sweeps them from her eyes to examine me again.

'To some extent. There's scope for negotiation.' It would be expensive, but it's not impossible to get out of.

'We've been living in the most fabulous romantic bubble since you arrived, Ryan, but I'm not sure how we're going to negotiate our way through the real world.' She sighs again. 'I'm not being negative here, just trying to add a touch of realism.'

She's right. It's a conversation I know we need to have, so why am I dreading it so much?

'When you said Victoria will be leaving for college in a few months, I thought you were suggesting you'd be free to move to the States with me, for a year or two maybe.'

Her sharp intake of breath assures me she was suggesting nothing of the sort.

'What about the castle? I can't just up and leave. It's my family heritage.'

'Can't you let Megan run it for you on a day-to-day basis? You could oversee it from anywhere once you have Wi-Fi.'

'So you want me to simply up and leave with you, is that

it? You just assume your career is more important than mine?' Arms cross over her bare chest.

Reaching for her, I pull her towards me, planting a kiss on her make-up-free face. 'I'm not assuming anything, except you might possibly have more freedom over the next year or so than I do. I'm not averse to living in Ireland. I just can't commit to it on a full-time basis at this moment in time. Perhaps we could do half the year here and half the year there? Or I could do what I have to do for a couple of months and get back as often as I can.'

It's not a prospect I relish in the slightest. I hate the idea of being away for a couple of nights, let alone months.

'But what if you don't come back?' It's barely more than a whisper. Through the soft moonlight I see the lump she swallows.

My arms tighten around her back, crushing her chest against mine, craving that delicious, unique skin-to-skin contact. 'Sash, I'll never leave you again. I swear it on everything I own.'

She nods against my torso. 'Sorry. I know I'm like a broken fucking record, but seeing you up there on that stage, shining, I honestly wonder how I could ever compete. I worry I'm going to wake up one day and you'll have disappeared out of my life again, gone like the wind.'

'Not in a million years, you'd never be that lucky. I spent the last ten years imagining what it would be like to have you back in my life – I'm not going to let that slip through my fingers again. You're stuck with me I'm afraid. The real me. Not the polished rockstar the rest of the world sees.' I stick my tongue out to lighten the mood. 'And it's not a competition. I can have a successful career and a successful relationship, but in order to do that, we need to talk about everything. Keep the channels of communication open. Always, okay?'

'I hate the uncertainty.'

'There is no uncertainty. I'll do what I'm obliged to do contractually and I'll always come home to you, wherever that may be, okay?'

She nods, but I get the feeling she's not entirely convinced.

'I'm going to fucking marry you, Sasha Sexton. And we're going to fill this castle with gorgeous babies, I promise. You'll never wake up and not know where I am.'

Her head tilts upwards, lips apart. I don't hesitate to meet them with my own.

CHAPTER TWENTY-NINE

SASHA

19th December

With only a few days to go until the ball, not to mention Christmas itself, things are busy at the castle.

Chloe is an absolute godsend. Firm, assertive and exquisitely attractive, she's the perfect woman to negotiate with the suppliers about our sudden increase in demand now the castle is booked out solidly for the first time in years.

Megan's redesigning the website with the help of a trendy new company recommended by Angela, Ryan's PA, who is flying in today to deal with the press and make an official statement on our relationship. She's going to negotiate all interview requests and possible public appearances. Though I have no intention of committing to any of it until the new year.

The building work's in full swing. The QS assures me it'll be complete by March, come hell or high water. With the way she commands grown men like children, I believe her.

Which leaves me strangely free at the busiest time of the

year. I say free, what I mean is available to entertain my aunts, Evelyn and Mags, for their annual Christmas visit.

'Don't think you're off the hook, Chloe,' I warn, as she sweeps by me in a cloud of perfume and paperwork.

'I have one more meeting with the dairy suppliers, then I promise I'll join you in the drawing room.' The unspoken *I've got your back* is conveyed in her astute aquamarine eyes. 'Where's Ryan?'

'He's waiting for Angela at the penthouse. She's due to arrive any minute. Her girlfriend is flying in at some point too. They're staying for Christmas. She's decided to trace her ancestry while she's here. You know the Americans love Ireland.'

'Great. The more the merrier.' She shrugs, heading towards the door. 'The turkey Conor ordered is big enough to feed the five thousand.'

Christmas is a notoriously difficult time of year for all of us. Like me, she probably assumes if the place is mad busy, we might not feel the weight of those who are missing quite as severely.

'It will want to be. Even though we won't have any paying hotel guests, the castle is going to be busy. Conor's staying on for the holidays. Megan's bringing her mother for Christmas dinner. James and his wife, Portia, will also be dining with us. You know he's sort of become a surrogate father to me over the years and they don't have any family of their own. Plus, Pierce, Frankie and Archie of course. Oh and Jayden's coming too. He arrives tomorrow.'

Chloe stops dead in her tracks, swivels on her heels, and her wide incredulous eyes bore into mine. 'Jayden Cooper? The arrogant little shit who used to tease me mercilessly when they lived in our cabin?'

'Ah, he wasn't that bad, was he?' I was so wrapped up in his brother, I didn't pay much attention either way.

'The man used to torment me until I'd practically combust.' An indignant expression furrows her eyebrows as she continues.

The memory of him kissing me to rise a reaction from Ryan flashes to the forefront of my mind. 'Yeah, he hasn't grown out that either.'

She huffs, a shapely arm resting on her hip. 'You only have to google him to see the man's a complete womaniser.'

'Says Mother Teresa herself, huh?' I shake my head, pressing my lips together in a tight line to suppress the rising laughter.

'I'm the way I am because of He-Who-Should-Not-Be-Named. Jayden was born that way. Did I tell you I caught him snogging the face off that chambermaid Mam couldn't stand, Janine, no wait, Jacinta, in the gardens?' Chloe visibly flushes at the memory. 'He thinks he's God's gift to women.'

It sounds like typical Jayden.

'From what I saw in Vegas, and from what Ryan's told me, I don't think he's changed much. He has this reputation for being like super arrogant but he's cut-throat in his job. By all accounts, he has a different woman on his arm every few weeks so he must be charming sometimes.'

'Those poor unfortunate women. Just keep him the hell away from me.' She turns on her high-heeled Jimmy Choos and stalks out the door.

Now probably isn't the time to point out they might have more in common than she'd like to admit.

Jayden isn't the only one who is notoriously cut-throat in his career, and also utterly allergic to a serious relationship. The only difference is, he says it like it is upfront, while Chloe takes her conquests' business first, then their body, before cheerfully informing them she doesn't do repeats. Ever.

. . .

***

Aunty Mags throws her arms around me like she hasn't seen me in years, instead of months.

'Come here, Sasha, let me look at you.' Stepping back, she takes my face in her hands and scrutinises. 'I swear you get more like your mother every time I see you. You have her elegance and grace, but your father's eyes, doesn't she, Evelyn?' Mags turns to her older sister, who glances in our direction, a distasteful sneer flaring her nose.

'She's like her mother alright.' Evelyn perches, rigid-backed in one of the castle's padded dining chairs and stares at the navy and white china cup before her, as if she expects it to magically fill itself.

Her less than subtle dig hits me straight in the sternum. Evelyn never liked my mother. She thought she was flighty with her boho style of clothing and interest in art. But my mother was a grafter, just like my father, and though the dislike was mutual, Mam always made her welcome in her home. Which is exactly why I'm trying to do the same now. Even if it is painfully arduous.

Mags takes the seat across from Evelyn and I pour the tea before slipping into the seat next to her.

'Oh, you are capable of pouring the tea. For a second there I thought we'd have to wait for one of your maids to do it.' Evelyn helps herself to a dollop of sugar. She could do with a few, though I doubt it'll make her any sweeter. The woman is bitter to the bone.

She glances at the festive displays of holly and fig leaves, beautifully bound and wrapped with scarlet bows. 'Thought you might have spruced things up a bit, what with all the media attention. It looks like the same lacklustre display as last year, and every year before.'

'Now, now, Eve. Play nicely.' Mags pooh-poohs her sister's prickliness, sweeping it away like a bad smell. 'Tell us, Sasha, quite the man you've bagged yourself. A rockstar no less! And oh my is he handsome! Your parents would be thrilled.'

Despite the awkward atmosphere from across the table, I can't help the grin at the mere mention of Ryan's name.

'He really is amazing, Mags, I can't wait for you to meet him. You're going to love him.'

Evelyn chips in, 'Is he here? I thought perhaps he was still in Vegas. A man like him must have a ridiculous schedule.'

As if she's thrown ice cold water directly into my face, my smile falters for a split second before I recover. She's right. He does have a ridiculous schedule, or he will do very soon by all accounts. But he's here now and we are going to have the best Christmas ever.

Trust Cruella to home in on my sensitive spot.

'Oh, he's here alright. He can't wait to meet my favourite aunty.' I deliberately beam at Mags.

'And he's performing at the Christmas ball, I hear.' Mags links her arm in mine, patting the back of my hand in a maternal gesture.

'Yes. He's been fantastic for business. The castle is booked out for the next two years solid. I've had wedding enquiries flooding in by the hour, the country's most affluent desperate to secure this venue for their big day. One of the Irish rugby players, Nathan Kennedy, has booked out the entire venue for his wedding on New Year's Eve, despite the work going on out back.'

'Amazing what a flash in the pan affair with a good-looking man can do for PR.' Evelyn snorts before sipping her tea.

I hope she chokes on it.

Now, now, Sasha, you're better than that. My mother's voice rings through my ear.

'I think it's more than a flash in the pan, judging from the photos in Vegas. The man looks at you like you're a goddess.' Mags gushes.

Evelyn tuts and rolls her eyes. 'Well, he is a performer. His job is primarily to put on a good show.'

Speak of the devil and he enters the room with the commanding presence of a man who knows half the world's in awe of him, and just enough grace to look grateful for that fact. Mags and even Evelyn rise to meet him, extending their hands to shake, but Ryan comes to me first, cups my face in his and plants a lingering kiss on my lips.

'Sorry, sweetheart, I got delayed longer than I thought.' Only when he's fully satisfied I've accepted his apology, does his attention turn to my two aunts, who I debriefed him about in bed this morning.

'You must be Mags.' He kisses the hand she extends. She might be sixty-two, but she swoons like she's sixteen.

'Oh my word.' Grinning like a Cheshire cat, she glances at her hand like she'll never wash it again and clutches her chest with the other.

Once again, I can only imagine what it's like to experience the Ryan-effect for the first time.

Ryan turns to Evelyn. 'Evelyn. I've heard a lot about you.' Though he offers her the same courteous kiss, an undercurrent in his tone imparts a subtle warning.

'Tea?' I hop up to pour it for him but his hand reaches out to halt mine.

'No, thank you.' Huge molten eyes express an implicit apology. 'I just popped in to say hi. I'm so sorry I can't stay longer. Jayden's plane is landing as I stand here. He insists we have urgent business to discuss.'

'Oh?' Surprise elevates my tone.

Evelyn sniffs a silent *I told you so*.

'It's probably something to do with the contract but,

whatever it is, I'd rather get it dealt with early, so I can spend the entire evening relaxing with you.' His lips search out mine again, delivering a sensual but comforting reassurance.

Mags' 'ahhh' echoes round the high ceilings.

'Mags, I expect to see you on the dance floor at the ball.' He winks and pats her arm.

'You can bet your life on it, boy. I might be twice your age but let me tell you, I've got moves.'

As he chuckles, his hair slips over his twinkling eyes. 'I can well believe it.'

He nods at Evelyn and pulls me towards him to walk him to the door.

'You'll give the poor woman a heart attack,' I whisper.

'Mags? You've got to be joking. I know a groupie when I see one.' His hand cups my face again. 'I'm really sorry, again. Jayden's got a bee in his bonnet about something. It's not like him. I promise I'll make it up to you later.'

'I like the sound of that,' I murmur in his ear.

'Trust me, you'll like the feel of it so much more.' His burning come-to-bed eyes and the hot breath that grazes my neck are a killer combination, making my stomach tighten with impatient longing.

'Just do me a favour...' I whisper.

'Anything.' Amusement dances eyes.

It's not what he thinks. 'If you see either of my sisters, send them in here right now before I cheerfully murder Cruella over there.'

A guffaw pierces the air as he blows me a final kiss.

Closing the door behind him, I turn my attention back to my aunts who are having their own hushed but heated discussion.

'I'm just saying, she'll never be able to keep a man like that.' Evelyn's bony fingers cup the china so tight they're in danger of snapping.

'Hush, now. Must you always be so mean?' Mags scolds.

'I'm only voicing what the rest of the world is thinking.'

Hot rage swirls and rises like a whirlpool within. How dare she?

What angers me the most is that somewhere deep inside, despite all his reassurances, I'm concerned she might be right.

CHAPTER THIRTY

RYAN

Funny how security in this fortress is heavier than it's probably ever been, yet I barely notice the guys at all.

The perimeters are well guarded. The guests are warned upon check-in that photography of anyone except their own party is strictly prohibited, which offers me a freedom I've never had in the States. Another plus on the list of ever growing pros of moving to Ireland.

Ambling out the castle doors, I walk straight into my brother and two of his security. Despite the long flight, he looks as smooth as usual.

Steely eyes assess the place we once called home. Expressionless, he soaks up every detail.

Abandoning his luggage, his hands rise, palms upturned to greet the light flurry of festive snow that has been steadily falling all day, now tumbling in perfect rhythmic timing with the brilliant festive lights.

'I'd forgotten how nice it is,' he admits with a gruff reluctance, his breath clouding the air before him.

'Nice doesn't cut it. Nice doesn't sell records.' I shoot him a grin.

A smirk curls his lip as he recognises his own words being thrown back at him. 'Christmas is meant to be cold. I never got used to that barbeque Christmas bullshit,' he confesses.

I slap him on the back in a welcome, not chancing the man hug after the last time. 'How was the flight?'

No one was more surprised than I was when he called yesterday to say he was boarding a plane. I don't doubt we have plenty to discuss but surely it could have waited until after Christmas?

Then it dawns on me. He's single again. Christmas is next week. I'm here. He's probably fucking lonely.

No scratch that, this is Jayden we're talking about. He's probably bored and looking for fresh meat.

'She's done a great job maintaining the place.' Thick black eyebrows arch as he admires the castle objectively. 'What is she? Twenty-eight?'

'Yep.' Pride swells in my chest when I think about all she's achieved alone. 'I still can't believe her parents are dead. You know she lost us all in the same day?'

'Unbelievable. I had no idea. You know, all these years I watched you pine for her. I knew why you couldn't settle for anyone else. It was written in every single song you produced, finely ingrained between the lines, or in the notes of those eternally haunting melodies.'

'Yeah?'

Jayden's emotionally intelligent side rarely rears its head, so I keep my mouth shut and see what else he might come out with.

'I was so fucking mad at her, you know...' He trails off and shrugs.

'You were mad at her? Why?' She mentioned she thought

Jayden didn't like her, but I explained he's like that with everyone, so this is news to me.

He swallows hard before answering. 'I suppose in my mind she had it all. This super fabulous, wealthy family. Parents who adored her. You adored her. And then the one time you could have been doing with some support, with her support, she didn't come. You handled sleeping on the streets better than you handled the loss of her. And even when we did make it to the big time, she still featured in every song you wrote in some subtle capacity. There was always a reference to that lost love, or first love. I felt like she had some kind of hold on you.'

'I never knew you felt that way.' My palm grazes over my stubble. 'And what about now? Now you've met her again.'

Gazing at me squarely in the eyes, he places one hand on my shoulder and squeezes. 'Now I know you have every bit as much of a hold on her as she does on you... You know I'm not the romantic type but even I can see the two of you are fucking head over heels in love.'

A stupid boyish grins spreads across my face, heating me from the inside out.

'The only problem is, what are you going to do about it? Like, do you intend to shack up here as lord of the manor for the rest of your days? Or is she going to become Evangeline Araceli's new BBF? Logistically, how the fuck are things going to work?'

'That's something we're still figuring out, but no matter what, I'm going to make it work.' It's almost a growl. 'Do me a favour... she thinks you hate her. Cut her some slack.'

'I will.' He nods earnestly. 'Look, I get it.' His expression is sincere. I'm actually touched at his unexpected empathy.

'Is that why you're here? Did Diamond Records put pressure on for tour dates?' I lead him towards the castle doors.

A frown flickers across his tanned face. 'Not exactly.'

'Just missed your little brother at the most wonderful time of the year?' My elbow connects with his rock hard abs. That fucker works out even more than I do.

'It's Dad.'

A heavy sigh reverberates between us.

'What's he done now? Don't tell me he ran out of money again?'

The man is a living breathing nightmare. Since we landed in Texas, all he's ever done is drink. Each year he gets progressively worse. For a man who was so polished, so together, he's been a train wreck since we left Ireland. And it was at his goddamn urgent insistence we left.

His only saving grace is that whatever he was wheeling and dealing in here, didn't make a reoccurrence in the States. Whoever he wronged must have put the shitters so far up his backside that he never dabbled in crime ever again. The only thing he does dabble in, is whiskey, specifically specialising in finding the bottom of the bottle.

We set him up in a comfortable four-bedroomed house not far from his sister's ranch in Texas. We make sure there's food in his fridge. That a cleaner goes in twice a week– to check he's still alive as much as to clean the place.

Still, apparently, it's not enough.

'I don't know what he's playing at, but he's insisting on speaking to you directly.'

The heat from the roaring fire hits us as we enter reception. I wave at Louise who emerges from behind the desk to hand Jayden the key card for his suite. It's not the penthouse but it has two bedrooms and also overlooks Velvet Strand, not that you can see much this late in the afternoon.

I haven't spoken to my father directly in four years. Jayden speaks to him now and again, but the last time we met in person he was off his face, and both aggressive and acrimonious. He swung a punch in my face. Unfortunately we were surrounded by paparazzi and the whole thing was all over the news.

Both Diamond Records and Angela insist I give him a wide berth. He hasn't come looking for me since and I certainly haven't sought him out either. I can't help him until he wants to help himself. The second he stops drinking, I'll talk to him, until then, there's no reasoning with him.

'Why now? What does he want?' I lead Jayden through the atrium to the huge walnut staircase.

'No idea, but he's threatening to go to the media if you don't take his call.'

Could his timing be any worse? The media are already all over me and Sasha. It's only a matter of time before they source the story of her tragic historical events, the last thing I need is him adding a backstory to mine.

'Great. Merry fucking Christmas.'

***

Sasha being Sasha, has organised dinner for everyone. By everyone, I mean my brother, her sisters, Megan, and even our closest security guys Pierce, Frankie and Archie, and Angela of course.

'Is this a good idea?' I button a crisp white dress shirt, in front of the mirror in my suite. 'I hate to sound like an entitled twat, but the staff are staff.'

Sasha's head tilts to the side and she arches a single eyebrow. If eyebrows could talk, hers just said *seriously?*

I watch as she crosses the room, her dress swishing in front of her, flashing the odd glimpse of her taut creamy thigh. 'You do sound like an entitled twat but I still love you.'

'It's not that I think we're any different to them, don't get me wrong. I don't have some sort of opinion of myself, but when shit goes wrong, it's these guys we expect to step into the firing line.'

'Precisely. They've agreed to stay on for Christmas to do exactly that. To work, so you and I can be together. The least we can do is organise dinner for them. We're as well to get acquainted.'

Evangeline Araceli dresses or not, I'm beginning to realise my girlfriend might not be cut out for the States, after all. The big Irish welcome is all she knows. She'd be lost in the rat race of the social climbers looking for their fifteen minutes of fame. Maybe she's right though. It's just one of many cultural differences I'd subliminally accepted.

'It'll be fun, I promise.' Sasha presses her chest against mine, tilting her head upwards for a kiss.

'If you keep pressing your tits against me with that look in your eye, we won't be making dinner with anyone.'

She steps back, reluctantly shaking her head. 'The night won't pass...'

'Damn right it won't.' Not when she looks good enough to eat.

Half an hour later, we're in a private dining room behind the main restaurant, waiting for the others to arrive. This room, so I'm told, is used for smaller intimate weddings. My mind strays to Sasha's carefully sourced Christmas present, the diamond ring stashed in my bedside locker, as I wonder what kind of wedding she might want. Even though she unintentionally steals the limelight wherever she goes, she's not the kind of woman who thrives on it. Yet another reason she might hate LA.

A humongous chandelier hangs over an ornate cherrywood table large enough to seat twenty, but set for ten.

'Take the seat at the head of the table.' Sasha reaches for a bottle from one of the wine coolers.

Taking the bottle from her hands, I pop the cork. 'I will not. You take the seat at the top. You are the lady of the castle, after all.'

'I'll take the seat at the head of the table, thank you very much.' I hadn't heard Chloe arrive, but no one will miss her in that vivid violet dress. It's low enough that it's borderline indecent. I avert my eyes from her direction entirely because it's too tempting to stare. And not because I have inappropriate designs on her – I'm madly in love with her older, sexier, slightly more respectably dressed sister – it's just screamingly eye-catching.

Don't get me wrong, she looks sensational. But she's dressed for a nightclub, not a family dinner. I can only assume she has plans for afterwards.

Victoria's at her heels dressed in a black high-neck dress with a pearl trim on the shoulders. Even though she looks so grown up tonight, there's an innocence about her that her sisters never had. She oozes a wholesomeness that I'd love to preserve for her forever. Standing behind the seat next to Chloe, she lays claim to it as she openly stares at her middle sister in discernible admiration.

Pierce, Frankie and Archie arrive together dressed in matching dinner jackets and jeans, like they collaborated on what might be an appropriate outfit beforehand. A collective awkwardness radiates from them.

As I said to Sasha earlier, we might all have become closer over the past few weeks, but this is taking things to a different level. Well, with Frankie and Archie anyway, Pierce and I have dined together a hundred times before. He lives in my house in LA after all.

'Sit down, please. You're very welcome here.' Sasha greets them individually with a single peck on the cheek. I snigger as Pierce's ears turn pink at the attention.

It's one way to break the ice anyway.

My eyebrows furrow as Archie makes a swift beeline for the seat next to Victoria. If I didn't know any better, I'd think he has a soft spot for her. A sense of protectiveness swells in my chest for Sasha's youngest sister, but Sasha said it herself, Victoria is almost eighteen. She'll be off to college in a matter of months.

Megan arrives looking like a sixties movie star, her auburn hair swept onto some sort of elaborate twist at the base of her neck. Pierce rises from his chair, automatically pulling out the one next to him. He's one man who will never be off duty.

Ever the gracious hostess, Sasha offers everyone beers, wine or cognac. The lads gratefully accept, all opting for something small and potent, which I pour from the crystal decanter on the drinks cabinet.

Angela arrives, minus her girlfriend who is working until the 22nd. She knows the security lads, but I introduce her to the others.

Two flustered looking waitresses arrive, smoothing down pristine white pinafores across the front of their formal black uniforms. The younger of the two halts in her tracks as her gaze meets mine. The wine glass she's clutching slips through her fingers and hits the floor with an almighty smash that sends clear sharp fragments skidding in every direction.

Sasha races over as fast as the sculpted Evangeline Araceli will permit. Placing a hand on the girl's arm, she comforts her. 'Don't worry, sweetheart. He has that effect on all of us.'

The poor girl looks distraught. 'I'm so sorry. I'll get the brush.'

Victoria pipes up from her seat at the table, 'Not quite all of us, can I just say.' Her nose scrunches in mock distaste and she pokes her tongue out, raising a tension-melting chuckle round the table.

Amongst the chaos, my brother slips into the room. He's changed into a sapphire shirt and chinos almost the exact same shade of blue. A five o'clock shadow peppers his chin the same as my own. He saunters across the room just as Sasha's pouring wine into her sisters' glasses.

'Just a small one for you, lady,' she says to Victoria. 'Remember we had to put you to bed the last time.'

Chloe thrusts her glass under Sasha's nose. 'Fill me up! You know I'd like a large one.'

'I could probably help you with that.' Jayden's deep husky voice slides past my ear as he takes the seat the other side of Chloe, as if he owns the place.

Chloe's head snaps round to seek the source of that heavily weighted promise. The initial hint of a smile is replaced with pure disgust as recognition rips across her face.

'Ugh. You!'

'Hello, Chloe. It's been a while.' His eyes roam across her body, unashamedly undressing what little material covers it.

Chloe rolls her eyes like she might die of boredom and huffs, not even bothering to gratify him with a response. Instead, she makes a show of returning to her previous conversation with Victoria and Megan, while Sasha fills the glasses and the waitress brings over another couple of bottles.

'Welcome home, Jayden.' Sasha pats his shoulder and he stands to kiss both of her cheeks.

'Thanks, Sasha. Thank goodness one of you Sextons has impeccable manners.' He grins and nods towards Chloe, who judging by her scowl, is eavesdropping on the exchange.

For a man whose mood swings are notorious, I'm seeing that grin a lot lately.

'Oh don't mind Chloe. She eats men like you for breakfast.' Sasha's irises glitter with amusement.

Jayden's ears positively prick with intrigue. 'Is that right?'

'Yep. Breakfast, but don't expect lunch. No one gets a second date. Ever.' Sasha presses her fingers to her lips as if it's a secret, but Chloe's scowl has been replaced with a defiant expression, which she wears like a coat of armour.

'There's a challenge if I ever heard one.' Jayden whispers in my ear.

'How about a toast?' Sasha scans the table, ensuring everyone has a full glass before raising her own. 'To the most fabulous Christmas ever.'

Crystal clinks, ricocheting around the table. 'To the most fabulous Christmas ever.' I tap my glass against hers and pray she's right. 'Thank you all for being here with us. For making this possible.'

Jayden slides his phone from his pocket, glancing at the screen with a frown, before cancelling whoever is on the other end. It lights up again before he can slide it into his pocket. I arch a questioning eyebrow in his direction, but he shakes his head in response. When I continue to stare, he mouths the name I've been dreading. *Dad.*

He's persistent this time and it's not sitting easy with me. Neither is the fact that no matter how fabulous this Christmas may be – even if I end up engaged to the woman of my dreams – the second it's over, we'll have to get down to the nitty gritty details of who will live where, and how the hell we're going to manage a long distance relationship. If only we could pause the moment and stay in this castle forever. It's so much nicer than the real world.

My own words from earlier come back to bite me.

Nice doesn't sell records.

CHAPTER THIRTY-ONE

SASHA

22nd December

'So, what are you getting lover-boy for Christmas?' Chloe leans over my desk, snatching away the plans for the new extension Ryan suggested. When we have the builders here, and the funds, it seems like the perfect time to upgrade the spa, install some state-of-the-art Jacuzzis and a twenty-five metre swimming pool.

'That is a good question. I have no idea.' Stretching back in my chair, I gaze out the window at the torrential rain.

I haven't given it much thought. I've been so snowed under with the building work, the last-minute ball preparations and sorting out Christmas presents for Victoria and Chloe. I can't wait to see their faces on Christmas morning.

I bought Megan a miniature Louis Vuitton handbag, I know she's going to love it. Conor got aftershave and a new shirt, the same as every year. But Ryan... I can't think of anything significant to buy him. I want it to be memorable, epic, but the man has everything he could possibly ever want.

At least I think he does. He's been preoccupied the past few days. Last night was the first he didn't initiate sex since we got back together.

'Hello? Who are you? And where is my super organised, estate micro-managing sister? You're cutting it fine, sis.' Chloe flicks her glossy hair from her shoulder, her bright blue eyes boring into mine. 'It's not like you.'

'I know, it's just been a month like no other.'

'How's your afternoon looking? Perhaps we could head into the city?' She shoots me a pleading look, as if I'm the grown-up she wants me to bring her to the playground. 'I'm dying to soak up some of the atmosphere. I'm getting cabin fever in this place. I've even begun working on preparations for the motocross event I have scheduled for the end of January, even though I swore to myself I was taking a break. It is a big deal though. The sheikh himself is attending. It has to be phenomenal.'

'Honestly, Chloe, you'll work yourself into an early grave.' I give her the big sister warning glare. Why does she do it to herself? I know for a fact she doesn't need the money and she employs a big enough team to do most of the hard work.

'I can't help myself. I love the thrill of landing a new contract. It just does things to me.' She shrugs, her irises glinting predatorily.

'I'm pretty sure Jayden Cooper would do things to you, given half the chance.' My face cracks into a rare widespread grin.

'Urgh. I'd bet my life that man only does things that benefit himself, in and out of the bedroom.'

'I don't know, if he's anything like his brother it might be worth adding him to your ever growing list of breakfast dates. Mind you, on second thoughts, it's probably best if you don't. I'd hate things to get awkward between us all. There's a chance he could be my brother-in-law one day.'

'A chance?' Chloe scoffs. 'I'd say it's written in stone at this stage.'

This time last week I'd have wholeheartedly agreed with her, but since Jayden's arrived, I have a niggling vibe something's not quite right, like the balance of things has shifted.

It could be nothing. I have a tendency to over analyse.

Maybe an afternoon out with my sister is exactly what the doctor ordered.

It's been forever since I was on Grafton Street. Brown Thomas is calling to me. Plus, I really need to buy Ryan a gift. But what do you buy the man who has everything?

'Ok, get your coat. You've pulled.' I stick my tongue out at her.

Chloe fist-pumps the air. 'Thank god! That's the best offer I've had since I got here.'

Two hours later we're strolling arm in arm through Grafton Street. Carol singers line the streets crooning all the classics, creating magical memories for everyone passing. A shiver ripples over my spine as I gaze up at the streets, dazzling Christmas decorations anchored from lamppost to lamppost, illuminating the way to our favourite shops.

It's been so long since I had a girly afternoon out, I forgot what it was like. I make a mental note to do more of it with Megan and Victoria. It's so easy to say no to everything, to put work before pleasure every single time, but don't I know more than anyone how precious time truly is?

'What are you thinking about?' Chloe squeezes my arm through my thick woollen teddy coat.

'Everything and nothing.' A contented sigh slips from my chest. 'It's great to have you home. I wish Victoria would have come with us. She's just at that age where she'd prefer to moon about her bedroom or watch videos of other teenagers doing stupid stuff on TikTok in a desperate attempt to go viral, rather than face actual conversation in the real world.'

'Are you sure that's what she's up to?' A small smirk slides the corners of Chloe's mouth upwards.

My head whips round incredulously. 'Well, what else would she be up to?'

'You don't think she might have a secret boyfriend? You know, only yesterday she asked me if she could borrow my make-up bag. Have you ever known her to show as much interest in her appearance as she has lately?'

Chloe has a point, one I'm not sure I'm entirely comfortable with. Though when I was her age, I was doing a lot worse.

'She's almost eighteen – it's about time.' Chloe pats my arm again and steers me into our favourite department store.

Everything seems to be changing and I know it's all for the greater good, but it still renders me slightly uneasy.

The astronomical level of heat from bodies jostling and overkill heating in Brown Thomas literally melts the shiver straight from my spine before I can waste another minute overthinking any of it. Searching through the men's clothing department, my heart sinks further with each item Chloe suggests. None of it is enough. None of it says what I want to say.

'Come on, let's go get a drink and put our heads together. Maybe something will jump out at us.' Chloe steers us towards the escalator, out into the twilight.

Outside, it's even busier than earlier. I didn't think it was actually possible. Hurried shoppers line the streets in search of last-minute gifts and essentials. It's a lot of fuss for one day.

A gang of teenage girls bomb towards us, shrieking and pointing. Chloe turns to me at the same time I turn to her.

'Oh my god, is he with you?' The girls literally hang from the tail of my teddy jacket.

'Bring us to the castle,' another girl pleads.

'She's not even that pretty,' another declares.

Before the situation can escalate, Chloe barges past them and pulls me to a side alley. One I'd never even noticed before, despite being a Dublin native.

'Quick, let's find a pub to hide in.'

We half run, half jog along the narrow cobbled streets. Though the crowd is thinning out the further we get from Grafton Street, I'm conscious others might recognise us.

Two more women in their twenties halt dead in their tracks, blocking the path in front of us. Darting eyes take us both in, before glancing behind us. Clearly everyone is looking for Ryan.

'Are you...' one starts, but Chloe yanks me into the nearest open doorway, which happens to be a music shop.

Slamming the door shut and turning the sign to closed, she rests against it, catching her breath.

A plump man in his fifties raises bushy grey eyebrows from behind a messy counter. Guitars of all description hang on the wall behind him in an unorganised display.

'We'll buy something, I promise. But we just need to hide out for a few minutes,' she explains.

Damn right we'll buy something. I just stumbled onto the perfect Christmas gift for my boyfriend. A brand-new acoustic guitar. Hopefully, given that it's a gift from me, he'll be able to put aside the sentiment of the old one and find some new value in this.

Pushing thick charcoal glasses further up onto his nose, he says, 'Errm, are you...'

I can only hope he has a genuine appreciation for music and isn't another infatuated fan wanting to climb my boyfriend. 'Yes. And I need to buy him a new guitar.'

. . .

When we arrive back at the castle, the final preparations for the Christmas ball are in full swing. I abandon my coat, the Brown Thomas bags, and the undisguisable guitar-shaped gift in search of Ryan.

The company renting out the marquee have spent the entire day constructing it. So elaborate in its design, inside almost feels like being in a proper ballroom.

They've set up a stage at the front of the room. Descending rows of seating circle the perimeter and in the centre of the room is a dance floor large enough to comfortably hold seven hundred people. It's unbelievable.

It's so solid, so well insulated, impenetrable even to the winter wind whipping the windows. Ryan stands in front of the stage where Matt and his band are fiddling with equipment in preparation for tomorrow night.

I slink up behind him, snaking my arms around his waist, and he flinches.

Spinning round, his hands catch my wrists and he visibly relaxes.

'Did you miss me?' I press a kiss to his lips. He responds but with not nearly as much enthusiasm as I'd like.

'I miss you every time we're apart.' Huge chocolate eyes gaze into mine. Their usual promising heat is missing and they seem to emit a sadness.

'Grafton Street was fab, but so hectic. We nearly got mobbed by some of your crazy fans. I won't be rushing back. I got you a Christmas present though...'

'Ah, Sash, why didn't you take Pierce with you? You can't just wander off like that. Not anymore.' His gaze softens. 'Besides, I told you not to buy me anything. There's nothing in this world I need or want that I don't already have.'

'That's what you think.' Grabbing him by the hand, I tug him away from the stage. 'This is absolutely class. I've never seen a marquee like it.'

Marvelling at the opulence of a glorified tent, I observe the staff hanging an abundance of fairy lights, mistletoe and intricately woven holly wreaths. No expense spared.

At the back of the tent a makeshift bar's being erected, it's even bigger than the stage. With eleven hundred tickets sold, every inch of it is going to be utterly essential.

Ryan's oddly quiet next to me, even more so than yesterday.

Jayden made no secret of his opinion on our relationship in Vegas. He warned me Ryan's schedule in the new year is going to be so hectic, he'll barely have time to breathe, let alone conduct a meaningful relationship, but I thought Ryan and I were above that. Admittedly, we still need to iron out the details but we're both committed to making it work.

Twisting to press myself against his chest, I angle upwards, seeking a sliver of reassurance. 'Is everything ok?'

Ryan's arms slip around my shoulders, returning the embrace, but his gaze wanders, eyeing everything but me. 'Everything's fine.'

'You seem a bit distracted. What's going on?'

Black narrow pupils pensively meet mine. 'I'm just tired that's all. It's been a hectic few weeks.'

He's right. Though I can't shake the suspicion there's more to it than that.

Is it me?

Has he finally remembered he's a living legend and way out of my league? Aunty Evelyn's comments ring freshly in my ears.

Has Jayden said something to put him off me?

Is it tomorrow night's concert? The one that's basically saving my family's castle and putting Huxley back on the map as one of the most sought-after hotels in Ireland?

Or is the bubble about to burst with the reality of

Christmas approaching and all that has to be decided in the new year?

Taking his hands in mine, I kiss the back of them, like he's done to mine a million times before.

'You would tell me if there was something up, wouldn't you?' I hate the hint of neediness that creeps into my tone.

'Everything's fine, Sasha, please, drop it.' He takes his hand back and pulls me towards the bar.

'Is the bar functional yet?' Ryan asks a bearded waiter stocking bottles in one of many fridges lining the back wall.

Either he doesn't know who Ryan is, or he doesn't care, because he barely glances at him, his eyes are solely trained on me.

'Miss Sexton. What can I get for you?'

Ryan harrumphs and bristles next to me, but he takes a seat at a frosted chrome bar stool.

'Two whiskeys, please. The Black Barrel will be fine, thanks.'

The server reaches for the top shelf, grabbing two tumblers. 'There's no ice yet, I'm afraid.'

'It's ok. I quite like the burn.'

Ryan knocks the honey coloured liquid back in one and hands it straight back for a refill.

Something's definitely bothering him. At the risk of annoying the life out of him, I don't dare ask.

A low buzzing sound catches my attention, patting the back pocket of my pencil skirt I try to locate my phone. The screen is black and silent. Not mine then.

The low hum of the relentless vibration continues. I eye Ryan's pocket, but he does nothing to acknowledge it.

When it rings for the fourth time I have to say something. 'Are you going to get that? It could be important.'

'It's not, trust me.' He takes another mouthful from his

rapidly depleting second glass, before removing his phone and switching it off.

Try as I might, I can't quite catch a glimpse of the caller identity.

CHAPTER THIRTY-TWO

RYAN

Four large whiskeys finally takes the edge off my unease. Jayden wasn't joking when he said Dad wanted to talk to me. My father's calls have been relentless for the past forty-eight hours.

I'm only grateful I'm this side of the Atlantic, because it wouldn't be the first time he's turned up at my door, a drunken howling mess. There's no way he'd arrive here.

For a man who was certain fleeing the country was going to solve all our problems, he sure made a terrible job of acting like it. He promised us the all American dream, yet he abandoned us the second we got there.

Jayden and I slept rough for months because he dragged us there on the promise of a home at his sister's ranch. He went on the missing list the second we landed and her hospitality came to an abrupt end shortly afterwards. We decided there and then if we were going to make it, we had to do it by ourselves, whatever it took.

Months later, when I was busking near the subway, a

talent scout approached with an offer. Wary to trust anyone, I immediately refused.

The next day, he returned with double his original offer. Jayden was with me the second time.

Sleeping rough changes a person. Hardens you in ways that can't be imagined. Any offer of kindness always had a cost. So again, I refused.

The following week the same man arrived with another suit in tow and after a particularly rough night on the harsh streets of LA, I agreed to go for coffee with them just to get a break from the elements.

The other guy was Richard Lambert, CEO of Diamond Records. He didn't appreciate having to slum in it in the roughest part of the city. Not when people usually snatched his hand off for an offer from his company. His offer was genuine. The scout saw something in me that no one else had before. Well, no one apart from Sasha.

It was a case of right place, right time.

But it should never have had to be.

The other teenagers roughing it on the streets alongside us were orphans, or runaways, all with pasts way crueller than ours. We'd already lost our mother, but for our dad to drag us to another country and then simply abandon us was abominable.

If he'd have left us in Ireland we might have had to lie low from the criminals he was involved with but surely that would have been easier than the alternative?

At least in Ireland I had Sasha. And her parents were the best kind. I know without a shadow of a doubt that Mrs Sexton would not have thrown us out. She might not have let me bunk in with her daughter, but she'd never have seen us on the streets the way our own family did.

When my debut album took the world by storm the following year, Dad reappeared in our lives, livid we hadn't kept a low profile as he demanded, barely acknowledging the way he abandoned us or the stardom we'd achieved.

After a blazing row, he fucked off again for another eighteen months. When he returned the next time he was desperately apologetic with a million excuses for his absence, none of which justified any of it. He claimed he had no idea his sister had thrown us out until it was too late and he had no way of contacting us.

I set him up in a nice detached house in one of the wealthier suburbs and that's when the drinking began again.

Over the years his behaviour only served to grow progressively more aggressive and unpredictable. Usually, I'm all about second chances. Especially since I just got my own with the only woman I've ever really felt anything for. But unless he commits to rehab, I can't let him back in my life. Been there, done that. Too many times.

Through multiple slurred gargling messages, he's insisting it's urgent this time. Apparently there's some stuff he needs to get off his chest.

I've heard it a million times before. It's always the same ending. Every time I think he might open up to me, to finally admit what the fuck happened to him, to all of us, he shakes his head, clams up and hits the bottle again.

'What are you thinking about?' Sasha's sea-green eyes bore intently into mine, dragging me back to the present.

The weighted sigh that echoes between us is unintentional. It's not her I'm frustrated with, but she's unfortunately bearing the brunt of it. A sorry side effect of being the person I spend the most time with. My mood affects hers and for that, I'm sincerely sorry.

Time to pull my head out my arse, before she regrets giving me another chance. Cupping her chin in one hand, I use the other to grab her backside and yank her towards me. Gazing warily from under those thick black lashes, I can see the way her guard's rising again and though I hate it, I'm powerless to stop it. My own emotions are running riot within.

'I was thinking that somehow last night passed without my tongue between your legs, and there's no fucking way it's going to happen again tonight.'

My words are rewarded with the subtlest thrust as she grinds her pelvis against my dick in a silent agreement.

'Let's go.'

We barely make it back to the penthouse before her skirt is up round her waist, my fingers slipping inside her.

Shaking her head, her mouth rocks against mine in a silent protest. Tilting her head back, she utters, 'I need you inside me, now.'

I fumble for my wallet in my back pocket in search of a condom, but she's already hoisting herself on top of my dick. It feels way too good to stop her but what if I get her pregnant?

I'm all for it, don't get me wrong, but is she?

'Sasha, wait.' I steady her, searching her eyes for reassurance, for permission.

'I want to feel you.'

'Are you sure?'

She offers a sharp nod, lust pooling in her eyes and between her legs.

It's enough.

It's everything.

I thrust into her with every inch of me.

***

. . .

A light tapping rouses me from a fitful sleep. Cocking an ear, I listen for a second, but it's silent again. The iridescent glow from the bright moon outside slips through the cracks at the edge of the heavy curtains I'd pulled in haste.

Patting the bed next to me, my palm lands on the creamy silky skin of Sasha's naked back. Tucking my knees into the crook of hers, I inhale the luscious scent of her skin, fingers skimming her thighs.

She's a fucking dreamboat. Everything I ever wanted wrapped in one beautiful package.

Just as my head relaxes into the duck-down pillow the tapping starts again.

What the fuck?

'Boss?' Pierce's hushed tone is unmistakable this time.

Flinging back the covers, I creep towards the penthouse door, inching it open with bleary eyes.

'Pierce?' My heart thuds rapidly in my ribcage. Pierce would never disturb me in the night unless there's a serious problem. The only thing I can think of is Jayden.

'It's your dad. We have to go'

Boiling blood surges through every vein and artery.

'What the fuck, Pierce?' I step outside into the corridor where Frankie, Archie and Jayden are huddled at the top of the stairs.

Jayden beckons me over, his facial expression the perfect imitation of the grim reaper.

Holding up my index finger, I silently convey I'll be one minute.

Slipping inside the penthouse, I pull on yesterday's jeans and an oversized hoody, all the while wondering what the fuck type of event I'm supposed to be dressing for?

Sasha moans in her sleep but doesn't stir. Should I leave a note? No, that's fucking stupid. Who do I think I am? Romeo

Montague? I have my fucking phone for Christ sake. The second she wakes, she'll call me.

I shoot her a fleeting apologetic glance before slipping out of the room.

'What the fuck is going on?' My irritation's increasingly evident with every syllable.

'It's Dad.' Jayden rolls his eyes.

'What's he done now?'

An image of his lifeless body being hauled out of a ditch flashes across my brain along with a ripple of guilt. Perhaps I should have taken his calls? Perhaps this was the one fucking time he really was ready to open up, and now it's too late?

I don't have time to contemplate for too long before Jayden speaks. 'He's here.'

'Here?' I'm aware my mouth is opening and closing like the proverbial goldfish but I can do nothing to stop it. 'What the fuck is he doing here? You know as well as I do it's not safe.'

My gaze flits around the castle walls, as if I suddenly expect him to step out from the shadows.

Jayden's got his I-mean-business-so-don't-even-think-about-trying-get-one-past-me face. 'Come on. I'll explain in the car. Shit's about to get real, brother.'

CHAPTER THIRTY-THREE

SASHA

23rd December

The familiar, soothing thrum of gentle but incessant rain finally drags me from slumber. The second my conscious mind stirs, an innate warning resonates from the tips of my fingers all the way to my immaculately pedicured toes.

Palming the cool sheets beside me, my eyelids prise open, squinting through the bleak sunrise. A chill reverberates over my spine and every minute hair pricks on my neck.

Ryan's gone.

I know with certainty.

His absence permeates the air surrounding me and no matter how much of it I desperately gulp in, the tightening in my chest intensifies.

Flinging the covers back, my feet hit the floor with a spring-like pounce. The fact his clothes remain hanging pristinely in his cupboards does nothing to reassure me of his whereabouts, after all, it's not the first time he's abandoned everything and walked out.

He didn't abandon you, he had no choice.

Maybe, but where the fuck is he this morning? And why does his absence instil such panic?

Nike runners glare at me from across the room. It shouldn't come as a surprise. My instincts have been screaming at me from the second I woke. Innately, I know he hasn't simply gone for a run.

Enveloping myself in one of the castle's fluffy robes, I open the door to the penthouse in search of security.

There are none. Which only heightens my anxiety.

Where has everybody gone?

It's the day of the Christmas ball. There's more than me just counting on him.

He's been acting weird as fuck since Jayden got here but surely he wouldn't just up sticks and go?

At the far end of the corridor I spot two chambermaids starting their rounds. Darting inside to avoid embarrassing myself, I scrutinise every inch of his suite in search for a note, a clue or something that might indicate his whereabouts.

No note, no coffee cup, no clue.

Hot nauseous bile rises in my throat with every second that passes.

He wouldn't leave. He promised.

I check my phone for a missed call or a text, but there's nothing. *Just ring him. What's the worst that could happen? Hell, the man could be out buying a sneaky Christmas present or anything.* If I thought for a second it was that innocent, I wouldn't hesitate. But what if I ring him and he says he gone? It would obliterate me.

The rational part of my brain finally kicks in, engaging a lot later that I'd like to admit. I have two choices. Phone him, and ask outright where he is, at the risk of sounding like a desperate, needy sap, or sit here and freak out all morning until he hopefully returns. Yet again, the gut instinct is screaming at me that it's not that simple.

My gut is ninety-nine per cent accurate. I trust my intuition more than I trust most people, even the ones I've known most of my life. And right now, it's screaming something's wrong.

The pad of my index finger unlocks the phone. The not knowing is killing me. If he's gone again, I'll deal with it.

Maybe.

But the need to know consumes me.

Jabbing the green button, my breath catches in my chest. Silence echoes in my ear, as it takes an unnatural amount of time to connect. Finally something clicks and I'm directed straight to an automated voicemail.

It didn't even ring.

Did something happen to him? Or did he switch it off?

Ten years' worth of insecurities violently rip through me along with both Evelyn and Jayden's words replaying like the soundtrack of my life.

She'll never keep a man like that.

He's not going to have much time for a relationship.

Things were going so well until Jayden showed up. What happened? What did he say? Or what did I do to drive him away again?

Events of the past few days assault my mind without any particular categorisation. Even though it goes against the advice of every romance article I've ever stumbled across, I dial his number again.

'You have reached the voicemail for—' I throw the phone face down on the bed in frustration.

Pacing the penthouse barefoot, the Christmas tree Ryan persuaded me to decorate with him flashes offensively before my eyes. Damn him, damn those flashing fucking lights and damn the stupid timer. I rack my brains for some sort of idea.

Thankfully it comes to me before I wear the skin from the soles of my feet.

Angela! The woman knows everything. She deals with every single detail of Ryan's life, no matter how big or small.

Picking up the landline, I dial reception. Louise answers on the first ring.

'Mr Cooper, how may I help you?' Her girlish coo rings straight through me.

'Lou, it's me. Have you seen Ryan at all this morning?'

'Sasha, hi.' The smile is evident in her voice. My staff are not used to me sleeping with guests, let alone one who's a fucking rockstar. 'No, I haven't seen him. Or his brother...' She pauses for a second, the clicking sound of her finger on the mouse on her desk travels over the line while she searches for something. 'Actually, now you mention it we're down two security guys from the front gate too. That's odd,' she says to herself as much as me.

'Can you email me the security footage from the night?' Cameras at the front door and front gate should provide me with the proof of what I need to know.

'Is everything ok?' Louise asks pensively.

'Fine. Well, not fine. But it's nothing you need to worry about.' Though it will be when today's guests check in to see the living legend Ryan Cooper perform one of the most intimate concerts of his life, and are sorely disappointed because, once again, he appears to have done a runner. After I let him come inside me. Again.

'Ok. Anything else I can help you with?'

'Can you connect me to the suite Angela is staying in?'

'No problem. I've emailed that footage to you now as well.'

'Great, Louise. Thank you so much.'

I wait on the call as she attempts to connect me to

Angela's suite. At least she hasn't checked out because Louise would have known if that was the case.

The shrill ringing continues before Louise's chirpy voice infiltrates the line again.

'Either she's not there, or she's comatose in the biggest jetlag-induced slumber known to man. Do you want me to send one of the porters up to check on her?'

'No, that won't be necessary thanks.' It won't be necessary because I already know she's not there. She's wherever Ryan and his security are.

I don't bother trying Jayden's suite. It's futile. Even if he was there, which I instinctively know he isn't, he wouldn't tell me a thing anyway. Placing the receiver in its slot, I head to the bedroom in search of my mobile again.

Thank god Victoria is on school holidays, and is blessed with the usual teenage habit of sleeping until midday, because there's no way I could put a brave face on this situation over breakfast.

The phone vibrates on the bed and in my hurried anxious state, I practically trip over my own feet to reach it.

I needn't have rushed. It's only Megan.

'Hello?' The irritation in my tone has nothing to do with Megan and everything to do with the likely possibility of Ryan Cooper leaving me for a second time, which every fibre of my being assures me he has.

'What's up with you? Only get three orgasms last night, instead of the usual four?' Megan snorts at her own joke.

'The missing orgasm isn't the problem. The missing boyfriend is.' My voice cracks on the last note.

A hiss seethes into my ear and when she speaks, her voice is dangerously low. 'What do you mean missing, exactly?'

'You know, absent, not here. Neither is his PR manager or any of his security detail. Gone. Vanished in the middle of the night. Sounds oddly fucking familiar, doesn't it?' A great big fat sob racks my chest. 'Louise sent me the security footage, but I can't bring myself to watch it.'

'I'm on my way up.' Megan ends the call.

Sixty seconds later the penthouse door opens. Her pale complexion looks almost as shaken as I feel. 'What the fuck, Sash?'

'He wasn't here when I woke up. Nobody was. And he's not answering my calls. Louise sent me the footage. I need to watch it, but equally I can't bear to.' Every cell of my body shrieks that it's the same as the last time. 'How could he do this to me, again?'

Dramatic trembling hands rake through her unruly curls. 'It's not just you, either. The castle's entire reputation is riding on tonight's ball. We have not one, but four, of the glossy magazines covering the event and *The Irish Independent*. No pressure or anything.'

She curses again. 'Maybe there's an explanation? Maybe they went out somewhere and they'll be back.'

'Well, why not mention it, or better yet, answer his phone when I call?'

'Try him again.'

'I can, but it's futile.' I throw her my phone and allow her to try. Again, it's directed straight to voicemail.

'The absolute bastard. Whatever about the ball, if he's left you again, I will never ever forgive him.' Megan strides towards the terrace, glaring at the newly assembled marquee blowing mockingly in the winter wind as if it might hold the answer.

'After all we've been through, and then Vegas and everything, I can't quite believe it.' Yet I know in the bottom of my heart that it's true. 'Why else would all of his security be gone too, and his PR?'

'There has to be another explanation.' Megan fretfully gnaws at her bottom lip. Turning to me, she pats my arm.

'Let's not jump to the worst conclusions. It's barely nine in the morning. There's plenty of time for him to turn up.'

The penthouse door bursts open, smacking the wall behind us with a bang that has me leaping a foot in the air. Chloe barges in, arctic irises blazing fire.

'Is it true?' Her voice is a low, menacing growl.

'Is what true? What have you heard?' My hands fly to the outside of my rapidly dehydrating throat.

Incensed pupils scrutinise the room, ruthlessly arbitrating the situation in under three seconds.

'So, it is true. It's written in every line of your face, Sash.' She charges towards me, enveloping me in an unyielding embrace, which only serves to panic me further.

'What do you know?' I manage to croak while Megan watches on in silence.

Chloe's arms reluctantly drop and she scans the room for the TV remote. Flicking it on, she flips to *Sky News* where an image of the back of Ryan's unmistakable physique fills the screen. He's marching into Dublin airport, flanked by Pierce, Frankie, Archie, Jayden and Angela. And the two missing security guards from the gate.

His head turns to look directly behind him, as if he's staring directly at me. His jaw is set in a tight determination and there's a coldness in his eyes I've only ever witnessed in the vividness of my worst nightmares.

CHAPTER THIRTY-FOUR

RYAN

'I suppose we should be grateful the authorities got hold of him before a mob did...' Jayden spits, shaking his head at Angela. 'You're going to have your work cut out for you spinning any positive PR on this one, sweetheart. I can see the headlines already.'

Her mouth sets in a grim line. 'I'll work it. That's precisely what you pay me for.'

An exasperated sigh whooshes from my chest. Glancing at the chunky titanium timepiece on my wrist, I wonder if Sasha's up yet. It's not even six a.m. and the day's already turning into a total shitshow.

Why the fuck would Dad get on a plane here when he was the one who insisted he could never come back? It makes no sense at all.

Striding through the automatic doors of the arrival lounge, a deep voice booms my name. Instinctively, and idiotically, I swing round before realising it's a dirty fucking paparazzi with a camera twice the side of his head.

'Where's your girlfriend?' His voice fades into the background, but not nearly fast enough. 'Had a falling out, have you?'

The doors close behind us and thankfully he doesn't follow. I wouldn't either if it meant trying to pass Pierce and the others. Unified in their mission to protect me, my security surround me, shoulder to shoulder. Though even their protection can't save me from whatever shitshow I'm about to walk into.

Excited travellers queue in line to check in, clutching carefully wrapped Christmas gifts, brimming with festive smiles at the prospect of returning to loved ones for the holidays.

How I wish things could be different. That I could feel a fraction of that enthusiasm. But it's hard to envision a happy ending here.

Four non-uniformed police approach, each flashing detective badges before guiding us across the white polished floors towards a security check point.

'I'm DI Jones.' A grey haired man in his fifties extends a weathered looking hand. I assume he must be the lead detective in Dad's case.

'What's this all about?' Jayden snaps, fingers massaging his temples.

'We have your father in custody, as you heard. He's confessed to several serious crimes.'

'Whatever he took or stole, we'll pay it back. No matter the cost.' Jayden glances at me and I nod in agreement. If there's any possibility of making this right, I'll do whatever it takes.

'It's a little bit more complicated than that, unfortunately.' Another officer hangs his head in a sobering motion. 'Sorry, but due to the nature of the offence and your financial means, he's a high flight risk. I need anyone who wants access to go through a security check and hand over everything. Wallets, buckles, phones, anything sharp or with the potential to be used as a weapon.' He motions towards the metal detectors.

Jayden rolls his eyes at me, but I'm already unhooking my belt. Whatever it takes to get this dealt with and over and see me back in Sasha's arms, I'll do it.

DI Jones steps forward, thrusting a plastic tray under our noses. 'All personal belongings in here please, including shoelaces.'

What the fuck?

Is Dad a suicide risk now as well as a flight risk?

None of it makes sense.

Stepping forward, I lean close enough to smell the tobacco on his breath. 'Can I ask what this is actually about? Whatever he scammed or took, I'll sort it. The man isn't dangerous.' Even as the words roll from my tongue, images of our last encounter assault my brain. Purple in the face, he was awash with rage. Until he crumpled into huge nonsensical tears and fucked off again.

'He wants the chance to tell you himself.' Jones cocks his head to the side in some sort of reluctant understanding. This is getting weirder by the second.

Angela's hand lands on my arm. 'Do you want me to come in with you?'

Jayden shakes his head, his finger twirls between my chest and his own as if to say it's down to us.

'Go back to the castle if you like. We can make a statement from there later.' Unfortunately, after the paparazzi this morning and my father's arrest, there's undoubtably going to have to be one.

'You can wait in one of the side rooms.' Jones points to two doors the other side of the security point. Angela nods and removes her jewellery.

'Anything else that you have in your pockets, please.' Jones motions to the plastic boxes again.

Reluctantly, I throw everything in, including my phone which I grudgingly switch off.

Dad really fucking knows how to make a scene, we'll give him that. For the millionth time this morning I wonder why the fuck he couldn't have just stayed put?

Stepping through the metal detectors, there's silence, bar the hammering of my heart, which resonates through my head, pounding in my ears like the ominous drum of an approaching attack.

Pierce, Frankie, Archie and Angela are led to one door, and Jayden and myself to the other.

'Holler if you need anything.' Pierce shoots me an understanding glance. It was he who ripped my father off me the last time he landed on the doorstep.

I nod, unable to form the words lodged in my throat.

The door clicks open and Jones ushers us in, Jayden leading the way.

Behind a tatty, scuffed desk sits our father, bleary eyed and pale, his wrists cuffed together, bound by metal hoops and a chain.

He rises as we enter, licking his cracked lips with what looks like nervous anticipation.

'Dad.' Jayden eyes him from head to toe as I nod the weirdest greeting of my life.

'Sit down, please.' Dad motions to the green shabby seats positioned on the other side of the table, as if he were welcoming us into his home and not what's essentially his cell.

'Such a fucking entrance into the country, Dad. What the fuck is this all about?' Jayden slams into one of the chairs and pulls out the other and gestures for me to sit down.

'Son.' He turns his attention to me, his eyes watery, but clear of drink for the first time in years. 'I had to talk to you.'

'So I see. Usually when a person doesn't answer the phone it signifies the feeling isn't mutual.' My anger's rapidly dissipating at the sorry state of him before us.

'Sorry, but there are some things that you need to know.'

'And it couldn't have waited until I got back to the States?' Raking my fingers through my hair, I note the absence of blood from the whites of his usually bloodshot eyes.

He swallows hard, his stare falling to the desk between us. 'Afraid not, like I said in the messages, it's important.'

'Clearly. So important you returned to the country you dragged us away from and insisted none of us could return to.'

His Adam's apple bobs as his blackening pupils rise to meet mine. 'It's time to face the music. I've been avoiding facing the consequences of my actions for too long, obliterating them with every drink and drug known to man in an effort to escape the reality of the situation.'

What a time to grow a conscience. Has the man been watching one too many Hallmark movies or what? There can be no happy ending here.

Why did he get on that fucking plane?

For years, I've dreamed of having a conversation with him sober. Now he finally is, it looks like it might be our last for a while, if the handcuffs are anything to go by.

Flicking my wrist towards Jones and another detective, I assure him, 'whatever you owe, whatever it is, I've already said I'll take care of it. If there's any way we can get you out of this, we will.'

Jayden nods in firm agreement.

'If only it were that simple.' Dad clears his throat to cover a noise that sounds suspiciously like a sob.

'I did something terrible,' he confesses. 'Worse than you

can imagine. Though I can never put it right, I need to pay my penance for it. I've been paying it mentally every day anyway. Serving time can't be any worse than the time I've served in my own head, replaying it. Longing for a different ending.'

A cold trickle seeps into my bloodstream, crawling sinisterly through my arteries.

Though I have no idea what he's about to come out with, I already know it's going to be life-altering for all of us, and not in a good way.

Jayden isn't quite so sharp on the uptake. He rolls his eyes and slams his fist on the desk making all of jump. 'For fuck's sake, Dad, it's not like you killed anyone...'

'That's just it, son.' His eyes intensively bore into mine and a sickening understanding rips through me.

Rocketing from the table, I bomb straight out the door, swallowing down the bile welling ominously in my chest.

CHAPTER THIRTY-FIVE

SASHA

Shock is as debilitating as a physical injury. My limbs won't move, bar the tremble that shakes relentlessly through them.

Even though every atom of energy inside recognised Ryan's disappearance was serious, witnessing it on television invokes another level of suffering.

What happened?

What did I do to drive him away? Again.

To not even take his belongings. For fuck's sake, I know the man isn't stuck for money but come on! What the actual fuck?

Combing through memories of the night before, I dissect every sentence he uttered, every distracted haunted look in his eyes. Sure, the whiskey relaxed him enough to make love to me – fuck that, you don't make love to someone and run out on them in the middle of the night. It might have been love for me, but he fucked me and fucked off when I need him the most – again.

Every instinct inside me warned me not to trust him.

Warned me not to get caught up in his enthralling charisma, again.

But I couldn't resist those huge, borderline black eyes, loaded with enough heat to spark a forest fire in the depths of Dublin's December snow.

That enormous physique that promised strength, support and so much fucking pleasure.

What he's done to me again is monstrously cruel.

He's the first man I let into my life, into my family and into my bed in ten years, and he's hurt me the exact same way he did the last time. Actually, it's worse, because the first time I had a childish sense of naivety, this time he wooed me with heartfelt lyrics loaded with promises he had no intention of keeping.

Fuck, is that it? It took him a few weeks but he finally managed to squeeze enough material to write the rest of his albums and now he's discarded me again.

He told me he hadn't felt anything for anyone in years. Did he use me to witness first-hand what emotion looks like so he could capture the very essence of how painful and powerful love can be for his songs?

I should have known it was too good to be true. A rockstar, in love with me? It'd be funny if it wasn't so fucking tragic. I only have myself to blame. I let my wants and desires override any sense of reality.

Ryan and I are from different worlds now.

Hugging my knees to my chest, I rock back and forth on the very couch he composed his wretched songs on. He's everywhere. Memories of him haunt every corner of this castle now. What he's done is utterly unforgivable.

Megan returns from the kitchen area and hands me a mug full of steaming black coffee.

'I put two sugars in it for the shock.' Dropping next to me

on the couch, she clutches her own mug, staring blankly over its rim. Whatever she's seeing, it's not in this room.

I can't even manage to utter a thank you.

Chloe's switched the television off and is busy pacing the floor. The rain's subsided and weak rays of winter sunlight bathe the room, yet I can't feel a flicker of warmth.

Overwhelming grief etches into my soul, searing every inch of me. I want to scream. Or lash out. Or something. But it's utterly pointless.

Chloe's pacing finally comes to an abrupt standstill a foot in front of the couch. Her jaw's set so tight she's at risk of cracking a molar.

'You know, if I ever seen Ryan Cooper again I *will* string him to the old oak tree beside the cabin they used to live in and tear him to pieces agonisingly, limb by limb, but I hate to remind you that today, we've got more urgent matters to attend to.'

She's right.

Unfortunately, I'm not the only one he's let down.

The success of tonight and the future success of the castle kind of depends on it. If we don't provide what we promised on the tickets, no one will ever trust us to deliver an experience again. Huxley's reputation is relying on this. Thankfully, I have a super successful events planner in my corner.

'How could he just…' Tears threaten to flood my face again but I don't even have the luxury of grieving right now.

Chloe folds her arms over her chest and blows out a weighted breath. 'There's no point in dissecting it today, Sasha. I feel your pain. I mean that literally. I'm your sister. We share a bond so powerful that my body aches with yours. But right now, we have a job to do. Starting with finding someone to perform at tonight's event. Someone even bigger, better, more successful than that spineless twat, Ryan-Runaway-Cooper. Or else we're going to have a tonne of disappointed guests and a lot of media fallout to deal with.'

'Hate to be a Negative Nellie here, ladies, but where on earth are we going to find someone like that? In a matter of hours? And even if we did, how will we entice them to perform here?' Megan chimes in, the voice of realism.

She's right.

Chloe's tongue clicks the roof of her mouth in a thoughtful tutting sound. 'The only positive about the whole goddamn awful situation is we have cash. Lots of it for once. Didn't he name you as a co-songwriter for the first album?'

I can practically feel the spinning of her brain as she tries to formulate some sort of plan.

'Money isn't a problem.' For now. If we have to refund the tickets and cancel all the bookings we received on the back of Ryan's visit, it might be. There's only so long you can plug the holes in a leaking ship.

Chloe extends a hand and plucks me from my woeful position on the couch. 'I know the pain you're feeling. But today, I need you in survival mode. Because that's what this is. Distraction is the best technique until you can process, and we have the biggest distraction known to man – an unbelievable amount of work to try and save this shit show of a ball tonight.'

Yet again, she's right.

'We'll get tonight over with and if tomorrow you want to get out of here, get away from it all, we can hop on a plane to Dubai, or anywhere else in the world you like. Megan can manage the New Year's Eve wedding. I just need you to hold it together for a few more hours.' Slim manicured fingers grip my shoulders as she pulls me into a tight hug. 'Do you think you can manage?'

Nodding, I take a step back from my sister, careful not to spill the coffee I'm still clutching like a lifeline. Downing it, I nod at both Megan and Chloe who peer at me like I'm a wounded bird.

The caffeine and sugar crusades through my blood. 'Ok, let's do this.'

Work's been my saviour for the past ten years. It's all I know. I can get through one more day. But after that, I don't know. Maybe a change of scenery is exactly what I need.

'What do you mean, you've tried everyone?' Hiding behind the only armour I own; my trademark pencil skirt and impressively ironed blouse is the only way I can face the staff. However, no amount of foundation will conceal my blotchy face.

Chloe shakes her head, her usually tanned face washed out with worry. 'I tried every contact I have, both in this country and abroad. I figured we have time to fly someone in but that's rapidly running out. She glances at the clock in our father's office.

'Even Victoria is stalking every celebrity she's ever come across on Instagram and TikTok in an attempt to convince someone to help us. Fuck, Sasha, I hate to say it but I think we might be screwed.'

This morning's flicker of optimism has well and truly gone up in smoke, along with every other hope and dream I'd harboured for the future. Megan's in the marquee overseeing the final touches. I couldn't face it, or anyone to be honest. Easier to work in here where no one can voice the same question that continues to plague me – *what happened to Ryan?*

A powerful knock sounds on the office door. I turn to Chloe as she turns to me.

'Come in.'

Even the sight of James' genial face does nothing to raise my spirits.

'Sorry to interrupt, ladies.' A wince crinkles his kind eyes. 'One of those journalists is here. Miriam. She's in the reception area screeching about Ryan being caught fleeing the country. She's causing a riot out there, disturbing the other guests, rallying up a witch hunt. Your Aunt Evelyn's in the thick of it too. There are at least sixty restless women in the reception area, all demanding to know where Ryan is and if he's still performing tonight.'

My head falls to my hands. 'Just what we fucking need.'

James steps into the room, closing the door behind him. In a hushed tone he says, 'Do you want me to escort her from the premises?'

'What I want and what I can have are two totally different things, unfortunately.' Drumming my fingers on the table, I rack my brains for some sort of solution. One that won't involve being named and shamed in this year's final edition of *Tatler*.

Another forceful knock lands on the office door. James steps away from it, gesticulating if I want him to open it. A shrug slips from my shoulders. Welcome to the spectacular shit show of my life.

Conor barges in wearing his chef whites and a thunderous expression on his face. 'Is it true? Has he gone?' Rage palpably ripples from him in relentless waves.

All I can do is nod.

'That spineless shit of a man.' He flies across the floor landing on his knees beside my desk. 'Sasha, I'm so sorry. Tell me what I can do to help.'

Swallowing back the lump forming in my throat, I wish for the hundredth time that I could have felt for Conor what I felt for Ryan. Conor who's so good, kind and strong. Conor who's never let anyone down in his life.

'I don't think there's a lot anyone can do at this stage,' Chloe interjects, eyeing the two of us.

I can barely meet Conor's penetrating gaze. 'I feel so bad for Matt and the band. It was supposed to be their big break too.'

'Ahh, Sasha. They'll be disappointed but they'll get over it. The question is, will you?' His huge warm hand lands over mine, halting the thrumming. One gentle squeeze promises a magnitude of love and support. I only wish I could accept it.

Ryan Cooper has ruined me forever.

James pensively clears his throat. 'Did I ever tell you who my second cousin is?'

Chloe's head whips round fast enough to give her whiplash. 'Who?'

'You might have heard of him. He's no "bachelor of the year" but he's part of one of Ireland's most successful bands of all time.'

'Who?' Chloe leaps to her feet, hands clasped in front of her chest.

'Bono.'

'FUCK OFF!' she shrieks, like a woman who's been pardoned three seconds before being executed.

James nods, a hint of pride rendering him an inch taller than before. 'Look, I don't know if he can help, I don't even know where in the world he is, but I can ask. We don't see each other often but I've saved his skin a few times and he always said he owed me.'

'You are a fucking legend.' Chloe throws her arms round him in a gesture that incites a hot blush to flush his cheeks.

Wriggling free, he slips a hand into his trouser pocket, presumably in search of his phone, but before he can pull it out all hell breaks loose from along the corridor.

Conor rises to stand protectively in front of me. 'What the...?'

High-pitched shrieks and wails reverberate through the castle's stone walls like an incoming attack. Feet pound the halls, shaking the floor beneath us. Chloe's alarmed expression mirrors my own.

I gather this is quintessentially what Ryan was talking about when he was referring to the downsides of his lifestyle. It's probably a good job he's on a plane back to the States because the way I feel right now, it would be awfully tempting to let them loose on him.

CHAPTER THIRTY-SIX

RYAN

'Don't go in the front door, Ryan. It sounds like there's a protest exploding in there.' Pierce flanks my right while Jayden borders my left, leaving Archie and Frankie to cover my back.

Angela went straight to a conference room to prepare some sort of speech on the whole fucking unfortunate debacle. Good luck with that, Ange.

'I have to get to Sasha. It's paramount she hears this from me and not the six o'clock news. Access through reception is the only way to her office.' Having finally heard Dad's big confession, I'm a fucking emotional wreck.

How am I meant to tell the woman I love that my father is the one who killed hers? And her sweet, eccentric mother in the process.

He orphaned her.

And I left her.

I had no idea what he'd done.

'And how come you're so sure that's where she is?' Jayden's

tone is arrogant and I'm not in the mood for it. He's taken the whole bombshell better than me, clearly. Then again, it's not his girlfriend's parents that ours ran off the road.

'Because whatever else is going on in life, she's still got a castle to run.'

'Are you sure about this?' I gather he's referring to telling her what we know, rather than battling a frantic crowd of women.

'She's going to find out sooner or later. It's going to be all over the news. Besides, she needs closure.'

She said she couldn't fully rest until they caught the culprits responsible for sending her parents' car hurtling over a cliff edge into a freezing stream below. I'm just not sure the knowledge is going to give her as much peace as she originally hoped.

It's the biggest shock I've received in years, yet it made perfect sense of everything that occurred ever since. Our rapid departure. My father's drinking. His emotional outbursts. His anger at my fame. His inability to find peace, no matter how luxurious a lifestyle we provided him.

The man's been tormenting himself so excruciatingly for the last ten years, he would have been better handing himself in at the time.

The way he relayed the events of the night, so clearly, I felt like I was watching a horror movie unfold in slow motion. The illegal deal he'd been cutting spiralled rapidly south. He was speeding away when he collided with Mr and Mrs Sexton at one of the tightest coastal bends in the county.

He had no idea Victoria was in the car. When I told him that she was, but she'd survived, he bawled like a baby.

The one person in this life you have to be able to live with is yourself. And he couldn't do it, no matter how inebriated he got. His self-loathing grew to a point that the drink failed to take the edge off.

Even bound in cuffs he looked more content than I've seen him in years. He'd been running for so long, it seems it's a relief to finally stop.

So even though I'm devastated my father's likely going to spend the remainder of his life behind bars, it's the right thing. By him, by Sasha and by the word of the law.

He said seeing Sasha and me photographed at the concert together in Vegas served as some sort of an epiphany. He recognised her immediately, in part at least. What he didn't apparently recognise was the haunted sorrow lurking in the depths of her eyes, a far cry from the bubbly teenager we all knew.

Seeing her further fuelled an increasing desire to confess.

I know the precise look he means. Sasha can appear detached sometimes. It was the exact expression she greeted me with in the atrium all those weeks ago. Desperately trying to demonstrate cold, soulless eyes, but if you get close enough the irrepressible energy exuding from her body gives her away. Not that my father would know that.

I've come to realise, for her, it's an act of self-preservation. I think her glassy expression was aimed at Jayden that night in Vegas, though he's still to tell me what passed between them in that box.

But either way, however Dad interpreted the situation, it brought him to this definitive closure.

The question is, will it bring closure to Sasha and me?

How could she possibly continue to love me, knowing what my family did to hers? Knowing that if it wasn't for us she'd still have her parents. Her life could have been so fucking different. All her struggles have directly resulted from my family. All her losses, even the baby she'd mourned was a result of me.

I'm not optimistic about the situation. It's not exactly the Christmas gift I'd planned to give her.

'I need to do this.' Taking a deep breath, I barge through the castle doors into absolute pandemonium. Louise and four other receptions attempt to placate around fifty or sixty women who are shoving and pushing like they're in a school playground or a very badly organised netball tournament.

Where the fuck are James and the other porters?

The atrium's squashed tight with fur coats and designer clothing. The sickly scent of floral perfume supersedes even the smell of pine from the sixteen-foot tree, which looks in serious danger of toppling over. Women jostle painfully close, carelessly knocking baubles in every direction.

'Where is he?' one woman shrieks, yanking the shoulder of the woman in front of her to force past her towards the front of a very loose line.

'We paid a ridiculous amount of money for these tickets. I demand a refund.'

'We saw him at the airport. Who is supposed to be the star guest now?'

We hover for a second, assessing the escalating situation and heads begin to turn. The deafening disturbance falls to a stunned burst of gasps for about three seconds before they lunge for me.

'Move!' Pierce shouts, his shoulder bouncing into mine as he rams me forward. Like pilgrims on a witch hunt, the crazed crowd begin to run after us, stampeding through the castle halls, knocking into the smaller trees lining the corridor.

The office door isn't far but fevered women nip at our heels all the way.

'Ryan, can you sign this for me?'
'Ryan, can you pose for a photograph?'
'Ryan, are you still performing tonight?'

I haven't missed this.

The senseless fanatical way women get in my presence.

Being here at Huxley, I've enjoyed writing the songs way more than performing them lately.

Perhaps it's time I bowed out and focused more on that side of things?

It's not a prospect I have time to consider as Pierce shoulders open the office door, propelling me through it. It slams with a bang a split second before he bellows, 'enough of this fucking madness. Pull yourself together unless you want to be physically removed from the premises.'

He's well able to defuse the situation. He's had plenty of practice over the years and he has Frankie, Archie and Jayden to assist.

The real question is, am I able to defuse the one in here?

Four sets of eyes blister into me, but there's only one set I meet.

Sasha looks an absolute wreck. Her usual porcelain skin is positively grey. Streaks line the area beneath her puffy eyelids.

Is it possible she knows already? That someone else got to her before I did? When I collected my phone from security I didn't dare turn it on in case she called because the second she heard my voice she would have known something terrible has happened.

'Sasha, I need to explain...' Taking a tentative step towards her, Conor rushes forward blocking the way.

'What the fuck are you playing at?' The man looks possessed with a rage I wouldn't have pegged him as capable of.

'I had no idea.' Side-stepping to stand in front of Sasha's desk, I silently will her to give me the chance to explain at the very least.

Sasha's wide-eyed gaze is filled with a misty confusion. She inhales a lungful of air and blows it out slowly in an attempt to gather herself.

Chloe lunges forward from behind. 'You had no idea

about what? That you were going to creep out in the middle of the night and fuck off to Dublin airport with your entire entourage? As if, Ryan. If you're going, just fucking go. Why the hell did you even bother to come back? She got over you once, she'll do it again.'

Fuck. Fuck. Fuck. Fuck. Just when I thought it couldn't get any worse, I realise the insensitive idiocy of my actions.

Sasha assumed I left her – again.

She never got over it. She didn't fully trust what we had. She doesn't know about my father, not yet at least. Her problem is solely with me at this precise moment in time.

'I'd never leave you.' My voice cracks with emotion. I'm three seconds from falling to my knees for this woman because whatever she's judged me for, it's about to get a whole lot worse.

Swallowing a fresh lump of bile, I turn to Chloe, James and Conor. 'Can we have the room please?'

'No,' Conor and Chloe voice unanimously.

Sasha's yet to utter a word.

'Please.' My eyes bore into hers and hers alone. I need to talk to her, I need to make her understand, even if she can't forgive the situation it's imperative that she knows I would never willingly leave her. That no sane man would. That she's the most important person in the world to me, even if she can never reciprocate those feelings.

One subtle nod creates chaos.

'Sasha, don't let him suck you in again. He can't be trusted,' Conor warns.

Chloe reaches over the desk to offer a supportive squeeze to her sister. 'I'll be just outside the door.'

James clears his throat in an awkward fashion. 'Do you still want me to text Bono?'

Sasha's nostril flare and she glowers at me. 'Are you planning on making an appearance at the ball tonight, or did you simply forget something?'

Does she seriously think I'd let her down on one of the biggest nights of her life?

'Of course I'll be at the ball, if you still want me there...'

A flicker of curiosity crinkles her eyebrows and she turns to James. 'I think we should be ok, but thank you. You never let me down.' Gratitude glints in her irises, but I don't miss the dig she shoots in my direction.

I deserve it.

I didn't expect to be gone so long today, and to be uncontactable. I should have known she'd be worried but I was preoccupied with fresh, more pressing, concerns.

Conor's shoulder connects roughly with mine as he barges out of the room with James and Chloe trailing behind.

The door clicks and then there's silence.

Ten years, so many secrets, it's now or never.

CHAPTER THIRTY-SEVEN

SASHA

Thunderous palpitations in my chest make me feel like I'm about to erupt like a simmering volcano. Insecurity fuels the bubbles, my rage is the lava.

What the actual fuck is going on?

'We saw you at the airport.'

Ryan rolls his eyes and sighs. 'Fucking paps. I'm so sorry you saw that, sweetheart. I'm only just beginning to realise what I put you through this morning.'

'You have no idea what you put me through this morning. Or you never would have done it. Ryan, I woke up this morning after having mind-blowing sex with you *without protection* and yet again, you were gone. Vanished in the middle of the night. Along with everyone else you brought to this castle.'

'But all my stuff was still here...' His words trail off. I can only imagine he's remembering it's not the first time he abandoned his belongings.

'You've been acting weird since Jayden got here. I know

he hates me. That he thinks I'm not good enough for you, or that I'm going to hinder your career or something. I was worried he'd been poisoning your ear. Then when I wake up and there's no sign of you, what else am I supposed to think?'

'Sasha, I—'

I hold my palm in front of his face signalling I'm not done. 'I had visions of being left pregnant and alone again, which was only reinforced by seeing your face all over every news channel in the country, glowering your way through the entrance of the airport. What was I meant to think?'

'Baby, please.' He grabs my hands across the desk and when I don't immediately yank them back, he takes it as an invitation to slide round the five-foot slab of maple and pull me into his arms.

'I told you before, I'll never leave you. I love you so much. Fuck, when I said I was going to marry you, I wasn't joking. We will have babies together. If you'll still have me, after everything.' He flinches as he says it, like he's willing it into fruition or something.

Much as I want to be angry with him, his familiar scent annihilates my willpower.

Slumping into his chest, huge heartfelt sobs rack through my chest. This time, the tears are filled with relief.

'I tried to call you. When your phone went straight to voicemail, I assumed the worst,' I confess.

'I had to go to the airport to take care of some delicate business. Security took my phone. I had no idea it was going to take so long. After everything we've been through, you should know I'd never do that to you.'

Sliding my palms across his ridiculously planed pecs, I angle my face towards his. 'Don't ever dream of putting me through anything like it again. If you have to go somewhere, wake me up. Or leave a damn note. Just don't leave me hanging. Trust takes time. I'm still a work in progress after the first time.'

All the tears, all the anguish this morning was for nothing.

I continue to breathe life into my own personal trust issues. Will I ever get over what happened the first time? Or will it sit between us for the rest of our lives?

Ryan brought me to London. He brought me to Vegas. He told the entire world it's always been me. And I panic at the first sign of trouble. Though I wasn't the only one who jumped to the worst conclusion.

'I swear, I'll never leave your side, if you'll still have me there...'

Pressing my lips to his, I slide my tongue inside his mouth and push him against the desk into a sitting position. My mouth and hands devour him. We only have a few hours before the ball and I need to make up properly, need the reassurance of him inside me.

But first, I need to ask one more question. A burning curiosity inside demands answers, even though it pains me to pull back from the kiss.

'What was the delicate business at the airport?'

Ryan's hands drop from my waist at the same time as his gaze drops to the floor.

'We need to talk about that.' Something in his tone makes every hair on my body prickle like an electric current.

'What is it?' Even as I demand answers, instinctively I know I'm not going to want to hear them.

Ryan guides me across the room, tiptoeing beside me like the world below his feet might shatter under his weight. Anxiety rips through my core. He nudges me into a seating position in the leather recliner, which only serves to fuel my alarm.

'Ryan, you're scaring me now. What is it?'

Crazy thoughts dance through my brain on a desolate cycle.

Is he sick?

Did somebody die?

Did he accidentally knock up one of those actresses and has a secret baby he wants me to adopt?

He takes a deep breath and kneels beside me.

'You know how you wanted justice for your parents' death? How you wanted to find the culprit responsible for running them off the road?' He takes my hand in his.

'Yes.' I can barely breathe. If they have that monster behind bars, it would be the best Christmas present ever. I know it's supposed to be the season of love and forgiveness but I'll never forgive what was taken from me. All the memories we were supposed to have made together.

Ryan's Adam's apple bobs and dips as his eyes brim with unshed tears. 'They have him. He's behind bars. He flew into the country and was detained by security and he confessed everything.'

Ten years' worth of hurt and injustice surges through every fibre of my body. My shoulders slacken with my relieved out breath and huge salty tears fall from my face to my lap below.

Finally, I can let it go.

Finally, justice will be served.

Just as I'm about to pull Ryan into a celebratory hug, my intuition screams at me. 'How do you know all of this? What does it have to do with you?'

Black pools of intensity bore straight through me, as if he's speaking to my soul. 'Because the man responsible is my father.'

Shock knocks the words right out of my mouth as the reality of the situation kicks me in the gut.

His father.

His dad killed my mam and dad. And ran.

He ran with him.

Shoving him away from me, repulsion crawls over my skin, cold enough to burn.

'You knew... this whole time...'

He jumps to his feet, following me across the room. 'I didn't know, I swear, Sasha. I knew he was involved in something so terrible he dragged us out of the country on the first available flight. It ate him alive every day since, that's why he turned to drink. I swear to you, I had no idea he was responsible for your parents' death. Not until about eight hours ago, anyway.'

'Convenient,' I spit.

A heartfelt sigh surges from his throat. 'Actually, Sasha, it's not convenient. None of it is. You lost your parents and I lost mine.'

'How dare you? It's wildly different and you know it.' A tempestuous rage burns inside my chest. Of all the people in the world, why did it have to be him? Images of my parents flash through my mind. Then the baby we lost. Everything he touches he seems to tarnish. Including me.

'How could you come back here? Touch me? Hold me, knowing he did that to them? To all of us?'

'I had to tell you myself, before someone else did. The press will get wind of the story at some point. I swear to you, Sasha, I didn't know. The second we landed in the States the man abandoned us with no explanation.'

Hurt, loss, frustration, disappointment and anger radiate between us in rippling unpredictable waves.

'He's my father. Nothing will ever change that, but I'm glad he's behind bars. And believe it or not, he's glad to be there too. He flew in specifically to turn himself in. He couldn't escape the guilt and shame. He tried damn hard for the past ten years. Sasha, I know this changes everything between us, but it doesn't change how I feel about you. I love you more than life itself.'

I feel the same. Unfortunately.

'I need to clear my head. Don't follow me.'

Ducking out the back door, I step into the crisp afternoon air. It's below freezing and the ferns bend under the frost, unable to fully support its weight and unable to shake it off. I know exactly how they feel.

Strolling over the gravel pathways, I instinctively find myself heading towards the cabins. They're the furthest spot from the castle and the opposite side to where the marquee's erected. The staff are bustling in and out, laden with supplies in preparation for tonight. The further away I get, the easier it is to breathe.

It was a shock.

A fucking huge one.

So many fragmented thoughts, images and broken memories whizz through my brain, it's hard to pick out one clearly to even attempt to analyse it.

Even if Ryan didn't know, loving the man whose father killed my parents seems like a betrayal to them. To their memory. For years, I imagined the elation I'd feel if justice was ever served. Now that justice is tainted with sorrow because try as I might, I can't help but feel sorry for Ryan.

He didn't ask for any of this. Jayden revealed enough about the hardships they suffered before they made it to the top.

It's just so messed up. So weirdly incestuous the way our lives have been interwoven, tethered with an invisible thread, yet not in a good way.

What happened will always be between us. And I don't know if I can ever get over that.

The wind picks up, howling through the old oak trees and a shiver rips over my spine.

The first cabin I reach is the one Ryan's family rented. The one I've been meaning to do something with for years, but never quite been able to face. Maybe it's time.

I let myself in with the universal key. Stepping into the dimly lit hall, the scent of dust and grime assaults my nostrils once again, but at least it's warmer than outside. And more importantly, it's quiet. Finally, I might be able to think straight.

Running my fingers over the dirty mantlepiece, I glance at the wall clock that long since stopped ticking. The Christmas decorations from years earlier are swamped with grime and silvery webs. They're a sorry state. A bit like myself.

A pitter-pattering noise begins rhythmically striking the Velux windows above. Glancing up, I see white sheets of sleet beating down.

A sound from further inside the cabin startles me.

Hesitantly, my feet carry me towards the bedrooms. Ryan's was the first on the left. My heart hammers in my chest, even though I know he's not here. Regardless that it's been ten years and I actually own the place, I still feel like I'm trespassing.

Opening the wardrobe, my fingers trace the clothes that have been hanging in the same spot untouched since that night. Inhaling the neck of one of his shirts, the scent of him has long since been replaced with a musty smell.

'I thought I'd find you here.' I leap into the air like I've been shot at the sound of Jayden's low, husky voice.

My hand clutches the material covering my chest. 'You scared the shit out of me.'

'Sorry, I guess you weren't the only one who wanted to take a trip down memory lane.' He arches a black bushy eyebrow. No trace of a smile lines his lips.

'Ryan told you?' His tone assures me he knows the answer already.

Nodding, I purse my lips to prevent from lashing out. It's not Jayden's fault his father ran my parents off a cliff.

So, why is it Ryan's then? a voice screams through my mind.

That's different. Is it though? Really?

What he said was true – he lost a parent too. The only one he had for most of his life.

'I'm so sorry, Sasha. We had no idea. Truly. Until a few weeks ago, neither of us even knew your parents had passed.'

A flashback of Ryan's initial return forces itself to the forefront of my brain with an unwavering clarity.

'Where are your parents?'

His shock and following condolences had been utterly genuine. If he had no idea they were dead, how could he have known his father was responsible?

My eyelids press tightly together as I try to sort through the tangled confusion in my mind. The oppressive outrage pressing in my chest softens, replaced with a fraction of sympathy.

The crux of it is, I don't know if I can trust him. Even if he didn't know about the tragic events of the past, there's so much history to wade through and it feels like deep, dirty water that has the potential to drown us.

And ultimately, after this morning's events, I'm petrified he's going to break my heart again. Because there's only so much one heart can take and mine is at its limit.

Jayden steps forward, his steely irises exuding an irrefutable sympathy. 'I know you might not want it, but Dad asked me to give you this.'

From the back pocket of his stonewashed jeans he draws a crumpled, musty envelope.

Disgust crawls over my skin and into my heart. I might be

able to forgive Jayden and Ryan for leaving and not knowing, but I don't think I'll ever be able to forgive their father.

Jayden barely moves as I try to push out the doorway he blocks. 'I'm nowhere near ready to read a hastily scrawled apology from the man who took everything from me.'

'This is a ten-year-old letter my father took from the kitchen the night we left. It's not from the man who took everything from you. It's from the man who wanted to *give* you everything. And from what I can see, he still does.'

He pushes the note into my hands before turning his back. Moments later, the front door bangs.

Shaky fingers tear at the time-worn envelope.

Truthfully though, it doesn't matter what it says. Its mere existence is the reassurance that Ryan didn't simply abandon me. The same way he didn't abandon me this morning. So why should I abandon him because of the terrible things his father did all those years ago?

CHAPTER THIRTY-EIGHT

RYAN

With a beanie pulled over my head and an utterly unnecessary pair of Ray-Bans wrapped around my face, I slip into the driver's seat of Angela's rental car. With Pierce, Frankie and Archie still resolving the situation in reception, there's no one to stop me.

While the entire country thinks I'm on a chartered flight out of Dublin airport (as if), I might get enough peace to do what I've longed to do since I landed back here. Walk the length of Velvet Strand, Portmarnock.

The sleet is just about subsiding, miscellaneous hints of blue emerge through the greyness of the sky at intermittent intervals. The unpredictability of the weather is the one sure thing that can always be relied on in Ireland, but even if it lashes from the heavens again, I couldn't give a shit. The need to escape is overwhelming. Sasha isn't the only one with a lot to get her head round.

Images of my father in cuffs haunts me. Yet, I can't deny

the peace it brought him. I only pray that eventually it will bring Sasha some peace.

Though there's nothing any of us can do for him, I'm going to use every connection I have to ensure he gets a smooth ride inside. He might have to serve time but I don't want him to have to do it in fear.

Angela's rental is a BMW with tinted windows. At the castle gates, the security guys don't even bat an eyelid. I hope they're more vigilant about who they're letting in than letting out.

As the heavy wrought-iron gate swings open, a van appears outside. The sign emblazoned on the side is for Homeless Ireland. Sasha's still committed to ensuring all produce that isn't used never goes to waste.

My first thought is that I wish someone had been as kind to me and Jayden when we were on the streets. The second is that Sasha Sexton really is a fucking saint. Pride swells in my chest at the generosity of the woman I love, even if she's unable to reciprocate that feeling.

She's too fucking good for me. She was ten years ago, and no matter how many records I sell or how much money I earn, she always will be. Because she's a decent person. A good person. Pure of heart. The kind of person who raised her sisters and runs a castle alone, even if it almost ground her to the bone, while I was busy driving fast cars, and even faster women. Mooning around complaining I couldn't *feel* anything.

What have I actually done that's meaningful with my life?

I can't undo the wrongs of the past, but maybe I could give something back, like Sasha.

Without any real recollection of the journey, I find myself in Portmarnock. It's almost three o'clock. I should be able to walk the length of it and still be back with loads of time before tonight's ball kicks off. Even though it's the last thing I feel like doing, I'm going to give the performance of my life. Not only do I need to ensure the night's a massive success for the castle, but I've got a growing feeling it's going to be one of my last few performances on stage.

As much as I've loved the journey, I think I'm finally ready to hang up my microphone. Writing music these past few weeks has ignited something else inside of me. Something I'm compelled to devote more time to.

The wind whips against my face, tossing sand across my reddening cheeks as the Irish Sea crashes against the shore, providing the soundtrack to my walk of self-imposed atonement. The salty scent of seaweed fills my nostrils and I feel so fucking alive. It's more invigorating than anything LA could ever offer.

This beach will always be my favourite, no matter where I go in the world, because it brings back so many amazing memories. It's where I first worked up the courage to kiss Sasha. She always thought I was so confident. It was all an elaborate act. She was way out of my league and I knew it. The confidence really only developed with our relationship. It was the only thing I was ever certain about in this life.

The clouds congregate thickly overhead, all hint of blue faded once again. While my brain mulls through my dire current situation, my legs manage to transport me five kilometres from where I abandoned Angela's car. I should probably turn back and face the music. Literally.

Though I think I've pretty much made my mind up. This country is my home and I'm staying. Whether that's to build a life with Sasha or not, is entirely up to her. I want to stay close enough to visit Dad. Whatever he's done, he'll always be my father.

The sky darkens ominously with every passing second. I pull my North Face jacket tighter round me, burying my chin into its collar, grateful for the less-than-fashionable beanie.

Multi-coloured lights twinkle across the horizon, so very different from the Christmas lights of the castle. It's a sharp reminder that Sasha hates multi-coloured lights. All because of me. I literally stripped the colour from her life.

I think it's safe enough to say I might be staying in Ireland, but any future with Sasha is utterly unrealistic. It's an impossible situation. She got what she wanted regarding justice, yet still there's no victory for any of us. There are no winners.

A furious flurry of snow cascades from the sky. Perfect fluffy circles settle on my coat, my face and my tongue as I stick it out in a childish gesture, my upturned palms catching flakes a fraction of a second before they melt on the heat of my skin. It's the story of my life. I seem to have a knack of chasing away anything beautiful.

The beach is practically deserted bar a few dog walkers. Most people have better things to do this close to Christmas, or more perhaps simply more sense than to brave the elements.

The approaching silhouette of a woman in the distance looks oddly familiar. Dark unruly hair blows in the breeze, snowflakes blur my vision, but I could swear it's Sasha. Clearly, I must be borderline hypothermic. There's no way she'd be out here.

Apart from all the things that have to be done for the ball, she doesn't know I'm here and if she did, she'd probably run a mile the other way.

Yep. Definitely delusional.

Though that scarlet coat looks like the one she had on in London. And those mahogany locks look exactly like the hair I've run my hands through a thousand times.

Upping my pace to a jog, I close the distance between us, trying to beat down the mounting hope growing in my heart.

She'll never forgive me, or my family, for any of it. Maybe something's wrong at the castle?

'Ryan!' The wind carries her voice towards me.

Another thirty seconds and I'll be in touching distance. That's assuming she'll let me.

'Sasha? Is everything ok?' Scanning her from head to toe, my gaze returns to hers. Sparkling jade eyes glitter with a magnitude of emotion.

Dragging her hands from her pockets, she flings them round me before thrusting a crinkled envelope under my nose.

'You didn't abandon me!'

Of all the things I thought she might say, it wasn't that. Squinting at the paper she clutches, I instinctively know what it is. I don't know where she found it, but it's the best Christmas present ever.

Clinging on like she might run at any second, I nuzzle into her neck as the snow flutters around us. 'I never would. Where did you get that?'

'Jayden gave it to me. Your father gave it to him. He took my parents and he took you. I'll never be able to get them back, but I can get you back... I hope...' With her lips millimetres from mine, she gazes up at me shyly from those elongated eyelashes, her cheeks a rosy pink from the wind or emotion, I don't know which.

'Sweetheart, you can't get back something you never lost. I told you, and the entire world in Vegas, it's always been you.'

'I should have listened. I never believed I was enough for you. When I lost everyone, I kind of got this idea that I was jinxed or something. Destined to go it alone in this world. Then when I got your note, ten years later, that dispelled that theory.'

I hate bringing it up, but if we're going to get any further forward, there's no point avoiding the elephant on the beach.

'And about my father...?'

She swallows hard and squeezes me. 'It's far from ideal, this whole tragic mess, but I'm beginning to accept that's what it is. He was reckless, but it wasn't intentional. And from what you said, you lost as much as I did that night. In time, we'll heal. Build a united family, I hope...' A small smile plays on her cherry-red lips.

'There's nothing in this world I'd like more.' Something unspoken passes between us, a binding agreement to work through whatever life throws our way.

My mouth fastens against hers, locking her into a kiss that tingles through my spine like a lit fuse. Her breath chills and heats me simultaneously.

She breaks away all too soon.

'We better move. We have a ball to get to. And I look worse than Cinderella before her fairy godmother arrives.' She motions at her sopping-wet hair before linking her arm through mine and half drags me back down the beach.

'Plus, I want to make a pit stop on the way.'

'Where are we going?'

'To leave a wreath for our son.' She squeezes my arm and I'm flooded with love, loss, and hope all in one all-encompassing tidal wave of emotion.

CHAPTER THIRTY-NINE

SASHA

The Christmas Ball

The marquee is wedged with anyone who's anyone in Dublin. Celebrities, politicians and even half the Irish rugby team seem to have secured tickets for this year's Christmas ball. I'm under no illusion who they came to see.

I don't blame them. The man is worth his weight in gold. And I'm not talking about his vocal talents. I'm talking about him. His integrity. His strength. Even as he shed a tear over our son's grave, he still emitted a sheer blistering masculinity. I didn't think it was possible to love him any more. Turns out I was wrong.

Dressed in a sharp tuxedo, Ryan mingles with the guests, sipping champagne from a crystal flute, occasionally sampling one of Conor's delicious canapés, which are thankfully both succulent and plentiful.

Pierce and Frankie linger in matching tuxedos, not letting Ryan out of their reach. He's pretty safe from what I can see, but from the commotion in reception earlier, it's better safe than sorry. There's no sign of Archie, though he's definitely here somewhere. Security teams cover each exit and entrance and the front gate.

Heaters with authentic looking flames have been thoughtfully positioned around the makeshift ballroom, but even without them there are plenty of bodies to ensure it's warm.

White string lights drape from every wall, glittering and glowing like the backdrop of a fairy tale scene. I suppose it is a fairy tale in some ways, finally it looks like I'm getting my happy ever after. Even though Ryan will have to go off on tour, finally, I've learned to trust he will always return.

Matt, Conor's cousin is doing a superb job on stage of entertaining the guests along with his uber-talented band. Christmas songs belt from the front of the marquee. The dance floor is full and has been since they began playing an hour ago. No one has even asked when Ryan is getting up there. Having him mingle amongst them is a novelty.

Chloe's glowing in a royal-blue floor-length silk gown, which has a relatively high neck but drops indecently low on her back. Who knew backs were so sexy? Men flock around her like moths to a flame.

I watch with a smirk as she laughs at something one of the rugby players whispers in her ear. He thinks he's a player. He's never come across anyone like my sister, on or off the pitch. I snort, wondering if he'll be staying for breakfast.

Standing with Victoria and Megan, it's an absolute pleasure to be surrounded by smiling faces and heartfelt laughter, cocooned by the love of my family, friends and my rockstar boyfriend.

Instinctively, Ryan turns from his conversation, striding towards us, his burning gaze trained solely on mine, loaded with an unmistakable look of love. Shimmying in between Megan and me, he slips an arm around my waist, fingering the delicate fabric of the brand-new crimson chiffon Evangeline

Araceli that arrived by courier this afternoon. If my recent deliveries are anything to go by, I think it's safe to say next time we're in the States, I'll have a friend to look up.

'You smell amazing.' Ryan's nose dips to my neck and he dots a row of light sensual kisses across my shoulder.

'Oh, get a room!' Victoria squeals with mock disgust.

'Oh, we have plenty. We're just counting down the days until you go to college so we can do it in yours, too.' Ryan winks at her as she makes a vomit motion.

From my periphery, I spot Conor approaching, a distinct look of apprehension in his oceanic eyes. Wearing a navy tailored suit that only enhances his stunning colouring, he drops a kiss on my cheek before shooting a glare at Ryan.

'The canapés were delicious. You are the most talented chef in the country and I'm delighted you're mine.'

He winces and my hand settles apologetically on his arm.

'Just take good care of her,' he growls at Ryan.

I send up a silent prayer that he meets someone who makes him feel like I do about Ryan. A need so feral it couldn't possibly be ignored for years. Then he'll realise what real love is.

'Thank you for everything this year.' I speak directly into his ear to be heard over the music. 'You've been an amazing friend as well as chef, seriously, I don't know what I'd have done without you.'

He nods, presses another kiss to my cheek and turns to get himself a drink. Megan follows him, winking at me as she departs.

The band break for a quick reprieve, which is Ryan's signal to get ready. He's due on stage immediately after the interval.

'I'll be the groupie screaming at the front of the stage.' Unable to keep my hands off him, I squeeze his pert, firm backside hard enough to make him jump.

'Come up with me, go on, I dare you...' Mischief gleams in his darkening pupils.

Arching an eyebrow, I take the champagne flute he's clutching. 'Exactly how much have you had to drink?'

'Not nearly enough.' His mouth catches mine again. 'Did I tell you that you look sensational tonight?' Hot breath trails over my shoulder again as he resumes those tiny infuriatingly short kisses.

It's an effort to form a coherent sentence. 'You might have mentioned something along those lines.'

The sensual assault on my skin continues. 'Did I tell you that I love you?'

My head rolls back, allowing him easier access to the sensitive skin of my neck, though I feel the heat of too many eyes scorching my skin, I'm utterly oblivious to who's witnessing this practically pornographic PDA, so thoroughly engrossed in the moment. 'If you did, I'd like to hear it again.'

With the sudden quiet of the band, the crowd begin to glance around. We're definitely attracting a significant amount of attention. From the glint in Ryan's eyes, he's enjoying every second of it. With my palms against his pecs, I push him away without much enthusiasm.

'We should probably save this for later.' It kills me to say it. We still have so much making up to do.

Hooded eyes smoulder as he shoots a crooked grin before dropping to crouch on one knee. Gasps fill the air around us. The biggest burst stems from my own open mouth.

'Sasha Sexton, I've loved you from the second I laid eyes on you. Will you do me the incredible honour of becoming my wife?' His hand reaches into his trouser pocket from which he produces a ruby coloured velvet box.

I don't wait for him to open it before I give him my answer. 'Yes. A million times over!'

The same words fall from our lips simultaneously. 'It's

always been you.' Mouths crash and tongues clash as soft hands locate mine, slipping cold metal onto the fourth finger of my left hand.

The gathering crowd erupts with applause, stomping loud enough to bring down the marquee. Ryan's joyous laughter rattles through his chest, breathing life back into my shell-shocked body. From my periphery I notice Miriam capturing the moment with her industrial-sized lens. Never thought I'd be grateful to see the woman but this moment is so momentous, it's only right it's documented for the world to see.

This man has given me everything. Saved my castle. Saved me from myself, ensured justice for my family even though it cost him his own, and still he keeps on giving.

The least I can do is give him something back.

Reluctantly breaking away, I glance down at the exquisite colossal diamond sparkling up at me. Around us words of congratulations flood from every direction. Hugs, kisses, back slaps and everything in between follow.

Chloe envelops me in a heartfelt hug, squeezing the air clean out of my lungs. 'I'd better be bridesmaid.'

'It goes without saying.'

'Maybe your new friend Evangeline will gift me a dress as gorgeous as this one.' Her hand slides over the material of my skirt. Clearly she hasn't been snooping amongst the presents or she'd already know I bought her one. Another reason to look forward to Christmas morning.

'Seriously, sis, I'm absolutely delighted for you. Nobody deserves it more than you do.' She beams at me.

'And we already know, I'm the best man.' Jayden's chest puffs in mock pride.

'Huh.' Chloe scowls as Ryan's bellowing laughter echoes around us.

Aunty Mags squeezes her way through the jostling crowd. Grabbing her hand, I guide her through to our intimate circle, closely monitored by Ryan's security, which has doubled in the past three minutes.

'Sasha, I am so damn proud of you, girl.' She kisses both of my cheeks, then squeezes them as if I'm a baby.

A cold bony hand takes mine and it takes me a minute to locate the attached body amongst the crowd. Evelyn's grimace glares back at me before curling into a thin lipped smile I never dreamed she was capable of. 'Congratulations, Sasha. I know we've had our differences at times but I'm certain your dad is watching over you, glowing with pride.'

If I wondered before if this entire evening was a dream, Evelyn practically confirmed it. Not a million years would I ever have expected congratulations AND a smile from the aunt who could give Cruella a run for her money.

'Thank you. That means a lot.' I squeeze her cold hand, trying to inject some warmth into it.

Ryan's hands gently grip my shoulders, commanding my attention. 'Sasha, baby, I have to go. But as you've seen with certainty, I will be back.'

'Actually, I'm coming with you.'

'To introduce your fiancé onto the stage,' he teases.

'No, to perform with you.'

His eyes light up like it's Christmas.

Oh wait, it almost is.

CHAPTER FORTY

RYAN

Christmas Eve

'You were unbelievable on that stage last night,' I say, nuzzling my nose against Sasha's naked back. I inhale the unique floral scent of her skin as memories of the most perfect night of my life float through my brain on an emotionally gratifying cycle, filling me with love, lust and enough material to write a hundred new albums.

'You never know, I might even join you on tour. Stranger things have happened.' She shimmies back under the covers, resting her fine ass on my lap.

'That won't actually be necessary.'

Widening eyes gaze at me with alarm. 'Oh my god, was I terrible? It's been years since I played and I was nervous and everything. I probably should have practised... learned to walk before trying to run again and all that...'

Pressing my index finger to her plump swollen lips, I shh her gently. 'It's not that. You were fucking amazing.'

'What then?' She scrunches her nose in a feline gesture.

Taking her left hand, I admire the diamond on her fourth finger. What makes it even more fucking beautiful is the fact it was me who put it there. If I don't wipe the grin from my face pretty fucking soon I'll be in serious danger of looking smug. 'I'm not going on tour.'

'What do you mean? Your contract states you have to.'

'Contracts are made to be broken. Jayden will get me out of it. I'll offer them a deal for another two albums if they drop the tours. We'll work it out. There are only a certain amount of tickets you can sell before filling the capacity. Album sales are unlimited. Which do you think the company would prefer? ' Nudging her onto her back, I slide on top of her, revelling in the sensation of her smooth silky flesh beneath mine.

'Oh, Ryan. You don't need to do that for me. I know how much you love it up on that stage. The crowd. The atmosphere. And I know you'll always come home to me, wherever home might be.' She bites her lip dubiously. I haven't had time to tell her, with everything else that's happened.

'Home is right here, if you'll have me. And there's nothing I love more than being here with you. The noise of a rowdy clamouring audience can't compare to the whimper you make when you come.'

Her mouth parts as my lips lock onto her nipple. 'I just don't want you to rush anything, you know, without thinking about it...'

'Sweetheart, I promise you, I'm not rushing anything. I've been thinking about this for the past ten years.' I wink up at her as my tongue traces over her belly button, then lower.

By three o'clock in the afternoon, the castle's emptied out, bar Sasha, her sisters, my brother, our security, Angela and her girlfriend who arrived yesterday. The last of the straggling guests have checked out. Most of the staff gone home to their families. The kitchen's crammed with enough food to feed the five thousand.

Impressively, all trace of the marquee is gone. If it weren't for the photographs plastered over every TV channel and newspaper, it would be forgivable to imagine it was a dream.

Mooching through the castle in search of my fiancée, (god that sounds so fucking good), I find my brother in one of the drawing rooms. He's kicked back in a navy armchair, his slippered feet resting on a coffee table.

His left hand clutches a whiskey glass with only a tiny drop of honey coloured liquid remaining, and his right, today's paper.

'Hard to believe the biggest story this Christmas is *GQ*'s most eligible bachelor is now off the market.' He thrusts it under my nose.

Rolling my eyes, I shrug off his remark. 'I hope you're going to welcome your new sister-in-law graciously into this family.' It's a warning to drop the grouchy act with her. The lot of us need to be united more than ever because at some point it will be a different story about our family spread across the paper, one that won't be so kind.

'I told you when I got here, I actually like your fiancée.' The word rolls from his tongue like it's an exotic fine wine.

'Whatever passed between you guys in Vegas didn't exactly give her that impression.'

Jayden sits upright in the chair, removing his feet from the table. 'I simply told her what she needed to hear to get you both to this point.' He reaches for the whiskey decanter on the rich walnut sideboard. 'Honestly, I'm happy for you guys, genuinely. I don't usually go in for all that true love kind of crap, you know how I personally feel about settling down.'

Twinkling graphite eyes glint over his glass. 'But you're different. I've never seen you so happy.'

'It could happen to you, when you least expect it...' I take the glass he hands to me, raising it in a silent toast.

'Ha, not a chance, brother, I'm actually—'

He's cut off by the arrival of Chloe. 'You're what, exactly?'

She flicks her chestnut hair from her chest in an aggressive motion, her cool blue eyes appraising us. Wrapped in a fluffy white coat, her tan complexion and delicately freckled skin is only further enhanced.

'Chloe, I never got the chance to talk to you about everything, to apologise.' Though I apologised to Sasha for my father's part in everything, it occurs to me I haven't yet cleared the air with her sisters.

She sweeps my apology away with the wave of her hand, the same way she swept everything else under the carpet, according to Sasha anyway. Everyone has different ways of dealing with things I guess.

'It's not the time or place to discuss. And besides, there's not actually a lot any of us can say on the matter. The whole situation's a flaming tragedy, but yet here we are to tell the tale.'

Her tough front isn't fooling either of us, but I respect her wishes to simply get on with things. 'Sasha is waiting for you in the atrium. She said to hurry.'

'Where are we going?' Glancing between Jayden and the glass of whiskey he just handed me, I'm reluctant to go anywhere.

She rolls her eyes as if it's been arranged forever. 'Ice skating, of course.'

'Ha! Good luck with that, brother.' Jayden clinks his glass against mine again and snorts.

Chloe snatches the glass from him a split second before

he presses it to his lips. 'I'm not sure what you think is so funny. You're coming too.'

'Me?' Jayden looks at me incredulously, like a child about to be dragged from a sweet shop.

'Yes. You. Much to my dismay. It's a "family outing" apparently. And unfortunately that includes you.' Pulling out a white fluffy beret from her handbag, she wiggles it one-handed over her head, refusing to risk placing down the glass anywhere Jayden could reach.

'Well? What are you waiting for? Go get your coat.'

'Don't tell me? I've pulled...' Jayden winks and blows her a kiss.

'Urgh. Not if you were the last man on this earth.' Her chest heaves in a deliberately exaggerated motion.

'What about the paps? Won't we get mobbed, especially after last night?'

I love ice skating, and I haven't been since we were kids, but the prospect of getting ambushed by a load of crazed fans is not how I envisioned spending Christmas Eve.

'It's closed to the public. Sasha made a few calls and apparently, they don't mind hanging on for an extra hour or so for Ryan-Rockstar-Cooper.' She shrugs nonchalantly.

Finally! I seem to have lost the Ryan-Runaway-Cooper title. It only took ten years, a whole lot of heartache and a whacking great diamond ring.

Jayden eyes his drink longingly. He's not used to being given orders. Especially not from attractive women who can't stand the sight of him.

Chloe takes a deliberately mouth-smacking slurp of whiskey, goading him over the rim of the glass. 'Go on. Chop chop. Christmas is coming.' It's her turn to snort. Jayden marches out of the drawing room without uttering a word.

An hour later, Chloe, Jayden, Victoria, Archie, Sash and I

are kitted out in our skates, tentatively braving the ice. Pierce opts to watch from the sideline with Frankie.

While Jayden's skidding round like a new-born fawn, and Victoria clings to Archie who clings to the barrier, I guide Sasha towards the centre of the spacious ring.

'Is there anything you're not good at?' Her hand squeezes mine as we glide through the ice underneath the cloudless twilight sky. The sleet and snow has finally subsided and hundreds of tiny twinkling stars appear overhead.

'I'm sure there is, but I'm yet to find it.' Her elbow connects with my ribs, trigging a wobble, but nothing I can't correct. At the risk of being a total show-off, I do a spin before landing in front of her. Skating backwards, I take her gloved hands in mine.

'I can't wait to be your wife.' Her teeth catch her bottom lip as it curls into a smile.

'And I can't wait to be your husband.'

It's the most fabulous Christmas either of us could have dreamed of.

EPILOGUE

SASHA

Christmas Day

The air in the bedroom is crisp and cold and subsequently, so is my nose. The rest of me however, is on fire, thanks to my fiancé whose chest is pressed protectively against my back. Strong, supple arms snake around my waist, then teasing fingers circle my ribcage an inch below my breast.

'Merry Christmas,' I murmur, catching his hand as it strokes my skin.

'Merry Christmas, gorgeous.'

In one swift cat-like spring he flips me onto my back, hovering inches above me, gazing at me with those intoxicating eyes.

'Do you want your present?' Powerful hips nudge against mine, parting my thighs to allow him access.

I grind against him with equal enthusiasm. 'You bet I do.'

Coquettishly nuzzling my neck, his breath skims my bare flesh, both chilling and heating me to the bone.

Before we get any further, the penthouse bedroom door bursts open hard enough to wake the dead.

'Merry Christmas!' Chloe and Victoria shriek in unison, wearing matching reindeer-print pyjamas.

Ryan groans, slumping face down on my breasts. 'Welcome to the fucking family.'

Yanking the duvet higher to cover my modesty, I reluctantly nudge him towards his own side of the bed. 'Later, I promise.'

'I'm holding you to that,' he growls.

I return my attention to my rapidly approaching sisters, who simultaneously cannonball onto the bed in a childlike fashion.

'Merry Christmas!' My excited squeal matches theirs.

'Have you got any clothes on under there?' Hazel eyes dart between me and Ryan with a mock horror.

'Does this count?' I thrust out the hand the diamond decorates so beautifully.

'No,' Chloe and Victoria shout in unison.

'In that case, no. Give me ten minutes and we'll meet you by the big Christmas tree in the atrium.' Traditionally, our parents always left our presents down there. They insisted it was the only time of year we got the castle to ourselves and we should use it rather than confining ourselves to our private living quarters.

Each Christmas, for three days solid we used to run riot through every corner of the castle, sleep in whichever bedroom we chose and pretend we actually were royalty. Somehow, I get the impression this year will be no different, except I already know which room I'm sleeping in.

Chloe wiggles her eyebrows suggestively. 'Don't tell me *GQ*'s previously most eligible bachelor is that quick?'

Ryan snorts, then presses his lips to my forehead in a

tender gesture before leaping out of the bed towards the ensuite, his bare backside a glorified piece of art for all to see.

'Ah, gross man!' Victoria covers her eyes while Chloe nods and gives me a suitably impressed glance that translates as *not bad*.

'He has a brother, you know...' I tease.

Huge blue eyes roll skywards. 'Urgh. Don't remind me.'

Victoria slips under the covers to my left, while Chloe slides under the right.

'It's so good to have you here.' I rest my head on my middle sister's shoulder while my youngest sister rests her head on mine in a sideways type of hug.

'It's so good to be here.' Chloe affectionately pats my arm.

'Do you think they're looking down on us?' Victoria's voice is so low it's barely audible over the sound of running water where Ryan showers in the next room.

'I know they are, sweetheart.' Taking my sister's hands, I squeeze gently, confident in the knowledge that I'm right. Their presence is everywhere. It doesn't matter how many changes we make to the decor, or the menu, or the grounds. A part of them will always live on here in this castle, in us.

Forty minutes later, I descend the wide walnut staircase to the atrium. The rich scent of cinnamon and pine filters through the air. Everyone I love waits below, primarily because I got delayed in the shower, receiving my first Christmas present of the day.

The open fire roars welcomingly. The jazz that usually radiates from the castle speakers has been replaced with Christmas party songs.

My sisters hold out their glasses, waiting for the first drink of the day. Bubbles on Christmas morning is one of my parents' traditions that we won't be dropping this year, or ever.

My heart swells at the manly form below, uncorking a bottle of the estate's finest champagne. He's a far cry from the boy who left all those years ago. He's inexplicably more exquisite. A magnetising aura radiates far and wide in every direction. His star quality is undeniable. With that jet-black hair and powerful physique, even from across the room he's impossibly striking.

If I didn't already know the man was a rockstar, it wouldn't be hard to imagine. He exudes a unique confidence with every breath.

My stiletto halts to an immediate, abrupt stop, hovering an inch above the bottom step as I drink him in. His coal-black hair. The way it frames the familiar contours of his face begs me to rake my fingers through it.

And that mouth.

Oh my god.

The subtle incline of his full Cupid's bow. Plush, plump lips. The memory of what they did to me not twenty minutes earlier springs to the forefront of my mind.

It doesn't matter what gifts are under the tree. The greatest gift I've ever received is his love, and the love of my family.

'Here she is.' Ryan's dark eyes glitter as he crosses the room to greet me as though we've been apart ten years, not ten minutes.

He takes my hand and guides me towards the sixteen-foot Christmas tree where Jayden, Pierce, Archie, Frankie, Angela and her girlfriend, Jasmine, congregate.

'Merry Christmas, everyone.'

'It certainly is.' Angela raises her glass in a toast. 'Thank you so much for hosting us in your beautiful home.'

'Thanks for being here.' Glancing round at our guests, I'm

grateful to each and every one of them for all they've done for us and all that they continue to do. For keeping my fiancé safe. For bringing him home to me.

My eyes land on Jayden who looks particularly well this morning in a crisp white shirt and navy jeans. 'Merry Christmas.' He drops a peck on my cheek and I can't help notice Chloe staring from across the room.

Methinks the lady does protest too much.

'Can we do the presents now?' Victoria eyes the embarrassing pile of lavishly wrapped presents under the tree. Ryan tops up the glasses like the gracious host he is.

My questioning glance at our guests is greeted with various nods and shrugs of acceptance, grins and smirks as each wait to give out their carefully chosen gifts.

'Sure.' I take a sip from the glass Ryan hands to me.

Leaning into my ear, his hot breath grazes my neck. 'I'm going to hazard a guess that one's for me?' His index finger points to a badly wrapped guitar resting underneath the pine needles.

'I hope you like it.' I rest against his chest while chaos breaks out around us.

'I already know I'm going to love it. It has sentimental value because you picked it for me. Thank you.'

A high-pitched squeal pierces the air, momentarily halting everyone in their unwrapping.

'Holy shit! We're going to see Adam Draker?' Victoria shrieks, palming her cheeks as she leaps into the air in a victorious jig.

'Language!' I chide, good-naturedly.

'Not that douchebag.' Ryan rolls his eyes and grins. 'Angela will probably be able to get us backstage too.'

Jayden saunters towards us clutching a tiny box wrapped in shiny green foil complete with a tacky looking crimson bow.

'A Christmas present for the happy couple.' He smirks.

'Oh god, do I even want to open this? If it's a condom you're about ten years too late.' Ryan elbows him playfully in the ribs, producing a small gold envelope from his back pocket.

'This is for you, from both of us.' He hands it over, pupils glinting with amusement.

I have no idea what's in either.

As Jayden's fingers close around the envelope, enlightenment shines in his steely eyes. Raucous laughter tumbles from his chest. 'Great minds think alike.'

Ryan tears open the wrapping, lifting the lid from the tiny gift box. In it is a futuristic looking car key emblazed with one logo. Ferrari.

Jayden slaps Ryan on the back in a manly thank you, which Ryan reciprocates, his grin exposing his Hollywood smile. 'Do what you like to this one.'

Chloe thrusts her very own Evangeline Araceli into the air with sheer delight. 'Oh my god, I love it!' She shouts from under the tree.

Pierce, Frankie and Archie seem suitably impressed with the gifts Ryan bought for them, matching Swiss timepieces so they'll never be late in their lives.

Tugging me away from the others, Ryan produces a small USB stick wrapped with a single golden bow.

'What do you buy the woman who has everything?' He muses thoughtfully. 'The answer is, anything she wants, any time she wants, but this here is something no one else can say is theirs, even if they buy it ten times over.'

'That sounds intriguing.' My head tilts in question.

'The ring was supposed to be for Christmas morning but I couldn't hold off for one more day. So this is something I made for you...'

'What is it?' It would probably be rude to slip away to

watch whatever is on the stick. Plus, if I don't get the turkey into the oven in the next ten minutes, we'll be eating crisps for dinner.

'It's my new album. It's for you. It's called "It's Always Been You".' Earnest eyes fill with emotion as he presses his lips to mine.

It's true what they say. The best gifts can't be bought.

The magnitude of what this man has done and continues to do for me cascades through me, filling me with more love than I ever thought I was capable of.

'Merry Christmas, Sash.'

'Merry Christmas, Ryan. Thank you for the most fabulous Christmas ever.'

He tips his flute against mine. 'Here's to many more.'

'Now, let's see if your many talents extend as far as the kitchen. I know a bird who needs stuffing.'

THE END

Not quite had your fill of Ryan & Sasha? Want an extra bonus epilogue?
https://dl.bookfunnel.com/rhbmts0042

Or Maybe it's Chloe & Jayden you want to see more of:

MY BIG FAT FABULOUS FLING (Sexton Sisters Series- Book 2)

I like to think I'm pretty level-headed but something about Jayden Cooper sends a hot flush of irritation pulsing through me every time I hear his stupid name.

His rockstar brother might be about to marry my darling sister, but that does not make us family. Thankfully, there's a continent shielding me from his ridiculously attractive but super-smug face- and his arrogant tongue.

As CEO of my own flourishing company, and one of Dubai's most successful female entrepreneurs I'm busy carving my name in the glittering world of celebrity events management... and what better event to manage than the final farewell tour of my sisters fiancé, Ryan Cooper.

It's the biggest gig of my career.

Eight cities.

Eight concerts.

Eight opportunities to prove my general awesomeness and enough PR to propel my business to the next level.

I couldn't turn it down if I wanted to.

The catch?

It means working closely with Ryan's agent- his brother, Jayden Super-Smug-Cooper.

Someone somewhere is testing me, but I've survived worse. And I'll survive him.

As long as I don't melt under that smug-but smouldering stare.. or fall foul to the talents of the aforementioned arrogant tongue.

Especially when technically...like it or not, we're about to be related.

Click here to read more...

My Big Fat Fabulous Fling is a steamy, enemies-to-lovers, laugh-out-loud romantic comedy, with no cheating, no cliff-hanger, and a guaranteed happy ever after (HEA).

My Big Fat Fabulous Fling

Eight concerts. Eight cities.
Eight chances to fall in love with a man I'm supposed to hate.

Lyndsey Gallagher

MY BIG FAT FABULOUS FIRST LOVE (Sexton Sisters Book 3)

Victoria and Archie both have a to-do list, but, technically, they shouldn't feature on each other's.

VICTORIA
To Do List

1. Finish placementon Accident & Emergency Ward without any further complaints re. my bedside manner. (In my defence, that patient definitely didn't require the mouth-to-mouth he requested. Sleaze!)

2. Invite chic new neighbours over for a house party- nobody likes a Sandra Serious - med student or not!

3. Get laid- ASAP. It's been a while.

4. Lose the bodyguard my celebrity sister assigned to babysit me, so I can work on point 3.

Note to self: Stop fantasising about aforementioned bodyguard. Difficult, given he struts around my house half naked most of the time. But I'm professional FFS! Almost, anyway...

ARCHIE
To Do List

1. Keep Victoria Sexton out of danger *at all costs.*

2. Keep Victoria Sexton out of trouble *at all costs.*

3. Stop Victoria Sexton from inviting half the city into her home for unruly house parties *at all costs.*

4. Stop Victoria Sexton from shagging the campus creep *at all costs.*

Note to self: Stop fantasising about Victoria Sexton naked *at all costs.*

I'm supposed to be watching her back, not imagining her on it.

Unless I want to lose my job, the first house I ever felt truly at home in, and my life as I know it... Nothing's worth that, is it?

Click here to learn more... https://mybook.to/MyBigFatFabulousFirstLove

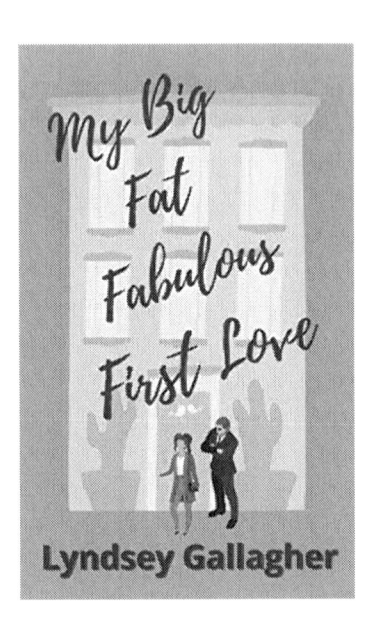

ALSO BY LYNDSEY GALLAGHER

PROFESSIONAL PLAYERS SERIES

Five Steamy Contemporary Stand Alone Sports Romance Novels. HEA guaranteed. Perfect for fans of Amy Daws, Meghan Quinn and Lucy Score.

BOOK 1: LOVE & OTHER MUSHY STUFF

One sassy radio agony aunt, one swoon-worthy rugby player, and one unlikely but alluring fake dating deal. Abby doesn't need or want a man, except to feature on her show and up her ratings. Callum's not looking for 'the one' merely 'the next one,' but he gets drawn into a bet to date the same woman long enough to bring to his best friends wedding.

Will Abby finally take her own romantic advice? Or will Callum nail his most elusive touchdown yet?

BOOK 2: LOVE & OTHER GAMES

Successful beauty business queen, Emma refuses to think about the rugby player who ghosted her after the best night of her life-much! Exactly one year later he shows up again. His pert backside hogs the seat next to hers on route to a mutual friend's beach wedding. Crossed wires at the hotel result in them reluctantly agreeing to share the honeymoon suite. Will Eddie's practiced tactics win out? Or will Emma stick to her game plan? Is there something else they both want more than each other?

BOOK 3: LOVE & OTHER LIES

Kerry's been sacked from her office job and evicted in the same week and she desperately needs to find a replacement for both, especially because her boyfriends about to be discharged from the military- a fact which she should be delighted about but is frankly terrifying.

Single dad, Nathan, is a successful rugby player at the pinnacle of his career. When he's left sole care of his daughter for the summer he realises he's going to need a nanny. A chance phone call results in Kerry accepting Nathan's job offer, without realising he's the only guy she kissed when her and her boyfriend were on a break.

Will Kerry let her past ruin her future? Or can Nathan convince her he's playing for keeps?

BOOK 4: LOVE & OTHER FORBIDDEN THINGS

When Amy lands her dream job as physiotherapist for the rugby team, she's forced to face the blistering growing chemistry with player number six, Ollie Quinn. Not only is he her patient, therefore utterly forbidden, he's also her brother's best friend. Injuries on the pitch seem minimal to what Eddie might do if he discovers their dalliances.

Is it simply the temptation of tasting the forbidden fruit? Or will forbidden turn into forever?

BOOK 5: LOVE & OTHER VOWS

Recently retired captain of the rugby team, Marcus is struggling to adjust to life away from the club. When his wife of ten years is paired up with his biggest sporting rival on the countries sexiest dance show, he realises he stands to lose a lot more than just his career. Marcus must act if he wants to save their relationship. They vowed to stay together in sickness and health but what about fame and wealth?

Professional Players Series.... FREE ON KINDLE UNLIMITED
click here to learn more...

THE SEVEN YEAR ITCH

Twenty-seven-year-old **Lucy O'Connor** has been asked to be her future sister-in-law's bridesmaid despite the fact they don't see eye to eye. The last thing she expected was to fall in love with a complete stranger at the hen weekend. Which wouldn't be a problem, apart from the teeny tiny fact that she's already married to somebody else...

Is it a case of the **Seven-Year-Itch**? Or could it be the real deal?

Lucy needs to decide if she's going to leave the security of her stale marriage in order to find out if the grass is indeed greener on the other side, or whether it's worth having one more go at watering her own garden.

Could this party-loving, city girl really leave the country she loves for a farmer from the west of Ireland?

Is there such a thing as fate?

What about karma?

Is John Kelly all that he seems?

★★★★★ *Love can be insane, gut-wrenching, and dizzying*

Lyndsey Gallagher captures the insane, gut-wrenching, dizzying first flush of love when all you can do is think about that other person and can focus on nothing else. Beautifully captured and expertly told. It's also a story of taking risks and proof that if you follow your heart, life usually turns out for the best. Highly Recommend.

Click here to download or learn more. FREE ON KU

THE MIDWIFE CRISIS

As a midwife, nothing shocks **Orla Broder**. She's seen it all; from fainting to forceps, epidurals to epiphanies, tears to triumphs.

Miles from her Galway home, immersed in the magic and madness of an Edinburgh labour ward, not to mention the wild hospital nights out, Orla had never given much thought to her own happy ever after....

That is until an unexpected financial contractor arrives at the hospital ruffling feathers, including her own. To complicate things further, Orla's previously estranged father re-enters her life with some heart-stopping news which will change Orla's outlook on life forever.

Cool, calm, collected Orla finder herself at the centre of her very own *midwife crisis*.

Will the labour of love ever win out?

★★★★★ *While at its heart, this story is a romance, it's so much more than that. It's a testament to midwives, families, friendships, and the importance of forgiveness. Gallagher captures life in the labour ward beautifully and immerses the reader in every scene. Without giving anything away, I cried at some bits and laughed at others. A very enjoyable read.*

Click here to learn more or download. FREE ON KU

MY BIG FAT FABULOUS FLING: Book 2 Sexton Sisters Series

I like to think I'm pretty level-headed but something about Jayden Cooper sends a hot flush of irritation through me every time I hear his stupid name. His rockstar brother might be about to marry my darling sister, but that doesn't not make us family.

Thankfully, there's a continent separating me from his ridiculously attractive but super-smug face. And his arrogant tongue.

As one of Dubai's most successful female entrepreneurs, I'm immersed with carving my name in the glittering world of celebrity event management... and what better event to mange than the final farewell tour of my sister's fiancé, Ryan Cooper.

It's the biggest gig of my career.

Eight cities.

Eight concerts.

Eight opportunities to prove my general awesomeness and enough PR to propel my business to a global level.

I couldn't turn it down if I wanted to.

The catch?

It means working with closely with Ryan's agent- his brother, Jayden-Super-Smug-Cooper.

Someone somewhere is testing me, but I've survived worse. And I'll survive him.

As long as I don't melt under the intensity of his smug but admittedly smouldering stare ...or fall foul of the talents of the aforementioned arrogant tongue...

Especially when technically...like it or not, we're about to be related.

My Big Fat Fabulous Fling is a steamy, enemies-to-lovers, laugh-out-loud romantic comedy, with no cheating, no cliffhanger, and a guaranteed happy ever after (HEA).

Click here to read more...

ACKNOWLEDGMENTS

I hope you enjoyed reading Sasha & Ryan's story as much as I enjoyed writing them! If you did, please consider leaving and amazon/ Goodreads or BookBub review. They really do make a huge difference to an author.

I need to say a massive thanks to my writing buddies- you know who you are. Thanks for the video calls, chats and advice, but most of all, thank you for your friendship. Writing could be a lonely job but thanks to you guys, it never is.

Thank you to my fabulous husband who's supported me unconditionally from the second I randomly announced, 'I'd love to write a book!'

Nine books later... I'm only just getting warmed up!

The biggest thanks goes to you, the reader- because of you I get to work at my dream job all day every day- sending huge hugs and love XX

ABOUT THE AUTHOR

Lyndsey Gallagher writes spicy contemporary romance starring swoon-worthy heroes, relatable heroines and guaranteed happy ever afters.

She lives in the west of Ireland with her exceptionally patient husband and two crazy kids. Lyndsey loves long walks, deep talks and more wine and chocolate than is healthy.

Subscribe to www.lyndseygallagherauthor.com for more info and giveaways.